SWIFTLY

❁

A NOVEL

'The blade of wisdom is turned against the wise.
Wisdom is a crime against nature.'
Nietzsche

SWIFTLY

A NOVEL

ADAM ROBERTS

The right of Adam Roberts to be identified as
the author of this work has been asserted by him
in accordance with the Copyright, Designs and
Patents Act 1988.

First published in Great Britain in 2008 by
Gollancz
An imprint of the Orion Publishing Group
Orion House, 5 Upper St Martin's Lane,
London WC2H 9EA
An Hachette UK Company

This edition published in Great Britain
in 2009 by Gollancz

A CIP catalogue record for this book
is available from the British Library

ISBN 978 0 575 08234 2

1 3 5 7 9 10 8 6 4 2

Printed and bound in the UK
by CPI Mackays, Chatham, ME5 8TD

The Orion Publishing Group's policy is to use papers
that are natural, renewable and recyclable products and
made from wood grown in sustainable forests. The logging
and manufacturing processes are expected to conform to
the environmental regulations of the country of origin.

www.orionbooks.co.uk

CONTENTS

❋

ONE

BATES

✻

[1]

5 November 1848

Swiftly, expertly, the tiny hand worked, ticked up and down, moved over the face of the miniature pallet. The worker was wearing yellow silk trousers, a close-woven blue waistcoat. It (for Bates could not see whether it was a *he* or a *she*) had on spectacles that shone like dewdrops in the light. Its hair was black, its skin a golden cream. Bates could even make out the creases of concentration on its brow, the tip of its tiny tongue just visible through its teeth.

Bates stood upright. 'It hurts my back,' he said, 'to lean over so.'

'I quite understand,' said Pannell. 'Might I fetch you a chair?'

'No need, thank you,' said Bates. 'I think I have seen all I desire. It is, indeed, fascinating.'

Pannell seemed agitated, shifting weight from one foot to another. 'I never tire of watching them work,' he agreed. 'Pixies. Fairies! Creatures from childhood story.' He beamed. *You smile sir*, thought Bates. *You smile, but there is sweat on your lip. Perhaps you are not altogether lost to shame. Nerves, sir, nerves.*

'What is it, eh, making exactly?'

'A mechanism for controlling the angle, pitch and yaw, in flight you know. I could give you its technical name, although it is Mister Nicholson who is the expert in these matters.'

'Is it a sir or a madam?'

'It?'

'The creature. The workman.'

'A female.' Pannell touched Bates's elbow, herding him gently

1

towards the staircase at the far end of the workshop. 'We find they have better hands for weaving the finest wire-strands.'

Bates paused at the foot of the wooden stairs, taking one last look around the workshop. 'And these are Lilliputians?'

'These,' replied Pannell, 'are from the neighbouring island, Blefuscu. We believe Blefuscans, sir, to be better workers. They are less prone to disaffection, sir. They work harder and are more loyal.'

'All of which is,' said Bates, 'very interesting.'

Up the stairs and through the glass door, Bates was led into Pannell's office. Pannell guided him to a chair, and offered him brandy. 'When my superior heard of the terms you were offering,' he gushed, wiping the palms of his hands alternately against the opposite sleeves of his coat as Bates sat down, 'he was nothing less than overwhelmed. Mr Burton is not an excitable man, sir, but he was impressed, very impressed, more,' Pannell went on, hopping to the drinks cabinet in the corner of the room, '*more* than impressed. Very generous terms, sir! Very favourable on both sides!'

'I am pleased you think so,' said Bates.

From where he was sitting the view was clear through the quartered window of Pannell's office. Grime marked the bottom right-hand corners of each pane like brown lichen. Each patch of dirt was delineated from clean glass by a hyperbolic line running from bottom left to top right, *as*, Bates thought, *x equals y squared*. The pattern on the glass further hemmed in the pinched view out upon which the window gave: the dingy street, the grey-brick buildings.

He shifted his weight in the chair. It complained, squeaking like a querulous baby. I too am nervous, he thought.

'Brandy?' Pannell asked for the second time.

'Thank you.'

'Mr Burton expressed his desire to meet you himself.'

'I would be honoured.'

'Indeed ...'

A bell tinkled, as tiny a sound as ice-glass breaking. A Lilliputian sound. Bates looked to the patch of wall above the door. The bell was mounted on a brass plate. It shivered again. Some more silver sound sprinkled free. Faery.

Pannell stood, staring at the bell like a fool, a glass of brandy in his hands. 'That means that Mr Burton is coming here directly. It rings when Mr Burton is on his way here directly. But I was to bring you to Mr Burton's office, not he to come here ...'

And almost at once the door shuddered, as with cold, and snapped open. Burton was a tall man who carried a spherical belly before him like an O of exclamation. His jowls were turfed with black beard, but his forehead was bald, as pink and curved as a rose petal. He moved with the burly energy of the moneyed. As Bates got up from his chair he tipped his glance down with a respectful nod of the head: Burton's shoes were very well made, tapering to a point, the uppers made of some variety of stippled leather. Standing to his full height brought Bates's glance up along the fine cloth of Burton's trousers, past the taut expanse of dark waistcoat and frock, to the single colourful item of clothing on the man: a turquoise and scarlet and *vulgar* bow tie, into which actual jewels had been fitted.

He faced the proprietor with a smile, extending his hand. But the first thing Burton said was: 'No, sir.'

'Mr Burton,' gabbled Pannell, 'may I introduce to you Mr Bates, who has come in person to negotiate the contract. I was just telling him how generous we considered the terms he offered ...'

'No, sir,' repeated Burton. 'I'll not stand it.'

'Not stand it, sir?' said Bates.

'I know who you are, sir,' fumed Burton. He stomped to the far side of the office, and turned to face them again. Bates noticed the bone-coloured walking stick, capped at each tip with red gold. 'I know who you are!'

'I am Abraham Bates, sir,' replied Bates.

'No, sir!' Burton raised the cane, and brought it down on the flat of Pannell's desk. It reported like a rifle discharge. Pannell flinched. Bates found sweat pricking out of his forehead again.

'No, sir,' bellowed Burton. 'You'll not weasel your way here! I know your type, and you'll not come here with your *false* names and *false* heart.'

'Mr Burton,' said Bates, trying to keep his voice level. 'I assure you that Bates is indeed my name.'

'You are a liar, sir! I give you the *lie*, sir.' The cane flourished in the air, inadvertently knocking a picture on the wall and tipping a stretch of the South Seas through forty degrees.

'I am not, sir,' retorted Bates, his heart dancing.

'Gentlemen,' whimpered Pannell. 'I beg of you both ...'

'Pannell, you'll hold your tongue,' declared Burton, emphasising the last word with another flourish of the cane. 'If you value your continued employment at this place. Do you deny, sir,' he added, pointing the cane directly at Bates, 'do you *deny* that you came here to infiltrate? To weasel your way in?'

'I came to discuss certain matters,' insisted Bates. 'That is all. Sir, do you refuse even to talk with me?'

'And if I do?' said Burton, his voice dropping a little. 'Then? You'll have your members of Parliament, your newspaper editors, your friends, and with them you'll turn on me? A pack of dogs, sir! A pack of dogs!'

'I admire your cane,' said Bates, lowering himself back into his chair in what he hoped was a cool-headed manner. 'Is it bone, sir?'

This took the wind from Burton's sails. 'We'll not discuss my cane, sir.'

'Is it Brobdingnagian bone? From which part of the body? A bone from the inner-ear, perhaps?'

'There is nothing illegal,' Burton began, but then seemed to change his mind. The sentence silently completed itself in Bates's mind. 'Very well,' Burton said, finally, somewhat deflated. 'You have come to talk, sir. We will talk, sir. Pannell, you will stay in this room. Pour me a brandy, in fact, whilst I and this . . . *gentleman* discuss the affairs of the day. Then, Mr Bates, I'd be obliged if you left this manufactory and did not return.'

'One conversation will satisfy me, sir,' said Bates, rounding the sentence off with a small sigh, like a full-stop given breath.

Burton settled into a chair by the window, and Pannell poured another glass of brandy with visibly trembling fingers. 'This *gentleman*,' Burton told his employee, 'is an agitator, sir. A radical, I daresay. Are you a radical?'

'I am one of Mr Martineau's party.'

'Oh!' said Burton, with egregious sarcasm. 'A party man!'

'I am honoured to be so styled.'

'And no patriot, I'll lay any money.'

'I love my country, sir,' replied Bates, 'love her enough to wish her better managed.'

'Faction and party,' Burton muttered grimly, raising the brandy glass to his face like a glass muzzle over his bulbous nose. 'Party and faction.'

He drank. 'They'll sunder the country, I declare it.' He put the empty glass down on the table with a *ploc.*

Pannell was hovering, unhappy-looking, by the door.

'We can agree to differ on that topic, sir,' said Bates, a little stiffly.

'Well, sir,' said Burton. 'What conversation is it you wish to have with me? I own this manufactory, sir. Yes, we employ a cohort of Blefuscans.'

'Employ, sir?'

'They cost me,' said Burton, bridling, 'a fortune. Regular food does not sit in their stomachs, so they must be fed only the daintiest and most expensive. Regular cloth is too coarse for their clothing, so they must be given the finest silks. The expense is very much greater than a regular salary would be. True, I own them outright, and this makes them slaves. The Ancients kept slaves sir! Plato, Caesar kept slaves. But mine are well treated, and they cost me more as slaves than employees ever could. I suppose Mr Bates here,' Burton added, addressing Pannell in a raised voice that aimed for sarcasm, but achieved only petulance, 'would see them free. Mr Bates considers slavery an *evil.* Is it not so, Mr Bates?'

Bates shifted in his chair. It squeaked again underneath him. 'Since you ask, I do consider such slavery as you practise here an evil. How many of your employees die?'

'I lose money with each fatality, sir,' said Burton. 'I've no desire to see a single one die.'

'And your cane, sir? How many Brobdingnagians are left alive in the world?'

'I have nothing to do with those monsters. Indeed not. One of their kind could hardly fit inside my building.'

'Yet you carry a cane made out of their murdered bodies, sir. Do you not consider that a wickedness? A contribution to their pitiable state?'

'*Some* people, Pannell,' said Burton, addressing his employee again, 'some people have leisure and predisposition to be sympathetic towards animals. Others are too busy with the work they have at hand.'

'Your Lilliputians . . .'

'Blefuscans, sir.'

'Your little people, sir – and the giant people also – are hardly animals.'

'No? No? Have *you* worked with them, Mr Bates?'

'I have devoted many years now to their cause.'

'Actually *worked with them*? But of course not. The midgets are mischievous, and their wickedness is in the bone. And the giants – they are a clear and present danger to the public good.'

'The Brobdingnagians have endured homicide on an appalling scale.'

'Homicide? But that implies man, don't it? Homo implies killing *men*, don't it?'

'Are not the Brobdingnagians made in God's image, sir? As are you and I? As are the Lilliputians?'

'So,' said Burton, smiling broadly. 'It's God, at the heart of your disaffection, is it?'

'Our nation would be stronger,' said Bates, struggling to keep the primness out of his voice, 'if we followed God's precepts more, sir. Or are you an atheist?'

'No, no.'

'Let me ask you a question, Mr Burton: are your Blefuscan workers – are they white-skinned, or black?'

'What manner of question is this, sir? You've just examined my workers out there. You know the answer to your own question.'

'Their skins are as white as mine,' said Bates. 'The Bible is clear on this matter. God has allotted slavery to one portion of his creation, and marked that portion by blackening their skins – Ham's sons, sir. There are enough Blacks in the world to fill the places of slaves. But it mocks God to take some of his most marvellous creations and enslave them, or kill them.'

'I do not kill my workers, sir,' insisted Burton.

'But they *are* killed, sir. Worldwide, only a few thousand are left. And the Brobdingnagians – how many of them remain alive? After the affair with the *Endeavour* and the *Triumph*?'

'I have met the captain of the *Triumph*, sir,' said Burton, bridling again. 'At a dinner party of a friend of mine. An honourable man, sir. Honourable. He followed the orders he was given. What naval gentleman could do otherwise? And,' he continued, warming to his theme, 'was it so great a crime? These giants are twelve times our size. Had they organised, had they known cannon, and ordnance, and gunpowder, they could have trampled us to pieces. Not only England neither, but the whole of Europe – they *would* have come over here and trampled us to pieces. Who'd have been the slaves then? You may answer me that question, if you please. With an army of monstrous

6

giants trampling England's green fields, who'd have been the slaves then?'

'The Brobdingnagians are a peace-loving people,' said Bates, feeling the colour strengthen in his face. 'If you read the account of the mariner who discovered their land ...'

Burton laughed aloud. 'That fellow? Who'd believe a word he wrote? Riding the nipple of a gentlewoman like a hobby-horse, by all pardon – it was nonsense. And the reality? A race of beings big enough to squash us like horseflies, and destroy our nation. Our nation, sir! Yours and mine! We had but one advantage over them, and that was that we possessed gunpowder and they did not. The King did well to destroy the majority of that population and seize their land. Our people are the best fed in the world, now, sir. Perhaps you do not remember how things were before the gigantic cattle were brought here, but I do. How many starved in the streets. Now there's not a pauper but eats roast beef every day. Our army is the strongest and manliest on the Continent. Would we have had our successes invading France and Holland without them?'

'You speak only of temporal advantages,' insisted Burton. 'But to do so is short-sighted. It is true that the discoveries of our navy have enriched our country in purely material terms – but the spiritual, sir? The spiritual?'

'God,' said Burton.

'Indeed, my friend. God created all these creatures as marvels. We have spat upon his gift. Lilliputians may seen small to us, but they are part of God's universe.'

'There are giants in Genesis, I believe,' said Burton. 'Did not the Flood destroy them?'

'The Flood may not have reached the northwestern coast of America,' said Bates. 'At least, this is one theory as to the survival of these peoples.'

'It hardly seems to me that God's Providence was greatly disposed towards these monsters. He tried to destroy them in the Flood, and again in the form of two British frigates.' His face twitched a smile.

'After much prayer,' Bates insisted, not wanting to be distracted. 'After much prayer, it has become evident to me ...'

At this Burton laughed out loud, a doggy, abrasive noise; each laugh parcelled into sections, like the 'ha! ha! ha!' of conventional orthography. It broke through Bates's speech. 'Pannell,' said Burton.

'Mr Bates has come to vex us, not to divert us, and yet how diverting he is!'

'Mockery is,' began Bates, his anger rising. He swallowed his words. Better to turn the other cheek. 'I come, sir, to *invite* you. To invite you to join a commonality of *enlightened* employers and financiers – a small core, sir, but a vital one. From us will grow a more proper, a more holy society.'

'A society? So that's it. And if I joined your commonality, I would not be allowed to possess any slaves, I suppose?'

'You might own slaves, sir, provided only they *were* slave— Blacks I mean. The Lilliputians are not slaves, sir, in God's eye, and it is God you mock by treating them so. God will not be mocked.'

'I daresay not,' agreed Burton, hauling his cumbersome body from its chair. 'It's been a pleasure, sir, talking with you. Mr Pannell here will show you out.'

Bates rose, flustered, uncertain at exactly which point he had lost the initiative in this interview. 'Am I to take it, sir, that you ...'

'You are to take it any way you choose, sir. I had thought you a spy for Parliament, sir. There are MPs who would gladly outlaw slavery in all its forms, and they have the power to do actual harm. But you, sir, do not – I doubt nothing but that you are harmless, as are your God-bothering friends. Good day, sir!'

Bates's ire spurted up. *God-bothering*! The insolence! 'You are rude sir! God is more powerful than any parliament of men.'

'In the next world sir, the next world.'

'You approach blasphemy, sir!'

'It is not *I*,' Burton growled, 'who attempted to infiltrate an honest workman's shop with lies and deceit, not *I* who broke the commandment about bearing false witness to worm my way inside a decent business and try to tear it down. But you knew that you would not gain admittance if you spoke your true purpose. Good day, sir.'

[2]

Bates paced the evening streets of London, the long unlovely streets. He passed gin shops and private houses. He walked past a junior school with ranks of windows arrayed along its brick walls like the ranks of children within. He passed churches, chapels and a synagogue. Up

8

the dog-leg of Upper St Martin's Lane and past the rag traders of Cambridge Circus, now mostly putting away their barrows and boarding up their shops. Bates, lost in his own thoughts, walked on, and up the main thoroughfare of Charing Cross Road.

Around him, now, crowds passed. Like leaves at autumn, drained of their richness, dry and grey and rattling along the stone roads before the wind. He thought of the French word: *folles*. A true word, for what was of greater folly than a crowd? The stupidity of humankind, that cattle-breed. Hiding, unspeaking, in some crevice of his mind was a sense of the little Lilliputians as daintier. More graceful, more *faery*. But he didn't think specifically of the little folk as he walked the road. There was an oppressive weariness inside him, as grey and heavy as a moon in his belly. Melancholia was, he knew it of course, a sin. The black bile sneered at God's gift of life. It was the sin against hope. It was to be fought, but the battle was hard. It was hard because it was the very will to fight that melancholia eroded; it was a disease of the will.

Over his head, one of the new clockwork flying devices buzzed, dipping and soaring like a metal dragonfly, long as his arm. It croaked away through the air up Charing Cross Road, flying north and carrying who knew what message to who knew what destination. Only the wealthy could afford such toys, of course; the wealthy and the government. Perhaps it was the noise, the self-important humming of it, that always gave the impression of a creature hurrying off on an errand of the mightiest importance. The war! The empire! The future of humankind!

Probably a financial facilitator, a manufactor, somebody with nouveau riches in the city, one of that type, had sent it flying north to let his servants know he would be late home from work.

The thought was sour in Bates's belly, an undigested pain. He should not have drunk the brandy.

He stopped to buy *The Times* from a barrow-boy, and ducked into a mahogany-ceilinged coffee shop to read it. Hot chocolate breathed fragrant steam at his elbow. Gaslight from four lamps wiped light over the polished tabletops, reflecting blurry circles of light in the waxwood of the walls. He brought his face close to the newsprint, as much to bury himself away from the stare of the other patrons as to make out the tiny printface. Miniature letters, like insects swarming over the page.

News.

British forces had seen action again at Versailles; the famous palace had been pocked with cannon shells. There was little doubt that Christmas would see the flag of St George flying over Paris. Anxiety of the French people; reassurance from the King that there would be no anti-Catholic repression after an English victory. The mechanics of the Flying Island had been thoroughly analysed by the Royal Society, and a paper had been read before the King. It seemed that a particular ore was required against which a magnetic device of unusual design operated. This ore was found only rarely in His Majesty's dominions, and in Europe not at all. But deposits were known to lie in portions of the North American and Greater Virginian continent. The way was clear, the paper announced, for this resource to be exploited and a new island to be constructed as a platform for use in the war against the Spanish in that continent.

Still Bates's spirits sank. He could not prevent it: some malign gravity of the heart dragged him down.

He turned to the back of the paper, and studied the advertisements. For sale, one Lilliputian, good needleworker. For sale, two Lilliputians, a breeding couple; one hundred and fifty guineas the pair. For sale, stuffed Lilliputian bodies, arranged in poses from the classics: Shakespeare, Milton, Scott. For sale, prime specimen of the famed Intelligent Equines, late of His Majesty's Second Cognisant Cavalry; this Beast (the lengthy advertisement went on) speaks a tolerable English, but knows mathematics and music to a high level of achievement. Of advanced years, but suitable for stud. And there, at the bottom, swamped and overwhelmed by the mass of Mammonite hawking and crying, was a small box: Public Lecture, on the Wickedness of Enslaving the Miniature Peoples from the East India Seas. Wednesday, no entrance after eight. Wellborough Hall. Admission one shilling.

Hopeless, all hopeless.

For Bates, this was the familiar sinking into the long dark of the soul. It had happened before, but every time it happened there was never anything to compare it to, there was never any way to fight it off. He stumbled down Oxford Street in a fuggy daze of misery. Where did it come from? Chapels littered both sides of the road, some polished and elegant, some boxy and unpretentious, and yet none of them held the answer to his indigestion of the spirit. If only some angel would swoop down to him, calling and weeping through the air like a swift, angelic and varicoloured wings stretching like a cat after a sleep, the feather-ends brushing the street itself in the lowest portion of its flying arc, its face bland and pale and still and beautiful. If only some angel could bring God's blessing down to him. Or perhaps the angel would be faery, a tiny creature with wings of glass and a child's intensity of innocence. Grace was Grace, even in the smallest parcels.

[3]

11 November

By the time Bates next rose from his bed he had been on the mattress for two days and two nights. His man put his insolent white head through the doorway of his cubby and chirruped: 'Feeling better today?'

'Go away, Baley,' Bates groaned. 'Go leave me in peace.'

'Off to your club today? It's Thursday – you told me most particular to remind you, Thursday.'

'Yes,' he muttered, more to himself than to his servant. 'Yes, Thursday. I will be getting up today. My . . . stomach feels a little better.'

'There you go sir.' The head withdrew, a smirk upon it.

Bates turned over in the bed. The sheet underneath him was foul with two days' accumulated stink, creased and wrinkled like the palm of a white hand. His bedside cabinet was littered with glasses, bottles, a newssheet, an ivory pipe. The curtain was of cotton velvet, and muffled off most of the daylight. The joints between knuckles and fingers' ends ached in both hands; the small of his back murmured complaint. His feet hurt from inaction. There was a series of bangs, miniature sounds, *goh, goh, goh*. Bates could not tell whether the thrumming sound was the spirit of Headache rapping inside his skull, or the sound of something thudding far away. The volatile acid of his melancholia had eroded away even the boundaries of self and world, so much so that Bates's misery spread out and colonised reality itself, it became a universal pressure of unhappiness. It occurred to Bates at that moment that the biblical flood had been, symbolically speaking, a *type* or *trope* for Melancholia itself, washing away strength, joy, will, hope, diluting the very energy of life itself and spreading it impossibly weakly about the globe. Grey waves washing at a rickety waterfront.

He pulled the pot from under the bed and pissed into it without even getting up, lying on his side and directing the stream over the edge of the mattress. Flecks of fluid messed the edge of the bed, but he didn't care. Why should he care? What was there to care about? When he had finished he did not bestir himself to push the pot back under the bed. He turned on his other side and lay still. There was the small noise again, a repeated thud-thud-thud.

It stopped. Bates turned over again.

Turned over again. Ridiculous, ridiculous.

He pulled himself upright, and snatched at the paper. Baley had brought it to him the night before, but Bates's fretful, miserable state of mind had not allowed him to concentrate long enough to read the articles. He started on the first leader, an imperial puff about the prospects for a British European Empire once France had been defeated. He read the third sentence three times – *our glorious history reasserts itself, our generals revitalise the dreams of Henry the Fifth* – without taking it in at all. The words were all there, and he knew the meaning of each, but as a whole the sentence refused to coalesce in his mind. Senseless. It was hopeless. In a fit of petty rage, he crushed the whole paper up into a ball and threw it to the floor. At once it started to unwind itself, creakily, like a living thing.

He lay prone again.

'Gentleman at the door, sir.' It was Baley, his head poking into the crib. 'I'm not at home,' Bates said into his mattress.

'Won't take that for an answer, sir,' said Baley. 'A foreign gentleman. Says he's High Belgium, but I'd say France, sir.'

Bates hauled himself upright. 'His hair black, in a long queue at the back of his head?'

'A what, sir?'

'Long hair, idiot, long hair.'

'Continental fashion, yes sir.'

Bates was struggling into his gown. 'Show him through, you fool.' He pressed the crumbs of sleep from his eyes and wiped a palm over his sleep-ruffled hair. Here? The selfsame D'Ivoi who had never before come to his rooms, had always insisted upon meeting in the club? Perhaps Baley had made a mistake – but, no, coming through to the drawing room there he was, D'Ivoi, standing facing the fire, with a turquoise hat under his arm, the sheen of his silk suit gleaming, and his ridiculous tassel of hair dangling from the back of his head. Baley was loitering. Bates shooed him away.

'My friend,' said D'Ivoi, turning at the sound of Bates's voice.

'I was coming to the club *today*,' said Bates at once. 'Perhaps I seem unprepared, but I was in train of getting dressed.'

D'Ivoi shook his head very slightly, no more than a tremble, and the smile was not dislodged from his face. 'There is no need for us to meet at the club.' His *ths* were brittle, *tare* is no need for us to meet at *t'* club, but otherwise his accent was tolerably good. 'I regret to say, my friend, that I leave this city this afternoon.' *Tat* I leave *tis* city *tis*.

'Leave?' Bates reached without thinking for the bell-rope, to call for tea. At the last minute he remembered that this was a conference to which no servant must be privy.

'I regret to say it. And before I depart, I bring a warning of sorts. Events in the war are about to take a turn ... shall we say, dramatic?'

'Dramatic? I don't understand. The paper says that we ... that, ah, the English are on the edge of capturing Paris. When that happens, surely the ...'

'No my friend,' said D'Ivoi. 'You will find tomorrow's newspapers tell a different story. France and the Pope have declared a common right with the Pacificans.'

It was all a great deal for Bates to take in at once. 'They have?' he said. 'But it is excellent news. Excellent news for our cause! Common right with Lilliputians and Brobdingnagians, both?'

'Certainly, with both. The petite folk and the giant folk, both are made in God's image. The talking horses, not; the Pope has decreed them devilish impostures. But of course he does so more because the English has its cavalry regiment of sapient horses. And the French army now has its own regiments. Regiments of the little folk would be useless enough, I suppose, but the giants make fearsome soldiers, I think.'

'The French army has recruited regiments of Brobdingnagians?' repeated Bates, stupidly.

'I have not long, my friend,' said D'Ivoi, nodding his head minutely. 'I come partly to warn you. There are other things. The President of the Republic has relocated to Avignon, as you know. Well, there have been great things happening in Avignon, all in the south you know. And these great things are about to emerge to the day's light, for all the world to see. It will be terrible to be an English soldier before them.'

'Monsieur,' said Bates. 'Are you ...?'

'Forgive me, my friend,' interrupted D'Ivoi. 'When these things happen, it will be uncomfortable to be a French national in London, I think. And so I depart. But I warn you too: your cause, your pardon *our* cause, for the liberation of the Pacificans, has aligned you with the nation of France. Your government may take action against you for this reason.'

'I am no traitor,' Bates asserted, though his tongue felt heavy in his mouth uttering the sentiment.

'No no,' assured the foreigner. 'I only warn you. You know best, of course, how to attend to your own safety. But before I depart (and time is close, my friend), let me say this: contemplate a French victory in this war. I advise it. Believe that, with the Pope and the President now allied formally to the petites and the giants, believe that a victory for France will spell freedom for these people. Perhaps one smaller evil counterbalances a larger good? Perhaps?'

Bates did not know what to say to this. 'I know that my actions here,' he started saying, speaking the words slowly, 'have benefited the French government. And I am not ashamed of this.'

'Good! Extremely good! Because it will be less time than you think before French soldiers arrive here in London town, and you would be well to consider how your duty lies. Your duty, my friend, to God above all. No?'

'Monsieur,' said Bates again anxiously.

But D'Ivoi was donning his top hat and bowing, stiffly. 'I regret I must depart.'

'French soldiers here?'

'Ah, yes. I will say only this, at last. There has been a very great series of inventions. We have a machine, a thinking and calculating machine ... have you heard of this?'

'A machine?'

'Mister Babbage, with his French mistress, they have been working in Uzès, in France's south, for many years now. You have heard, perhaps, of Mister Babbage?'

'The name is familiar ...' said Bates. His head was starting to buzz unpleasantly. This conference was a shock, there was no mistaking that.

'He has built a machine. It can undertake a week's calculations in a moment. It is nothing more than a box, the size of a piano I think, but it gives great power of calculation and ratiocination, of the power of thought in this box. Forgive me, I am forgetting my English already. But our engineers now use this box, and with it they design fantastic

14

new machines. Our generals use it, and with it they plan all possible military strategies. This box will win the war, for us.'

And he bowed again and was gone.

[4]

Where does it go, the melancholia, when some startling event evaporates it, sublimes it into vapour that dissolves into the wind? Bates's downheartedness vanished. He washed, shaved, dressed, ate and bustled from his rooms in an hour. Everything had been turned topsy-turvy, and the evil spirit squatting spiderish in his head had somehow been shaken free.

He hurried. D'Ivoi had been his only contact with the French, and perhaps by limiting his contact to a single individual he had, at some level, believed that he limited his treason too. And for a day or two the very notion of a French victory – of French troops marching up the Mall – was too shocking for him to think about it at all. But the idea percolated through his mind anyway, and soon he was almost welcoming it. It would at least bring his cause to fruition. The Lilliputians would be freed, the Brobdingnagians reprieved from race-death.

He was up, up, up.

He went to his club, and wrote three letters. Then he caught a cab (a rare expense for him) and visited a sympathetically-minded gentleman in Holborn. He spent the evening with a gaggle of churchmen, duck-like individuals who paced about the room with their heads forward and their hands tucked into the smalls of their backs, talking ponderously of God and Grace and Sin. He told the sympathetically-minded gentleman little, but he told the churchmen all. Their worry, it transpired, was not of French political rule so much as the danger of an oppressive Catholicism being imposed as the official religion. Bates was too excited, too elevated in spirit, to worry about this.

'Are you certain that these events are going to come to pass?' one of the clerics asked him. 'Are you sure?'

'I am sure,' gabbled Bates. He tended to talk too rapidly when the mood was on him, when his blood was hurtling through his body, but it couldn't be helped. 'Now that they have declared themselves for the humanity of the Lilliputians and Brobdingnagians, all of the civilised world will support them, surely. And their alliance has meant that they could recruit a regiment of giants to fight us. To fight the English. Moreover,' he went on, wide-eyed, 'they have perfected a device, a machine, a thinking machine. Have you heard of Mister Babbing?'

Babbing? Babbing?

'Do you mean *Babbage*,' said one elderly churchman, a whittled, dry-faced old man who had been a main agent in the campaign since its first days. 'The computational device?'

'The French have perfected it,' said Bates. 'And with it they have constructed new engineering devices, and plotted new techniques of war-making.'

'Incredible!'

'It is credible indeed.'

'The computing device has been perfected!'

On the Saturday he attended a tea-party at which he was the only male present. He sat on a chair too small for him, and listened politely to half-a-dozen wealthy matrons and maidens expatiate upon how beautiful the little people were, how marvellous, and how wicked it was to chain them with tiny fetters and make them work in factories. Bates did not mention the Brobdingnagians, of course, who lacked the daintiness to appeal to this class of person. But he smiled and nodded, and thought of the money these women might gift to the cause.

One woman confided in him. 'Since my husband passed through the veil,' she said in a breathy tone of voice, 'my life has become divided between these darling little creatures and my cats.'

The Sunday, naturally he went to chapel. But he could not bring his mind to focus on the sermon. Something fretted at its margins, some piece of thought-grit. *These darling little creatures*. But, Bates thought, there was so much more to the Lilliputians than this! They were messengers, in a manner as yet uncertain to him. He had not managed to distil the thought thoroughly enough through his brain to fully understand it, but he *felt* it, he felt it genuinely and thoroughly. Messengers. There was something about them, something special, that deserved preservation in the way few ordinary-sized people did.

She had sat next to him, with purple crinoline and a lace cap covering her hair, but with these intense, beautiful air-blue eyes, and had said: *these darling little creatures and my cats.*

Cats preyed on them, of course. One of Bates's acquaintances said that he had first become interested in their cause after watching two cats fighting over a stray Lilliputian in the kitchen of his uncle's house.

And so it slid again, dropping like leaves from a tree until the tree has lost all its leaves. Bates went to bed Sunday night with a heart so heavy it registered not only in his chest, but in his throat and belly too. And waking the following morning was a forlorn, interfered-with sensation. The urge not to rise was very strong: merely to stay in bed, to turn the heavy-body and heavy-head and lie there. So it was that after a spurt of energetic living Bates's was again usurped by melancholia.

His rooms, on Cavendish Square, looked over an oval of parched winter grass and four nude trees. Some days he would sit and stare, emptying one cigarette after another of its smoke, and doing nothing but watching the motionlessness of the trees.

When he had been a young man, some six or seven years earlier, Bates had had an intrigue with a tobacconist's daughter called Mary. The romance had included physical impropriety. To begin with, Bates had felt a glow in his heart, something fuelled by equal of parts pride and shame. The necessary secrecy had enlarged his sense of himself. He felt the sin, but he also felt strangely elevated. He could walk the streets of London looking at others and knowing something they did not know. The aftermath, the potent stew of good and bad emotions, was more pleasurable than the physical enjoyment of the act itself, pleasurable though that act was.

Then Mary told him that she was carrying a child. This altered the balance of feelings inside him to a form of fear. He could not bring himself to confront his own father (still alive at that time) to declare himself the destined parent of an infant. It was impossible. Inner shame is, perhaps, a sensation so powerfully mixed of delight and disgust that it approximates glory – but public shame is a very different matter. A very different matter. Bates senior was not a wealthy man, but he was proud. Marriage to a tobacconist's daughter was out of the question. And Mary was a sweet girl. But what could he do? What could be done?

Of course nothing could be done.

There was a very uncomfortable interview between the former lovers. There were tears and recriminations from her. These made it easier for him to adopt a stony exterior manner. Afterwards he spent the evening in his club, and drank most of a bottle of claret. A walk home and a half-hour in a chapel along the way. Prayer blended his awkwardness, his shame, his self-loathing, his weakness, into a cement of strength. He would be strong from this moment, and Christ required only repentance, in that moment, and clean living the future. He would go and sin no more.

His resolution required a blanking-out of Mary, which he managed by pretending that she did not exist. For weeks this strategy worked well. For hours at a time he forgot that there was such a person in the world. Only when he indulged in his occasional night-time bouts of impure thought and manual stimulation did her image insert itself into his mind, and this only encouraged him to quit that degrading business anyway.

Then, a month or more later, he saw her at the booth, paying to cross London Bridge. He hurried after her, uncertain whether the face glimpsed under the bonnet was indeed hers. 'Excuse me, Madam,' he called. And she turned.

She looked blankly into his face, neither pleased nor displeased to see him.

'Mary,' he said, catching up with her.

Her stomach was flat.

'A gentleman,' she chided, following his gaze, 'would not stare so.'

Light made painterly effects on the river, speckles of white brilliance spread in a swathe against the dun.

He didn't know how to ask the question. They walked together.

'Don't worry yourself, sir,' she said, blushing plum-red, her voice as angry as Bates had ever heard it. 'No child will come and threaten you and your loved honour.' At first he heard this last word as *on her*.

'No child?'

She was quiet for a time. 'A friend of mine knows a doctor, see. Not that I'd call him a real doctor, see.'

'Oh,' said Bates, soft, realising what had happened. They were a third of the way over the bridge now. The sunlight swelled, and the Thames was glittering and sparkling like a solid. Bates's mouth was dry.

'What did you do with it?' he asked, a pain growing in his chest as if his ribs were contracting like sphincters and squeezing his lungs.

'It?' she replied.

'The,' he said, his voice sounding alien to himself, 'child.'

She stopped and stared at him, stared for long seconds, her face immobile but her eyes wide. 'I buried him,' she said. 'I dug under a hedgerow in Hampstead, beside the churchyard, and buried him there. To bury him I thought in proper ground.'

For days afterwards Bates had been unable to get this image out of his mind. His child, his son, buried and mixed into the earth. Like ore. He dreamt of the little creature, its eyes closed and its mouth pursed against the chill. He imagined it with hair, long blond strands of hair. He imagined it miniature, Lilliputian in size. In the dream he scuffed at the dirt with his feet, knowing his child was interred beneath the spot. A strand of gold grazed his wrist. Boys in brown, crossing-sweepers, leant together to talk, somewhere in the distance. Through a window, perhaps. One of them yawned. But he was in a room, with velvet curtains. The strands of gold were woven into a cobweb. A strand of gold grazed his wrist. The baby's tiny hand was reaching for him, and when it touched him its skin was so cold he yelped out loud.

At that point he awoke.

[5]

On the 19th of the month French forces crossed the Channel. The fighting in the northeast of France had been the hardest, British troops having pulled back with a military alacrity to trenches dug earlier in the campaign and then stuck to their positions in and around Saint Quentin. But the French army was renewed. Three battalions of regular troops attacked the British positions; but then the *premier corps de géants* stormed the eastern flank. They carried enormous weaponry, great hoops of iron ringing massive staves of treated wood, cannonaders that the Brobdingnagians could fire from their shoulders, sending fissile barrel-shaped charges hurtling onto troops below. The packages were filled with Greek Fire. The giants proved remarkably resistant to rifle fire; although cannon-shells could fell them.

The battle fought at Saint Quentin was the major engagement of the whole war, with conventional troops charging the English line of defence from two sides at once, and a platoon of Brobdingnagians wading amongst the fighting with studied, slow-footed seriousness, smashing and killing about them with long, weighted pikes – sixty feet long, and carrying nearly a ton of metal shaped at the killing end. And the cannonaders wrought havoc. One Colonel growled like a dog as he read the paper containing the casualty figures after the battle. 'If this number were pounds rather than corpses,' he told his aide-de-camp, 'we would be wealthy indeed.' His *bon mot* went around the camp. The English army, the soldier joked grimly, was wealthy indeed in corpses, but poor in terms of the sovereign. The Commander in Chief was still hanging men for High Treason because this joke had passed their lips when the rest of the army had retreated to the coast. He himself escaped on a sapient horse as French forward troops broke through the camp and past the dangling bodies.

From Saint Quentin the English fell back across the Pas de Calais. Orders to establish a series of redoubts were ignored, or heroically followed to the death of everyone concerned. Commanders attempted to co-ordinate an evacuation on the beaches around Calais town, but the French pressed their advantage and embarkation turned to rout. Eventually the Brobdingnagians swam through, pulling English boats down to perdition from underneath. Commanders fled the scene in small skiffs. There was screaming, weapons fire, commotion and confusion. Clots of Greek Fire burned on the sea like shining seaweed. The English losses were even worse than they had been at the battle of Saint Quentin. Corpses sank to the bottom of the Manche as stones, or bobbed on the surface, tangled with the waves, or rolled and trundled dead in the surf, sand in their mouths and in their hair and in their sightless eyes.

Bates followed the news, reading the hastily printed newssheets with a fearful avidity. He wanted the French repulsed, like any Englishman. But then again he wanted the French victorious, and with it the noble God-endorsed cause to which he had devoted so much of his adult life. He didn't know what he wanted. He wanted to sleep, but he could only toss and roll on his dirty sheets.

His servant disappeared. This abandonment didn't surprise him. Everywhere, people were leaving the capital.

The *premier* and *troisième corps de géants* walked and swam the Channel, pulling troop-barges behind them. The army beached at Broadstairs. The English army, with all reserves called up and all available men under orders, assembled on the hills south of Canterbury. Travellers and passengers began carrying word-of-mouth reports of the fighting into the capital. *Terrible, like the end of the world*, they said. *It can but be the world's end*, a preacher was saying on Gad's Hill. *These gigantic men are God's wrath.*

The flood of people out of London increased.

Bates found his mood undergoing one of those peculiar bubblings-up that correlated only poorly to his surroundings. He took to rising relatively early, and walking the streets of London with a dispassionate, observer's eye. He watched servants load belongings onto carts outside lankily opulent town houses in Mayfair; watched shopkeepers fitting boards over their windows, whilst their wives wrapped whimpering Lilliputians in handkerchiefs for the journey. On the Great North Road a great worm of humanity pulsed slowly away to the horizon, people walking, trudging, hurrying or staggering, handcarts and horse-carts, men hauling packs stacked yards high with clinking pots and rolled cloth, women carrying children, animals on tight tethers. Bates stood for an hour or more watching the stream of people moving on, as seemingly sourceless and endless as the Thames itself. Militiamen trotted by on horseback, hawkers cried wares to the refugees, clockwork aerial craft buzzed up and down the line left and right across it.

Eventually, Bates wandered back into the city, and went to his club to take luncheon. Only Harmon was there, and one cook in the back room. 'Dear me,' Bates muttered. 'What's the matter, here?' Harmon was all apologies, a good man in trying times. 'Luncheon should not present problems, sir, if you'd care to eat.'

Bates ate. He smoked a cigar. His thoughts kept returning to the war. Could he, perhaps, persuade the generals that England was losing the war *because* it had flouted God's ordinance? A general proclamation from Parliament freeing the Lilliputians, and God's radiance would smile on His people again – surely? Surely?

He wandered, pensive, taking twice his normal time back to Cavendish Square. A stranger, dressed in an anonymous brown, was waiting outside his front door.

'Sir?' he said, starting forward. 'You are Mister Bates?' His accent was French.

Bates felt suddenly panicky, he knew not why. 'What do you want?'

'Calm yourself, sir, calm yourself,' said the stranger. 'You are a friend of Mister D'Ivoi, I believe?'

'D'Ivoi,' said Bates. 'Yes.'

'I bring a message from him. Could we go inside your apartment?'

'Your army is in Kent, sir,' said Bates, his fight-or-flight balance teetering towards the aggressive again. 'It loots Kent as we speak, sir.'

The stranger only said: 'I bring a message from him.'

The stranger did not introduce himself, or give a name. He carried a leather attaché case, and his boots were well worn at toe and heel. Inside, as Bates unclasped his own shutters (having no servant to do the job for him), the man placed his case carefully on a table, took off his three-cornered-hat, and bowed.

'Swiftness is to be desired, sir,' he said. 'I apologise for my English, for the speaking. You will pardon my poorly speaking?' Without waiting for an answer, he went on. 'Mister D'Ivoi has you asked for particularly.' He enunciated every syllable of this latter word with care. 'He, and I, ask for help. You have faith in our cause, I believe.'

'Cause?'

'For the Pacificans. For the little and the great, of the people. The Holy Father has declared the war a holy war, to free these creatures from their bondage. Yes?'

'Yes.'

'Our army will soon be in London. We wish for you to do something for us, which it will make more swift the ending of the war. If you do this thing for us, the war will end sooner, and the holy cause achieved.'

'Yes,' said Bates. His mouth was dry.

'In this satchel there is a person.'

'Satchel?'

The stranger bowed. 'Is the word incorrect? I apologise. This sack, this bag.'

'No, sir, I understand the word.'

'Please, will you take this satchel to the Tower of London. It is this tower which is the command position for the defence of London, as we believe. The generals, the munitions, the forces, they gather there. The person inside the satchel will be able to work such things as to ... to make more swift the ending of the war.'

'There is a Lilliputian in the bag?'

The stranger bowed, and opened the flap of the satchel. A Lilliputian unhooked himself from a small padded harness inside and climbed out to stand, at attention, on the tabletop. Bates, as amazed and as unsettled as he always was in the presence of these tiny beings, smiled, made his smile broader, opened his mouth to show his teeth as if he were going to eat the thing. The Lilliputian stood motionless.

'He has a training, a special training,' said the stranger. 'He is a warrior of great courage, great value. If I were to approach the Tower I would be shot, of course. And the naked streets are dangerous places for the little men, with traps and cats and all things like this. But if *you* were to bear the satchel, you would be able to release him inside the fort. Yes?'

'I know nobody in the Tower of London,' said Bates. 'I have no contacts in the army.'

'You go to the Tower, and tell them that you bear a message from Colonel Truelove.'

'I do not know the gentleman.'

'He is captured, but we believe that the ... English, excuse me, that *you* ... do not know that he is captured. You will present to the guards and tell them that you bear a message from him, for attention of General Wilkinson only, for the general *only*. Once inside, find a quiet place to release the warrior from the satchel.'

Sunlight laid squares on the floor. Light is a weight upon the earth, a mighty pressure from above, and yet it is constituted of the tiniest of particles.

Bates felt as if the moment of choice had already passed behind him. He did not have the language to phrase a rejection. All he could say was: 'I will do this thing.'

[6]

27 November 1848

You are a strange figure, somebody told Bates. Sometimes your spirit is enormous; sometimes it shrinks to nothing. To nothing, Bates thought, and I lie abed for days. But not now, he thought. Now I have a task, to test myself, to prove myself to God.

The Frenchman had insisted on the urgency of his mission, and had pressed Bates until he offered up a promise to undertake it the following dawn. 'Dawn, mind, sir,' said the Frenchman, before leaving. 'If we co-obstinate ...'

'Co-ordinate,' corrected Bates.

'Just so. If we co-obstinate, such that the little warrior is inside the Tower at the right moment, then we can complete the war much sooner. Much sooner. There shall be less deaths, so.'

He departed, with a gait that looked to Bates like an insolent jauntiness. But it was much too late for regrets. He shut his door, pulled up a chair and sat opposite the miniature human on the tabletop.

'Good evening, my friend,' he said.

The Lilliputian was silent.

There was some uncanny aspect to them. Bates had often thought this. He could not feel comfortable in their company. They unsettled him. He tried to visualise them as toys, or marionettes, but then they would shiver in some inescapably human way, or their little eyes would swivel and stare, as if penetrating beneath the decorous levels of manner and behaviour. They carried within them a strange elision. They were sylphs, but they were also and at the same time devils.

But it was too late for regrets.

'You are reticent, my friend,' he said. 'I cannot blame you if you harbour resentment against the English peoples. My people have committed . . . terrible crimes against . . . your people.'

The Lilliputian said nothing. Was his silence the outward sign of some savage indignation?

'Believe me,' Bates went on, 'I am your friend. I have devoted my life to your cause.'

Nothing.

It occurred to Bates that the Lilliputian might not speak English. 'Mon ami,' he began, but his French was not good. 'Mon ami, j'espère que . . .'

The Lilliputian turned on his heel, clambered back inside the satchel, and was gone.

In the small hours of the morning Bates discovered that the Lilliputian did indeed speak English. He had somehow mounted the arm of the *chaise longue* on which Bates was sleeping, and called in his wren-like voice: 'Awake! Awake! For the sun will soon scatter darkness like a white stone scattering crows in flock.'

Sleepy-headed, Bates found this hard to follow.

'We must be on our way,' cried the Lilliputian. 'We must be on our way.'

'It is still dark,' Bates grumbled, rubbing the sleep from his eyes with his forearm.

'But it will be light soon.'

'You speak English.'

The Lilliputian did not say anything to this.

Bates rose and lit a lamp, dressing rapidly. He used yesternight's bowl of water to rinse his face, laced his feet into his boots and looked about him. The Lilliputian was standing beside the satchel.

'You are eager to go to war, my little friend,' Bates said.

The morning had a spectral, unreal feel about it: the citrus light of the lamp, the angular purple shadows it threw, the perfect scaled-down human being standing on the table.

'I am a warrior,' it piped.

'But we must remember that Jesus is the Prince of Peace.'

The little figure slanted his head minutely, but did not reply.

'Well well,' said Bates. 'Well well, we shall go.'

The little figure slipped inside the case.

Locking the door to his rooms felt, to Bates, like sealing off his life entire. Perhaps I shall die, he said, but his mind was so muzzy with tiredness that the thought carried no sting. Perhaps I shall never return here. But he didn't believe that, not truly. He did not truly believe that.

His fingers slipped and fumbled at his coat buttons, and then hoisting the case with its precious cargo he strode out.

His heels sounded on the pavement in Cavendish Square. The air was chill. The western horizon was still a gloomy and impressive purple, but the sky to the east was bright, the colour of tawny wine, with the morning star a dot of sharp light like a tiny window, immeasurably far off, open in the wall of an immense yellow citadel.

At the top of Charing Cross Road Bates saw a solitary person in the otherwise deserted streets, a hunched-over infantryman stumbling or hurrying north. He drew back automatically into the shadow of a doorway, and then rebuked himself and reemerged. He imagined sentry questions. *Who goes there?* An Englishman! A loyal Englishman! God save the King! *What's in the bag?* Nothing – sir – nothing at all, save some personal belongings ... but that would be easily disproven, a quick search would reveal his true cargo. Papers! Papers for the General ... to be perused by him alone. To be seen by his eyes only! Would that satisfy a sentryman?

He walked on, and the dawn swelled in brightness all around him.

By the time he reached Holborn the sounds of fighting were unignorable.

From a distance the cannon-fire sounded like the booming of bitterns over estuary flats, or the stomach-rumble of distant thunder. But once down the dip and up the other side of Holborn the battle seemed to swoop out of the imaginary into the real with appalling swiftness. Knocks and bangs three streets away, two, and then rifle fire tattering the air, men in beetroot uniforms with bayoneted rifles trotting en masse, or hurrying singly from firing position to firing position.

Bates was fully awake now.

He ducked down one side street, and then another, trying to stay clear of the scurrying military action. He was vividly aware of the stupidity of his position; a civilian, an unarmed and inexperienced man wandering the streets in the midst of a war. A bomb swooned through the air, exploding somewhere away to his left with a powerful crunch. It actually bent the air, staggering Bates like hot breath from the ovens of hell. He almost fell quite over, danced to recover his balance.

A siren sang a pure note inside Bates's ears.

Panic took him for a space of some minutes. He dropped the satchel and tried to claw his way through a barred oak door. When his right fingernails were bloody the panic seemed to ebb from him, leaving him panting and foolish. He retrieved the satchel, hurried to the end of the street, turned a dog-leg and found himself on the riverside.

The sun at its low angle, with sunlight trembling off the water, turned the river to metal. Bates hurried on. Fifty yards downriver and he was at the deserted tollbooth of London Bridge's Middlesex side.

'You there!' called somebody. 'Hold yourself! Friend or foe!'

Bates stopped. 'An Englishman!' he called.

From where he was standing he could look down upon the bridge, and across the pale brown rush of the river. The Thames's flow seemed enormous, the water standing up at the leading face of the bridge's pillars in burly lips, the trailing edge leaving deep scores in the surface that broke into wakes and ripples hundreds of yards downstream. Riflemen hurried along the half-completed embankment, ducking behind the unplaced stone-blocks, or jumping into the holes where such blocks were yet to be placed. The sound of horses' whinnying, like metal skittering over ice, was in the air from somewhere on the other side of the river. An artillery unit laboured with a recalcitrant field gun, poking its snub over the bridge's parapet. On the river's surface, a boat jockeyed against the fierce pull of the water, three sets of oars flicking up and down like insect legs, hauling the craft alongside a small quay onto which soldiers were alighting.

And then, with the sounds of multiple detonation, smoke flowered into the air. French dart-shells hurtled over the horizon, threads against the sky, and careered into the masonry alongside the river with astonishing vehemence. The ground shook. Ripples shuddered across the face of the water. Stone cracked and puffed into the air as smoke. Bricks, pillars and blocks tumbled and clattered. More explosions. The tick-tock of bullets, British rifle fire, although Bates couldn't see what they were firing at. Then the giants came; heads rearing up like the sun over the horizon, but these suns followed by bodies, and the bodies supported on enormous legs. They strode up the river, the water blanching into foam about their thighs. They were dressed in crazily patched leather clothes, padded with numerous metal plates that were too poorly bur-nished to gleam in the light. With the sun behind them, four marched.

He was so stunned by the sight as to not understand how much in shock he was. He blinked, and turned. People were rushing on all sides, faces distorted as they shouted. He blinked again, turned again. The French, soldiers of ordinary size, were visible on the south bank, some firing over the water, some attempting to cross the bridge. English troops were defending the position. Bates stood in the midst of it, a single gentleman in modest but expensive clothing, his coat buttoned all the way to his chin, carrying a leather satchel briefcase. One of the English soldiers, hurrying to the bridge, caught his eye. 'You!' he yelled. 'You!'

Still numb to his surroundings, Bates turned to face him. Smoke misted up and swirled away, to an orchestral accompaniment of clat-tering explosions.

Everybody was looking north. Bates followed their glances. Another thunderstroke.

One of the Brobdingnagians had climbed up to the dome of Saint Paul's. He had driven his metal-tipped staff through the shell of it, as if breaking the blunt end of an egg. He lifted it out, and struck again, and the dome collapsed, leaving a fuzzy halo of dust.

Bates turned to look for the soldier who had accosted him. He was not standing where he had been standing. Bates looked around, and then looked down, and saw him lying spreadeagled on the floor. Blood, as dark and sluggish as molasses, was pooled all around him.

Bates stumbled, half-awake, from the tollbooth and down a side street. A crazy trajectory. He ran past a row of scowling arches and turned into a doorway, pressing himself up into the shadow against the side wall.

The sounds of battle had become chuckles and creaks. It took him a moment to realise that the fighting was moving away, sweeping round beyond the wrecked cathedral and into the fields to the north. He fiddled with the catch on the briefcase and whispered inside, and as he did so he was struck by how peculiar it was to be whispering.

The street was deserted.

The Lilliputian's high-pitched voice warbled from its hidden place. 'You must go on.'

'I will be killed,' said Bates, a trill of nerves shaking the last word. He was near tears.

'Death is the soil of the world,' said the Lilliputian, the oddness of the sentiment made stranger still by the ethereal, piping voice that uttered it.

'I will wait here until the fighting has stopped,' said Bates. Saying so brought him a trembly sense of satisfaction: to be safe, not to die, to stay hidden until the danger had passed.

'No,' said the Lilliputian. The timbre of his voice had changed. Somehow, Bates could not see how, he had slipped out of the case and climbed up his overcoat. In an instant he stood on Bates's shoulder, and with a shimmer was on his face. Pressure on his ear. The horrid tickling sensation as if of a mouse on his cheek. Bates could not repress a shudder, raising of his hand to swat the creature that had the *gall* to touch his face! – to touch his *face*! It required the fullest effort of will to hold from slapping at the little creature. I must not! He thought. God's creature!

Blurrily close to his eyeball, the pink-yellow shape of a head, a lash-like hand, dissolved by nearness. 'This thorn,' warbled the Lilliputian, 'is a weapon. I can thrust it into your eye, and it will explode the eye, as a bomb explodes.' Bates's eyelids froze. 'If you attack me,' the creature urged, 'I will have your eye.' Bates blinked, forcefully, and again, but it did not dislodge the assailant. His eye was watering; his breaths were coming much more swiftly. 'If you do not move now, go to the Tower, I will have your eye.'

'My dear little friend,' said Bates, high-pitched. 'Man share amy.'

'The Brobdingnagians live to be a hundred and fifty years of age,' came the sing-song rapid little voice. 'They are wary of death, for death is a rarity to them. But we of Lilliput live a quarter as long, and hold death in a quarter as much worth. We are a nation of warriors.'

'My dear little friend,' said Bates, again.

'Go now.' And the tickling sensation vanished from his face, the ornament-like pressure removed from his ear. When Bates had regained his breath the Lilliputian was back in the satchel.

The battle seemed to have passed entirely away. Cautious as a mouse, Bates ducked from doorway to doorway, but the only people he saw were British soldiers, all of them hurrying. He hurried himself, jogging down Eastcheap, and came out from between the houses directly in front of the Tower.

He had no idea of the time. Certainly the morning was well advanced. The sky was crowded with ivory-coloured thunderheads. Spots of rain touched his face, and Bates was put in mind of a million contemptuous Lilliputians spitting upon his skin.

There was a great deal of military activity around the Tower. Mounted troops skittered by over the cobbles, their horses glittery with sweat, or rain, or both; cannon were positioned at all places, sentries doing their clockwork sentry business, chimney smoke and noise and business and camp followers, all the melee. It seemed odder to Bates than the battle he had just witnessed. He shouldered the satchel, its occupant a fierce wasp, striped in its uniform. Yet who could say? Why not angelic as well? Mightn't angels' wings have the sheen of an insect's, the blur and light of it? The buzz-buzz? And there was the Tower itself, London's Tower as white as ice, blocky like teeth, standing taller over him, his parent, his nationhood's parent. It was Brutus's tower.

It did not look inviting.

Nobody challenged him as he marched up the causeway until he had come within ten yards of the closed main gate, with its lesser gate inset and open. 'Who goes there?' yelled the sentryman, although he was only a foot or so from Bates. 'General Wilkinson!' shouted Bates, startled into life. 'I bring a message for General Wilkinson!' His heart stuttered. 'I have a message for the general's ears only! From Colonel Truelove!'

[7]

He spent much of the rest of the day hiding inside a well-appointed house whose door had been blown, or beaten, from its hinges. The kitchen was wrecked and the food looted, but the other rooms had been left untouched: beautiful furniture, with legs curled and slender as angels' wands, ornaments with the intricacy of clockwork but without function or movement, globes of glass holding preserved flowers, a new design of tallboy-clock, whose metronomic timekeeper rocked back

29

and forth on its hinged base like a tree swaying in the breeze. The walls were hung with oils of society beauties.

Entering the Tower had, in the end, been a simple business. The guard had looked inside the satchel, but only cursorily and without penetrating deep enough to unearth the miniature warrior concealed inside. Bates had walked into the Tower through the inset door, the flap a twelfth the size in the corner of the great gates. The great gates were not opened. Bates had hurried past the buzz of people within, over the inner quad, through another door and to a coign in an empty corridor. And there he had released the Lilliputian warrior, who had emerged from the bag with threads of rope coiled over his shoulder, and his own miniature satchel on a belt around his waist. He had not bidden Bates farewell. He had scurried off without a word.

Bates had loitered, nervously, around the Tower, and then had slipped amongst a crowd of engineers and kitchen servants as they exited the Tower, and after that had made his way into deserted streets in Whitechapel.

Perhaps he expected to hear some titanic explosion, the arsenal beneath the Tower exploded by the fierce little Lilliputian; perhaps he expected the cheers of French troops. But although his ear was repeatedly distracted by bangs, knocks, creases of sound in the air, yells, tatters of song, aural flotsam, he heard nothing that matched the imagined cataclysm of his heart.

Much later in the afternoon, ashamed at his own manifest cowardice, he had ventured out from this house, and wandered the city. He came across one dead body, in a British uniform, and then a clutch more of them. A print-shop's windows had been broken in to make a placement for a field gun, but the gun's barrel was sheared and broken like a daisy, and its crew lay in a tangle of blackened arms and legs around it. Southward brought Bates out on the river again. Here there were more bodies. Bates went to the water's edge and sat down. On the far side of the river ruined buildings bannered smoke into the evening air.

There was nobody in sight. It was as if London were a mort city.

The river hushed below him, a sound like breathing.

I have killed my city, thought Bates, his mood flowing away from him now like the river itself, his spirits draining into the sinks of despair. I am a traitor, and I have killed my city.

An irregular splashing to the west intruded on his attention. Upriver he could see one of the giants, sitting on the bank with its legs in the water for all the world like a small boy beside a tiny stream. The giant kicked his legs, languidly, intermittently, sending up house-sized bulges of water to trouble the surface. Behind him, the tip of the sun dipped against the river. Its colour bled from it into the water, like paint from a brush washed after a day's work.

With desperate, self-detesting resolution, Bates started towards the figure; this giant surveying the ruins he had made of the world's greatest city. 'Monsieur!' he called. 'Monsieur!'

He ran for ten minutes before he was close enough for his gnat's voice to reach the great flappy ears. 'Monsieur! Monsieur!'

The Brobdingnagian turned his head with the slowness of a planet revolving.

'I am here, Monsieur!' squeaked Bates. 'Down here, Monsieur!'

The eyelids rolled up, great blinds, and the carpet-roll lips parted. 'Good day,' the giant said.

And now that he was standing beside the creature, Bates realised he had no idea what he had intended in coming over. 'Forgive me, sir,' he said. 'Forgive me for approaching you. Is the battle over?'

'I can barely hear you,' grumbled the giant, its sub-bass voice rolling and coiling in the evening air. 'Allow me to lift you.' And with sluggish but minute patience the enormous hand presented itself, so that Bates could step into the palm. The quality of the skin was not in the least leathery, as he expected it to be; it was douce, though strong, with some of the quality of turf. And then he was lifted into the air, and brought before the enormous benign face. Bates could see the pores, a thousand rabbit-holes in the cliff-face; could see the poplar-stubs of unshaved beard, the tangle of hair in the nostril like winter scrub.

'Thank you, Monsieur,' he said. 'Is the battle over?'

'It is,' said the giant.

'Are the French victorious?'

Every flicker of emotion was magnified, as if the great face were acting, over-acting, each expression. 'You are French?'

'No, sir, no, sir,' Bates gabbled. 'But a sympathiser, sir. I am an ally of France, an ally, that is to say, of its great cause, of freedom for Pacificans, of freedom against slavery and the upholding of God's law.'

'Your voice is too small, and too rapid,' rumbled the voice. 'I cannot follow your speech.'

'I am a friend to the Brobdingnagian people,' said Bates more slowly and more loud. 'And to the Lilliputians.'

31

A smile, wide as a boulevard. 'The tiniest of folk. Our fleas are bigger than they. Some of my people,' he grumbled on, benignly, 'do not believe they exist, never having seen them. But I am assured they do exist, and I am prepared to believe it.'

There was silence for a moment. The light reddened deeper into sunset.

'The day is yours?' Bates asked again.

'The army of France is victorious.'

'You do not seem happy.'

'Melancholia,' said the giant, drawing the word out so that it seemed to rumble on and on, a sound like heavy furniture being dragged over the floor. 'To observe a city broken like this. We Brobdingnagians are a peaceful people, and such destruction . . .' He trailed off.

'But your great cause,' chirruped Bates. 'This victory is a great thing! It will mean freedom for your people.'

'The France army,' said the giant, 'possess a machine of the greatest ingenuity. I have seen it; no bigger than a snuffbox, yet it *computes* and *calculates* and solves all manner of problems at a ferocious rate. So swiftly it works! It is this machine that has won the war, I think. This machine. Its strategy, and its solution to problems. This machine.' He hummed and hoomed for a while. 'My people,' he continued, 'my people are ingenious with machines, but never so ingenious as your people. You are small, but cunning. Perhaps the others, the Lil, the Lilli . . .'

'The Lilliputians.'

'Just so, perhaps *they* are more ingenious even than you? The smaller the more cunning? This may be God's way of ordering his universe. The smaller the more cunning.'

'I have long been an ally of France,' Bates declared. His spirits, sunken only minutes before, were rising again, following their own unfathomable logic. Perhaps, he thought, perhaps my betrayal truly followed a higher good. Perhaps it is for the best. After defeat, England will abandon its persecution of the Pacificans, and soon after that its greatness will reassert itself. In ten years . . . maybe less. And it will be a more worthwhile greatness, because it will not flout God's ordinance. 'I have long been an ally of France, and a friend of the Count D'Ivoi.'

'D'Ivoi,' said the giant. 'I know him.'

'You know him?'

'Indeed. Shall I take you to him?'

'Yes!' Bates declared, his heart flaring into fervour. 'Yes! I will congratulate him on his victory, and on the new age of justice for Lilliputians and Brobdingnagians both!'

The enormous hand cupped him against the giant's shoulder, and he rose to his full height. The sun seemed to pull back from the horizon with the change in perspective, and then in lengthily slushing strides the giant marched down the river. He paused at the wrecked arches of London Bridge, stepping up onto the concourse and over it into the water again. In moments he was alongside the Tower. The troops outside the citadel were in French uniform; they scurried below, insect-like, apparently as alarmed by their gigantic ally as the British had been by the giants as foes. Cannon were hauled round to bear on the figure.

'A visitor for Monsieur Le Comte,' boomed the Brobdingnagian. 'A visitor for Monsieur D'Ivoi.'

He placed Bates on the charred lawn before the main gate, and withdrew his hand.

[8]

Bates was kept waiting for an hour or more, sitting on a bench inside the main gate. The evening light shaded deeper into full darkness, and a November chill wrapped itself around the skin. Soldiers passed back and forth, perked by their victory. Every face was grinning. Bates allowed the sense of achievement to penetrate his own heart. Something great had happened here, after all. He thought of the little warrior he had carried past this gate only that morning. Such valour in so small an individual! Was he still alive? When he met D'Ivoi again, he would ask. Such valour. He deserved a medal. Would miniature medals be forged, to reward the part brave Lilliputians had played in their own liberation?

'Monsieur?' An aide-de-camp was standing in front of him. 'The Comte D'Ivoi will see you now.'

Bubbling with excitement, Bates followed the fellow across the court and down a series of steps. Gaslit corridors, the stone wet with evening dew, or with their own cold slime. Finally into a broad-groined room, lit by two dozen lamps, brighter than day. And there was D'Ivoi with his absurd pigtail bobbing at the back of his head. A group of gorgeously uniformed men was sitting around a table.

'Bates, my friend,' called D'Ivoi. 'France has much for which to thank you.'

33

Bates approached, smiling. The generals at the table were examining maps of the southern counties. Around them strutted and passed a stream of military humanity. In the corner, somewhat the size of a sentry box, was an ebonywood case.

Of the generals, only D'Ivoi stood up. The rest of the generals were still eating, and pausing only to drink from smoky coffee-cups as wide as skulls.

'Bates, my friend,' said D'Ivoi again.

They were eating pastries glazed with sugar. The pastries glistened as if wet.

'D'Ivoi,' said Bates. He felt cheered to see his old friend, but something was wrong somewhere. He couldn't put his finger on it. He could not determine exactly what was wrong. It might have been that he did not want to determine what was wrong, for that would mean dismantling his buoyant feeling of happiness and achievement. And yet, like a pain somewhere behind the eyes, Bates knew something was wrong.

One of the generals looked up from the table. His ugliness was remarkable, the left eyebrow and cheek scored with an old scar, the eye itself glass and obnoxious. 'Sit,' said D'Ivoi.

The air in the room was not sweet: close and stale-smelling.

'I am glad that my small action,' said Bates, 'was able to hasten the conclusion to this wasteful war.'

One of the generals at table snorted.

'Did the Lilliputian warrior I ported here . . . did he survive?'

'He did his job very well,' said D'Ivoi. 'Although, alas, the war is not over yet. The English are resisting at Runnymede, on the hill by the river there, with some skill and some force. But it will not be long! It will not be long, in part because of your labour. We, France, salute you.'

'Ours is a nobler cause,' said Bates, the words for a moment swimming his head with the thrill and honour of it all.

'Cause?' asked the general with the glass eye. It was impossible to look at his bunched, seamed face without one's glance being drawn to his hideous eye. Bates pulled his gaze away, and it fell on the box in the corner of the room.

'The Pope's latest decree,' said D'Ivoi, and stopped. He noticed where Bates was looking. 'Ah, my friend, your eye discovers our most valuable ally. The computation device!'

'So this is it,' said Bates, distantly. The fact that there was something wrong was intruding itself again. 'The famous computation device.'

'Truly,' said D'Ivoi. 'It has brought us further, and faster. It will change the whole world, this beautiful machine. Beautiful machine!'

'The Pope's latest decree?' queried the General. '*C'est quoi ce que t'as dit?*'

D'Ivoi gabbled something in French, too rapidly for Bates to follow. His own smile felt false, now. The light was too bright in this underground cavern. It slicked the walls. Centuries of the Tower, a prison. The giants Gog and Magog, and Bran also. Was it not Bran the giant? Buried under Tower Hill, that was the story. Buried under the hill and the Tower built above it, pressing down on the enormous bones. A giant prison oppressing the buried form. How many people had seen the inside of this chamber, and never seen the light again? Centuries of people locked away, barred and closed and buried in the ground like blind stones in the mud.

Bates was stepping towards the device now. 'It is marvellous,' he muttered. 'How does it work?'

D'Ivoi was at his arm, a touch on his elbow. 'Ah, my friend,' he said. 'I cannot permit you to examine it too closely. You are a friend to France, I know, but even you must respect military secrets.'

The box was coffin-black. It did not display any of its secrets on its exterior. 'Of course,' murmured Bates.

'As to how it works,' D'Ivoi continued, steering Bates back towards the door of the room. 'For that you will have to ask Mister Babbage. It is something like an abacus, I think; something like a series of switches, or rolls, or gears, or something like this. I do not know. I only know,' he beamed, and took Bates's hand in his own, 'I only know that it will win us the war. Goodbye, my friend, and thank you again.'

Bates was half dazed as he walked from the room. A guard eyed him. He walked half aware up the stairway. There were certain things he should not think about. That was it. That was the best way. Bury thought, like the giant buried under the hill. Certain things he should not think about. He should not think of the French troops ranging out across the fields of England, of other towns burning, of the smoke rising as a column from the heart of the kingdom. Should not think of the blood draining out of bodies, tomato-bright in the sunlight. Should not think of giant men working to the extinction of their race at brute tasks, menial tasks, hauling logs or working great engines until their sturdy bodies gave out in exhaustion. Should not think of the Computational Device in the corner of the oppressive underground room. Not imagine opening the front of the device and looking inside. Or if he did think of this last, if he must think of it, then he should think of some giant clockwork device, some great rack of toothed-wheels and pins and rods, something wholly mechanical. But not think of a tight, close, miniature prison-cage, in which sweating rows of labouring tiny people worked at wheels and abacus racks, tied into position, working joylessly in the dark and hopelessness to process some machine for computation. Not that. He was on the top step now, and about to step back into the light, and the best thing would be to leave all that behind him, buried away below.

TWO

ELEANOR

❀

[1]

Eleanor was eighteen years old when she learned whom she would marry. His name was Jonathan Burton. He was an industrialist. Her mother (seven years a widow) wept actual tears when she talked of it, as if perfectly overjoyed at the prospect. And yet Eleanor was certain her mother knew how deeply she was repelled by this Burton. How could she not? Burton owned a manufactory down by the river. He was vulgar, and he was old, and he was ugly. Worse, he was a mere arriviste: his father had been a printer's devil, and his grandfather a servant – a servant! – in Derbyshire. Yet by his own efforts, employing the tiny Lilliputian men and women to make fancy machinery and cunning devices, he had become rich. And wealth, of course, brought its own privileges. Even at eighteen, sitting beside her Mamma in the open-topped clarence that they could not afford (but which Mamma continued to rent) – even at so early an age Eleanor understood that the economics of love were based on a principle of exclusive binaries. You might have a handsome husband, but he would be poor. You might have a wealthy husband, but he would be ugly. There were, it seemed, no other permutations of that particular equation. You might marry for the love of your betrothed and give up the love of your family; or alternately you might marry a man without owning a tittle of love for him and by doing so cement your Mamma's love for you. This balance was what the mathematicians called *zero-sum*. Eleanor understood all this without needing to tax her mother's nebulous hypocrisy with question and answer. 'He is a kind man,' her Mamma said one Thursday, as they rode out in the clarence carriage.

Eleanor had been thinking of mathematics, and was not paying proper attention. 'He, Mamma?'

'Mister Burton,' said Mamma, with a fluttery intimation of displeasure in her voice that said plainly, *Pay attention to me when I speak.* Eleanor thrust mathematical thoughts from her mind.

'Indeed, Mamma,' she said. 'He is kind.'

'And wealthy. In the world of industry he is greatly respected.'

Eleanor wondered how her mother could possibly be privy to the opinion of the world of industry. But she only said: 'I do not doubt it.'

'He is almost a gentleman,' said Mamma, wistfully. They were trotting now, bumpily but with a pleasant sensation of swiftness, along Oxford Street. There was a great blueness in the sky, and a congregation of bright white clouds. The very air felt blue and clean passing into Eleanor's lungs. Sunlight winked at them through a grid of streetside poplars. They were going, as they did most weeks, to watch the soldiers parade and practise in Hyde Park, the carriage joining a select audience formed of two dozen other carriages (most of which were much grander than their own) parked on the green.

These little excursions represented a high point of Mamma's week, and although Eleanor always found them tedious she endured them for her Mamma's sake. But lately, since the engagement to Burton had been formalized, Eleanor had been finding them less tolerable than before. Her Mamma seemed to have no understanding of the ironies of the circumstance. There was, in her limited imagination, no conflict between her own gawping at these handsome men and her daughter's prospects of life with the soggy-faced, flabby-bodied old factory owner. Eleanor looked away from the park as the men filed past. Her heart complained within her. There would be no slim, handsome husband waiting for *her* by the altar; no hero of the Continental wars; no officer with twenty thousand a year. Her mother's eyes positively latched on to each of the young men as they passed. Was not such behaviour indecorous? Surely it verged on the improper. Of course, if Mamma were to be challenged (and of course Eleanor would not force her mother to so humiliating a circumstance) she would talk about the trips as her *tribute to the army*, or somesuch expression – as relating to her national pride at this time of war, or admiring the precision with which the men drilled, the glamour of their uniforms and the honour they embodied. But Eleanor, though young, was not so foolish as to miss the truth of it. Her mother admired the young men for their good looks, for the slimness of their figures, the straightness of their limbs. The carriages lined along the park were full of wealthy women casting the same admiring looks for the same reason, and many of them were not widows – many were actually married. Being joined to their husbands did not stop those women. Eleanor's disapprobation was a puny force against such consolidated appetite.

From time to time, an officer would pull his horse up alongside one or other carriage and exchange a few words with the people within. On occasion such a figure pulled alongside even their humble carriage. *Good morning to you, fair ladies*, some young lieutenant would beam. *A glorious morning, ain't it?* At this Mamma would giggle like a girl, and Eleanor's heart would shrink. The embarrassment! Once a Captain leant, practically, inside their carriage, still in the saddle, and said *Why I do declare there are two sisters herein, they've come out unchaperoned!* And Mamma had laughed, and the Captain had laughed, and Eleanor had simpered and wished that he would go away and leave them be. After he had trotted off, Mamma had been virtually bursting with excitement at the encounter. 'Did you hear that?' she had gabbled. 'He thought me your sister – and in such a strong light, too. It was worth spending the money on my paint' – her face-paint, she meant – 'if it can work such effects.' 'I'm sure, Mamma,' Eleanor drawled in reply, 'that he was being only polite.' 'Bah,' dismissed her mamma with a wave of her gloved hand. 'You said eighteen shillings and six was too much for a pot of the stuff, did you not? What do you say now, my girl?' Such a little pot, Eleanor remembered. And so oddly coloured on the skin. And now, sitting next to her in the open-topped carriage, with the morning sunlight shining hard on her face, Eleanor could only think uncharitably how old her mother looked, how many twiggish lines had spread over her face, how her hair-dye smudged onto her scalp at the roots. But she said: 'You're quite correct, Mamma.'

The problem, Eleanor decided afterwards, was the way her mother's manner was so different when it came to her daughter's impending marriage with Burton. With the handsome young officers she was silly and self-deluding as a girl; with Burton as hard-nosed and practical as a moneylender. Did she not see that they were two examples of the same general case? Only that the former applied to Mamma's cloud-hearted dreams, and the latter to pounds and shillings and pennies. Could she not at least be consistent? Eleanor felt like a commodity to be traded, and felt that her Mamma – now home, her face now free of beauty-paint – was merely her agent of sale. It was a common enough situation, Eleanor knew. But she told herself that she could have borne it better if Mamma had only shown some honesty about it.

Of course, in one respect at least Mamma was perfectly correct. They could not live without money. Eleanor did not know how they had lived as long as they had. And Burton – though disgusting, physically, with a nose shaped like cheese squashed in a muslin bag, and with the habit of sucking his teeth smackingly – Burton, it could not be denied, was wealthy.

Mother and daughter lived together with a maid of all work in three rooms on Poland Street; one room at the front, which received a pleasant portion of sunlight during the day, and two at the back, which did not. It was a first-floor apartment. Mamma had taken the front room, and by having a curtain hung from the ceiling so as to partition off a corner contrived to double the room into bed- and sitting room. Eleanor's own room looked over the yard at the back of the house, a cobbled irregular pentagon shape, in which the clarence was kept underneath a tarpaulin (its horse was owned and stabled in a yard on Euston Road, and brought down by the boy when it was needed). Next to her was what Mamma called 'the morning room', although it was actually the maid's room, the larder and kitchen, and served other functions too. Sally was under instruction to clear away her pallet-bed and the canvas bag containing her belongings immediately upon rising and store them in one of the room's large cupboards. The maid received a salary of fifty shillings and two dresses each year; but Mamma had not had enough money to supply the dresses for eighteen months now. Sally – a meek, complaisant little thing most of the time – bickered about this neglect from time to time, the more so when she was stitching a repair to her own threadbare clothes. Eleanor, indeed, considered it demeaning to cheat a servant of her wages, but the few occasions when daughter spoke to mother on the subject led only to tears and a bad atmosphere between them.

'There must be some way we can buy poor Sally a new dress,' she would say.

'You know nothing of it,' her mother would snap at her. 'The finances are a constant worry and burden to me.'

'Yet we suffer the expense of maintaining the clarence.'

'Don't be foolish, girl!' replied her mamma.

'But don't you think,' Eleanor essayed next day, thinking the stratagem more likely to succeed, 'it reflects but poorly on us if our servants are so ill-clothed? Do you not agree, Mamma?'

'Agree?' replied her mother, and then hallooed: 'Ha! You'd have an army of servants all dressed in our own livery, I suppose? Dressed,' she repeated (she often repeated her own comments if she thought them particularly witty or telling, as she often did), 'in our own livery, I suppose?'

'Now,' placated Eleanor. 'Mamma, please don't misunderstand.'

But her mother was crying now. 'As if I haven't shouldered the burden of raising a family since your poor papa left us, sole and solitary. As if it hasn't put lines into my face and shrunken my figure, shrunken my figure, with care and fretting. As if I don't wrestle with the tiresome figures and sums and all that accounting like Jacob with the angel every day I breathe. Like biblical Jacob and the angel.'

Eleanor embraced her mother.

'Mamma, Mamma, I did not speak to vex you.'

'I don't believe any woman of quality in the whole of London has suffered as I have,' whimpered Mamma. 'Since your papa left us.' She never spoke of Eleanor's father *dying*, always spoke of him *leaving*. It was a more blaming locution.

'But I only wish to help,' Eleanor insisted, smoothing down her hair with the flat of her hand as her head pressed against her shoulders. Smears of her mother's hair-dye streaked her palm. 'I only wish to alleviate some of this worry. Perhaps if we moved to less expensive accommodation ...'

Mamma jerked up, accusation in her eyes. 'This again?'

'If, Mamma, only if ...'

'You'd have us leave this fashionable address, and move to Somers Town?'

'I only mentioned Somers Town that time before because Mr Froude at the soirée had the good sense to suggest ...'

'That beast!' hissed Mamma. 'I'll not have his name mentioned. Somers Town is seedy and repulsive to my sensibilities.'

'But it is less than a mile from here, Mamma, and so much cheaper ...'

'You know nothing of the expense of renting decent accommodation,' said Mamma. 'Besides, I have an understanding with Mr Newsome.' Then her anger, momentarily solid enough to sit her up straight, collapsed away in a tumble of tears. 'Oh my darling girl,' she sobbed, her head sinking against her daughter's breast. 'My darling girl!'

Newsome was their landlord, a doleful little man, but an individual – or so Eleanor assumed – sympathetic to the vagaries of finance that supported, or barely supported, his two female tenants. At any rate, he had not evicted them yet. The more Eleanor thought about it, the more remarkable this became to her. Father had left them no money. They had no other relatives to support them. They did no wage-earning work. Eleanor absolutely could not fathom from where her mother got her money. Not that they ever had *much* money, of course, but Eleanor could not guess where even that little came from. Mamma could not, presumably, conjure gold and silver from thin air; yet there was always silver, and sometimes even gold, in her purse. The silver was only thruppences and sixpences and shillings, it was true, and the dull gold of a half-sovereign was a rare visitor, but all these coins must have come from somewhere.

In many ways Eleanor knew herself innocent of the world. Appropriate to her caste, she had been raised to take a degree of quiet pride in this very ignorance. And from what little she saw of the world outside her bubble she had no great desire for closer acquaintance. It was a grim place, she saw, and dangerous – animals battling with animals and humanity little better, dirty and grimy and every last farthing fought over. Eleanor preferred the sterile beauties of Science – mathematics and engineering in particular, but any book of natural philosophy, or of technics, that she could borrow or buy. But the one field applied to the other. After a day of reading algebraic notation and arithmetical shorthands it was hard not to meditate, half consciously, on the banal arithmetic that governed their precarious gentility in Poland Street, the sums that her mother insisted, with faint absurdity, were too mean for her daughter to be acquainted with. The rooms must cost a pound a week; probably more. Call it £60 per annum. Add in a pound a month for hire of the clarence, and a crown or more each time mother wanted to take it out down Oxford Street to admire the soldiers marching in Hyde Park. Probably two crowns, now Eleanor thought of it: a crown for the horse, and another for the driver. Dresses, coffee, food, surely added up to another pound a week, or perhaps more. Membership of the Portland Street library was a guinea a year, with each volume borrowed for a week costing a shilling: three shillings for a three-volume 'fashionable' novel of the sort that Mamma enjoyed, another three for

Eleanor's various books of science and mathematics. Membership of the Fitzroy Society was four guineas for the two of them, although Mamma would surely insist that that was a necessary expense, for the quest to find Eleanor a wealthy husband could not be maintained in a social vacuum. Tot it all up, pennies, shillings, pounds, and the complete amount could hardly be less than £150 a year. Not a princely sum, but money nonetheless.

Where did it come from?

But as Eleanor thought about the subject she found herself wondering where *any* money came from. She had read Ricardo, had read Mill's *Lectures Upon Political Economy*, had read Martineau's *Essay*, and had grasped many of the points in these books, for she was a fast-witted girl. But this new science of 'political economy' seemed concerned with the *distribution and effect* of wealth, not with its *origin*. For Ricardo wealth was simply a solidified form of work. The worker labours for ten hours to make the hat, and when the hat is sold for ten shillings those chiming silver coins are just icons of the time put in by the labourer. Frozen clock-faces. Mutations of time into metal. Without the time and the labour they would be meaningless. Martineau agreed with this assessment, describing money as 'the concretisation of social relations, the sixpence distilling (as it were) your desire for a loaf of bread and the baker's desire to sell one to you'. Of course, it had been several years since a loaf cost sixpence. The war pushed prices up. But the general point was clear enough.

But there seemed something, somehow, wrong about this to Eleanor. It seemed to conjugate coinage in too passive a manner. When she took out her small purse and tipped its contents into her palm, the copper and the silver weighed down her hand with a more than material tug. Coins possess a magical quality, surely – an *active* rather than a passive power, as if each of them were alive in some way, as if the King's head on the obverse were filled with real silver-thread or gold-cell brains. These coins, though tiny enough to hold in the hand, could assemble into great armies, could call forth mighty buildings to rise from the soil, could conjure machines to plough the oceans or thunder over the ground, or even to fly though the air. Was there anything money could not do? Eleanor could even half-believe that there was something divine about currency: something *ideal* in the sense Plato had meant the word. As if God had scattered coins down one day like hail, rattling on the rooftops of dumb humanity for them to take up and use and make the world a better place. Each penny, she thought, holding the coin between thumb and forefinger, held a portion of this grace. Might it not be so?

Of course *she* had no reason to consider money in so benign a light. To her and to her mother money was a tyrant, not a redeemer. The king stamped in Grecian profile on the coin ruled their lives with a Babylonian severity. Money dictated what they could do, and forbade them from doing a great deal more – it was money that commanded that she marry the repulsive Burton. She held the shilling at arm's length, till it was small as the moon, and contemplated it. So small a thing, to exercise such power over them all. The sovereign is sovereign over all of us, she thought to herself. Then, pleased with her pun, worked through further examples. The *crown* sits on a tyrant's head, not our own. The penny *pens* us in like animals in a cage. But she could not think of any further examples.

That night she played cards with her mother. Sally brought in supper from a chophouse round the corner, potatoes hot under a tin lid. The gravy was a little too salt, and the meat was overcooked, almost biscuit in texture. But Eleanor did not complain.

Afterwards there was a little Madeira wine for mother and daughter whilst Sally took the plates back to the shop. They played another hand of cards, and Mamma took a second glass of the sweet wine.

'You know, dear Eleanor,' she observed, 'that Mister Burton will call on us tomorrow afternoon?'

'I recall, Mamma.'

There was a silent moment between them. The wind brushed against the window outside, and rattled the panes with a noise like a slow shuffle of cards. Eleanor tidied things away. Mother poured herself another Madeira, and drank it in one gulp. 'He will treat you well, my love,' she said. 'That can't be said of all men a woman might marry. But he has a kind heart, I think.'

'I know, Mamma.'

'Perhaps he will not be the most ... the most *dashing* of husbands ...'

'It is all right, Mamma.'

Another silence. The stub of the old candle chuckled to itself. It pulsed its light in flickers against the walls. Eleanor almost called for Sally to bring a new candle, before remembering that she had gone out to take the plates back to the chophouse. She had been gone a long while. What could be keeping her so long away? Better, anyway, to save the expense of the candle.

'I shall retire, Mamma,' Eleanor said.

'Sleep well, my darling,' said Mamma, a clucking little catch in her voice that threatened tears, the Madeira promoting the flow of sentiment through her foolish heart. 'My darling, darling girl!'

Eleanor embraced her mother. 'Don't upset yourself Mamma,' she said, softly.

'You are so darling,' the older woman moaned, her eyes wet. The candle stuttered again, and the light danced crazily. 'My darling girl.'

'Don't upset yourself Mamma,' Eleanor repeated. She helped her over to her divan, and pulled the curtain to. 'Goodnight, Mamma.'

'Darling guilt,' murmured her mother. 'My darling, darling guilt.'

This jarred. 'What was that, Mamma?'

The older woman seemed to jolt more awake. 'What?'

'Did you say?' But Eleanor thought better of pressing the point. 'Nothing, Mamma, nothing. Goodnight.' She fetched the snuffer from the cold mantelpiece and put the dying candle out of its misery. Mamma's breathing had steadied to the rumble of sleep by the time she was at the door.

Eleanor made her way through the dark into her own room, and lit her own candle. She heard the front door, and came through to the little hallway to confront the serving girl. The candle stroked weird trembly ellipses and intersecting arcs of light against the walls. Sally's face looked flushed. 'Where have you been, Sally?'

'Just round the corner to the chop palace, Ma'am.'

'You took your own long time in coming back.'

'There was a wait on, Ma'am.' But the girl was smiling.

Eleanor was almost too tired for the scene. 'None of your impudence, Sally,' she said, in a forced whisper. 'Mamma's asleep, or I'd call her through to reprimand you.'

'I'm sure I don't know what you mean, Ma'am,' said Sally, looking affronted. But the smile was still vestigially present.

'I know what *you* mean, however,' hissed Eleanor. 'I know how it'll happen, and you'll be sorry. You'll fall into a shameful life.'

'Ma'am!' Shocked.

'Oh, there's no good in beating around the bush. You've been in a public tavern with some fellow from the chophouse. I have a care for your reputation, even if you have none. Do you wish to lose your place? Is that what you want?'

Sally glared, but kept her insolence dumb.

And all of a sudden Eleanor was too tired for the confrontation. 'To bed Sally,' she said, in a flat voice. 'To bed now, away with you now.'

Eleanor came through to her own room and sat on her bed. She could almost envy Sally. She could dally with whatever man took her fancy, and not worry that he was poor. But then again, she could barely read. She knew nothing of mathematics, or of physical sciences, or political economy. Her life was small, to Eleanor's eyes. Then she remembered her mother's drowsy voice: *my darling guilt*. Had she misspoken 'guilt', or 'gilt'? Either related to the matter in hand. Both commented upon the mercenary unspoken motivation behind her mother's actions. Perhaps Mamma did after all possess a bad conscience at her daughter's circumstance.

After making sure that both Mamma and Sally were asleep, Eleanor wrapped a shawl about her and made her way out of the house. Down the stairs and through the creaking main door, onto Poland Street.

It was a cloudless night, with a burly wind pushing up and down between the rows of houses. She pulled the shawl tighter about her shoulders and looked up. The stars were extraordinarily clear, as if the wind had rubbed and rubbed them against the black of night like a jeweller's cloth.

She turned into Oxford Street, and wandered eastward. The road was lit with occasional gas lanterns, and the light seemed to draw human activity. People gathered in the bright ellipses on the pavement, wandered up and down the road. Coaches and carriages passed and re-passed. At Saint Giles Church she turned down Charing Cross Road and into less fashionable districts. The only light here came from lit windows, and there were few of those. The moon itself seemed a more starved sliver. An empty belly. Fallen women loitered along the street, and men – some in gentlemanly garb, some dressed as workmen – stopped to converse with them.

Eleanor felt a thrill, compounded of a sort of delicious horror, at the sight of them. A voice, male or female (it was difficult to tell), addressed her with the word 'Evening', and she wrapped her arms about her and hurried on. These nocturnal walks had become an increasing feature of her life. As the prospect of her nuptials approached she felt the need for the sense of *release* that accompanied them more and more. The sense of danger, although nebulous, was thrilling. It was not a strictly improper thing she was doing, but she was flirting with the unacceptable.

My darling guilt, Mamma had said. Gilt, or guilt? Athough, of course, she had *meant* neither. But some fumble of the tongue had shifted girl to guilt. How intimately, Eleanor thought, how *bodily* guilt is worked into the weft of life! A city pulses in sunshine with the life of empire, men of business and honour stepping briskly about their business, past elegant marble arches and needle-thin church spires under a blue sky. The same city, the same men, accumulate their guilt in the night-time, chasing their own shame and self-hatred with a devotion worthy of a better cause. How could they not feel guilty, these people? These men, pressing themselves up against bawdy women; these women, selling their daughters in the Babylonish slave market of polite society under the hypocrisy of marriage. As Eleanor crept back along Poland Street her spirit flared purple as the night, like the flame that burns from iodine or the lithium metallic compounds.

[2]

The following morning, after breakfast, Eleanor washed herself in the bowl containing her mother's second-hand water. She dressed, and spent two hours reading in the front room, to keep company with Mamma. Mother was reading a piece of silvery fiction, *The Lord of the Forest*, in which a governess married a baronet, or an orphan was revealed to be heiress to a fortune, or some narrative of that sort. Eleanor was trying to concentrate on a difficult passage in Lieut.-Col. Charles Hamilton Smith's *Natural History of the Human Species, its Typical Forms, Primaeval Distribution, Filiations and Migrations, with an Appendix on the Relation of Pacifican Miniature and Enlarged Forms of Humanity to the Physical History of Mankind*. She was not helped by Mamma's fluttery and unsettled manner. Every five minutes, it seemed, she hopped up from her chair to look out the window.

At noon Eleanor put her book away. 'Shall we take luncheon, Mamma?'

'No luncheon today, dear Eleanor,' was the reply. 'I expect Mister Burton at any time.'

'I thought he was not coming until later this afternoon?'

'I distinctly recall him saying that he would call by for luncheon.'

This was alarming. 'Will he not, then, expect luncheon to be provided?' Eleanor made a quick mental calculation. She had less than six shillings in her purse; enough for a loaf of bread, some cheese, two pints of beer, but not enough for a decent spread of luncheon – cold meat, some pie, tea.

'I was hoping,' said Mamma, her agitation more palpable, 'that he would offer to take us out.'

This was too nakedly mercenary for Eleanor's comfort, but she held her peace. In the event, Burton did not call by until after two, by which time Mamma was in an almost agonised state of agitation. Eleanor's stomach was griping with hunger, but she said nothing.

Burton had that shyness that appears especially ridiculous in a large and burly man. He moved awkwardly, half-shrinking then pressing suddenly on. At the door he hesitated, started forward, stopped, before surging finally into the sitting room. He bowed too deeply to Mamma, nearly stumbled, and in grasping to stay upright he disarranged the carefully drawn night-time curtain, revealing the divan within. This awkwardness caused him to blush claret-red, and bumble back towards the door as if he were about to leave. He hovered there a moment, then lurched back in. 'Mr Burton,' said Mamma, in as soothing a tone as she could manage. 'Mr Burton.' She took him to the window, directing his eyes to the significant features of the street scene outside as Eleanor rearranged the curtain.

Finally Burton sat himself down upon the chaise longue with his legs pressed together in front of him as if to provide a platform for his overhanging belly, and his right hand propped on his red-and-gold-topped cane. Even his sitting was strenuous, as if it took an enormous physical effort to relax in a chair. His jacket looked new, the brushed felt of his lapels almost gleaming. His bald forehead shone in the daylight as if it had been polished. A strong scent of macassar came off the hair at the back of his head.

'Mrs Davis,' he said, mumblingly, his tongue seemingly too big for his mouth. 'Miss Davis.'

'Mr Burton,' said Mamma.

'It's ... good,' he said, and then revised his sentiment with a little irritated shake of his head, 'it's very good to see you both again.'

'Thank you, Mr Burton,' Mamma replied. 'You are very kind. And we are delighted to receive you.'

There was a silence. It lengthened.

Mamma drew a breath, but Burton said nothing.

Eleanor felt the spiderish rustlings of embarrassment in her innards. Was she truly to marry this man? It was too hard to believe. Such a man! Mamma drew another breath, and then launched into some politely meaningless utterance to at least fill Burton's silence; but as she spoke Burton coughed into speech himself, and they overlapped one another.

'I trust you are well ...'

'I hope I am not forward in ...'

They both fell silent. Burton was blushing a deeper portwine shade.

'After you sir,' said Mamma, lowering her eyes.

'After you Madam.'

'Please, Mr Burton'.

'No, Madam, I insist.'

Mamma gave a little shriek of laughter; Burton flinched as if stabbed. 'But this is ridiculous! We are all friends here, sir ... your betrothed, sir!' She smiled, and gestured languidly in Eleanor's direction. Eleanor smiled in turn at the prompt. Burton's beard waggled minutely, ambiguously. It was possible he was smiling underneath it. There was sweat on his brow. Little star-dots of sweat.

'What was it,' he said, doggedly, in a low tone, 'what was it you were about to say, Mrs Davis?'

'I was merely enquiring after your health, sir.'

'My health is good, Madam. And yours?'

'We are both well.'

Another silence grew, mould-like, between the three of them. Eventually Mamma prompted him. 'Mr Burton? You were about to say something?'

Words tumbled out. 'I was hoping that Miss ... Miss Davis would accept a small gift, a small gift, a little book that I purchased at Arthur Shipley's bookshop upon the Strand, Ma'am.' He fumbled in his jacket pocket and brought out a small red-bound volume. As he held it out for Eleanor to take up his hand was visibly trembling. 'I was hoping that Miss Eleanor ... that Miss Davis ...' The sentence floated away with conclusion.

Eleanor plucked the volume from his fingers. 'Thank you indeed, sir,' she said 'This is very kind.' She checked the spine: *Poems*, by Elizabeth Barrett Barrett.

'Is it a book of science, or political economy?' enquired Mamma, with another piercing shriek like a whistle. 'Is it a book of mathematics? My darling Eleanor loves mathematics. 'Tis hardly natural; I sometimes think I have brought a *calculating machine* into the world, not a feminine being at all.' She laughed at her own joke with a little whinny. Nobody joined her. 'Sometimes think I have brought a *calculating machine* into the world,' she repeated.

'Do you not read poetry?' Burton asked, his face bent in two by sudden concern. Eleanor, irritated, nonetheless could not help but console him.

'It is a fine present, sir, and I shall enjoy reading it very much.'

'I enquired at my club,' said Burton, 'and they ... the members, I mean ... thought that poetry was an appropriate gift for a young lady.'

But Mamma, with one of those startling absences of tact of which she was often capable, said in a giggly voice: 'Oh, Eleanor's the least poetic girl in Europe!'

'Mamma!' Eleanor rebuked her. 'Don't listen to her, Mr Burton. She is teasing you. I like poetry a great deal.'

'Like it?' echoed Mamma, mockingly. She seemed to have worked herself into one of her occasional little hysteric states. 'Lord, she could no more like it than a *natural* girl could like books with numerical tables and diagrams of levers. Like it!' She laughed again. Then, belatedly, she blinked, peered about her. 'Not,' she said, looking a little confused, 'not but that your gift is not greatly appreciated.'

'Indeed, I am very grateful for the book.' She opened the volume, but the pages were uncut and she did not have a paper-knife to hand. 'I do not know the authoress, however,' she said. 'Is she famous?'

'I am informed so,' mumbled Burton.

Of the whole volume only half a dozen pages could be read without cutting the paper. Eleanor opened the volume in the middle. The phrase 'deep-hearted man' caught her eye, and she thought to read the verse aloud in tribute to Burton himself. She cleared her throat and read:

> *Deep-hearted man, express*
> *Grief for thy dead in silence most like to death;*
> *Most like a monumental statue set*

> *In everlasting watch and moveless woe,*
> *Till itself crumble to the dust beneath.*
> *Touch it: the marble eyelids are not wet —*
> *If it could weep it would arise and go.*

She stopped; Burton and her mother were looking at her with widened eyes. 'Perhaps that is not a very well chosen piece,' she said.

'Is that poetry?' said Mamma. 'But that is merely dismal! Dear me, how dismal that is. That's not *my* idea of poetry at all.'

'It is a *little* dismal,' said the wretched Burton. 'I should apologise again.'

'Tush,' said Eleanor. 'It is fine poetry. Fine. I'm sure other pieces in the volume have a lighter tone. Thank you, Mr Burton.'

She closed the book.

The Dutch clock on the mantel ticked quietly to itself. It had a miserly and a muffled tick, as if it were hoarding seconds to itself and counting its fortune out to itself, tick by tick. Burton shifted in his seat.

Eleanor started to draw a breath, and was abruptly aware that she was breathing roasting fire and violence. Why? Wherefrom? It hardly mattered. A sudden, piercing sensation of hatred ran up and down Eleanor's body like a galvanic shock – she wanted Burton to leave, wanted him away from her *for ever*, wanted him *dead* – wanted to strike the blow herself with a switch of her arm across his face, his idiotic and ugly-flabby face. The feeling swept through her, like fluid forced through a pipe-section at tremendous pressure. She froze in her chair.

The intensity of the emotion shocked her, scared her, even, but at the same time it carried her away, like a modern Saint Theresa in an angelic ecstasy. The sheer weight of this Burton-man, the huge, lumbering physical presence of him in their little room, was too provoking, just *too provoking*. It was all too provoking, the mass of him, an immovable deadweight dropped upon their lives. She held herself perfectly still in her chair, afraid that any movement would cause her to burst out, to leap up and scream. She could feel her cheeks colouring slightly but otherwise the internal tempest vortexed round and round with such velocity that it seemed to acquire a stillness of its own, of the sort that they say is to be found in the middle of tornadoes. Every blockage in her life, every repression of passion and every sacrifice she had ever made in the name of necessity and respectability became focused intensely in the awkward male form seated before her. On some savage inner level she thought that if this man could be knocked aside then all her life would lighten and brighten – everything would then be all right. And why not? Why couldn't her mother and she live together, as they had done for seven years now, just by themselves, without interruption or adulteration? They lived modestly enough, didn't they? They never asked for luxury or expensive flimflam. Eleanor knew many people for whom £150 was a mere trifle – why should those people have that money and she and her mamma none at all? How was that fair? It was a crushing weight laid across them, and the weight was this large man, with his absurd bear-like beard and his sack-of-meal belly. *He* was the weight.

The inevitability of Burton, the inescapability of him, stung her again and again, a vicious horsefly inside her head. And, yes, she knew the reasons: but they all boiled down only to money, to money. One hundred and fifty pounds; three hundred half-sovereigns; three thousand shillings; and (three-twelves-are-thirty-six) 36,000 pennies, the money multiplying like biblical locusts in her head, pennies swarming down from the sky copper-skinned to plague her and her mamma. And Burton owned more money than he could possibly need, he had sacks of coins as large as his own belly, had them scattered around his ogre-palace down by the river, that ogre-palace he called his manufactory, in which all the little faerie people were enslaved. And so, only because he had money, she must marry him, and spend not just one afternoon but every afternoon, and morning, and evening, in this gross company. Only because *he* had the money, a superfluity of money, more than the £150 they needed, so *much* more, doubtless more than £15,000, than £150,000, more (for all she knew) than £1,000,000; and the zeros spawned in her mind like maggots.

Her clenched self-control quavered, and a little gasp escaped the enclosure of her teeth. Burton twitched forward in concern.

'My dear?' said Mamma.

Eleanor looked up, with feigned innocence in her eyes. 'Mamma?'

'Are you alright?'

'Quite alright, Mamma. Perhaps you could ring for Sally? She might bring us a glass of water. I feel a little dry.'

'It *is* dry,' said Burton, fumbling for a comment. 'I feel a little dry myself.'

'Water,' said Mamma, and tinkled the little handbell that stood, in their reduced circumstances, for a proper bell-pull. Sally, who (of course) had been waiting directly on the far side of the door hoping to overhear the conversation, came straight through, and was dispatched for water from the pump downstairs with some severity.

Eleanor breathed out, and the passion to squeeze the life from Burton's flesh relaxed within her, her hatred diminishing and diminishing. And by whatever mysterious process that governs these subterranean and irrational emotional forces, after a few moments Eleanor felt calm again, calm enough to turn to the man and smile at him. His beard twitched. Perhaps he was returning the smile.

The Dutch clock ticked on.

Ten minutes grew into twenty, and then thirty. From time to time Burton essayed a clumsy conversational gambit: the weather; the latest British success in the Continental war; the last lecture of the Fitzroy Society (John Percy FRS had talked on the metallurgy of lead, with added remarks on desilverisation and cupellation, 'a most interesting talk', Burton said), at which neither Mrs nor Miss Davis had been able to be present. A shame. Such an interesting talk. But each conversational exchange died quickly, and the parched silences between them grew longer and longer. Eleanor, her head still buzzing faintly with the aftershocks of her violent inner flux, settled only slowly back into boredom. But the boredom claimed her eventually.

Eventually it was clear that time had elapsed to sustain the polite fiction that Burton had enjoyed Mrs Davis's company. He shuffled in his seat, coughed, and said: 'I wonder whether Miss Davis would enjoy a stroll around the square?'

Eleanor almost sighed with relief; not because she relished the prospect of walking with Burton, but because it marked an end to the parlour-torture of merely sitting there. She rose abruptly, and hurried through to her own room to dress herself for outside. She called Sally in with her to give the impression that she was being dressed by the maid, but in actuality she dressed herself, because Sally was inept at the task. Away from her future husband she gasped with a release of pressure. Maddeningly there were tears somewhere behind her eyes. She had to focus, to lock them away there.

Burton and she stepped out together into the grey afternoon. Eleanor felt a little light-headed, with a touch of nausea in her abdomen, but that could doubtless be ascribed to the fact that she had eaten no luncheon. They strolled to Soho Square, Burton's cane tapping the pavement as he walked.

'I am so glad to find you well, Miss Davis,' he said.

This might have been the occasion for her to say *Call me Eleanor, please do*; but she found herself disinclined to encourage such further intimacy between them. She was to marry the man, after all. That was surely enough.

'And I,' she replied, looking briefly in his direction, 'you.'

For several minutes they walked in silence around the central green of Soho Square. Then Burton spoke, more forcefully than before.

'I confess myself anxious, Miss Davis, that my gift to you was ill-chosen.'

She smiled, but the anger was hard as a conker in her belly. She had already thanked him for the present. Was he fishing for more gratitude? Did he expect her to reassure him for ever? 'It is quite alright, Mr Burton,' she said. 'My mamma has perhaps misled you a little. It is only her teasing manner, she means no harm. But, truly, I shall enjoy the poems very much.'

'I remember our first meeting was at the Fitzroy Society,' said Burton. 'And I see now that your interest in science is genuine. Perhaps I would have pleased you better by bringing you a copy of Mrs Somerville's *Molecular and Microscopic Science*, or something along those lines.'

This struck home. Eleanor had seen that very book advertised in the endpapers of the latest *Quarterly*, which she had read at one of Lady Fonblaque's soirées – and upon seeing the advertisement she had surrendered herself immediately to a hopeless covetousness. The book had been advertised as two volumes, post octavo, 21s. A fortune. It might just as well, for Eleanor, have been twenty-one pounds. And two volumes would mean *two* shillings for a week's perusal out of the library; even that petty sum could not have been expended without hardship in some other quarter. And yet she wanted to read the book very much indeed. Could such work be hers, truly, as a gift?

She tried to keep the eagerness from her voice. 'Do you have that work, Mr Burton?'

Burton looked away as if embarrassed. 'I do, Miss Davis. The,' he added, with a little spurt of anxious expression, 'the publisher sent me a copy.'

'The publisher?'

'Mr Murray. I know him through a mutual acquaintance. I, in

turn, provided some of the microscopic equipment used to make the illustrations. My workers, my Blefuscans, are extremely skilled in fine optics work. If it would give you pleasure, I will lend you ... pardon me, give you ... the book.'

Eleanor's bibliophilic avarice flared in her breast. She wanted the book intensely. 'That,' she said, with a tightly controlled inclination of her head, 'would be very kind of you, Mr Burton.' Two volumes! With illustrations! Glee moved inside her, she couldn't quell it. But immediately behind the delight came a sense of humiliation – that she was dependent on such a man as Burton for gifts of books. And with the humiliation came the anger again. That she could not buy the book herself! – twenty-one paltry shillings. That Burton could dangle the thing in front of her, as a treat for a faithful lapdog. That she was now *beholden* to him. Her hate crystallised inside her again; not so vehemently as it had done before, but with a sharp edge to it.

Burton stopped suddenly, and stepped in front of her. 'Miss Davis,' he said, earnestness making his big face look ridiculous. 'May I call you Eleanor?'

There was no avoiding it. 'Of course,' she said.

'Eleanor ... I know it is conventional when a man makes a proposal of marriage, and when that proposal is accepted ... conventional for the man to declare himself the happiest creature on the planet. But believe me, in my case the phrase is no mere form of words. You indeed make me, you have made me, happier than any man in the world.'

His eyes, moist with unshed tears, glinted slimily in the sunlight.

'Mr Burton ...' Eleanor said.

'It is hard for me to express, because I am no orator. I am not eloquent. But I never thought to find a woman ... to find a wife ... who would share in any way my own interests. My own passions.'

'Interests?' queried Eleanor, choosing the less indecent word.

The bare skin above Burton's beard warmed orange-red again. *The man blushes*, Eleanor thought with annoyance, *at the drop of a hand-kerchief.* 'My interest in the mechanical sciences, I mean to say,' he gabbled. 'I only meant ... but I am putting it poorly. I know I am an old man, my dear Eleanor. I know that I am but a poor catch for a beautiful young woman such as yourself.'

He paused. Eleanor knew that she ought to frame some conventional contradiction at this point, to murmur *No no*, or *Not at all*, but the words stuck in her throat. Burton's observations were nothing but the truth, after all.

'I know,' he went on, stammering a little now, 'that I am come from no fine family, that I bring no great dignity with me – except money, I suppose, and trash such as money can have no appeal to a woman of your breeding.' He ground to a halt, coughed, cleared his throat, and started again. 'But I bring a true heart, Eleanor,' he said. His eyes were glistening. 'I hope you will believe me, for it is the simple truth.'

'Mr Burton,' Eleanor murmured.

'Jonathan!' he cried, almost shouting. His blushing cheeks deepened their shade. 'I'm sorry,' he stammered, 'Please call me Jonathan.'

His emotional distress was so intense that Eleanor began to feel almost alarmed at it. It was painful to watch a full-grown man reduced to such a state.

'Jonathan,' she said.

'Allow me,' he said, straightening his spine and endeavouring to speak with a more level voice. 'Allow me to finish what I was saying, Eleanor. Perhaps it is foolish, but I feel I must say it, for my own peace of mind if for no other reason. I know that people gossip about our match. A man, although wealthy, of no family marries a woman from a better class than his own. They gossip that I have consented to the match only to raise my social standing. But it isn't true! It isn't true! I must tell you why I have fallen so in love with you …'

'Jonathan,' she said again, vaguely rebuking.

'I feel a commonality of spirit between us, Eleanor. It is not that you are young and beautiful, although you are both those things. It is not that I have come to a period in my life when I have the money and the inclination to start a family, although that is also true. It is that I *sense*, I sense, that you share my own passion for the sciences. For the mechanical sciences. For mathematics – your mother said so. Women so rarely see the *beauty* of science. Women are so often vain and foolish, so caught up in nonsense and vacancy. But not you, my darling.'

He stepped towards her, as if he would embrace her, or even kiss her – right there, in the street: *that would be just his sort of vulgarity*, Eleanor thought, despising him with a panicky intensity. She could not stop herself stepping backward, and Burton pulled rapidly back as well, as if dancing cumbrously.

There was a pause. Some of the urgency seemed to drain out of the man.

'All I am trying to say,' he said in a lower tone, 'is that I hope you will continue your interest in sciences. I hope you will allow me to assist you in cultivating it – any books you require, any lectures or societies. Any journals.'

Eleanor looked around her. The vista was of low trees and greensward in the little park, and hard by that the towering façade of housing. Windows slightly bowed like pouches of glass. Stucco as textured as skin. The wind was making trickling sounds in the trees as it shuffled itself through the leaves. A clergyman walked quickly past them and hurried down Greek Street.

'Thank you,' Eleanor said slowly, not meeting Burton's eye.

'It's all,' said Burton, turning away, 'that I wished to say.'

He resumed his walking, and Eleanor fell into step beside him. They exchanged no more words. On the far side of the square they paused. The iron railings outside one of the tall houses caught Eleanor's attention. The metal was callused with rust at every intersection, and had been imperfectly painted with tar-paint. Little spots of red-brown, like the scabs on grazed skin, clustered. Like sores, almost, though dry and crusted with little nubbins of metal dust. A poor public frontage for a grand house.

They started the stroll back to Poland Street. Turning off the square onto Carlisle Street Burton resumed his confessions, although in a much more subdued voice. 'I meant to add also,' he said, 'that I do not expect you to leave the apartment you share with your mother. After our wedding, I mean. In the *immediate* aftermath, I mean. In time, of course, your mother will come and live with us; but of course my bachelor apartments are wholly unsuitable, and until the purchase of the house is completed, I know you will remain in Poland Street. I do not wish to . . . intrude,' he added, sheepishly.

'That is very kind of you,' said Eleanor, distantly.

'The purchase is set for next month,' Burton added. 'You must allow me to show it to you, before that time. To show you round, I mean. And your mother, of course.'

'We would be delighted.'

They were walking up Poland Street now. 'Splendid,' Burton mumbled. 'Splendid. It is on Gower Street you know,' he added, with animation. 'Not far from the new university. I have attended several public lectures at the university, of considerable interest.' He stopped again. 'May I suggest Friday? I will call for you both at eleven. I'll come,' he added, hurriedly, as if it needed saying, 'in a carriage, of course.'

'Friday,' said Eleanor, firmly.

There was another ponderous pause. Then Burton bowed his whole bear-like body at the waist, said goodbye, and walked quickly away. Eleanor watched him for a moment. She could detect in his gait a physical relief, as if a burden had been lifted from his wide shoulders. That he could be so pleased to depart piqued her once again. She had disliked his presence and looked forward to his going, but she hated him more for feeling such relief to be out of her presence. How vulgar he was.

[3]

It did not occur to Eleanor that there was anything unreasonable about her dislike of Burton. The more he tried to ingratiate himself with her, the more she despised him. In this she felt no compunction whatsoever because – after all – he was the one with the money. His wealth provided Eleanor with the right to hate him, or so she told herself. Because he had the wealth and she had none, he possessed the power. Because he was the powerful party and she the weak, she was justified in kicking against the pricks, in asserting herself by whatever means she could. The fact that he cloaked his power in a shambling display of social awkwardness and foolishness only justified the hatred more. She might marry him – there was no helping that, of course. She might be well-bred enough to ensure her hatred never slipped past the mask of her face. She might *act* the part of the good wife, good mother, good hostess; might act any part required of her. But her hate would always be there inside her, a miniature version of herself sitting inside her head and looking through the portholes in her skull with eyes of fire.

The volume of poetry was placed on the little shelf of books in the apartment, its pages still uncut.

She read Smith's *Natural History of the Human Species*, but the book was a disappointment. The author rehearsed the old Lamarckian theories that forms of life altered and evolved, but rehearsed them only to dismiss them peremptorily. The proof of the argument was in the Lilliputian and Brobdingnagian races, he said; the proof of God's intervention in the natural world.

It has been known since the days of Galileo Galilei, and his great study on the strength of materials, that a square-cube law applies to the magnification of materials. Volume, and therefore weight, increases as the cube of linear dimensions, but strength increases only as the square. Were a horse to be enlarged to the size of an elephant its legs would be insufficiently strong to support its new weight, and would snap underneath it. Anatomical study of the elephant reveals that providence has given it legs markedly shorter and thicker, in proportion, than other animals. And yet this square-cube law appears contradicted by the Brobdingnagians. We might conceive that giant men would bear the same relation to ordinary men as an elephant does to a dog, namely that their legs would be short and broad, their bodies compressed in proportion, their metabolisms slow and sluggish. But this is not what we discover.

Were Lamarck's evolution the true case, he said, the giant-men might have 'evolved' from men of the proper size over time. But in this case they would be made of the same stuff as ordinary men – and they were not. Their bones were knit differently, of a stronger material than human bone, or they would break under the weight of their oversized bodies. The only explanation for the giants was that God had created them just as they were, created them with the organs they needed to survive perfectly arranged with one another.

Eleanor found the reasoning weak. She had read, and been very persuaded by, Buffon's treatise on the 'generation and degeneration' of alteration in the form of species. She believed, with Buffon, that life created increasingly complex organisms over time. The Pacificans clearly presented a special case, and any scientist would need to accommodate their physical peculiarities into his science: Eleanor had hoped that Smith would do this. But Smith's arguments consisted of nothing but flat contradiction of the established science, contradiction without further evidence being adduced, save only chapter-and-verse quotation from the Bible. As if the Bible were science!

She and Mamma visited the house in Gower Street that Burton hoped to purchase; a four-storey family home, with large rooms, with a basement, with a grass-and-flower; garden. 'How beautiful it is,' ejaculated Mamma. Eleanor nodded and smiled.

After the tour the three of them paused in the hallway whilst Burton stood before her stammering and stepping from foot to foot. In the carriage outside, riding home, Mamma giggled and said to her: 'I hear that he is a terrible tartar with his underlings in the factory.'

'The little people?' said Eleanor, her interest piqued.

'No, the real people, *I* mean, they who work under him. They say he is a tartar, nothing less. And yet!' Mamma interrupted herself with another chortle. 'And yet to see how nervous he is before you, my dear! Love, it is, love. He is reduced to a stammering schoolboy because he loves you.' The comedy of this point struck her again, and she laughed. 'He is become a schoolboy and you the Dame, only because he loves you.'

Two days afterwards Eleanor took another night-time walk through the streets, observing the nightlife with a dispassionate, a scientist's, eye – or, at least, attempting to be as disengaged as that ideal, though the excitement of the night scene ruffled her objectivity, pumping the blood faster through her veins. She hid in a shop doorway somewhere in Farringdon whilst two men fought in the street illuminated by the light from a window. Two drunken men staggering at one another and stumbling apart, aiming great wide sweeps of their punching arms and connecting with one blow in three. It was absurd, and even amusing, but it was also thrillingly exciting. One man boxed the other in the face, and there was a distinct noise of impact, like a single clap, and a fuzz of airborne blood-droplets visible momentarily in the lamplight. The violence was real. Eleanor almost felt the impact in her own body. The fight ended when one of the men pushed the other hard against a small unshuttered casement, breaking the glass. The sound, thought dainty and tinkling, was enough to scare the aggressor off. The second man sat in the road for a while touching and touching the back of his head, bringing his hand away (Eleanor thought) wet. Then he too got up and staggered away.

Eleanor breathed more deeply. She was free on these walks. It was a feeling inexpressibly fine and elating, as if she had escaped from her cage. It was something about the lower orders, their lack of restraint; or else it was the privileging of her position as observer – the scientist's superior vantage-point, examining animalculae through the optic glass. She saw ugliness in the vulgarity of these people, and yet it made her heart dance in her breast. The sky plum-black, the stars shrinking like sphincter muscles of light puckered up in fright. The streets like gashes cut in the fabric of house and business and prison that constituted the city. The moon surveilling every illicit step.

She crept through the streets, moving from doorway to doorway, alive and excited with the fright – although she could not have said what frightened her, exactly. The dark, perhaps. The city itself. At Blackfriars Bridge she stood and stared at the lights of Borough, over the river. She would have gone over there, but she could not afford the toll. It was pennies, but she could not afford it. Instead she looked down upon the black rushing slick of the Thames. Its ceaselessness. Apart from the half-moon, the lantern from the tollbooth was the only light reflected in the dark water. The river could have been ink flowing. The lanternlight showed the miniature ripples, like tiny dunes in the fluid.

The day of the wedding approached.

Burton took Eleanor and her mother around his manufactory. It was located down a street running from the Strand down to the river, a teetering old wooden building, its back parts were actually over the water, supported on wooden pillars that had been carved by the Thames's flow and painted green with algae. Burton's own office was spacious and well furnished, the walls hung with heavy cloth. It was situated at the rear of the place, with a south prospect. His door opened onto a little platform overlooking the body of the manufactory, from which a stair ran down to the desks and boxes, the machines and tanks. Burton's assistant, Mr Pannell, had a smaller and dingier office on the opposite side of the building. His windows gave out over nothing more than the grimy brickwork of Villiers Street.

What struck Mamma the most was the low manners of Pannell, who bowed and scraped in a positively oriental manner, flattering both women implausibly and leaning too close. After Burton had led them away and taken them amongst the machines, Mamma kept dropping *sotto voce* disparaging comments. 'You'd think Mr Burton would employ a better class of worker,' she hissed. 'A most unpleasant fellow.'

'Hush, Mamma.'

'Did you see the look he gave me?'

'Hush now! Mr Burton will hear!'

'He's no Englishman, that fellow,' said Mamma, more to herself than Eleanor. 'I'd wager a guinea he's not.'

But Eleanor was fascinated not by the machinery, nor by the evidences of Burton's wealth. She was fascinated by the little people themselves. They were arrayed in a variety of cubbyholes and boxes, working at all manner of miniature tasks. Many were confined, but some seemed to have the run of tabletops or open spaces.

Eleanor had seen such little folk before, though not very often. Some of the people in her circle of acquaintance owned them as pets, but they were expensive pets, and only the very wealthy could afford them – the wealthy, or those (like Burton) who required the specialist skills the Lilliputians brought with them. Eleanor had never examined one properly, had never been able to pin one down and bring an enlarging glass over it and have a proper look. She resolved that, after she was married, she would have Burton give her one of the little people as her own, her pet. She began to think of experiments she might undertake upon the creature.

Burton was saying something. She forced herself to pay attention. 'Highly specialised,' he said. 'Their hands are so small and dextrous that they can undertake very fine work indeed. The flying machines would be quite impossible to manufacture without them.'

'Oh those machines,' shrieked Mamma, without thinking. 'Vulgar things. Buzzing up and down the streets, like busy bees. Vulgar and horrid.'

'But,' said Burton, 'important, my dear Mrs Davis. Important and valuable.' There was the faintest shadow of rebuke in his tone. For the first time Eleanor caught a glimpse of some part of the man not entirely despicable. She turned to him and smiled – and the manliness wilted and evaporated before the heat of even that small sign of approbation.

'That is to say,' he stammered, 'not ... to be rude. I'm sure you're right, Mrs Davis. Vulgar and low. Not for the ... genteel.'

Eleanor's heart sank again. 'This,' she said, to cut off his abysmal gush rather than because she possessed any actual interest in the device. 'What does this do?'

'It's a fascinating object, Miss, eh, Eleanor,' he said. 'These machines wind up, like watches, you know. The springs – four of them – provide the motile power. It is only possible to make them of a small size, you know; larger and the devices become disproportionately heavy. It's the square-cube law, you know.'

'I know the square-cube law,' she said, severely.

At this Burton smiled, and Eleanor realised that he considered this mutual knowledge of essential scientific principles to be a sort of bond between them. She might have shuddered with disgust, but she had more control over her body than that.

Later that day it occurred to her that this belief of Burton's that there was a special connection between the two of them made the prospect of the marriage *less* tolerable than otherwise. When her mother had first persuaded her to accept the man, pressing the many benefits financial security would bring to their lives, Eleanor had thought of Burton as distant, as a theoretical husband rather than an actual mate with saggy flesh, with hair growing on the backs of his hands like mildew and smut. An actual man with the odour of perspiration always about him. She had considered him as a theorem, a mathematical abstraction (so many minutes together at breakfast, so many together at supper, a total of so many hours in his company each week). The marriage seemed almost bearable on such terms. But now she had a horrible premonition that Burton would expect the two of them to share all manner of intimacies. That he regarded the transaction not in the light of a mutually advantageous business deal, but rather as the coming-together of soulmates.

That night, in her bed, she could not sleep. A sensation akin to panic kept her awake. Was she consenting to being truly buried alive? As she half-slept, the very cloth covers on her bed seemed to assume prodigious dimensions, pressing down upon her like the weight of cold soil. She felt, with that bizarre sensation of corporeal dislocation that sometimes creeps over us when we are half asleep and only half in touch with our bodies – she felt as if her limbs were thickening and elongating, as if her head were swelling like a vitreous globe puffed out by a glassblower. The sensations were so unsettling, as if she were being transformed into one of the gigantic Pacificans, that she twitched herself into movement to dissipate it. But this brought its own difficulties. She grew hopelessly fidgety. She turned on her left side and turned on her right side and turned to her left side, wishing that she had some third side onto which she could turn, some comfortable and restful side on which she could settle. There was a ticklish warmth in her lap – low down, in her lap, where her waste waters were voided, the necessary process of kidney, bladder, and expulsion. It was not the sensation of a need to pass water, though. This was something else. It was a sensation that sometimes came upon her, an incommoding thing. She lay on her back and separated her legs a little, and using the flat of her four fingers pressed together, she smacked it, as if it were a naughty child. The buzz caught and faded.

Sleep.

[4]

Thoughts of the wedding merely depressed Eleanor; but her mother became more actively anxious, convinced that some disaster would intervene to wreck it. 'The consummation,' she said, one morning, 'is so near. So near! We must make sure nothing destroys all our hopes, at this late stage.'

'What can go wrong, Mother?' said Eleanor, sourly, resenting the way in which her mother was drawing her in to the role of co-conspirator.

Mamma could not be definite; yet her fears grew as the date agreed on approached. 'What if he should withdraw from the arrangement?' she fretted.

'Then he would breach his contract, Mamma.'

'That's true,' said Mamma, as if hoarding the fact to herself. 'That's true. He'd not dare breach his contract with you.'

And yet, at a meeting of the Fitzroy Society, something occurred to screw Mamma's anxiety up to an extreme pitch. The lecture had been upon 'Interplantetary and Vacuum Travel by Means of Artillery Propulsion', the talker a religious man from Yorkshire who insisted that it would be possible to project a chamber into interplanetary space by means of a large cannon.

Burton, wearing yet another new coat and hat, accompanied Mrs Davis and Eleanor, sitting uncomfortably all through the talk. Afterwards drinks were available, wine for those who desired alcohol, Vichy water for those who preferred sobriety, in the adjoining room. This was the usual pattern for the Society's weekly talks. Burton seemed in a good mood, and had chattered out his opinion of the science of the proposal (which he regarded as fanciful) with hardly a stammer. Mamma, clutching her glass of wine, nodded and cooed at every one of his words.

Eleanor, her smile locked in place, was looking about the room, and so noticed a newcomer amongst the usual society members: a tall and handsome man with an air of greater breeding than many of the attendants. He looked up and caught Eleanor's eye, and instead of nodding and averting his gaze he looked at her – practically stared at her – with a sly smile on his face. Eleanor looked away, a little startled, but when she looked back the fellow was making his way across the room towards them.

'Excuse me,' he said, drawing himself up before Mamma and bowing. 'I apologise for intruding.' His words betrayed a slight Continental accent.

All three turned to look at him.

The stranger said: 'I believe I knew your late husband, Madam.' He was smiling. A well-made man of middle years, his blocky face made all of flat planes like a carpenter's model; pale yellow hair and skin of a uniform pinkness all over from his chin and forehead to his eyelids and lips. Handsomely made, in a conventional manner, except for his eyes, which were much more than handsome. They were amazingly blue eyes, as blue as the spurt of a lighted match. To notice them was to find oneself drawn to them.

Mamma turned. 'You knew him, sir?'

'A fine man, Madam. A great loss.'

Burton squared up to the man. 'What's that? You knew Mrs Davis's husband?'

'Davis?' said the stranger, a twitch of puzzlement about his eyelids. 'Ah, I understand, you have changed the name.'

Mamma sucked a breath in with a little panicky noise.

'Changed the name?' queried Burton.

'From Davidowic,' explained the stranger, smiling again and pronouncing the 'David' in the French style and drawing out the remaining syllables of the name, 'Da-vede-of-each'.

'And who are you, sir?' blurted Mamma, in a more forceful and higher-pitched voice than perhaps she intended to use.

'I beg your pardon, Madam. I am Count Baron Idigon von Leloffel.' He tipped his head smartly in salute. 'I admired your husband very greatly.'

'Your husband was a Hebrew?' asked Burton, a slightly pinched expression on his face.

The Count noted Burton's expression, and smiled more weakly. 'But perhaps Madam you were wise to change the surname. There is, I think, some prejudice amongst many English people against . . .'

'I am no Jewess,' shrilled Mamma. 'Please understand the circumstance.'

'Mother,' said Eleanor sharply. 'You embarrass me. You embarrass yourself.'

'Nor is my daughter,' added Mamma, her voice becoming louder by degrees. 'Jews inherit through the female line, and I am no Jewess.'

'I beg your pardon most sincerely,' said Von Leloffel, bowing his head again. 'Sincerely, I did not wish to cause offence.'

'There is no offence,' said Eleanor hurriedly. 'I believe there to be no shame in a Jewish ancestry. Rather, surely, it is something of which to be proud. Many great men of science and philosophy have sprung from that race.'

'Eleanor!' cried Mamma.

'I agree with you completely,' smiled the foreigner, tipping his head one further time. 'Your father was not least amongst them.'

'We are communicants at the Anglican Church of Saint Giles,' said Mamma, piercingly.

'Please excuse me,' said Eleanor, as smoothly as she could. She gripped her mother by the cheese-soft upper part of her arm and pulled her away. A few yards off her mother wriggled free, like a disobedient child. 'This could bring ruin on us!' she hissed. 'Burton will desert you!'

'Don't be ridiculous,' Eleanor said, although she felt a little bubble of hope float up through her body. What if Burton were indeed one of those who hated the Semitic peoples? He might break off the arrangement. And then (her thoughts leaping ahead of her) they might be able to extract some money from him – the threat of a court action for breach of promise would be enough, surely. Perhaps a sizeable sum. They could get at his money without her having to actually marry him. Perhaps—

But Burton had stepped over to join them. 'Mrs Davis?' he said. 'Eleanor?'

'Mr Burton,' said Mamma, hurriedly. 'Please understand that . . .'

'It's quite alright, Madam,' said Burton, a little stiffly but with a certain dignity too. 'I assure you it makes no difference to me – no difference at all to the deep love I feel for your daughter – whether there be any Jewish blood in the family or not.'

Eleanor smiled as her castle-in-the-air collapsed.

It took a moment for Burton's words to penetrate Mamma's carapace of anxiety. She almost sagged with relief. 'Sir,' she said, 'you are kind, sir. Kind.'

'Not at all, Madam. I'll confess that I was a little startled. But I had not known your husband to be the celebrated Davidowic.'

'You have heard of my departed husband?'

'Indeed, Madam. Some call him a mere gunsmith, but in my eyes he was nothing less than an artillery scientist. One of the greatest. The grand cannon he forged for the Prussian king ...' Burton expressed his admiration for this notable triumph with a wordless shake of his head.

'This was before our marriage,' said Mamma. 'Before he came to this country, though he told me of it.' Her relief was manifesting itself in an incontinent stream of words. 'He often told me of those great guns, la!, as if a lady would take interest in such a thing! But I understand that he was greatly esteemed by the crown prince of Germany, of Prussia I mean to say, and royalty is royalty after all, though it be foreign royalty.'

Burton bowed, awkwardly.

'*My* family,' Mamma rushed on, as if Burton has not heard this narrative twenty times before, 'are of the oldest English stock, however. Domesday Book, they are mentioned thrice in the Domesday Book. The Mintos of Shropshire. My cousin thrice removed is Lord Minto, you know.'

Eleanor excused herself. She made her way through to the rest room, fitted with one of the new-model water-closets, and relieved herself of some of the wine and Vichy water she had drunk. The suddenness and the intensity of the hope she had experienced at her mother's absurd fears – the almost visceral hope that Burton would disappear from her life leaving behind only a satchel of money as fat as his belly – now dejected her. These spurts of potent feeling seemed to rush upon her, out of nothing, and to consume her whole body in an instant, like a taper gobbled by flame. They departed as quickly, leaving her shuddery. Why did it happen this way? One day, she feared, the rush of emotion would overcome her. She would shout out. Or do something worse.

It disturbed her.

Returning to the main room, she was again intercepted by Count Baron Idigon von Leloffel. His face wore a strange, unreadable smile. 'Miss Davis,' he said, bowing and – with Continental floridness – kissing her hand.

'Count,' she returned.

'I trust I did not incommode your . . . situation?' he said, the sly smile giving the words a brimstony, dangerous aspect.

'Not at all.'

'It was not my intention. You are affianced to the gentleman?'

'I am.'

Von Leloffel's smile widened.

'Pray why do you smile, sir?' she asked, trying for a severity of face but barely able to prevent a smile coming to her own face. How handsome this German Count was!

'I mean no disrespect,' he said. 'I believe I heard your mother mention that she is related to Lord Minto – I take him to be the same Minto who served so honourably in the previous administration?'

'Yes.'

'I ask because I have met Lord Minto on several occasions. And I knew your father, as I mentioned. Though Jewish, he was from a noble and long-standing family. The family circumstances had become reduced, as sometimes happens with even the best family lines. But he was a true aristocrat.' He smiled, and waved his left hand, a controlled and ambiguous gesture.

'I don't follow what you are saying, Count.'

'My dear Miss Davis . . .'

Acting on an unfamiliar impulse, she said: 'Please call me Eleanor.'

'Eleanor, then,' he said smoothly. 'I am saying merely that I appreciate the exigencies of this world. My own family is an ancient one. My ancestors led their people against the Romans. They rode at the right hand of Charlemagne. And yet here I stand before you, virtually impoverished, living in a tiny room in Mary-leBone.' He shrugged. 'Fate takes our money – takes it all away – from people such as you and me – and our only consolation is that money don't define us. Whether we have the money or do not have the money cannot change who we are. Breeding is always breeding, no? Even if the scale of our living is *reduced* by poverty, breeding is still breeding.'

There was something rather flattering, to Eleanor, in this oblique account of the Count's own familial decline. She smiled.

'The gentleman,' the Count went on, fixing her gaze with his own, 'the gentleman . . . the name is Burlington?'

'Burton,' said Eleanor.

'No relation, then, to the Marquis of Burlington?' asked von Leloffel, though patently he knew the answer to his own question. The absurdity of the conjunction made Eleanor giggle. She could not help herself. She placed her gloved hand before her lips. How charming this German was!

'Burton, then,' said von Leloffel, his blue eyes twinkling. 'I understand he has a great deal of money. And he is surely a kind-hearted man. I have only met him this very afternoon, but he seems a decent fellow.'

'A decent fellow.'

'Money has such power in this world,' said the Count, with a little mock sigh. 'Breeding has so little, in comparison. Beauty pays its respects to money. How could it be otherwise? If only I had the money that Mr Burton possesses, then a beautiful woman such as yourself . . .'

'Count! Fie!' Eleanor almost hummed the word.

'You'll forgive my impudence, I hope,' the Count continued easily. 'When a man such as myself meets a woman as beautiful as you are, my dear Eleanor, he cannot control his expressions of admiration, even though they border on the improper.'

'I am betrothed to another man,' said Eleanor.

'And, naturally, you owe your future husband certain . . .' said the Count, rolling his right hand over and over, drawing a circle in the air with his forefinger. 'Certain *forms*. If I feel that you owe your own class something deeper, it is only because I am a *wretched foreigner* in England, and I don't know any better. Nevertheless, I do assert that you owe your own class – you owe *yourself* – something that cannot be claimed by a man of such small breeding.'

'But,' she said, wanting to egg him on rather than contradict him, 'I will be married. Is there not some small matter of a contract of marriage?'

'True,' he smiled. 'But can a contract entered into by a woman of breeding and a man – forgive me – without breeding . . . can such a contract be anything other than what the Jesuits call a *contractus turpis*?'

'*Contractus turpis*?'

'An immoral bargain,' said the Count. 'As, for example, for murder or theft. Such a bargain need not be respected, since it is by its essence null. Do you not think so.'

'How shocking you are, Count,' she said, but her voice was soft.

He smiled again, semi-satyr. 'Permit me,' he said, 'one further indiscretion.' And he bowed and kissed her gloved hand a second time. 'It is this request, that I may be permitted to call on you after your marriage, and that I may kiss your hand once more. But I am detaining you,' he concluded, stepping aside. 'Forgive me.'

Eleanor smiled at him and walked past. Her Mamma was still explaining the ins-and-outs of her own family to Burton. '... and her second cousin married Sir Jeremy Smiles, the baronet you know, who owns the tall house on Bond Street, you'll know the one Mr Burton for it has a yellow roof ...'

'My dear,' said Burton, greeting his fiancée with a broad smile.

[5]

Inexorably time moved, miniature second by miniature second accumulating without cessation into great blocky weeks and months, and it was the eve of the wedding itself. On the morrow, Eleanor would become a wife.

The encounter with Count von Leloffel had stayed in Eleanor's mind. She found herself spinning elaborate fantasies out of it. How unfortunate that the fellow was not wealthy. In various silver-fork alternate versions of reality, conjured by her imagination, he was a millionaire; or he inherited a million; or he was given an outright gift of a million by a grateful Prussian monarch – and then he called at Poland Street in a gold-leafed carriage to carry Eleanor directly to church and marriage and a fine life. In another little fantasy, he swept her away on horseback, though still poor, and the two of them ran off together, left the stifling confines of London life far behind them. But a more persistent fantasy, one that kept returning and returning to Eleanor's mind, was much more disturbing, because it was much more plausible. In this fantasy Eleanor married Burton, and conducted a secret liaison with von Leloffel.

She shocked herself. But it was exciting, too. And did not such things go on, in society, all the time? With Burton's money, perhaps Eleanor would be able to engineer a double life, her husband squatting spider-like in his manufactory whilst she and the Count took a closed carriage around Hyde Park together.

Was such a thing possible?

The truth was that Eleanor remained uncertain as to the precise practical dynamic of married life. She had been brought up, as her class and breeding required, to respect the veil drawn over the nature of marriage. Novels ended with weddings; they did not reveal the secret life of husband and wife that followed. It was not that Eleanor was stupid, of course. She could imagine a great deal. And she wanted to be able to plan out, with the scientific rigour that played so large a part in her thoughts, how this arrangement could be finalised.

It was evening. Burton had called round earlier in the day, with a man called James Silverthorne who was to stand with him at the church. The two men had stayed for twenty minutes, and then departed. After the visit Eleanor played cards with her Mamma, and the two of them drank most of a bottle of claret.

'The big day is tomorrow,' said Mamma, folding the cards together and putting them away. 'Are you anxious, my darling? It is,' she added, immediately, 'most natural for a girl to be anxious on the eve of her wedding day.'

'A little,' Eleanor conceded.

'It is most natural, indeed,' she said again, 'for a girl to be anxious on the eve of her wedding day.'

Eleanor smiled. 'Mamma, you seem more anxious than I.'

'And why shouldn't I be?' Mamma shrilled. 'My only daughter married on the morrow, my only support in this bitter world. Such pain I had in bringing her into this world, and there is so much pain in being a mother.'

'You're becoming maudlin, Mamma,' said Eleanor, but not severely. 'Perhaps it is time for us to go to our beds now?'

'My darling,' said her mother, as if she had not heard. 'My darling. Do you know about tomorrow?'

'Tomorrow, Mamma? Tomorrow is my wedding day.'

'Do you *know*?'

Eleanor was a little puzzled. It struck her that Mamma might be once again expressing the emotion that had been captured in her slip of the tongue when she had said *my darling guilt* instead of *my darling girl*. 'I am reconciled to it Mamma,' she said. 'You need not be anxious on that account. Burton is no hero from romance it is true, but I feel our relationship will be,' she found the word quickly, 'practicable.'

Her mother's face looked drawn, almost haunted. She stared at her daughter. A silence stretched out between them, with Mamma's weird expression penetrating Eleanor's affectation of calm. 'Mamma?' she said. 'Mamma, what is the matter?'

'Do you know,' repeated her mother in an uncharacteristically subdued tone of voice. 'About tomorrow?'

With a sort of tumbling realisation, Eleanor understood her mother's meaning. There was a little interruption in the smooth functioning of her polite-demeanour mask, a little sagging of the edges of the lips, a tiredness that moved over her eyes. Then she breathed in, smiled more broadly, and said: 'It is alright, Mamma. I do indeed know about these things.'

Her mother seemed to shiver. 'I know it is a distasteful topic, my darling,' she said in a low tone. 'Of course it is. But a mother has duties, you know, a duty to explain this sort of thing to her daughter. Somebody must explain this sort of thing, and it falls to the mother, you know. But I was thinking, perhaps,' she added, with a hopeful expression, 'that you have read of these things, in one or other of your books on science, you know.'

'I have read about these things,' said Eleanor.

Relief rushed into Mamma's face.

Eleanor's first intimation had come, obliquely enough, in Thomas Ryburn Buchanan's *Contrivances by which Orchids are Fertilised by Insects*, a botanical study that she had borrowed from the library some two years earlier. She had borrowed the volume with a vaguely sentimental apprehension that she thought orchids beautiful flowers, and an inchoate desire to know more about them from a scientific point of view. And the book had been extremely instructive, although the black-and-white engravings of the flowers had not at all captured the sensual, louche beauty of actual blooms (such as the Countess Blessington had a servant bring to her London house from her husband's hothouses at Richmond). But it so happened that this was a book that had piqued her interest beyond what she had expected. She learnt that flowers required a third party (insects) to spread their male sex material to the receptive female parts of another plant. In this way, the author had discreetly observed, the plant shares the same aim as the whole botanical and zoological world, save only a few lowly self-budding organisms – that the male germinative principle be conveyed to a receptive female. She had thought how comical it was that plants should share the terminology of male and female when they were so patently and radically different from actual men and women. And then, a moment later, prompted by a description of the way certain orchids mimic the female sex-parts of certain insects, she had the epiphany that, though a more primitive form of life, these plants (on the one hand) and men and women (on the other might) carry in common the general, Platonic, ideal of fertility. It had struck her with the force of a revelation. She actually sat back in her chair, letting the book fall to her lap. It wasn't her intimation of the human sex-act itself that shocked her; it was rather the sense of how foolish she had been, how blind not to have understood it before. Because that single trigger was enough to constellate a hundred little hints and clues that she had picked up during her young life, but which had never until that moment impinged fully on her mind. The male disseminates his spermatic material to the female. The man to the woman. This material is is combined in the female, nature to nature, and a seed, a child, is engendered. The acquaintances of whom her Mamma had boasted that 'they had a child on the way now' had acted out the human form of this same practice. A million people a year enacted the same ritual. King George himself had done the same, six times (the sense she got of sexual activity from Buchanan's book was that it was invariably successful in producing new life). Even her own parents had done this thing, whatever it was, to produce her.

This realisation that there was such an arena of human life, and that she had been too childishly short-sighted even to perceive that it existed – this realisation stung her. It offended her own pride in her scientific curiosity. She decided the proper scientific thing to do was to study the phenomenon more fully. But the library possessed no books on the subject – no books, that is, on human sexual life. Her reticence, bred carefully into her all her life, of course deterred her from actually asking the librarian outright. And the catalogue of books, a handwritten folio, listed no relevant titles. It was, of course, an indecent topic: the lack of books did not surprise her. But she did not give up the quest for knowledge. The best she could do was to read general works of instructive biology. She attended carefully to each of Dr Hartwig's *Popular Accounts of Natural History*, beginning with *The Tropical World*, and going on to *The Polar World, The Aerial World* and *The Sea and Its Living Wonders*. Each book, with three hundred woodcuts and eight of the new-fangled coloured chromoxylographs, provided immense quantities of data, but only the tiniest proportion of this was concerned with reproduction. By poring over the volumes and comparing their different descriptions Eleanor came to the conclusion that *all* males of whatever species possessed sex organs, external to their bodies, attached to gonadic glands that produced sperm. She also learnt that the female's sexual organs were receptive rather than active, that the sperm was deposited in the uterine cavity, and that the young grew in this place. She took out Herbert Howe Bancroft's *Native Races of the Pacific States of North America*, but it contained no mention of reproduction at all, and Eleanor felt that she had wasted her shilling. Then she chanced upon a small book, evidently designed as a practical manual for farmers (she wondered, indeed, how it had found its way into a London lending library): *Pig Breeding, with additional remarks upon Swine Fever* by George Tregelles. From this book she gleaned that the male organ in pigs is 'considerably larger than in most Mammals when erect'; and from this last word she deduced that the male organ assumed an erect posture during mating as a necessary part of the process.

She lay in bed and explored her own body. She had concluded, by a process of elimination, which were her own sexual organs. The various fragmentary allusions to the whole business, which had always been by necessity oblique and veiled, assembled themselves in her head. Somehow the man, becoming 'erect', deposited sperm in the small cavity at the base and the front of her torso.

She felt a disinclination to touch herself between her thighs, as if it were somehow wrong or shameful, and yet she could not remember ever having been specifically rebuked for doing so. Where had she learnt the interdiction? She remembered when her father had been alive, and she had been nine years old – the last months of his illness, in fact, when they were still living in the house in Greenwich. There had been many comings and goings, doctors with their servants, apothecaries and tradesmen of every description. One playful serving man, waiting in the kitchen for his master to come down from upstairs, had joked and jollied with Eleanor for an hour. She had been only a child, not yet old enough to be discouraged from loitering in the servants' quarters, and this servant had been immensely attentive, asking her questions, stroking her hair, laughing. Then, suddenly, the cook had blustered in and shooed him away, afterwards rebuking Eleanor with severity for spending time with the fellow. At the time it had been that severity that stuck in her head, and the shame of the tears she had cried. But now, in bed, she remembered the cook's actual words. *A lady has to watch herself with men*, she had said. *Men want one thing, and they'll try anything to get it, they want to put themselves in you and they'll try anything to do that, and you mustn't let them. Do you understand?* None of this had meant anything to the nine-year-old. But as a young woman, after her menses had started, after reading the books, Eleanor had a flashing sense of what the cook had been getting at. The male organ, which was (evidently) no thicker than a little finger, must be inserted in here. There seemed, to her exploratory fingers, very little room, but doubtless nature had arranged for that. She wondered how long the process should take – seconds, she supposed.

It was strange. She felt she had solved that particular problem, and thereby added to her sum of knowledge. Therefore she could move on to other scientific learning. But the issue refused to leave her mind. She found herself wondering about the exact protocols of the procedure. She found that a delicate touch of her hand on those parts in her bed at night was pleasurable; and again she had the instinctive sense that this was shameful, that she must not speak of it to Mamma. Every time another piece of the jigsaw came her way she stored the information in her mind. Mrs Fox Talbot's serving maid was dismissed for getting herself with child. Mamma and Mrs Fox Talbot talked about the scandal of it in hushed tones, thinking Eleanor absorbed in her book. But Eleanor, listening, learned that the *foolish little minx* had fallen for a soldier. That he was *already married*, but the *little trollop* had pursued him anyway, declaring herself *in love with him* like a penny romance, and that the two had gone off to Shrewsbury together. She came back, of course, said Mrs Fox Talbot, in tears, though I guessed what she had *been up to* (*Shocking*, Mamma had whispered, nodding), and had cried and begged to be taken back. And I took her back, but her condition became only too clear in a few months. And Eleanor learned one further detail, for Mrs Fox Talbot related that her husband had wanted to find out the father's identity and report the fact to his regiment, to his commanding officer, for punishment; but that Mrs Fox Talbot had persuaded him not to – after all, she said, it is the girl's fault, not the man's. Men can't help themselves, of course.

Their landlord at Poland Street was a man called George Newsome, a paunchy man of diminutive stature with a fox-like fuzz of ginger for hair and pale, mournful eyes. He was barely a gentleman, though always quiet and polite in Eleanor's company. But he would call at the apartment once a month, or sometimes more frequently, to collect the rent from Mamma, and discuss any subject that related to the rooms.

On those occasions Mamma would shoo Eleanor from the front room, send her to her own room, or out to the shops with the strict maternal command not to disturb her conference with Mr Newsome. 'Mr Newsome has no desire,' she would snap, 'to be bothered with the prattlings of a girl like you. He and I must discuss the ground-rent' (or the pipes, or the roof, or the yard, or whatever it chanced to be), 'and we are not to be disturbed.' Of course Eleanor accepted this on face value. Why should she not? She curtsied to Mr Newsome, who bowed shallowly in return, and then she went out into the open air.

It was a sunny day, a June day, and Eleanor – knowing her mother's preference in the matter – had volunteered to walk out to sit in Soho Square and read for the duration of Mr Newsome's visit. She had tripped down the stairs, feeling light in her heart and happy, and had reached the end of Poland Street before realising that she had brought the wrong book. She had meant to bring the first volume of Mrs Markham's *History of France, from the Conquest by the Gauls*; but she had actually picked up a volume of *Lisette's Venture, by the Author of 'Thomasina'*, which was of a similar size and had similar-coloured binding. Had her mother's novel been a little more interesting to her, or had she not become quite caught up in the narrative of early French history, she might have simply sat and read *Lisette's Venture* in the sunshine, and that would have been that. But she wanted her own book. So she came back up the street, up the stairs, and let herself into the apartment. She told herself that she might ease the door to the front room open, slip inside, retrieve her book and depart without interrupting her mother's conversation with Mr Newsome. And so she turned the knob with that tentative, controlled touch we use when we want to operate a door-handle without it squeaking. She exerted the slightest pressure on the door and inserted her body a little way through the opening she had made.

The scene inside was nothing she had seen before, but it did not bewilder her. She knew straight away what was occurring, what it must be, and at first the fact registered in her brain without shock. The curtains were drawn across the windows. Her mother was lying face-down over the chaise, her skirts thrown forward over her body with the crenulated hem lying across her shoulders. Her legs were bare all the way up to her waist, and those two pale shapes' rising Λ were what first caught the eye. Then Eleanor took in her mother's whole posture, and then she saw Mr Newsome's relationship to the whole. He too was naked from the waist down, his own legs darker and thinner than Mamma's, his bottom squarely saggy. At the moment that Eleanor opened the door he was in the act of stepping backwards, at an angle to her point of view. His male generative organ (the first that Eleanor had ever seen) waggled a little, forming an angle of no more than fifteen degrees from his stomach. It was of considerable size, or so it seemed to Eleanor. It was darker than Newsome's sallow legs and hands. In the shadowy room it seemed almost black. Newsome spoke a single phrase, 'Lie *still* Madam', to which Mamma replied only with a little half-sigh. And then Newsome stepped over towards the chaise and took his male generative organ in his left hand. He positioned it between Mamma's legs and inserted. Immediately he began swaying his hips forward and backwards, making little grunting noises.

Mamma lay absolutely motionless.

Eleanor extracted herself from the room as silently as she could, and drew the door closed behind her. The latch caught with a loud click.

It might have been a gunshot for the effect it had on Eleanor's nerves.

It was that click that was, for her, the most terrible aspect of the entire encounter. Without it the thing she had seen might have remained a sort of waking dream, a glitch in the ordinary parade of magic-lantern scenes that made up the sights of a day. But the click sealed the occasion.

Eleanor fled the apartment.

Mamma, and Mr Newsome, must have heard the door clicking shut, and would know therefore that they had been observed. It seemed to Eleanor, pacing the streets in a sort of frenzy of anxiety, that they *must* know it had been her. The latch of the door had sounded a sort of death-knell. Everything must tumble now. In her mind she recited the ways in which she was going to have to justify her spying, reciting over and over the innocence of her intention to retrieve the book, only that and nothing more, and adding, in her own head – with ferocious emphasis – that she had *seen nothing*, that there had been *nothing to see*. Hours passed and passed. She wore the pavements down with walking round and round, all the length of Oxford Street and back several times. She loitered in Marylebone Park.

Finally, she could put off the return no longer. She crept up the stairs, her heart palpitating like a death-rattle in her breast, and opened the door. Sally greeted her in the hallway. As if stepping up to face headsman, block and axe, she went through into the front room and greeted her Mamma.

She was sat, in the same chaise over which Eleanor had observed her prone earlier, with the newspaper in her hands. The curtain was drawn back from the window and the evening sky was bright through the glass. As Eleanor came into the rooms he looked up and said: 'Hello my dear. You were gone for ever such a long time.' The words seemed free of accusation. There was no cloud over her mother's face, and no savour of accusation in her manner.

'I went for a walk, Mamma,' Eleanor returned in as blithe a voice as she could muster.

Mamma's attention went back to the newspaper. 'The weather has been very pleasant today,' she said.

And so life went on, exactly as it had done before. For about a week Eleanor fretted and worried, when lying in her bed at night, over whether her mother knew that Eleanor had observed her with Mr Newsome. She might, it was possible to imagine, have thought the door opened by Sally (although Sally never entered a room without being first summoned). Or perhaps she had thought the wind had moved the door, or that it had been a different door in the apartment, or that the click had been some other noise. Eleanor fretted and fretted, but even she knew, in some small place inside her mind, that she was shifting her anxiety from the act itself onto this associated worry of having been detected. Agonising over the clicking of the latch blocked out any too vivid mental picture of her mother prone and Mr Newsome half-naked. That was what she could not allow herself to picture.

Yet the image kept entering her mind. Unconnected items in the world seemed to trigger the involuntary memory: a chair seen at an angle so that its legs seemed to make the shape of an A. The hind quarters of a horse in harness with the cabman snapping his long whip down. Sally, observed from behind as she reached forward to un-snib the latch to the window. Eleanor would see these things, and the image of the darkened room, and Mamma's posture, and Newsome's thin, dark legs, and the vine-stick protuberance of his male organ, would illuminate itself inside her head again.

Subsidiary questions sometimes occurred to her, unbidden – why would her Mamma submit to such a treatment? Had it happened to her before? What of the other gentlemen with whom Mamma occasionally had private conversations? –what of Sir George Cornewall

Lewis, for instance? Or Professor Ludwig Urlichs in Mayfair? But these questions had to be forcefully eliminated from her mind, overlaid with thoughts of mathematical theorems, or *The Steam Engine and Miniature Steam Engine*, or *The Naturalist in Nicaragua, a Narrative of a Residence at the Gold Mines of Chontales, with Observations on Animals and Plants*, or *Half-Hours with the Stars: A Plain and Easy Guide to the Knowledge of the Constellations*, or whichever book she happened to have taken from the library for that week. She attempted to plunge into the books like a diver into a freezing sea, so that nothing but the astringent nature of the element could impinge on her consciousness. That was the way to avoid the insidious imagining of Professor Urlichs – enormous, pastry-fleshy Urlichs with his dewlaps big as goitres and his bulging eyeballs – imagining Professor Urlichs naked and Mamma naked and the two of them arranging together for the male spermatic material to be disseminated into the female after the fashion that Eleanor had herself now witnessed. Rather than think of that, Eleanor was content to devote the most minute attention to her reading. How it was that Mamma did not become pregnant was beyond her, but Eleanor did not want to think about that. Perhaps Mamma was past the age at which pregnancy was possible, but Eleanor didn't want to think of it.

Several weeks afterwards they took out the clarence and trotted along to Hyde Park to watch the soldiers form and march and wheel and reform. For the first time Eleanor found the experience actively upsetting. There was an avidity in her mother's perusal of the officers on their horses that she found repulsive. A veil had fallen. She pictured the naked male forms beneath their uniforms; imagined their male organs of generation growing erect, sizeable as a swine's, and in her imagination her Mamma was watching and thinking precisely the same thing.

Eleanor pressed her gloved hand to her lips. Her mother asked if she was ill, but she could press her teeth very fiercely together, and she could insist that she was well, she was fine, she was in perfect health, and so she did.

No mention was ever made of the clicking of the latch.

Slowly the idea grew in Eleanor's mind that perhaps Mamma had not heard that sound. Perhaps it had not been as loud as she had, at the time, feared. Maybe Mamma had been distracted. But without the latch to focus upon she found it harder to block out flickers of memory relating to the scene itself. A month later Newsome called again, and

Eleanor had a sort of hysteric attack, almost fainting in the hallway, supporting herself against the wall. She raised herself, drawing on all her willpower to put her brave face on, to smile away expressions of concern. She hurried out of the apartment as soon as was polite. She hurried through the streets as if pursued by a djinn from the Arabian Nights, and found herself on Charing Cross Road. There, though a single lady alone, she went into a coffee shop and took coffee, ignoring the glances of the other clientele.

Thoughts in her head, of whatever sort they might be, seemed always related to the male generative organ. She fretted over the matter of how it became hardened – for she knew that this organ was not hard all the time, but rather that it alternated between a flaccid and a hard state (although *why* Nature had decreed such a circumstance necessary was beyond her). Did a bone, or cartilaginous protrusion, insert itself? She could not think how else it might happen. She thought of it jabbing, dagger-like. She daydreamed it as a gormandising, a gluttonous and devouring act. The male *devoured* the female, chewing and masticating and crushing utterly the softer female flesh. Was the male organ equipped, perhaps, with a little mouth, with little teeth? It was clear to her why women, or women of a high enough class, were kept in the dark on this topic. *Lie still Madam*, Newsome had said to Mamma, in the quiet of that room; and normally he was so softly spoken and polite. There had been menace in those words. Why was Mamma required to lie still? Was she wriggling with pain, with discomfort perhaps? And Newsome was at the apartment now – was Mamma repeating the encounter now, at this very minute?

It took deliberate effort to hold back tears. Eventually, walking back, her disgust and anxiety boiled into a kind of hatred of her mother for submitting to it. How could any self-respecting woman submit to it? She could see no justification.

And on the evening before her own wedding, here was her mother attempting – unsolicited – attempting to raise this grisly, gristly matter again. Her anger fizzled upwards, and she had to crush her teeth together again. She hated her mother, briefly, for mentioning it. She did not need to bring up such a matter. She ought not to talk on such a topic. Not that Eleanor was wholly blind: she knew, in a half-unacknowledged part of her mind, that her Mamma had been, in her foolish and incoherent way, passing on this task, this woman's work, to her daughter. It was evidently how Mamma viewed her duty. Eleanor, from tomorrow, would have to share the bed of Burton, and by doing so would have earned the right to his money, to enough money to support both herself and her mother, as her mother had done before. This was her labour. This was where the coins were generated.

But on the evening itself, however, the eve of her own marriage to Burton, Eleanor did not and could not see it in those terms. As Mamma stumbled and mumbled over her explanation of what Eleanor might expect on her wedding night, she felt the coldest sort of revulsion inside her. 'It is quite alright, Mamma,' she interrupted. 'I fancy I have a good sense of what to expect.'

Mamma looked at the fire for a while. Then she said with a pitiful meekness: 'Might I offer one piece of advice, dear daughter?'

Eleanor did not want to hear the advice. She wanted her mother to say nothing at all about this topic. But there was no way to shut her up.

'Mamma?' she said.

'The trick all womankind learns, sooner or later,' Mamma said, still looking at the fire. 'To submit. Do you see what I say? It goes easiest if you merely—'

'I understand,' barked Eleanor, her voice louder than she had meant it to be.

There was a silence.

'I was only going to say,' Mamma continued, in an even lower tone, 'to grant the man his way. It goes easiest, then.' Mamma was crying now, in the firelight, the tears sticky and adhering to her face – the surface-tension potential of fluids such as salt water, Eleanor knew, rendering it most likely that a film or sheen of the substance will attach itself to smooth surfaces, although this cohesive force – the same that the tiny insects called water-boatmen use to support themselves on the surfaces of ponds – may be disrupted by the application of certain detergents.

[6]

The morning of her wedding came. Eleanor woke early. She had experienced bad dreams, and had slept poorly – but naturally, she told herself, naturally I am apprehensive. It would be peculiar if I were not apprehensive. Today is my wedding day. Nevertheless the bad dream stayed with her. It stained her waking thoughts too.

In the dream she had been with Burton in the Poland Street apartment, although it did not resemble the apartment. It was a much bigger room, with fantastical and expensive red silk drapes on every wall, and three tall narrow windows in the Gothic style. Yet she had known that it was her apartment, so much so that she had wondered where her mother was. Burton was standing in front of her, and he said: 'It is imperative that a commanding officer be a real Tartar with his men, for how else,' he added, seating himself on a black chaise longue, 'how else is our Continental war to be won?' She had replied something conventional, in agreement, when Burton had stretched himself on the chaise longue, in an utterly uncharacteristic manner. His voice was that of the German Count's. 'Do you understand the meaning of the phrase "*in exactly the same manner*"?' he asked. Dream-Eleanor had wondered if perhaps he had wanted the phrase translated, and was about to reply that her German was not adequate to the task when Burton pulled open the front of his trowsers. The trowsers, indeed, seemed to dissolve and vanish, and there were Burton's legs, thin and stick-like (in the dream), and at the apex of leg and leg, instead of the usual male organ, stood a Lilliputian man, a tiny six-inch man in a toy red uniform, standing straight up with a tooth-filled grin on his face.

Eleanor woke feeling ashamed of herself. But she couldn't rid herself of the image.

Burton had, taking Mamma's detailed advice, bought two dresses for Eleanor to wear. The first was a cream silk wedding dress with lace trimmings and a twelve-foot train. It was more gorgeous than any Eleanor had owned before, but was far outshone by the magnificence of the second dress, which was for formal wear on honeymoon. This was a petticoat of green silk entirely covered with Brussels point, and a loose drapery of lilac silk, covered also with lace, and drawn up in festoons with large bouquets of fashioned mother-of-pearl, each bouquet consisting of one large rosette from which rose bending sprigs depended in imitation of snowdrops. The dressmaker had fitted Eleanor only with the underdress for both patterns; she did not see the finished products until the morning of her wedding. And when the dressmaker called at the apartment that morning, even she – with her studied bluestocking manner of scientific detachment – even she could not restrain little cries of delight. The dresses were so beautiful! Mamma burst into loud tears at once, and could not have put on a more formidable show of weeping had it been her daughter's funeral rather than her wedding.

They took a covered carriage – not the clarence, but a carriage Burton had hired specially for the occasion – the four hundred yards down Oxford Street to Saint Giles Church, where the groom was waiting with Silverthorne. Mamma had talked animatedly for weeks about how Louisa, Marchioness of Waterford, was to be Maid of Honour, but in the event she did not come – her inducement, unkind gossips said, was insufficient (or perhaps Mamma had felt uncomfortable about approaching Burton for money to do so dubious a thing as bribe a Lady to attend). But Misses Moore and Rogers attended, smiling and lively and almost pretty, though the one was obese and the other – the wits said, cruelly – skinny and shaped like an alligator.

Eleanor's experience of the ceremony was of a vague detachment from everything, as if she were watching somebody else getting married rather than going through the process herself. The Rev. Jeremiah Lawless married them with a sombre, almost fierce expression on his face, seemingly disapproving of the match; but afterwards he preached a beaming sermon on the beauty of new love, especially praising Burton and Eleanor for the self-evident attachment and affection they both demonstrated. Outside, as shredded paper was cast over them and the small crowd cheered thinly, Eleanor turned to look at her husband, half-expecting – irrationally – there to be some change in him, as if the fact that he was now legally her husband must magically transform him into a creature she could not help loving and respecting. But he stood winking and blinking in the sunlight, a dusting of sweat on his wide brow, and the crease in his double chin as sharp as a cut in his neck. He seemed as ludicrous as ever. The thought of him as husband seemed as preposterous after as before the sacrament.

The wedding feast was taken in the Ogilvie Hotel. Fourteen of Burton's Lilliputians served on the table, pulling miniature carts up and down the length like tiny drayhorses for the convenience of the diners: a wheeled gravy-boat; a silver sled containing asparagus; four of them in harness pulling an open carriage filled with potatoes. Each of the tiny people had been dressed in doll-clothes livery of scarlet and gold. They averted their tiny eyes from the full-sized people, they strained and worked in their tiny universe. Eleanor, smiling and making banal conversation, was repeatedly struck by the absurdity of the *mise en scène*. The shift in perspective between the human beings sitting around the table eating and the miniature Pacificans upon the tabletop gave her the uncomfortable sensation of being a giantess, of swelling and engorging every limb as if with hot air, of rising up (like Mr Harcourt Johnstone's hot-air balloon that had floated above Marylebone Park for a fortnight the previous year) until she was a mile high.

'My dear,' she said, turning to Burton – to (she scolded herself silently to remember) her husband – 'the Lilliputians look so charming in their uniforms.'

'Blefuscans,' said Burton, 'my darling. These are Blefuscans, and not Lilliputians.'

She smiled and nodded. Her husband, as he now was, had drunk three glasses of claret. She had never seen him drink alcohol before.

The toasts; the speeches; the three-cheers and thrice-times-three; and afternoon wore into evening. Eleanor did not drink much, for she had always found the flavour of alcohol distasteful. But Burton drank glass after glass, as if he hoped to fill the barrel of his belly with fluid. Eventually Eleanor kissed her Mamma and retired to their suite at the top of the hotel. Despite everything, despite a whole day spent steeling herself internally, she was nervous. Her fingers would not stay still. The maid Burton had engaged for the occasion (not Sally, who was in Poland Street attending to Mamma) undressed her, and she went to bed with a candle to wait for her husband. When he came up he was unsteady on his feet. He appeared to be growling like a bear. Eleanor realised almost at once that this was a sort of half-awake snoring. He stripped off jacket and trousers, and fumbled for a long time with his necktie. 'My dear?' Eleanor called tentatively from the bed. 'Mmm,' he replied, the susurrus rumbling on from his throat. 'Married now,' he said. The tie came away like a snake, to be discarded on the floor. Burton collapsed on the bed. He lay like a dead man, his snoring more regular. Eleanor watched him for fifteen minutes, before settling under the covers and going to sleep herself.

In the morning, Burton was abjectly apologetic, meekly enduring the miserable symptoms of his over-indulgence from the previous night. He shaded his eyes with his right hand, nibbled feebly at the breakfast that was brought in, and drank only Vichy water. The experience, the anticipation of which had (Eleanor now realised) built up layer upon layer of anxiety in her mind over the previous months previous, now seemed laughably anticlimactic. Her condescending disdain for her husband had been cemented by the non-encounter – by (she realised, understanding the phrase fully for the first time) the *non-consummation*. For her marriage, she could see, had not been consummated.

'I really must apologise for my behaviour last night,' Burton muttered for the sixth time.

'Really,' she snapped back at him, dabbing her mouth with a napkin. 'Say no more about it.'

That afternoon they caught the Channel packet for the Continent. Burton had promised her a honeymoon wherever she wanted – Rome, America, she had only to name the destination. But she had not wanted to be so far from home, to travel to some inaccessibly distant place only to be trapped there (as she could not help thinking of it) with her husband. So she had chosen Brussels, and Burton had been very pleased to agree. It would harm the business, he said, were they away longer than a week.

That night they stayed in a Calais hotel, and although Burton stayed sober he was too embarrassed by the previous night's debacle to press his attentions. The next day, on the coach ride through the French and Belgian countryside, Eleanor saw giant men, the Brobdingnagians, labouring in the fields. One drew a massive hundred-bladed plough through the sticky soil; another tossed a house-sized hayrick with a rake as long as Satan's spear in *Paradise Lost*. 'Why do they plough the fields in autumn?' Burton wondered, aloud.

'The new strains of winter wheat,' replied Eleanor, with a sneer on her face at her husband's ignorance.

Burton, blushing, said nothing more.

They arrived in Brussels in time for supper. During the meal, which was in conducted in silence, Burton sucked a deep breath into his chest, sat up straight, and said: 'My dear, I hope it will be convenient for you tonight.'

'Convenient?' she replied. For a moment she really had no idea what he meant.

Both his cheeks blushed bruise-dark. 'Convenient for both of us, I,' he muttered, 'I-I should say.'

She looked at the green bottle from which he had been drinking. 'And this is why you have drunk nothing but water and coffee all evening?'

He nodded, looking grave. Then he laughed, a single laugh. She did not join him, and the mirth died.

'I have no wish,' he said, 'to force my attentions.'

'And I no wish to be forced,' she replied, fiercely. But as soon as she had said this, she felt something like regret. It was perhaps too cutting. After supper, when they retired, she kissed his beard, rather primly, and led him to the bed. Better to get it over with. He said nothing, but his breath was coming sharp and shallow in little gasps. She slipped her dress off without calling for the maid, and sat on the bed in her petticoat. He was pulling off his clothes awkwardly and throwing them aside until he stood before her in only an undershirt and silk socks. Eleanor's apprehension seemed to have dissolved. Her only emotion was a kind of detached curiosity. Her husband's legs were much fuller than Newsome's had been. His belly hung down like a fold of uncooked pastry. His male organ poked out at a right angle. It had a rather different appearance than the only other she had seen: where that had been squat and short, this was lengthy and quite thin, with a reddish, purplish, knuckle-shaped knob at the end. As Burton approached the bed this organ rocked a little from side to side, and Eleanor's detachment was enough for her to peer a little more closely, hoping to identify the gonadic organs, of which she understood there to be two, the provenance of the male spermatic material. But Burton was on top of her before she could make her observation.

'My darling,' he grunted, 'my darling.'

He pressed his face against her, and she was conscious of the prickliness of his beard, and then of a wetness on her chin as he kissed her. She felt the weight of his body, and the jag of his organ against her thigh. 'My darling,' he grunted again, and then half-coughed, as if something were caught in his throat, 'Ah-ah-ah!' Suddenly he was still.

He rolled to the side and lay on his back. For several minutes Eleanor did not dare move. But then, raising herself a little, she noticed a glutinous, pale substance sticking to the skin of her thigh. She almost asked him 'What is this?', but realised suddenly that it was sperm. She could have laughed out loud at it. She had assumed, without thinking too closely about it, that 'sperm' would be a dry substance, like plant pollen. It had simply never occurred to her that it would emerge in fluid form.

She lay down again beside her husband. Minutes passed. The occasion was not at all as she had expected. 'Is that all?' she asked, finally.

Burton did not look at her. 'I fear,' he said, his voice small, 'that I must apologise once more.'

'I don't understand,' she said.

'Did your mother not explain to you . . . ?' he said.

She spoke quickly. 'Yes, yes, yes, of course.'

Burton shifted his large form, turning on his side, sending bouncy waves through the mattress until he settled. He was lying with his back to Eleanor. 'We can try again tomorrow, perhaps,' he mumbled.

Eleanor waited for him to speak further, until she realised that he had fallen asleep. But she could not sleep. Was she now a wife? A wife, and no longer a virgin? It was absurd that she did not know, but no book she had read prepared her for this moment. The man had deposited his sperm upon her, so perhaps she was now deflowered. But the whole encounter had a half-finished feeling about it. She had expected the sperm to be deposited inside her organ of Venus – she touched that place now with her fingers' ends, touching herself very gently as if afraid of waking her husband. It seemed to be buzzing, a thrilling and slightly uncomfortable sensation. Had Burton attempted to place his seed in that place and, somehow, missed? That seemed incredible. Or was it the proper thing to do to deposit the seed on the thigh? Perhaps it was a sort of sexual etiquette; or perhaps it was some feature of human sexuality of which she was ignorant, some feature with no analogue in the animal or plant kingdoms. She touched the sticky material, touched her own organ. The sensation there was something like a kind of itch, although not exactly an itch, a warm feeling, an ache for pressure. Her finger moved in tiny circles, trying to fathom the connection between the experience she had just had and the reproductive cycle, trying to work out the anatomical connection between thigh and that place and – without warning – she felt a hot shudder pass up her body, hurrying up through her torso to her face where it emerged in a series of little gasps.

She lay for a while, until her breathing returned to normal.

She had not experienced such a sensation before. It unsettled her. She ought, she decided, to leave her husband's sperm upon her skin. It might be a faux pas to wipe it away, might interfere somehow with the sexual process, although it felt clammy and unpleasant on her leg.

The following night Burton tried again. This time he did indeed attempt to insert himself between her thighs, but he was tentative and clumsy and she could not stop herself calling out in her discomfort. It seemed impossible to her that the operation could be successful. His organ was simply too big for the space. He could no more fit it into so small a hole than he could fit it in her nostril or ear. He pulled away, anxious, apologetic, 'I'm sorry my dear, sorry to have hurt you.' She didn't reply. Then he tried again, and again he deposited his sperm upon the outside of her body, this time between her legs.

The following night he stayed late downstairs, playing cards in the smoking room with some men he had met, whilst Eleanor sat in bed reading and eventually fell asleep.

The night after that he came to bed drunken again, and fell asleep fully dressed on the settee.

During the day the two of them toured the sites of the old city, lunched in a fine old restaurant, and strolled in the parks. Eleanor read *The Imperial Gazetteer*, and dipped into Professor Alain Privat Deschanel's *Natural Philosophy*. But her mind kept returning to the question of the consummation, or non-consummation, of her marriage. She came to the private conclusion that there was something malformed about her own organ of Venus. It was clearly too small to admit her husband's member. What she had seen of Newsome and Mamma (although she did not like to dwell on the memory) suggested that a man's member could be easily inserted into a woman. That Burton's did not fit meant that either his member was abnormally large, or else her organ abnormally small, and she inclined towards the latter conclusion. A sort of dismal fatalism fell upon her. It was impossible. She would never consummate the marriage.

On the final night in Brussels Burton came into the bedroom drunk, but this time did not simply fall asleep. He seemed belligerent, even costive. He blundered about the room muttering to himself. The sight of so large a man in a bad humour, and the fact that such behaviour was so unfamiliar to Eleanor, who had only ever seen Burton as bumbling and shy as a child, alarmed her very much. She reacted to her fear by becoming aggressive herself. 'Drunk again, sir?' she baited him. 'I did not know I was marrying a drinking man.'

'It must be tonight, madam,' he replied, fiercely. 'You'll not put me off again.'

'Put you off!'

'You'll act your part, Madam. I was talking to a fellow downstairs, a good sort. A brevet-major. As fine a fellow as I've met. I've been talking the matter over with him.'

'Talking, sir?' she said, outraged. 'Talking of matters personal to you and me? How could you!'

'Talking to a *fellow*,' Burton said, leaning towards her and putting slurry emphasis on every other word, 'who *gave* excellent advice concerning *the female*.'

'Are our personal affairs to become a talking point for every common soldier in the British army, sir?'

'He said your womanhood would be tight to begin with ...'

Eleanor gave a little shriek of horror.

'... tight to begin with,' Burton continued thickly, 'but I must simply push past it, simply push past it.'

'Tonight, sir, I am in no amorous mood,' said Eleanor firmly.

'Tonight it *will* happen, Madam,' he replied fiercely, and launched himself, or collapsed, upon her. She shrieked again and struggled, slapping his face and his shoulders, but he bore down on her. 'He said,' he muttered to himself, as he fumbled under his own body to undo his trowsers, 'he said that your maidenhead would be tight to begin with ...'

'Get off me, sir,' insisted Eleanor.

'... you'll act ...'

She felt his male organ, hard as a stone, pressing between her legs, against her venereal organ. With a horrible, invasive sense of physical danger she began crying, slapping with redoubled force. The pressure grew until, suddenly, something inside, in that part of her body, burst, with a stabbing sensation of pain. She shrieked again. Burton shuffled, twitched, twitched again, and then pulled sharply back. He rolled over and lay on his back, panting.

Eleanor shrank away, scrabbled to the far edge of the bed. She almost did not dare look down, to see what damage had been done to her body between her legs. A tart throbbing sensation suggested actual injury. She looked at her husband, fearful and angry, only to see that he was crying. What she had taken for gasps of passion were actually sobs. His face was wet with tears. He turned his face to her. 'I'm sorry my darling,' he said, in a maudlin-drunk voice. 'My darling wife.'

She steeled herself and looked down. Blood was on her thighs and had red-inked a maple-leaf shape onto the sheet beneath her. Her face flushed, her stomach tingled with horrible apprehension. What if some deep injury had been effected inside her? What if she bled on and on, bled to death? 'I fear,' she said, in a trembly voice. 'You have injured

89

me, sir.' But Burton's sobbing had slid imperceptibly into the snores of sleep.

She was awake for more than an hour, resolved to call for a doctor if the bleeding did not abate. But it reduced over a quarter of an hour or so, and finally it stopped altogether. She washed herself as best she could in the porcelain bowl, using the whole of their jug of water. She would have rung the bell for more water, but did not like the thought of the hotel staff seeing the bloodstained sheets. They would surely assume some crime had been committed.

Finally she returned to the bed. There was, after all, nowhere else for her to sleep. For a long time she sat looking down at her husband, fully dressed, on his back, his male member poking through the slit in his trowsers, flaccid now though crusted with her blood. It was a most distasteful image.

She lay down, with her back to him, and tried to sleep. But images of her father occurred and reoccurred to her. Why should she think of her father at a time like this? It made no sense. Yet the churning sensation in her belly was like the one she had always felt visiting his sick bed.

Papa had always been a gaunt man, a tall man, severe of manner. But after he fell ill his sharp features and long body became, as it were, whittled away to the bony essence within. Sitting in bed the long shallow curves of his flanks, his arms, took on a hammered, metallic aura. The illness seemed to be metamorphosing him into a creature made of white metal. He might sit, propped with woolsack pillows, for hour, turning his eyes slowly to face the light of the window, and back to rest on the form of his daughter, sitting on the bedside. A white man, tucked between white sheets in which he made hardly a bulge. Then the coughing would sweep over him, a punishing sequence of powerful coughs that crunched his face up like a piece of waste paper balled in a fist. His body would twitch, as if a muscular demon within him were punching outward against his ribs with all its force. His right hand would go to his mouth, the white cotton handkerchief clutched in it, and cough after cough would come bursting through. On the handkerchief, first a dewdrop spot of red; then a thruppenny-sized circle; then a spreading patch of scarlet. The coughing would slowly subside, and his hand would sag, exhausted, to his side, dropping the kerchief onto the sheets, where the creased cloth would roll and settle, and the fluid mixture of saliva and blood would mark the sheets. The red staining the white. And papa another painful inch closer to death.

She looked down at Burton's snoring body. His member looked as innocuous now as a worm. Her papa, she thought, had been the strongest man she had ever known; valiant-for-truth, an inspiring model of rectitude. Death had levelled him, of course. We all carry death within us, of course, and eventually it must emerge, howsoever we struggle to hold it within.

In the small hours Burton awoke with a jerk, mumbled 'So, so,' turned and fell asleep again.

In the morning, Eleanor bundled the stained bedclothes into a drawer. She rang the bell for the room-servant, and when he arrived, bringing a tray, sent him out to fetch an English paper. Whilst her husband still slumbered, she sat in bed eating breakfast from the tray and reading about the latest events. British forces were about to go into action at Versailles. There was little doubt that Christmas would see the flag of St George flying over Paris. The Belgian government had reaffirmed its alliance with the King – the burghers of the country alarmed, Eleanor thought to herself cynically, at the prospect of royal troops and sapient cavalry marching into Brussels.

When Burton finally awoke, he moaned like a dying man. Eleanor, brisk and distant, went for a morning stroll through the new Arcade, and spent forty pounds of Burton's money on pointless fripperies. When she returned, Burton had washed and changed and looked a little better; but he looked sheepish too, as if deeply ashamed. As, she thought fiercely to herself, he ought. As he ought.

They departed the city after luncheon, staying in a hotel on the coast. The following day they returned to London.

[7]

Once before, when Burton had come wooing to the apartment in Poland Street, Eleanor had experienced an epiphany of hatred. The urge to throttle the man, to beat him and stab him, had rushed through her with maenad intensity, although she had maintained her external poise. The lust for his death had passed quickly, but now that they were married she found little stabs of anger bursting through her composure all the time. Her experience of him had been compounded of the clumsy violence of their honeymoon and his subsequent fawning, his abject feebleness of manner – the latter, she now saw, the most prominent mode of Burton's existence. She hated him more fiercely than she had before.

They moved into the house in Gower Street, and Eleanor adjusted to the new manner of living: a head butler, a housekeeper, three under-butlers, six maidservants, cooks and gardeners and various menials, all waiting on the three of them. Mamma had a little suite of rooms at the rear of the ground floor. Although Burton had urged her to dismiss Sally, even offering the girl a generous payment in severance, Mamma, growing increasingly sentimental, had insisted on keeping her. Eleanor found the presence of so many people in one house, even a large house, such as hers now was, disconcerting. Wasteful. It seemed, obscurely, another thing with which to rebuke her husband.

But her rebukes were now silent, expressed through the media of bodily movement and facial expression. She exchanged hardly a word with Burton. They slept in the same room, but in separate beds, and her husband was too cowed to approach her in any amorous sense. They took breakfast together, and dined together in the evening, but conversation was sparse and functional. Otherwise the most that husband would say to wife was 'I see an interesting book is now published, by Padre Secchi of Rome, containing the latest astronomical observations of the moon'; or 'Mr Dammell has published a tract on Electro-Plating, my dear, which I may purchase.' Eleanor understood that these comments were covert appeals to what Burton regarded as common ground between them, attempts to draw out her interest. She resisted them, sometimes despite herself. She wanted to punish him yet awhile; to blockade, as it were, any of the finer emotions that might otherwise be traded between them. She was not sure how long this punishment ought to last. In her milder moments she thought, perhaps, a year. But then Burton would do something clumsy, something crude, and her hatred for him would bubble up inside her again, and she would resolve never to permit him intimacy on any terms.

He stayed, increasingly, late at work. She noticed that he was drinking far more. One afternoon she called at the manufactory, to be met by the grinning Mr Pannell. 'I'll announce you, Madam,' he said, his face a rictus. 'He'll be delighted to see you, I'm sure. He's been a new man since the wedding. A new man.'

But Burton was not there. 'I don't understand,' Pannell told her, the concern in his voice at odds with the grin he maintained on his face. 'He must have travelled out on business, I think. Or so I suppose, Madam.'

'Very well,' said Eleanor, gathering her skirts around her and stepping down the dirty steps from the main entrance. 'Tell him that I called.'

'Of course.'

'Mr Pannell,' she said, turning on the bottom step. 'Did my husband drink before the marriage?'

This question was peculiar enough, and personal enough, to flatten the smile from Pannell's lips. 'Drink, Ma'am?'

'Drink liquor. Drink alcohol.'

'Why,' said Pannell. 'No, I don't believe he did. I don't believe he did.'

Eleanor made her way back to the carriage and allowed herself to be helped in by the footman. She felt a quickening in her belly, a wicked sense of satisfaction – not a pure or gleeful emotion, perhaps, but one mixed with enough dark joy to make it more pleasant than unpleasant. It was the knowledge that her husband was miserable. Which could only mean that, in some oblique way, she was having her revenge. For what else could it mean?

But her personal unhappiness polluted this joy. There was no escaping her moods. And then there was Mother. After the move her mother had been gleeful as a child for three days, flitting from room to room in the large house, ordering the servants. But, as the novelty faded, she grew morose. She drank more than ever before.

And another night passed, with Mamma too intoxicated even to play cards, and Eleanor staring at the fire, a book open on her lap. 'Where is Jonathan?' Mamma asked, querulous, from her chair. 'At the manufactory, Mamma,' Eleanor replied, 'as he often is. It can hardly be called,' she added, angrily, 'a politeness that he so markedly avoids our company. Can it, Mamma?'

But her mother was snoring.

One afternoon, von Leloffel called to pay his respects, accompanied by a gentleman called D'Ammassa, from Rome. Mamma was not pleased to see him, but the four of them took tea in the front room. 'I must congratulate you, Mrs Burton,' Von Leloffel said smoothly, 'on your marriage. And you, Mrs Davis, also, on your daughter's connection.'

'Thank you,' said Mamma, chilly.

'A jewel requires the proper setting, if its lustre is to be properly appreciated,' the Count drawled. 'Even a beauty as striking as yours, Mrs Burton, gains sparkle from the proper environment.' He looked about him, smiling.

They talked for half an hour, the Count making a series of elegant and witty observations, and D'Ammassa interjecting curtly from time to time; then they took their leave. Afterwards, Mamma was in a bad mood. 'They'll be back, I'll wager you,' she said. 'They'll be like ants to honey, they will. Like ants to honey.'

'Whatever can you mean, Mamma?' replied Eleanor, half-deliberately imitating the Count's elegantly drawling manner of speech.

'To borrow money, of course!' cried Mamma. 'He's poor as a Spaniard, that Count, for all that he puts on fine airs. Money, such as we now have, carries its own responsibilities you know.'

But Eleanor did not gain much solace from having money. All through the thirty minutes of conversation with the Count she had found herself thinking how much more presentable he was than her own husband. Such thought was reprehensible, she knew, and yet her glance traced out the line of his jaw, his slim figure, his startlingly blue eyes. There would be no clumsiness with him, she told herself; he would know how to act in every situation. He, or somebody like him, would have been the proper consort to her life.

And – the thought occurred to Eleanor frequently now – were her husband to die, to have a heart seizure or to fall in front of a train, then his money would become hers. If she had money, she might make the Count her own. She could live life as she wished. Such a possibility was so perfect, so well shaped, that the obstacle to it seemed to shrink in her mind. Even the bulk of a man so large as Burton became gossamer to her fantasising mind. The thread that tied her to this miserable life was, after all, no thicker than the vital thread of Burton himself; and that was no thicker than any man's, a delicate red line of a pulsing artery. And this red line was thinner than some, for Burton was not a young man.

Her daydreaming got no further than this vaguely wished-for vanishing of her husband, however. She made no concrete plans for his departure. How could she? Such thoughts were not civilised. Such thoughts were not womanly.

Mamma was playing patience, and Eleanor reading. 'My dear,' Mamma said, without looking up from her cards. 'The room directly above this? With the Di Fiore windows?'

'Yes, Mamma?'

'That would be the best room for a child, I think.'

'A child?'

Her mother looked up at her. There were moss-branch traceries of red in the corners of her eyes. 'Of course, my darling. When you and Jonathan are blessed with children. A son or daughter, you know, must have an appropriate room. I must think of these things. I would want only the best for my grandchild, you know.'

It had simply not occurred to her that children might follow her marriage. But of course, it was expected. She felt foolish for not thinking of it before. Without further congress between husband and wife a child was unlikely, she knew; and yet how could she guarantee that? Burton, drunken and enraged, had pressed himself upon her before. He could do so again. And what of that first time? Less than a month ago: how could she know that she did not already carry a child?

After Mamma had retired, Eleanor sat up for several hours, revolving and revolving the possibilities in her head. Was there a tiny person inside her now? It was intolerable. To be Burton's wife was bad enough, to bear his children was too much. She decided, the thought locking inside her head with its sense of rightness, that she would wait no longer. The marriage was a sham. She would confront Burton that very night, and tear down the facsimile behind which they were both living. Better to do so now, before it was too late.

Burton's day had not gone well.

The morning had been spent with a Mr Haughton, a fiduciary. Two contracts for the military had been cancelled. Burton had no idea why this had happened, and Major Phillips (with whom he usually discussed such procurements over dinner) was not in the country at the moment. But the loss of the work, combined with the various expenses associated with his marriage, placed the company in a slightly awkward financial position. Haughton thought matters reparable with new contracts, and fortunately Burton had received a letter from a Mister Bates enquiring after work that might well lead to a contract for ten, perhaps twelve, thousand pounds. 'This would be most advantageous,' Haughton had sniffed, 'this sum. Most advantageous for the financial health of the company.'

Burton had never before heard of this Mr Bates, which was perhaps unusual given the size of the proposed contract. But he assured Haughton that the deal was more or less assured. 'Mr Bates is visiting the premises this very day,' he said.

'I will be able to write to you by the evening post, I believe, and confirm the contract.'

'I hope so, sir,' said Haughton, standing. 'For your sake, your company's sake, I hope so.'

After he had gone, Burton read through Bates's letter again. He tried to tell himself that it would solve his problems, but by ten he was drinking deeply from the bottle of brandy that he kept in his office. The fluid, golden in the morning light, burned pleasantly in the mouth. As molten, though cold, as the fluid metal bubbling in the vats on the manufactory floor. The drink, as ever, unhooked some latch in his brain. The financial difficulties seemed to recede. The dozen thousand pounds from Bates's employment would make all right again.

The sunlight burned a little brighter on his desk.

Burton's good moods were fleeting, however. He toured the factory. A crane bolt was close to shearing, the foreman told him. That was eighty pounds to mend if it was a farthing: a scaffold must needs be built to support the superstructure whilst the old bolt was cut away and a new one fitted. It would take a day and a night, and precious little real work could be managed during that time. Moreover, the foreman said, one of the Blefuscans was dead. That was an expense in itself running into many guineas. But it seemed that this Blefuscan was an aristocrat. A count, a prince, a king – who could fathom their mysterious little hierarchies. 'The workers are unhappy, sir,' said the foreman.

'Unhappy,' Burton sighed. 'They are forever unhappy.'

'This time, sir,' said the foreman, 'it is more acute than normal.'

The foreman was a good fellow. Called Marcus Antonius, or somesuch Antique Roman affectation as is common in the West Indies, he was known to everybody with whom he worked as Mark. His promotion had been rapid, and Burton depended upon him more than on any other worker. Above all he knew the Pacificans, knew their ways. 'If you say there is real concern here, Mark, I shall believe you.'

'Thank you, sir,'

'How did the creature die? Do we know?'

Mark shook his head. 'They're fragile, sir,' he observed.

'True, true. But no sign of . . . depredation?'

'No rats, sir. No cats. I've spoke to the representative, and he says only that the Prince has died, and that they must have three days for proper funeral.'

'Three days,' tutted Burton. 'Impossible, of course.'

'I'll tell 'em so,' said Mark.

As he went away Burton almost yielded to the impulse to call him back, to have him give the Blefuscans their funeral time. A day, at least; a half-day. But the moment passed. They did not rule the factory, after all. He did. Three-day holiday? Doubtless the dead Blefuscan was no prince at all, merely some miniature equivalent to tramp or servant, and the Pacificans were merely hoping for three days' idleness. They were, all of them, the most idle of creatures.

Burton returned to his office, with a sunken sensation in his stomach. He had a premonition that the little folk were going to disrupt production that day, and for days after, on this trumped-up account. He reached for the brandy to pour himself another glass, and found the bottle empty.

He could not send an underling out to buy another. His drinking, much more pronounced now than it had ever been before his marriage, was not a matter to which employees should be privy. Discreetly, and obscurely angry, he fitted himself into his overcoat and slipped out of the manufactory.

He strode briskly up to the Strand, and across up to Agar Street, to the grog shop he had taken to frequenting. The old woman behind the counter beamed at him as he came in. The fact that she recognised him made him more annoyed.

'French,' he said brusquely. 'None of your cheap stuff.'

'Sir,' said the old lady, with a wheedling and faintly rebuking inflection. She went into a back room and returned with a boxed bottle, opening the lid to display its contents to her customer. The straw packing the box looked mouldy, but Burton was in no mood to complain.

'Ten shilling and fivepence exactually,' said the old woman.

Burton paid, and hurried away.

He crossed the Strand again, noticing as if for the first time how many couples there seemed to be, how many contented men and women walking arm-in-arm. In his sour mood it struck him almost as a sort of mockery. A thought ground its way out of the machine in his brain: how had his marriage gone so wrong in so short a time?

Burton prided himself on his honesty. Some, he supposed, called it brusqueness, but Burton could not see it as a fault if such directness was merely a function of truthfulness. Truth was great, and would prevail, for all the hypocrisies of politer society. Yet it was hard to be honest with one's self. Eleanor was beautiful, yes; and Eleanor was intelligent, yes; but she was unhappy. He had made her unhappy. He was unhappy himself. Perhaps his unhappiness had, somehow, infected her, like rust spreading from a rotten girder to a sound. Were it so, how could he forgive himself? To have caused suffering to a creature superior to him in every regard?

Back in his office he uncorked the brandy and poured himself a full glass.

Nevertheless there is, he thought to himself as the sunlight pushed gleaming swords diagonally down through his window, some sort of hypocrisy woven into the very fabric of life. To think it had come to this. When he had first elevated himself, by his own efforts attained a more respectable position in society, he had been as shocked as a schoolboy by the manifest *cant* of the upper classes. He encountered such people at his club, where they drawled and chuckled over their wickednesses; revelling, for instance, in adulteries – actively revelling – comparing other men's wives as if they were racehorses, boasting of unchastities. They lived a life quite different from the elegant surface they presented to society, a life of immorality, of wickedness and indulgence. The revulsion Burton had experienced had been genuine. How ironic, then, he told himself (pouring another glass), that he should find himself trapped into a life similarly hypocritical. To the world he was married, but of course the relationship between himself and his wife was not marriage as the term should be properly understood.

Even the brandy was not removing the tartness of misery from his thoughts.

He must do something. And yet, what could he do? He might be no gentleman in the eyes of polite society, yet he prided himself on acting as a gentleman should, and he could not abandon Eleanor and her mother. Might there not, he asked himself, might there not be a way to discuss the matter with his wife? To come to some rational arrangement between them? He pictured Eleanor's face, the beautiful face distorted with disdain for him. His heart twitched as if stabbed with pins. It was too terrible.

Pannell put his idiotic head round the door frame. 'Sir?'

'A gentleman,' Burton bellowed, 'knocks! Knocks, sir!'

'I did knock, Mr Burton,' said Pannell timorously. 'I knocked several times. Perhaps you did not hear me?'

Burton's fury hovered on the lip of emergence, then withdrew inside him. His situation was not the fault of Pannell, after all, foolish though the fellow was. 'I have been,' he said, gruffly, 'in a reverie. I have been thinking, deeply.'

'I only wanted to say,' said Pannell, 'that Mister Bates is here.'

'Very good, sir,' said Burton. 'Entertain him, sir. Show him the works, give him a drink, make him sweet. Make him sweet. Then bring him to me here.'

'Very good, Mister Burton. The midday post has arrived, sir, also.'

'Good,' said Burton. 'I'll look it over whilst you show Mister Bates about. Does he seem,' Burton added, unable to keep the anxiety from the edges of his voice, 'does he seem a gentleman?'

'Oh yes, sir.'

'A gentleman, I mean, of means?'

'Oh yes, sir.'

'Very good.'

Pannell slipped properly into the room, deposited a bundle of letters on the desk, and stole away again.

Burton stared at the little string-bound package. There were, he estimated, half a dozen letters. A year ago the midday post had brought forty letters most days. There was a palpable sense of diminishment. He did not know why.

The light had faded a little. Burton stood and looked through his window, over the ceaseless river to the warehouses and roofs of the south bank. Grey clouds had smoked out the wintry sunshine. Bundles of clouds, like bales, moved stately through the sky. The sun was uncovered for a moment, and then covered again. Light grew, filling the glass with brightness, and then shrank away again. Somehow it was like a yawn. A ruddiness blurred the clouds close to the rooftops over the way.

The Thames was the colour of tea.

Burton seated himself and started reading through the correspondence. The first two letters were dull, business communications, but the third letter was of a very different sort. It made Burton sit up sharp in his chair. A friend of his, a fellow businessman who made and brokered high-class Church paraphernalia (clergy dress, ornaments, carved pews, stained glass and the like), had written. It was not uncommon for the two men to correspond, but this letter carried a warning.

> You mentioned a certain Mr Bates, promising a generous contract for your manufactory to produce gyroscopic devices. Let me warn you: Bates is not what he seems. I'll wager you a hundred pound he is not interested in any contract of work with you, my friend. He is a political agitator, well known in Parliamentary circles for always harping on at the rights of the Pacificans.

This crowned the day. Burton heard himself, as if he were a third party, growling like a dog. It was too much.

Burton stood straight up from his chair, and grabbed his cane. He felt doubly angry for the feeling of having been fooled. Bates was doubtless not even the fellow's name. And he came here to try and put an honest businessman out of work? Freeing all the little devils? Burton pulled savagely on Pannell's bell-cord. Pulled again, and then, unable to contain himself, stomped from his office, his anger heating and heating inside him.

That evening, after he had seen Bates off the premises, Burton returned to his own office. The thrill of the fight drained out of him over a half-hour or so, and he was left glum. He opened another bottle of brandy and reflected, with melancholy little shakes of his head, that he had not drunk before his marriage. His marriage had been only unhappiness. What had he thought? What had he been thinking?

At nine by the American clock on the wall Pannell knocked at the door of the office. 'Yes?' Burton drawled. 'Yes?'

'I'll be on my way home, sir,' trembled his subordinate's voice through the door.

'Have you locked up the Blefuscans? Have you seen to it personally?'

'Yes sir.'

'Till tomorrow, Mr Pannell.'

'Tomorrow, sir.'

Burton listened, remotely, to the receding sounds of Pannell's footsteps. He uncorked the brandy bottle again. As he poured, the bottle's neck glugged like a gourmandising man.

[8]

Eleanor could not sleep. She lay in bed and stared at the plaster knobs and ornaments on the ceiling. From time to time a carriage would clatter past the window, down in the street; or the sound of pedestrian voices would crescendo and diminuendo as people passed outside.

It was gone midnight by the time she had dressed and left the house. The butler implored her, as forcefully as his position allowed him, not to go out, but she felt stifled, buried, in the house. 'I will visit my husband,' she said.

'It is late, Madam,' the butler observed, his face screwed up with concern as if he were tasting something unpleasant on his tongue.

'It *is* late,' Eleanor retorted, as if with a clincher, 'but not so late that my husband has yet returned from his manufactory. I will visit him there, since he chooses not to return.'

'Allow me, at least, to call the carriage, Madam,' the butler murmured.

'No,' said Eleanor. 'I choose to walk.'

She marched out of the house and along the well-lit pavement of Gower Street. The night was chill, and she tugged her shawl tighter around her shoulders. She made her way briskly but unhurriedly. London, she thought sourly, was in its glory. The crowd of carriages and pedestrians was swollen by the contributions of the theatres, which now gave forth their audiences in dense volumes up and down Oxford and New Oxford Street. Talking, laughing, sometimes singing, these metropolitans passed cheerfully along their illumined streets with all the security that noonday would have provided.

The Strand was similarly well lit and thronged, but ducking down a side street took Eleanor into another world. There were no street lamps here. The dark was palpable as black silk. The noise of merrymaking shrank back, became increasingly drowned by the night the further she went down the alleyway.

At the main entrance to the manufactory Eleanor caught a whiff of Thames water, a tart, sewer smell of water that was nonetheless mixed with something clearer, something ozoney. The nightwatchman was standing in his alcove. 'Ma'am,' he grunted, recognising the owner's wife. 'Here alone, Ma'am?'

'I have come to see my husband,' Eleanor said, rather primly.

'Very good, Ma'am,' said the old man, unlocking the door and letting her through.

Inside the air smelt musty, cool. Megasaurian shadows, machines and tanks, loomed around her. At the far end of the barnlike space, on the level of the first floor, the light was visible through the window of her husband's office. It was the only light in the place, four squares of gleam marking out a shadowy cruciform cross-bar. It would guide her to her husband, like the star of the Nativity.

Such thoughts were not appropriate.

She took a step forward. With another of those jolts of inner knowledge she realised that she had come to murder her marriage, to end it, to bury it once and for all. She took another step. The stairway up to the office was faintly visible, as if under grey tracing paper in the blackness. She would mount the stairs, and confront Burton. The memory of her honeymoon would give her strength. She would kill their marriage. She could murder him. Him? *Him*, though? – and why not? Think of the biblical Judith. Then his wealth would be hers, but she would not be inconvenienced with the man himself. Her heart thrummed. To murder the marriage.

At the foot of the stairway she stopped. There was a scrabbling sound to her right, and she thought – panic startling her – of rats. She turned to face the noise. The manufactory was hard by the river, after all. There were surely rats here. Vaguely, lit poorly by the single illuminated window from above, Eleanor could see a stack of large boxes, big as kennels. She peered closer. They were fronted with wire mesh.

A light flared inside one of the boxes; dolls, standing in row, loomed into sight as her eyes adjusted. The middle doll was holding a lucifer, a miniature firebrand.

Her heart still thumping, Eleanor tiptoed over to the cages. Within, the Lilliputians were all arrayed in ranks, as if on miniature army parade. All were awake, their eyes wide, and all were looking at her.

'Do you speak English?' she whispered, throwing a guilty look up at the lit window of her husband's office. She crouched down, bringing her face on a level with the little folk. Their motionlessness was truly uncanny. Like toy soldiers. One of them, in pale trousers and a dark waistcoat, leapt at the wire-mesh of the cage. The motion was so sudden, so rapid, that Eleanor jerked back in alarm.

The tiny figure piped: 'Release us.'

It was gripping the mesh, its fingers delicate as eyelashes.

'Your pardon . . .' mumbled Eleanor, her heart hurrying.

'Release us,' repeated the Lilliputian.

'My . . . little friend,' whispered Eleanor, bringing her face close to the wire. 'I do not carry the keys to your prison. I am sorry for it.'

The little creature made a theatrical sweep of its arm, pointing past Eleanor. 'There,' it cooed. 'To your rear.'

Eleanor twitched her head round. She could see nothing in the darkness behind her.

'What?'

'There,' came the tweeting voice again. 'On the bench behind you. You may see a pouch of jeweller's tools. You may pass these to us.'

The thought leapt up in Eleanor's head – and why shouldn't these little people be free? The parallels between their circumstance and her own struck her forcibly. Were they not also imprisoned by Burton? Slaves to his weight, to his money, as she? Natural justice would see them released. Without allowing herself to follow the chain of consequence along its length in her mind, she stood and felt her way to the workbench behind her. Her hand touched the felt purse of tools almost at once.

She returned to the cage; the Lilliputian carrying the lit lucifer was holding it higher now, as the flame – large as his head – burned down. The light throbbed against the sides of the little cage. Eleanor could see pigeonholes lined with bedding, could see a pencil-length water-trough along the back. Mice or rabbits might be kept in such a cage.

'The pouch,' she said, breathily, 'is too large to fit through the mesh of your cage.'

'Open it,' urged the first Lilliputian. 'To take the tools out. To pass them through one at a time.'

The tools each had their own cloth pocket inside the pouch; tiny screwdrivers and gravets no bigger than her little finger, ivory handles with needle-fine pins and shafts. Eleanor hurriedly pushed half a dozen through. 'Is that enough?' she asked. 'Is that enough?'

But the Lilliputians seemed to have lost interest in her now. They were huddling together, a tiny high-pitched murmur in some foreign tongue. For moments Eleanor watched them, but soon enough she began to feel she was, somehow, intruding. She moved away.

Her eyes were better adapted to the dark now, and the steps were clearly visible to her.

She felt prepared, now, to confront her husband. Now was the time.

Her foot struck the lowest of the wooden steps with a thud, like a blow connecting with a body. She breathed in deeply, her ribs hooping out underneath her chemise. Another step. She did not know what she was going to say to Burton when she got to the top; but the spirit would move her. Screw courage to the sticking point.

But the encounter was anticlimactic, as these much-anticipated occasions often are. Eleanor pushed through the door of Burton's study and stepped inside. Her husband was sitting slumped in his chair. At first she thought him awake, but then she realised that he was asleep with his eyes open.

Eleanor took in the scene. The uncorked bottle of brown glass standing on the desk; the dirty tumbler with a fluid cylinder of brandy, half an inch tall, inside it. The story told itself.

Burton trembled in the seat, let out a drumroll snort, and lolled his head from left shoulder to right. His eyes were wide. Perhaps, Eleanor thought, he was not asleep after all, but rather in a half-stupefied waking state. Perhaps he could see her, could hear her. Her stomach buzzed with a strange excitement.

She crossed to her husband and laid a hand upon his shoulder, thinking indistinctly to rouse him. The pressure of her arm rolled the chair backwards, pushed the seated man a foot back across the floor.

His chair was upholstered with green leather, and mahogany arms arced from back to seat. It was supported underneath on a single wooden pillar that led down to a claw-like spread of four spars, each fitted with a small wheel. The wheels were so well oiled that it was an easy matter to move chair and man across the floor. Eleanor took hold of one of the armrests and heaved the whole round. Burton grunted as his feet trailed over the floorboards.

When he was positioned by the door, Eleanor sat herself on the edge of his desk so as to face him. The room's single window was open behind her, letting in the chilly finger of a night breeze to stroke the back of her neck, making the hairs of her nape stir and rise. Did hairs stiffen according to the same mechanism by which the male generative organ stiffened? Eleanor wondered – the thought coming to her from some obscure corner of her brain. How did *they* manage to stand proud of the skin at moments of cold, or of excitement? – tiny thorns poking from the skin to raise them up? There was so much mystery about the human organism.

A plan occurred to her then and there. She saw a path. This marriage was no marriage. She would explain affairs to her husband: she could never love him. Better by far that he provide her with an income – nothing excessive, a thousand a year perhaps – and that she live her own life. She could devote herself to science; buy all the books and the equipment she desired. The prospect animated her; she felt her heart move more swiftly with the prospect. Surely Burton would agree. She would explain it to him now, when he was incapacitated. When she was in a superior position. How could he deny her now, seated intoxicated and degraded as he was? How could she fail, when the fizzing in her stomach told her how much power she possessed? Revenge, justice, righteousness. She could feel her face reddening with excitement, as if with shame.

Behind her, through the open window, the river hushed her, hushed her.

She took a breath.

'Husband,' she said, her voice a croak. She cleared her throat and spoke again, more audibly. 'Husband – Jonathan. I am sorry to see you like this.'

His eyes were certainly fixed on her, but his mouth drooped like an unbuttoned pocket and his body was still.

'This drinking is a poor habit to fall into,' she said, matronly. 'It has ruined better men than you in its time. Shame, shame on you.'

Nothing.

'I released your Lilliputian workers,' she declared, with a swelling of pride in her chest. *There's nothing you can do about that!* sang her inner voice. *See what I have done to you now!* 'They're free now, and I am not ashamed at my actions.'

Burton's only reply was the washboard scrape of his breathing.

'Well,' she said. 'I'll say what I must say. Our marriage, sir, is not a success. Can you deny it? I want for us to come to an arrangement, sir. It will not cost you overmuch.'

Shush, said the river behind her. Sshh, sshh, sshh.

'I'll tell you,' she went on, becoming more eager. She was spurred on by his stupefied silence, by the impossibility of his interrupting or contradicting her. 'I'll tell you, husband, my mother was speaking today of her *grandchildren*. Do you find that notion as absurd as I do myself, sir?' There was a sort of triumph in her body now, in her posture, in the fire in her heart. She could not contain herself. She hopped off the desk, and began pacing up and down. 'The idea of us having children, of you and I. Of my carrying your child in my *belly*, sir – for that is where I would carry it. I'd sooner,' she said, with a little spurt of anger, 'sooner *eat* one of your Lilliputian workmen *whole* than endure such a thing. But she *would* talk of it, she would prattle on, you know my mother sir.'

She stopped, smoothed her face with the flat of her hand.

'I do not mean to lose my composure, Jonathan,' she said, more quietly. 'Let me tell you of something I read lately. I read it in a book you yourself purchased for me – I may, I can add truthfully, thank you for your gifts of books. They at any rate have been much appreciated. There is, you know, a species of hymenoptera of which I read, and saw colour illustrations, in a volume by Fabre. A species of wasp, sir, called the burrowing wasp. In order to provide a ready supply of fresh food, of fresh meat, for her offspring after her own decease, this creature utilises her knowledge of the subject of anatomy. She gathers other insects and spiders by paralysing them, and the touch of her abdominal sting is so precise, sir, that she can pierce with it exactly the line of insectile nerves upon which the power of locomotion depends – but none of the other vital functions. The captured prey is paralysed, sir, but otherwise wholly alive and sensible. The wasp may then lay her eggs upon this living creature, such that the larvae, when hatched, have before them a docile and inoffensive quarry incapable of flight or of resistance, but perfectly fresh for the larder.'

She stopped. 'Fresh,' she said again, and now the sibilance of the river's noise through the open window seemed to echo her. Fresh.

Fresh.

'I fear,' she said, subdued now, 'that I am not quite making myself plain to you.'

She made her way to the desk again and sat upon it. On an impulse she picked up the glass and took a swig of the fluid inside; it scorched down her throat, and revived her a little. But a slump followed on. It was late, a long way past midnight, and she realised belatedly that she was very tired. Perhaps this interview was nothing but an absurdity, nothing but empty noise. Burton was surely taking nothing of it in. And, besides, was she even certain herself what her words signified? It was hard to put into words, and doubly hard to explain to a man such as Burton.

'Are you hearing me,' she asked. 'Husband?'

And there did seem to be a dreamy, distant sort of consciousness in Burton's eyes. One of his slack arms twitched, and his head lolled back the other way.

Eleanor yawned. It was one of those yawns that possess the whole head, like a malign spirit, and cannot be turned away. Her mouth stretched so wide the hinges of her jaw hurt. She finished with a shudder, and closed her mouth. Perhaps she should call a cab, should return home.

'Perhaps,' she said, 'we should talk tomorrow.'

She stopped. The door to the office was yawning, the dumb objects of the world mimicking her own actions. It swung slowly open until it gaped completely open. Nobody came through. The action had, it seemed, been effected by a ghost, by a mere ghost. A perturbation in the fabric of things. Eleanor sat very still, sat frozen, very very still. The German word, she knew, was *Poltergeist*. *Geist*, she assumed, was a variant of ghost. She did not know, and could not guess, *Polter*.

A frisson hurried up Eleanor's backbone. Fear bristled in her chest. She was, sharply, vividly awake again.

'Hello?' she called. 'Who's there?'

But the door stayed open, and nobody visible came through. Her husband snorted, the noise as startling as a whipcrack. He began receding. Her eyes were surely playing tricks with her: he was diminishing, shrinking in front of her, still sitting motionless in his chair, his eyes still staring at her.

She looked down towards the floor. A dozen – more – of the little people were at the base of the wheeled chair. They were pushing, pausing, pushing, in silent unison. With each heave chair and passenger moved backwards, over the floor, through the doorway. Eleanor could not move. She stared, mesmerised. The chair rattled over the rim of the door, and disappeared.

She was alone.

For long moments she sat. Her husband, stupefied with alcohol, had been taken by his own workers. They could not intend him good. Surely, they intended him harm. How could it be otherwise? She ought to rouse herself, ought to do something. And yet: the most tenacious lethargy had taken her body, had sunk its teeth into her very bones. She could barely lift her hand to wipe away the curls from her forehead. What could she do? She had herself released the Lilliputians from their night-time cages. But she had not anticipated that they might act in this manner. Surely the few she had released had now released all the little people. What business did they have with Burton? Why were they drawing him away?

A series of sharp knocks was audible outside, as of somebody stomping rapidly down the wooden stairs.

With an heroic effort she shook her limbs free of their tiredness – paralysis – and slid from the desk. She stood for a moment, and then drifted forward. It was all dreamlike. Had she fallen asleep? Perhaps this was all a dream. Indeed, it lacked the tang of reality.

Through the door, from the bright lit room into the darkness beyond, she almost stumbled over the chair. It sat, empty, on the little landing at the top of the wooden stair. She shoved it, so that it rolled back into Bates's room, and turned to look down upon the factory floor.

A fire had been lit. She could see its flame, masked by some containing metal structure, in the centre of the manufactory space. Looking again, she could see little people hurrying up and down miniature stairways and ladders, evidently designed for their use, urgently pursuing some mysterious business of their own. It was not clear what this might be.

The whole was a phantasmagoria. The littleness of the Lilliputian workers gave a feeling of forced perspective, as if she were watching the operations of some gigantic forge manned by full-sized men from a great, great distance away. As if she were floating in the clouds.

Ratlike motion at the foot of the stairs attracted her notice. There was the body of her husband on its back, slumped like a discarded sack of grain. Lilliputians hurried around it, clambering up onto its arms and chest.

There was a gleam in the centre of the room. Eleanor saw a great wooden lid, ten foot broad, swinging free from a mighty cauldron: the little people must be moving it in some mechanically assisted manner, for it was so large that even a full-sized man would have found it difficult. A bright disc, flattened to an oval by the angle of her point of view, was visible beneath the lid. It shone, like the retina of a cat caught in a beam of light – the back of a cat's eye being provided, as Eleanor knew, with a reflective layer called *tapetum lucidum*, 'bright carpet'. Six Lilliputians, wearing strange headgear, appeared on the lip of the cauldron, and pulled together on a lever; again, evidently provided for their use, for it operated a pole via a series of levers, and the pole stirred the silver gleaming material in the cauldron with easy strokes. Something similar must have facilitated the removal of the cauldron's lid.

Even from her distance Eleanor could sense the heat now emanating from this shining fluid; and she understood that this must be molten metal, that the device must be some manner of crucible. She knew that Burton's establishment produced a variety of fine-engineered metal devices, and so (she supposed) there must be equipment for firing and moulding metal. This, it seemed, was what the workers had activated.

A boom, long as a ship's mast, swung slowly through the space below her, supported on wires from the shadow-obscured ceiling. Lilliputians were hauling on wires, she could see, manoeuvring the long spar into position. One end of it fell and slotted into a notch beside the cauldron. Its far end moved slowly, and then stopped. It stopped directly above the supine body of her husband, on the floor at the foot of the stairs.

The lid of the cauldron swung, slowly, back into position. The silvery gleam of liquid metal was eclipsed. The room became darker; yet there was still enough light for Eleanor to watch two Lilliputians who were sitting astride the pole that had been positioned above Burton's head. They scrambled along it, pulling themselves forward hand-over-hand, and fitted some snake-like appendage to the end of the pole; it fell in chiming links onto Burton's head, draping itself over his forehead and past his ear. Other Lilliputians pulled it up, and positioned it carefully at Burton's open mouth. Burton shuddered, but did not move, as the little people forced the end of this tube between his lips.

Why did he not move? He must be tied. The Lilliputians had tied him.

There was a strange sense of burning anticipation in Eleanor's stomach; a sensation indistinguishable from heartburn, or the butterflies-in-the-midriff that young girls often experience. She understood, now, what was happening; or she thought she did.

The little people were pushing hard on the tube, forcing it into Burton's throat. His body twitched, shuddered, but did not move. He was clearly tied.

Eleanor's hands were gripping the rail at the top of the stairs.

She said to herself, the words forming themselves distinctly in her head: I must do something. I am a woman, and could not combat these little folk; but I could call the nightwatchman from the front door. Surely I could make my way through the body of the manufactory, and alert the nightwatchman. He could rescue Burton; or perhaps fetch police or militia. This could all be stopped. I must do something, to stop this, or they will kill my husband.

But the weird, half-lit phantasmagoria continued. Eleanor did not move. Her fingers gripped the rail at the top of the stairs.

There was a splash of light from the cauldron in the middle of the room, like a lightning's flash. But it was enough, somehow, for Eleanor to see Burton beneath her in etched detail. The strands of the hair from his head pinned into the wooden boards of the floor, strands of wire tethering his wrists and ankles. Little people swarming over him.

Her glance travelled up the length of the pole to the central mass of machinery. The molten metal would slide down that pole, and into her husband. This would kill him. This would surely kill him. She had to do something.

And yet she did not move. She should fight them. Wrench Burton free. But could she combat a whole population of them? They were small, but legion; and she a woman. What could she do?

Then, nipping at her mind, came the thought: with Burton dead the factory would be mine. With my husband dead, his wealth would be mine. And, accompanying this thought – the image so vivid upon her inner eye that it almost seemed as if the spirit of the man had suggested it to her – came a memory of the handsome face of Count Baron Idigon von Leloffel.

She hated this thought, for it meant that her inaction was no longer merely a strange dream-trance, a leaden lethargy in her bones. It was also carried by the base motivation of self-interest. Now the action of saving her husband's life would also be the action of depriving herself of wealth and comfort. If she did nothing, then the Lilliputians would lift from her life the great weight of her husband's corporeality. Each of the swarming little people would be metamorphosed into a golden coin, and all the coins would hurry into her purse.

All she needed to do was to stand, motionless.

She couldn't simply stand there and watch her husband murdered. And yet, she did not seem to be able to move. Frozen, statuesque. The baseness of this motive, revealed to her then – of this motive of personal

gain – corroded her thoughts. Base, vulgar: money could not be allowed
to overcome her breeding, the proper thing to do.

Still she could not move.

But she was asleep, surely. That must be it. Her whole body as
soundly asleep as a child; and yet she was awake in her mind, in her
eyes. 'No,' she croaked, trying to break the malign charm that held her
solid. Lot's wife. 'No.' But her voice was far too small to carry.

There was a pause. Eleanor could see that the little people were
waiting now for the metal to heat to a properly fluid state. Every now
and again the body of Burton shuddered a little, as if he were straining
against his bonds; but he was well fastened, and besides which he was
very drunk. Drunk and incapacitated.

The great lid swung away from the cauldron, and a breath of heat
reached Eleanor's face. The Lilliputians moved the great ladle, by some
complex of levers and pulleys, stirring the ingredients. The lid swung
back into place.

She could pull her hand free. She was surely capable of that. She
could, if she were to try, take her hand from the balustrade. From there
she could move other portions of her body. She could take the steps,
one after the other, down the stairs and over the floor to the door. The
nightwatchman was waiting there. He, surely, could fight through and
free his master – kicking and slapping at the Lilliputians and pulling
Burton free from his restraints. It would take a minute, at most. She
would do it.

She *would* do it.

She did not move.

And, with a guttering slurp, a trickle of metal flashed in the tube. It
slid further and further along the pole – Eleanor could see now that
this pole was actually an open-topped narrow duct of some kind. The
gleaming grew and grew, like an angel's spear of light, longer and longer,
and finally it reached the end and ducked down. Burton's body heaved,
his fat stomach bucking up and down; once, twice, and then he was
still. Metal appeared at the corner of his mouth, and spilled scaldingly
down the sides of his face. Cries, stifled, high-pitched and small but
nonetheless audible, sounded across the factory. There was a pause;
some barrier must have been inserted in the tube to prevent the flow of
the metal, although Eleanor did not see where this blockage had been
effected. The little figures on Burton's body were pushing at something,
pushing (she could see now) to force the tube deeper down her husband's

throat all the way down, practically into his very stomach. More cries, and the metal flowed again.

Eleanor's knuckles were hurting.

She released her grip on the wood of the balustrade.

Then, with the uncanny swiftness that often characterised their motions, the Lilliputians were finished. They hauled the tube upwards, and its remaining metal drained back into the cauldron. The spar swung away into the shadows, and little people hurried to and fro. With a loud plock, like a door latch clicking home, the fire underneath the cauldron was extinguished. Eleanor took a deep breath. The air tasted strange; a metallic scent, and the distinct odour of roasted pork, the sort of smell one notices when one passes a chophouse.

There was a scraping sound, and Eleanor looked down. Burton's body, released from its ties, was moving. Her heart thumped; was he still alive? Crawling over the floor? But, no, his motion was being imparted to him by teams of Lilliputians.

Where were they moving him?

Eleanor realised that her legs were unsteady beneath her. She stepped, precariously, to the top of the stairway. She could, of course, hurl herself down – an act of suttee, of sorts, to complement her husband's death. Perhaps the Lilliputians would even clear her corpse away, as they seemed to be doing with Burton.

But instead she sat, as heavily as a toddler falling onto its behind, on the top step. Her head felt waverly. The dream, if that was what it was, had taken an unpleasant turn. Burton's corpse continued inching, like a slug, towards the wall. Lilliputians hurried hither and thither over the floor, in some commotion like a nest of spiders disturbed by a farmer's spade and turned into the light. Hands, Eleanor thought. They were called hands, the workers in a factory. And this was part of the uncanny unpleasantness of the Lilliputians themselves. It was as though various portions of a full-size human body had broken off and assumed independent life. They were like hands and feet, like noses and ears, given independent life by a sorcerer, scurrying about on their mysterious errands.

With a start, Eleanor stood and hurried down the stairs, but at the bottom she stopped. All the Lilliputians had frozen in their places, scattered about the half-lit floor, and all were looking up at her. Only those tugging her husband's body carried on, heaving together in little pulses. She stared at the body. From where she was now, she could see the destination: a sort of trap opened in the floor at the back of the room leading down into the river. They were going to dump Burton's body into the Thames. His belly was filled with metal; he would sink to the bottom. He would be swallowed by the mud at the bottom of the river.

It would be as if he had never been.

His belly was filled with metal.

Eleanor felt the urge to call out, to shout she knew not what, but she managed to rein herself back, to preserve her composure. Her husband was dead now, after all. There was no point in becoming hysterical. She couldn't stay here. The little doll-like figures, standing quietly all over the floor, were obnoxious to her, horrible to contemplate, terrible. She could not stand it. She had images of them swarming over her body in her mind; swarming all over her body, climbing into her every crevice, scuttling over her face.

She turned, and hurried back up the stairway, into Burton's office, shutting the door behind her. There was no lock on the door, but she sat herself in the chair with her legs against it. She sat for a long time, her mind circling and recircling the events she had witnessed. Eventually she dozed.

When she woke, stiff from her upright posture, she wondered if everything that had passed had been a sort of phantasm. The memory seemed friable. It crumbled like old sandstone. Had it really happened?

And yet here she was, in her husband's chair, with her feet against the door. She got unsteadily to her feet and stretched. The lamp had burnt itself dry, but daylight was coming through the window. With a deliberate motion she pulled the door open.

She stepped through. The workplace was bright with early light, and empty of the little people. It was on this same landing that she had gripped the rail so hard it had hurt her knuckles. The workshop was laid out below her, morning light falling onto it through the skylights. There was the cauldron, cold now. There were the workbenches, the cages.

She came down the stairs as if floating. None of it had been real. As she descended she was, vaguely, building an alternative narrative. She had come looking for her husband, but he had not been in his office. Yes. So she had settled down in his chair to wait for his return. She had fallen asleep, and had experienced a strange and violent dream. Now she was going to walk out into the fresh air of a London morning, and return to her house. At the bottom of the stairway she examined the floorboards. They were scuffed, marked with scorches and scratches, but that could have been from any of the working days of the place. There were myriad little pearls and teardrops of metal, tiny ones, lodged in between the planks themselves; little solidified splashes of metal. She wandered along to the corner and its alcove. The trapdoor that gave access to the river beneath was closed.

She turned and walked, slowly, past the Lilliputian cages. There was no motion inside them, but perhaps the little people were asleep, hidden in their cubbies.

At the main entrance she pulled the heavy latch with a careful slowness, and eased the big door open. The nightwatchman was slumped in the corner of his booth, wrapped in a tartan blanket. His eyes were clenched tightly; his snores assumed spectral, cloudy form from his open mouth, like smoke from an invisible pipe. Eleanor crept past him, made a catlike way up the street.

The air was very cold, needle-sharp. Her own puff haunted her face. Two spikes of chill reached up the sinuses of her face as she breathed. Dawn frost dulled and matted the cobbles, making her footsteps precarious. Only at the turn of the road, when she emerged into the sunshine and the morning traffic and bustle of the Strand, did she feel that she was returning to the world. People around her again. For she had the sensation that she had spent the night in some fairy-tale realm, some dire subterranean kingdom like a heroine from a Grimm's tale. Now the clatter of a milk-cart along the road was more real to her than anything that had happened since the previous midnight.

There were no cabs to be had at that hour, so she crossed London on foot once again to make her way back to Gower Street. The underbutler was, at least, still awake. He let his mistress into the house, and roused the maid, who made hot chocolate and brought it up to her room. Eleanor sat by one of the bedroom windows, watching the increasing volume of traffic as the morning progressed with studious attention. She was, equally studiously, not thinking about the previous night's events.

But she must tell somebody. She could not keep it in. The possibilities revolved and revolved in her mind. She decided at luncheon that it would be a mistake to inform the authorities. Quite apart from the awkwardness of having to spin so bizarre a tale to a policeman or a militiaman, there was the thought – she did not know how founded in Law it might be – that the truth would deprive her of her inheritance. She had stood by and done nothing. Was she not, somehow, an accessory? But if nobody were to know, her husband's disappearance would not be connected with her. She could play the innocent.

None of it was real, anyway. The whole edifice of the cosmos seemed dreamy, seemed insubstantial to Eleanor's listless eyes.

As the two of them sat down to supper together, her Mamma offered some comment at the non-appearance of Burton. 'Is he not to join us for supper again?' she said, querulously. 'He has absented himself two nights running.'

Eleanor dismissed the maid and butler, going over to the door after they were gone to fasten it shut. 'Mamma,' she said, coming back to her mother and kneeling on the floor at her feet. 'Mamma.'

'Gracious,' said her mother, looking down unsteadily. She had been drinking already that day. 'What can this mean? My own daughter kneeling at my feet.'

'Burton will never come back.'

'My own daughter kneeling at my feet,' Mamma repeated, more slowly.

'Listen carefully to what I say, Mamma. Burton will never come back. Never.'

Mamma's trembling hand reached for the red cone of the filled wine glass. 'Never come back, you say.'

'That's right, Mamma. We shall never see him again.'

The older woman took a long swig of wine, and said in a very small voice: 'What can this mean?'

'You must promise, Mamma,' said Eleanor hurriedly, 'that you will tell *nobody*. Nobody must know. But you *must* understand that this is a wonderful thing to happen in our lives. Burton's money is ours. You must understand we can live here until the inheritance is assured, and then we are free. Free and rich.'

'My own daughter,' said Mamma, as if to an invisible interlocutor. 'How she teases me.'

'I am not teasing, mamma,' said Eleanor, earnestly, squeezing her mother's knees. 'Last night at the manufactory I saw the little people, the Lilliputian people, rise up against him.' She did not say that she had released them from their cages in the first place. 'They tied him up and . . . drowned him in the river.'

With a little scream, Mamma pushed the chair back and dropped to her knees, bringing her down to a level with her daughter. 'Don't say so!'

'Think, Mamma, think, and stay calm. Think that this makes us rich, and that we are no longer beholden to Burton.'

Her mother's eyes were wide. 'You are sure he is dead?'

'Quite sure.'

'And the little people, they killed him?'

'Yes.'

She looked closely at her daughter, and then, with a girlish, almost insouciant toss of her head, she clambered back into her chair. 'Well well,' she said, draining the rest of her glass of wine. 'Well well.'

Eleanor, faced with her mother's equanimity, began – to her own astonishment – to cry. She got to her feet hurriedly and hid her face. She did not feel the grief; if anything she felt a fury at herself for the loss of control. And yet here were the tears! Some part of her that was beyond being reasoned with or intellectualised believed that she had herself murdered Burton: believed that her own spirit had called those tiny creatures into existence, and that her own anima had effected its violent revenge upon the man. Her guilt was more than a passive thing. And in later time – sooner than her rational calculation estimated – it was to make a deeper trouble for her.

This was the evening of the 6th November. The events in the workshop had happened on the night of the 5th and the early hours of the 6th.

Pannell came to call on them in the Gower Street house on the afternoon of the 11th to tell them – his seamy, sweaty face collapsed with fear – that Burton had vanished. The police had searched for him; notices were in the newspapers; but nobody knew where he could be. Mamma made melodrama out of the role of a woman receiving news as an unlooked-for blow: wailing and throwing her hands in the air. Eleanor adopted a stony expression.

The day after, Pannell returned, with an inspector of police. Burton had still not emerged. An extensive survey of the premises, and surrounding properties, had been undertaken. Mamma cried. Eleanor thought it best to preserve her stony face.

*

The days stretched on. Eleanor had found a cubbyhole, somewhere deep in her consciousness, for her feelings of guilt. She knew they were still there, somewhere out of sight, coal in her mind's cellar, but the feelings did not trouble her immediately. There was the longer-term question of how she might deal with that, but for now she found herself slipping closer and closer to her desired goal. She told the Inspector that she had visited her husband on the night of the 5th – the nightwatchman would confirm as much. She had found him in good spirits, she said, working at papers, and had left him. At what time? At a little after one. The nightwatchman had been asleep, Eleanor added. I noticed that on my way out. He swears he was not, said the Inspector. Swears not. And I, insisted Eleanor, bridling a little in a gentlewoman's proper style, I *swear* he was. I'm sure you're right, Ma'am, said the Inspector. Of course the fellow would not confess to sleeping on the job. But your husband was in good spirits when you left him? Yes, Inspector.

The Lilliputians had vanished.

Pannell, interrogated by Eleanor the following day, confirmed that a great deal of cash-value had vanished with them. We're ruined, screeched Mamma. Ruined! We're destitute! No Ma'am, said Pannell, hurriedly. No, no no. New Lilliputians can be bought as necessary capital outlay, and the value of Burton's assets and other holdings was still very considerable. Seventeen thousand in consolidated bonds, Pannell said. Seventeen thousand in consols, repeated Mamma in a calculating voice. Yes Ma'am, said Pannell. And the factory is an asset indeed.

Not ruined? asked Mamma.

Certainly not, Madam, said Pannell. Quite the reverse.

The week wore on, and Eleanor found herself cautiously – tentatively – looking forward to what the future might bring. Eventually she would be declared the legal heir. It might be years; but until that time she and her mother might enjoy a materially improved existence. And eventually it would all be hers. Her future was assured. Wealth.

She wondered whether she ought to pray to God to thank him for this twist in her fate. Or would that be in itself a shocking thing to do – to thank God for a murder, for an insurrection? God did not require such thanks, surely. Or was this the true nature of God? Was God a Thug, relishing murder and death? Possibly. Besides, Eleanor thought, if not thank him for ill-chance, why thank him for the good? God was large enough to account for all fates, and not merely the pleasant ones.

On the 19th day of that same month, French forces landed on the Kentish coast. Consols were written off by the government. A week later French soldiers were marching up the Mall. A week after that, an official of the new Government of Occupation called at the house, informing Eleanor and her Mamma that the manufactory was being confiscated by the Government of Greater France. Mamma wept, protested, fruitlessly begged and exhorted. Eleanor treated the Frenchman to a display of the most distant and coldest English politeness.

That night she drank more than her mother. She spoke aloud, to herself rather than in conversation: 'As like thank Him for the bad as the good. As like rail against Him for the good as for the bad.' 'What are you saying, my love?' Mamma had asked, in a frightened voice. 'What are you saying?' 'We are insects to God,' said Eleanor, with a sudden intense emphasis. 'He sees insects and he sees us. He is so gigantic that to His eye all we crawling miniature things are the same. As flies to wanton boys,' she added earnestly, but she could not remember how the quotation continued, or even from where she was quoting.

This time it was Mamma who began to cry. The sound of her mother's distress was grating and unpleasant to Eleanor. 'Hush, Mamma,' she said, without tenderness. 'Hush.'

Alone together that evening (for all the servants save the butler had deserted the house and fled the city; and the butler had been pressed for roadwork by the French) – alone together, Mamma kept repeating the phrase: 'It was all for nothing, his death for nothing, it was all for nothing.'

'For nothing,' repeated Eleanor, almost triumphantly.

She wanted to reassure her mother, to tell her that they were no worse off than they had been – better off, for they still had the house in Gower Street. But the words refused to come. She knew in her heart that she was indeed worse off, greatly worse off.

She received a letter from Count Baron Idigon von Leloffel. It read:

The French authorities have me under arrest, my dear lady, as it seems the ancient friendship between the two Saxon nations of England and the Germanies is viewed with suspicion by the new occupying power. I have been permitted to write to you, to ask you for certain monies – you will, I am sure, forgive the vulgarity of so direct an approach; but without fiscal security the French will not permit me to walk at my liberty. My parole does not satisfy them. Dear lady, for the sum – small to you – of two hundred pounds, I would have the pleasure of attending upon you. I have long been desirous of continuing our conversations. I feel sure that new horizons await our friendship. Leloffel.

Postscriptum. I offer my condolences on the death of your former husband. But – of course – any such moth who dared approach the flame of your beauty could not have expected a lengthy life.

His intentions were clear. Eleanor had no money to give him, unless she mortgaged her house, which was of course out of the question. She had no money to give him and for some reason this caused her a sharp pain in her forehead. It felt almost like shame.

She wrote a brief reply, and went to bed. But she could not sleep, however much she prayed for repose. Thinking of the letter brought tears to her eyes, although she did not know why. When she reread the document, and read it another time, she winced at the last sentence of the postscript, for, she told herself, only at that point did the nobleman abase himself. It was too crudely flattering a sentiment. It did not sit aright with the eidolon of Leloffel she had in her mind. He ought not to have stooped, she told herself. It pained her that he had stooped.

And the pain was genuine. It spread across her temples, and round to the back of her skull, like a hoop of suffering. She closed the curtains and tried to sleep, but could not.

That evening she received a second letter from Leloffel. Its hand was less perfectly formed, the lines slanting down, the letters compressing in the haste of their scribbling. Instead of writing paper, it had been penned on the reverse of a handbill, torn in half, but offering financial inducements to any Briton who enrolled in a new organisation, *Les Amis de la France*. Eleanor handled the paper, turning it over and over, before summoning the courage to read the note.

Madam – your reply has been delivered to me. I must beg you to – must insist you reconsider. I must insist, Madam. You cannot resist my appeal to our fellow breeding. Though a Jew, your father was of the noblest blood. My ancestors led their people against the Romans. They rode at the right hand of Charlemagne. It is most literally intolerable – intolerable – for a person of my birth to be confined by such people as now have me under their lock and their key. They are such little people, Madam, these jailers and soldiermen, such little people. It is contrary to natural justice they confine one such as I. Be assured, were our positions reversed, I would work every sinew to release you. And when the open-sesame is a matter so small, a matter only of ten score pounds, I will not believe — I choose not to believe — that you will deny me. L.

Eleanor was not sure what it was about this second note that compelled her to dress and leave the house, but there was something in it. They are such little people, Leloffel wrote, of his gaolers. The phrase chattered in her head like clockwork. She walked to the first banker's office she found, and went in. The sunlight was bright and cold through the main office windows as she sat, her hands in her lap. She could barely see the banker himself, and had some difficulty in explaining her circumstances. Two hundred pounds, she said. A mortgage upon my house, she said. To release a man imprisoned by the French.

'This man,' asked the banker, his face blurred and shadowed as he sat there, with the sunlight hard behind him, 'is he a relative, Ma'am?'

No, she replied, no relative. There was an odour of apples somewhere in the room. The floor was rough-planed wooden planks. The whole western wall was washed with light. 'Not a relative, but,' she added, hoping to elucidate, but she did not complete the sentence. In her head was a free-floating quotation, from the Bible although she could not recall exactly where, about migrating birds, *the stork in heaven knoweth the time of their coming.*

'Do you understand, Ma'am,' the faceless banker said, leaning a little forward at his desk, 'that in the present occasion — during the military uncertainties of these days — the amount of money our institution might loan upon a property, even so substantial a property as your own, must be reduced? In more peaceful times, we might offer better terms. But in the current climate—'

Yes, she said. Yes, she said.

A sweet and cidery smell. Her head swam a little, but she was in no danger of passing out.

'—and that such a loan,' the shadow-faced banker continued, 'carries the very real prospect of the collateral being seized,' and he coughed, corrected himself, 'becoming *due* to the creditor, in lieu of payment? In these days, in particular. I must enquire, though the question be delicate, whether you have the means to repay the loan?'

'I must have the money,' said Eleanor, simply. And she knew that she must have it. To disassemble the whole house into bricks, and break open each brick in turn, and find a sovereign inside every single one. She wanted to explain to this man about the nature of imprisonment, and the impossibility of it – that any cost was acceptable to free a certain soul (she thought she meant Leloffel's, but of course she wasn't truly thinking of him) from its cage. And it even started to seem to her that the house itself was a kind of cage, a cage in which she was imprisoned, with her mother as the broken-down gaoler, her mother saying my darling guilt in place of my darling girl. But these thoughts were confused and broken about, and she did not give them voice. Instead she nodded, and listened to the banker, as the precise terms of repayment, and the precise terms of losing her house, were explained. Her attention drifted to the windows behind him, their intersection of clear glass with the red light of sunset.

THREE

THE DEAN

❀

[1]

London was the city of birds, pigeons and pigeonhawks the true possessors, but poorly tolerating human cohabitation. London was Pigeonopolis. It was bluetopia and greytopia with those flashes of emerald in their necks, and the flurry of wings, and a vocalic cooing from all directions. The birds colonised every ledge, whitewashed every surface with their droppings, they bickered in the skies, they scratched at stone with their beaks. The chilly folded-over sounds of wings in motion, myriad *brrs*, occupying the air like a very blizzard. They rose in great drifts, as biblical locusts, from Covent Garden. And in their midst the hawks zipped diagonal up, diagonal down, like shuttles in a loom.

Bates found his thoughts – his dreams, too – reverting to birds. How *dual* their quality. The mutual embodiment of beauty in ugliness, and ugliness in beauty – so foul they were, so very rattish, each with its shabby little beak underneath that revolting fold of pink flesh, its two ink-drop eyes, soulless. Pestilential. And their feet were all decaying and pestilential, stars of cankerous flesh. And yet – and yet! – Bates could not help staring at them, for the fragment of rainbow that was tangled in their breast feathers. The rainbow was the sky's domain, it was air and flight, flight. In flight they were lovely as poetry, applauding the sunlight and the sky with their wings and soaring. Escape and revulsion and beauty, and all at once. The blur of their wings in flight folded together earth and spirit, the diabolic and heavenly.

Although everybody knew that they spread disease. Surely they were a pollution.

And now he sighed. *Hhh*.

And now he was in the realms of Tartarus and the void. There was a voice in his head, and it said: 'We're going to get you, kill you, cut your parley-loving *throat*.' As if those three things were three separate things. Get you. Kill you. Cut your throat. What was the point in slitting the throat of a corpse? And yet the threat made sense according to the logic of these people: outraged patriots, these hissers of words. He must not think of it.

Now he was standing on Bury Street, looking across the open square of Covent Garden, watching the birds rise, watching them turn through the sky and settle again on the ground. The ribbon of AF, *Ami de la France*, was pinned to his lapel. The spring was palpable, on the very edge of dissolving itself into the clear fresh air. Everywhere one looked showed intimations of a new warmth, a fragrance even here in the centre of London. April showers were readying themselves in the parti-clouded sky: those clouds purely white and those stained purple upon their cream breasts eagerly shouldering one another afore the blue. People were coming and going, in and out of the row of houses to his right, a crowd as numerous, it seemed, as the pigeons themselves. Bates stood for a quarter of an hour, and every person who saw him, he knew, hated him on sight. None offered him greeting. They glanced at his ribbon and they scowled, hurrying on. The hawks circled his head. The hawks went through and through the sky above his head. The time would come, his dreams told him, when a hawk huge as the sun would descend upon him and blot out his life. We call this hawk *death*, and the name of his wings is oblivion.

He could delay no longer. He had delayed too long.

On the Strand he tried to call down a cab, but no carriage stopped for him. Though small, yet was his lapel-badge noticed. True Britons despised him. He thought again, as he often did, of simply removing the ribbon. But, you see, it would have been a foolish gesture. The London Johnny d'arms knew him by sight. Oh, it would reflect but poorly upon him if he were seen abroad *without* the badge. He professed pride in his association. He had sworn loyalty to the French people. The consequences would be terrible if he were discovered forsworn. He would lose his position with the new administration; and without that, amid the undying animosity of English-born Londoners, he would surely starve.

He loved his country. Nevertheless his continuing existence depended upon the success of the domination by a foreign power. How complicit his *circonstances*.

He fetched up his stride and walked down past Charing Cross and into Pall Mall. The steeple clock at St Martin-in-the-Fields began its ponderous tolling of ten, dropping each of the chimes into profound and stilly depths of sound to sink, sink. A flying machine, brass and greasepaper, flew past him and after it scampered a young boy, leaping up to snatch at the toy. As it banked to fly up Glovers Lane the boy's fingers caught its tail fan, and with a yawp he hauled it out of the sky. The propeller snapped on the ground and the motor whiningly spun and unwound. Bates stopped. The machine bore no French colours, but it was indeed likely that it was on official business. If a Johnny d'arm had seen the lad, who was to say he would not have rifle-shot him – killed him dead? Such risk! And for what? The boy was wrenching open the device's chamber and pulling out its burden: papers, nothing but papers, not money, no valuables. He hurled this useless litter to the ground and ran as fast as he could up past Charing Cross.

The final bell tolled. It had all happened within the tell of the chimes.

Ten was the hour of his appointment. Yet still Bates held back. In St James's Square, outside the very building that the French authorities had requisitioned as the base for their governance, he loitered, pulling his hat down about his brow and watching the military men and the dark-suited civilians come and go.

Three flags: the French national banner here, military colours there, and on the far side a Saint George's Cross. Each pennant wriggled on its pole, like the wind shaking crumbs out of a tablecloth. Bates had not before noticed how the arrangement of *blue* and *white* and *red* on the French flag make it look as though the extremity of the cloth had been dipped in blood.

D'Ivoi was standing beside him, as if appearing from nowhere, as if he were a genie raised suddenly by stage-machinery through some trapdoor in the earth itself. 'You are thinking, my friend,' he said, beaming, 'of the fellow they caught last night?'

'I have not heard of the circumstance,' said Bates.

'You have not? He was attempting to climb the pole and deface the flag. He has been executed, to encourage others to obey the laws. We must all obey the laws, after all. But there is bad feeling, I understand, on some streets of this city that the punishment was too harsh.' D'Ivoi turned, smilingly, and Bates had a foreflash of the hawk, the hawk – descending upon him and destroying his life – and then, in the instant the vision was gone and it was only a Frenchman, gesturing towards the doorway with his hand to show Bates the way.

'Was he a rebel in arms?' asked Bates, his heart trembling. 'Or was he some other form of vandal?'

'He claimed to be a revolutionary,' said D'Ivoi. 'But perhaps he said so only to win our sympathies.'

And the flag on its flagpole in front of him wagged from side to side like the shaking of a gaily-coloured head.

Bates walked in the direction D'Ivoi had indicated.

'In what manner would declaring oneself a revolutionary,' asked Bates, 'win the sympathies of the authorities?'

D'Ivoi widened his smile. 'To you English the prospect of revolution appals, perhaps. But we French have sympathy in our hearts. We had our revolution after all, we – would you say? – *revolved*.'

'And bloody it was,' replied Bates. They were in the hallway now, feet clucking on the marble like pigeons' voices. Two guards stood at attention besides the stairway.

'Ah,' said D'Ivoi, refusing to relinquish his good humour. 'But blood is a needful part of the revolution. You had a revolution too, you in England, did you not? And was it not bloody? Besides, your revolution brought forth a tyrant – your Cromwell.'

'And in France also?' reorted Bates. 'Did not your revolution result in the tyranny of—' But his memory wasn't sharp enough to recall the name. 'The Generalissimo, he who, during the civil war . . .'

'He was himself called Buonoparte,' said D'Ivoi. 'But he was no tyrant; merely a general too small to fulfil his ambition. Even had he lived, he could never have subdued a nation as vivid, as passionate as France. Do you know why? I ask it of you.'

'I could not hazard an answer.'

They were mounting the stairs. Windows of plain glass, filled with sunlight, stood severely before them, like two luminous and blank and unfillable pages from the book of life.

'Because he lacked the support of the Church. Your Cromwell, he made his own Church, I believe. This was good policy. Truly, without such support, without the Church on his side no ruler can last. Church,'

D'Ivoi concluded, sententiously, 'is bigger than nation.'

'Bigger?' said Bates. 'Do you mean *bigger*, or *greater*?'

'It is not,' said D'Ivoi, puzzled, 'the same word?'

They were at the top of the stairway now, and D'Ivoi led him through to a high-ceilinged room, glorious with twenty-foot-tall mirrors and gold wainscoting at top and bottom of every wall. D'Ivoi's desk looked petty indeed in the midst of such splendour.

He settled himself behind it. 'I should of course have commenced the conversation with the pleasantries,' he said. 'We know how important it is for you English that the proper forms are observed. I should say, *How do you do?*'

'It is not necessary,' said Bates.

'I should say, *Please be seated*,' D'Ivoi said, a feline smile on his face. Bates sat.

'In Combray,' said D'Ivoi, stretching back in his chair, 'there is an astronomical observatory, with a grand telescope, and they report that a comet has been seen in the sky; bright in the night sky, with its tail flowing out behind it like a white feather. It portends disaster, do you think?'

'Disaster,' Bates said, disdainfully.

'It is always so? Before the last French invasion of these islands, with your King Harold, was there not a comet that portended disaster for the English?'

'Superstition,' said Bates.

D'Ivoi sat forward. 'Ah, but you have no stomach for small-conversation. Small-talk, I should say. I have heard, my dear friend, that you have become considerably more attentive in your religious observance. Is it so?'

'I attend church,' said Bates, shortly. 'This is no crime, I trust.'

'Not at all. Even to attend a Protestant church.'

The smile on the Frenchman's face seemed to Bates to be growing more insolent. A spurt of boldness in his English chest: 'I have heard talk,' he said, 'that the forces of French occupation will shortly set about unmaking English Protestantism. I have heard such a rumour ... that you will enforce capitulation to the Roman faith. It is not so, I trust?'

'Rumours,' said D'Ivoi, with a dismissive shrug. But the smile did not go away.

'You can understand the anxiety of the population,' Bates pressed. 'Your own history – to return to the question – has an unfortunate aspect, when viewed by a follower of the Protestant faith. I refer, naturally, to the fate of your Huguenots.' He pronounced the word *Huge-enoughs*.

At this D'Ivoi laughed a clanging laugh. '*Les assez-grands!*' he said. '*Oh c'est très bien, ça. Nous sommes* assez *comme ça, nous n'avons pas besoin de ces Huge-enoughs*. My dear Bates,' he said, leaning forward. 'This is to worry about matters about which you have no cause to worry.' Had he placed a slight emphasis upon the *you?* Was he implying that, however dismal the fate of the Anglican communion, Bates himself need not worry?

'I am merely,' Bates replied, stiffly, 'reporting to you, as is my obligation as Ami de France.'

But D'Ivoi was still chucking over the humour. '*Les "huge-enoughs"*,' he repeated. 'This is very good. These of Brobdingnagia, they are huge enough, I hope? Your Royal Navy attempted a Saint-Bartholomew-Eve massacre upon those huge-enoughs, did they not? Like the Holy League of the Guises, you were.' He laughed a second time.

'Mister D'Ivoi,' said Bates, feeling desperately uncomfortable to be the butt of the Frenchman's joke. 'I have come to report to you, as is my duty. I hope I do not deserve mockery for merely fulfilling my duty.'

D'Ivoi stifled his smile. 'Forgive me,' he said. 'Yes, your job. Yes, you are not content, I think, in your job. Yes.'

'I do my duty,' replied Bates, stuffily.

'But to be a spy . . .' D'Ivoi shook his head. 'It is but a poor occupation for a gentleman.'

Bates said nothing.

'You will be pleased, I think,' D'Ivoi continued, 'with my news. We no longer require your services as a . . . spy I was going to say, but perhaps I should use the more formal title.'

'You are not happy with my work?' Bates demanded. He spoke sharply. A shudder and wraith of shadow passed the window, perhaps pigeons flying. A blue devil was gripping in his guts. The sensation was dismally familiar. Of course he was despised by his countrymen, and how could it be any other way, for he was despicable. But he had at least possessed the melancholy satisfaction of thinking his French employers were happy with his reportage. Perhaps they were not. Perhaps he was quite without worth.

'Your . . . I am not sure of the word in English. Your *personnalité* – is it the same word in English?'

Bates nodded. He felt sick inside himself.

'You have a sort of sickness of the *personnalité*, I think. Your moods are variable. Even now, my friend, you chew at your lower lip. It is a caprice, like a child's caprice, I think. And another time you will be happy, very happy. But this is not a problem for us. On the contrary, we are extremely content with your work.'

'But nonetheless you wish me to cease?'

'You have worked as an *Ami de la France* for, it is how long? For six months? Not so many; five months. And before the occupation, you were an ally of the French cause. We have reason to be very content with you, my friend. The French people are grateful.'

'But nonetheless,' Bates repeated, doggedly, 'you wish me to cease?'

'What I wish, is,' said D'Ivoi. 'I wish for you to go to York.'

A darkness hovered beyond the window. Bates sat in silence, but D'Ivoi was smilingly patient. The comet, coming to earth, was God's pigeonhawk, coming to prey upon the sinners. 'To York?' he said, eventually.

'That is so. You will leave tomorrow. A party of military men will accompany you. They are travelling to the north, so perhaps I should say *you* will be accompanying *them*. They carry with them a calculation device, you understand?'

'Indeed I do,' said Bates. And suddenly, and without warning, like flame applied to alcohol, the lower mood had evaporated all away. This was an adventure; he was admired, prized even, by his French masters. He would accompany a Calculator!

'You will travel fairly slowly, but this is of necessity a military consideration. We must take every precaution that the Calculator not fall into enemy hands.'

'But surely the land is wholly under French control now,' said Bates. 'As far north as Derby. The newspapers report it. Is it not true that the army controls the roads all the way to Preston?'

'Our generals,' said D'Ivoi, his expression sphinx-like, 'have enjoyed formidable victories. But nonetheless, there is much hostility, especially in the north. Alembert took Scarborough' – D'Ivoi sounded every letter in the name – 'a fortnight past, but the countryside in Yorkshire is adversarial towards him still. *Les ennemis de la France.*'

'I shall go,' said Bates, a sense of purpose filling him again. 'I shall accompany your Calculator, my friend.'

'Oh,' said D'Ivoi. 'The Calculator is incidental to you, my friend. This is not why I wish you to go.'

'Then why?'

'Another gentleman will be a member of the party. It is the Dean of York. You will accompany him.'

'Accompany him?'

'As his aide-de-camp, if you will.'

This sounded, to Bates, considerably less glorious. 'To what end?'

'He is a friend of France. He will lead us to a great prize in Yorkshire. The calculation machine will facilitate the use of this prize. We shall seize the prize and make use of it.' D'Ivoi's scrupulously unidiomatic pronunciation, bringing out the 'r' in every word, gave his words a queerly Scottish flavour. 'But we do not trust him. We cannot. So we will observe him, of course. And you – *sans* your ribbon, my friend – you will befriend him, and act as a bridge between himself and ourselves. Do you see?'

'I understand,' said Bates. 'And this prize?'

'This prize,' repeated D'Ivoi, in a neutral tone.

'What is it?'

D'Ivoi cast his right hand into the air, his fingers wriggling, as if the prize were the least important thing in the world. 'It is something,' he said folding his arms, 'of military significance. You have heard rumours of a great military device in Yorkshire?'

'I have not. In Yorkshire? I have not.'

'A cannon,' said D'Ivoi. 'It is a cannon of great size. Constructed by the English several years ago; constructed, indeed, over many years. The great Davidowic designed and cast several of the components. But then the project languished. But after this, events in India, and the hostility of the princes of Russia, persuaded the English to proceed. The Dean of York was eager in its construction.'

'He was *eager*?'

'I mean to say he was, I mean to say that there was *enthusiasm* in him for the project.'

'The Dean of York?'

'The science of ballistics is his hobby, his hobby horse, is that the correct word? He has helped assemble the giant cannon.'

'How large is this ordnance?'

'A mile long, perhaps.'

Bates gasped. 'Impossible!'

'One would say so,' agreed D'Ivoi. 'I have not seen it with my eyes.'

'No horse could pull such a gun,' said Bates. 'Not even a Brobdingnagian one!'

'I understand that the Giant people have indeed been involved in the construction of this device,' said D'Ivoi. 'I understand that it could not have been built without them, of course. But the cannon is not a motile device, or so I understand it. It is fixed against a hillside.'

'And is it finished – this cannon? Ready to fire?'

'So we understand it to be.'

'I wonder,' said Bates, 'that the English, that my people, did not use it against the army of France.'

D'Ivoi shrugged. 'Indeed. Perhaps it is not oriented in the correct direction. I believe that it has been constructed to aim shells at Afghanistan.'

'I had heard of this land as a place in fable. It is beyond China, I think?'

'The north of India,' said D'Ivoi. 'The south of Russia.'

'So far? But what could launch a cannon ball so far?'

'Howsoever,' said D'Ivoi, with a brisk tone that suggested the interview was complete. 'you will go with the party, and liaise between the Dean and the French commander, a Monsieur Larroche. You must attend to them by the Tower tomorrow, and the party will proceed from there. No later than noon.'

Bates stood up. 'I accept,' he said grandly.

'Of course you do,' said D'Ivoi, his face crumpling out a smile. 'What else would you do?'

[2]

At dawn the following day news came that the journey to York had been postponed. 'By how long?' Bates demanded of the messenger, in an agony of impatience. 'Postponed by how long?'

'I don't know,' said the boy. He was perhaps ten years of age, and was dressed in the livery of the newly created Public Servants, with the letters EFP – *Employés de la Fonction Publique* – printed on the tunic.

Doubtless, Bates reflected, he received a portion of that same general disdain and hostility from ordinary Britons as was also served up to Bates himself. He looked fiercely at Bates, at any rate, as if outraged by his fate.

Bates held the scrap of paper in his hands: his journey postponed, no more detail. 'Do I,' he asked the boy, 'do you – expect a tip?'

The boy scowled again. 'You ben't supposed to tip EFPs,' he said. 'We get a considered ration from the government.' But he held his right hand out anyway, and Bates fumbled out a penny.

After he had gone Bates fussed around his rooms. Without a man-servant (he could not, despite prolonged effort to do so, entice a servant to work for him), his lodgings were in a poor state. Paper, rinds, old clothes, all manner of litter on the floor. How long would the delay be? What was he to do? He had, mentally speaking, prepared himself for the adventure.

Later in the day he stepped out to buy a *Mercury*, but it was an emaciated newssheet, shrivelled to two small pages by the strictures of war and occupation, containing nothing of any importance save official notices by the occupying forces and some town gossip. As he returned from the street vendor the rain, which had threatened for so long, finally began to fall. It came at first like a miniature artillery attack, large drops falling as shells to explode on the dusty road in starbursts of mud. The temperature dipped, and the light went dark grey. Then, as the torrent gathered vigour, a tumbling airful of heavy water came hard down upon him. Bates ducked and sprinted, but was drenched to the skin by the time he returned to his rooms.

It rained. The rain was constant for six days, sometimes growing in intensity and sometimes diminishing, but never ceasing. Bates rarely left his room during this week, venturing out once a day to buy some hot food and a pitcher of gin, but otherwise sitting at the window in a state of torpor. He spent a great deal of time in bed with a cold and with shrunken, aching spirits. He felt as if his very soul were becoming mildewed, as if fungus were sprouting on his heart. The window leaked, and water dribbled down the walls. The furthest points of the floor-boards had swollen and were starting to coil and warp like slow-living things, like tree roots or great mushrooms. The wall was slimy to the touch, its paintwork sprouting horrid-looking boils.

It was dismal, dismal. The whole cosmos was dismal.

Bates did nothing. He could not rouse his spirits beyond slouching to the chophouse, or plying his exhausted soul with coffee from Harman's. He slept a great deal. He lay on his bed a great deal, like an invalid. What else was there to do?

Then, on the seventh day, the rain stopped. Bates rose from his bed and went to the window again. The sun shone through the glass. The light came straight through, it came through the glass bright and strong. The sunlight struck his skin with such force as if it were a great jet or spout of water – fire and heat in place of water and cold, perfectly opposite to the deluge that had occupied the previous week, yet somehow akin. Bates blinked, gazed, saw the world anew. The week was almost over. Below him, mud had been washed completely over Poland Street by the water. It glistened in the sunlight like a great hide of polished leather.

The following day Bates made his way through sunshine to St James's. He waited on a lower functionary, and drew his salary as *Ami de la France*; eight pounds for the month. Some months he might be given a bonus, but he had done nothing this month to earn such a *gratuité*, merely danced attendance upon D'Ivoi and loitered in his rooms. Still, as he walked out into the sunshine, the coins chinking in his purse gladdened his heart. He took luncheon at one of the most expensive restaurants on Piccadilly, amongst French colonels and fawning English traders. Bates watched the waiters with a spy's detachment. He observed them stretch smiles across the drumskins of their faces and bow deep when serving the French. He observed them stand stiffly when serving the English.

Bates's stomach sang its froglike song.

He sauntered back to Poland Street, his belly full and his heart light. An EFP boy, a different one from last week's messenger, was waiting by the doorway. 'To go at once, sir,' he gabbled. 'The party yer awaiting is press-cur.' He hopped from foot to foot. 'Bin waiting a hour,' he brayed. 'A hour I bin ere – awaitin for you to come 'ome. I shall be in trouble, lest you go straight sir. You're to leave directly, directly, and go to the Tower.'

'The Tower of London?' asked Bates. The boy's anxiety was infectious. 'Now? Immediately, now?'

He danced anxiously about his rooms as he plucked together the contents of a travelling satchel, his omnium gatherum, whilst the EFP nagged at him from the doorway. Then he was surging up Holborn and losing his breath in the effort, walking at forced-march pace down side streets and towards the river. The Tower raised its crenelated crown over the rooftops, and then Bates was at the gate.

The EFP, who had run the whole way to keep up with Bates's furious step, tugged the sleeve of a military officer, a Colonel. This officer turned. 'Good day to you sir,' he said. 'You are Sir Bates, I think?'

'I am plain Mr Bates, Abraham Bates,' panted Bates. 'I have been ordered to report . . .'

'Indeed sir,' said the French officer. His English was more heavily accented than that of D'Ivoi, though it seemed fluent. 'I regret I am occupied with loading up this train.' He gestured at three carriages, and half a dozen men hauling boxes. 'I travel in the first. You, sir, will travel in the second. The third contains our – object of importance.'

'Sir,' gasped Bates. He was uncomfortably aware that he was perspiring. 'If there is any way I can be of help, in preparing the . . .'

'Mr Abraham Bates,' said the Colonel, sweeping his hand round towards a tubby and black-suited man standing against the wall of the tower. He was twitching his head left to right, as if nervous. 'I must introduce you to the Dean of York.'

[3]

The Dean was named Henry Oldenberg. He was, he was quick to tell Bates, descended from the celebrated Oldenberg who had helped found the Royal Society, and who had been, Bates remembered, apprehended as a spy for the Deutsch and the Dutch. The present Oldenberg inheritor did not have the look of a spy. He was a too-plump gentleman of late middle age and there was a gelatinous quality to his flesh. His whole corpus, if jolted by, for instance, the carriage bumping over an impediment, jiggled like firm-set pudding. Except when *actively* scowling his face carried a continual expression of vague anxiety, as if conscious of a distant but terrible fate that was certain to overtake him. The thumb's width of skin between his eyebrows was marked with a deep vertical worry-line. His nose was fat, a yellow pear in the middle of his yellow-red face. On his upper lip he affected a carefully trimmed apex-shaped moustache; but to Bates this looked merely ridiculous, as if the delicate, almost feminine brown hairs had been blown out of his nostrils during a sneezing fit. His lips were pink as his fingernails, and his jowls sagged from the line of his chin.

Their first meeting did not begin well. Bates walked over to the man and bade him good day. At first the Dean did not look at him. Bates coughed, discreetly.

'And you, sir?' Oldenberg demanded suddenly, with a querulous tightening of his worry lines. 'Who are you, sir?'

'Permit me to introduce myself,' said Bates. 'Abraham Bates. Do I take you to be the Dean of York?'

'You *take* me?' retorted the Dean, his voice soprano. 'Impudence, sir? Who are you to *take* me, sir?'

'I pray you not to be offended where no offence was intended,' said Bates, attempting a mollifying tone.

'Order me, sir?'

'I *beg* of you, rather ...'

'Order me? Who are you to order?'

'No sir, I do not so presume. I beg ...'

'No?' the Dean squeaked. '*No sir*, you say? You contradict me? Contradict *me*, sir?'

Abraham tried again. He bowed his head, lifted it and said: 'Dean?'

'What do you do here, sir?'

'I believe I am to accompany this train, and yourself sir, to York.'

The Dean pulled himself up to his full height. He was by more than a foot the shorter man. 'You have been sent,' he said, 'to spy on me, sir. To spy! To pry!'

'I refute the allegation,' said Bates, startled.

'Oh you *refute* it?'

'I do.'

'You *refute* it?'

Bates paused. 'Sir ...' he said.

Oldenberg executed a strange little movement. He fluttered his feminine fingers at his chest, spun on his heel, waddled away from Bates a distance of four or five yards, turned on his heel, waddled back up to him, and repeated: 'You refute it?'

Bates was uncertain what to say. 'I intend no disrespect, sir, truly not. But I must say that I think you mistake me.'

But, startlingly, Oldenberg was now laughing, a gurgling and babyish sound. 'With your talk of *refutation*, sir, you have the manner of a logician. I beg your pardon, I beg your pardon,' he grabbed Bates hand. 'You'll pardon my high spirits, I hope?'

'Of course,' said Bates, cautiously.

The Dean took hold of Bates's elbow and pulled him, almost by main force, away from the carriages. They walked towards the river. 'You must excuse my high spirits, sir,' he said again, standing on his toes' ends to talk directly into Bates's ear. 'I am prone to high spirits, I know. But I'll say this, young sir, I'll say that we can both *pretend* an allegiance to the French at the moment – eh? – eh? What else can we do? There's no shame in such pretence.'

'Indeed,' said Bates, a little flustered.

'They think I'll help 'em,' whispered Oldenberg. 'But *we* know better. Don't we? Don't we? What? It's a setback – the army, I mean – the French army, I mean, in English fields – but God will not permit it to last for ever.' He stepped back. 'Let us greet one another like English gentlemen. You are as handsome a young fellow as I've seen in a long time – a handsome face, a handsome face. *I* am Henry Oldenberg, Dean of York, and I am honoured to make your acquaintance, sir.'

'Abraham Bates, at your disposal, sir.'

'There!' The little ritual seemed to have pumped up Oldenberg's spirits to preposterous levels. He did an inelegant little jog on the spot, twiddling his feet. 'There, like *English* gentlemen, like Marlborough, or King Richard, or Saint George.'

'Indeed,' said Bates.

'Though Saint George was a Turk!' the Dean squealed, so loudly that several of the party loading the carriage stopped when they were doing and looked in the direction of the two men. 'But let that pass! Let it pass. Come, we had best return to the carriage. The Frenchers will want us to depart soon enough. They'll want to be away, and we'd best be away with them.'

Another twenty minutes, and all three carriages were fully loaded. With a command, the French Colonel saw the attendant troop mount their horses, and the drivers fetch up their reins. Bates settled himself into the second carriage and the fidgeting Dean of York squirmed in the seat beside him. He seemed as giddy as a child.

They rolled through the city, and onto the North Road. Few of the Londoners they passed deigned to notice them. 'Their insolence is their only fight,' said the Dean, pressing his nose against the glass. 'Their only fight! They know no other way to tackle the French, save ill-manners.'

'I think it is so, sir,' said Bates.

'Now,' said the Dean, rotating in his seat to face Bates directly. '*Now* we'll talk, sir. I'll say, to commence it, that I am sorry to have called you a spy, before.'

'Think nothing of it,' said Bates, a little stiffly.

'Oh, it's a slur, a slur. But it's a slur might describe us both, I think. We contrive what arrangement we must with the French, to carry on as we must. But 'tis not *that* I wish to speak of. Let us establish our grounds.'

'Our grounds, sir?'

'You are to be my *assistant*?' Oldenberg said, pronouncing the word in the French manner.

Bates hesitated. 'If you desire it, sir.'

'But you are a gentleman, a gentleman,' gabbled the Dean. 'I know it, I know it. I'll not treat you as a servant, no. But assistance will be greatly appreciated – as one gentleman to another, eh?'

'Certainly.'

'Then I accept your offer of assistance. And I'll tell you something more.' He wiggled his plump body along the seat until it was close against Bates's, as if he would whisper again in his ear, but instead he sang out: 'We'll give these French the slip, we will. I have a plan. My cannon will *propel* us ... propel us! Clean out of their clutches. In India, we'll be free.'

'Dean,' said Bates. 'I must confess I do not quite ...'

But Oldenberg's attention had been taken by something else. 'See,' he cooed, twisting round to look out of the carriage window again. 'Spitalfields! Fields of Spital! *Sputum civitatis!* Observe the butchers carrying their carcasses into the city. Ah, might the city not be an organism and each of us but cells in the whole? Do you not agree? But then there are no shadows upon the face of the sun and it casts shadows, whereas the moon existeth in shadow yet can still – on a full and moonlit night – and the moon might cast the sundial's shadows, yet we do not call that a moondial, do we?' He snorted. 'Do you not,' he added, abruptly, 'see the resemblance between a church steeple and the bayonet upon a soldier's rifle? Excuse me if my thoughts gallop – and gallop. Does it distress you, my dear sir?' Before Bates could answer he said: 'I have been awake all night! I have not slept since yesternight. Not a moment's sleep!' His voice seemed to imply pride at this fact, as if it were an accomplishment.

'Not slept?' said Bates. 'Why not?'

'Too excited. Grand adventure, away, over the hills and far,' said the Dean, and started bobbing up and down on his seat.

Bates later discovered that Oldenberg's high spirits were temporary aberrations in his demeanour, brought on (as the Dean himself admitted, or rather *boasted*) by a particular variety of snuff of which he was especially fond. He took out his snuffbox and displayed the contents to Bates as they passed into the countryside north of the city. 'The opening of the Pacific has brought many such goods into our ken,' he said.

'I have not seen this before,' said Bates, looking carefully. The ebony box contained a fine white powder, like milled salt, or like flour. He took a dab on the end of his finger and tasted it; it had a sweet quality, and it made the end of his tongue tingle. 'What manner of tobacco is this?'

The Dean shrugged. 'Some albino form, I assume. I am no expert on the varieties of the tobacco plant. But I find it more invigorating than my usual snuff.' He put the snuffbox away, and turned to look out of the carriage-glass at the passing countryside. Already he seemed a little calmer.

A little later he yawned, settled himself, and fell asleep with his chin tucked into his neck. He slumbered deeply, despite the worst rattles and bumps of the carriages motions, for many hours.

As they moved away from the city and into the rustic expanse of Hertfordshire, Bates's spirits rose. His heart leaped up. All his despondency was left behind in the sink of London, the crease at the bottom of the city where the river followed its lowest declivity. Now he was moving ahead, and Bates permitted himself to consider positive possibility – for perhaps his life was about to improve. Might it not?

Climbing up Highgate Hill, when the French soldiers dismounted and walked to ease the burden for the horses (the two Englishmen were, of course, exempted from such footwork), Bates felt his body relaxing in consonance with his rising spirits. They passed a church whose steeple looked not so much like a bayonet as a blade of bronze grass. The sunlight fair sang in the blue sky. A stream flowed alongside the highway, hemmed into a brick channel here and there, at other places flowing through feathery rims of grass grown long enough to bow down over the water. And here, near the summit of the hill, the stream fell down a short cataract, a culvert of sorts, as their coaches mounted alongside, like salmon. The water was glassy and leaden-coloured except where a protruding rock slit the belly of the flow whitely. Such liveliness in water! When Christ had blessed water, choosing it as the sacramental embodiment of spirit, he had surely blessed *all* waters – as precisely as aware of this little Highgate stream as of the *Oceanus Pacificus* and the *Mare Tranquillitatis* – the thought gave Bates all the physical symptoms of excitement.

The Dean snored as if he had the east wind in his throat.

Down the far side the drivers put on the brakes and passage became more jolting. Bates let his thoughts slip forward. Perhaps the successful completion of this adventure would raise his reputation amongst the occupying force. Perhaps he would be given some more dignified role than mere *Ami de la France*. A counsellor, perhaps; liaison between the benign occupying force and the English – offering guidance on how best to maintain the welfare of the Pacificans. Once the French knew he could be trusted, then he might begin to use his influence for good. He glanced forward to a possible future in which the unpleasantness of the invasion was past, England restored in partnership with the French – two Christian nations in brotherhood together, both equal, portions of the *universalis civitas humani generis*. And the Pacificans converted, brought into that harmony. The Dean muttered something in his sleep, and the hawk swooped with its customary suddenness inside Bates's thoughts. What of Oldenberg's plans to betray the French? What of that? Would Bates become caught up in some sedition – hanged, who knew, from a flagpole? Bates felt his good mood dissipate. He spent long minutes considering ways in which he could distance himself from the Dean – should he not, perhaps, betray the betrayer, inform on him to the French? Or if that would be too despicable, then was there some other way in which – in which—

The Dean sneezed in his sleep, and this woke him up.

The procession stopped at an inn for luncheon in the countryside well north of the city. The Dean was silent the whole time. Bates attempted to engage in conversation with him, but he merely grunted in reply and lifted his glass of wine. But Bates's good spirits returned nonetheless. It seemed futile to fret about what the Dean might or might not do – he, Bates, was master of his own destiny, was he not?

After months of stagnation in the city he felt himself now free – away, in motion, moving like Odysseus towards the ever-receding horizon of possibility. He finished his eating, and stepped outside the inn.

Sunshine filled him.

There was an enormous oak outside the inn, plunging upwards out of a broad circle of close-mown grass. It took Bates's fancy and he strolled over towards it. The clear spring light smoothed the sky into a flawless paleness of blue, and came through the leaves of the tree like clear water splashing down, to dapple the lawn beneath with a scattered network of shadow and brightness. The French Colonel (his name was Larroche, Bates recalled) was standing against the trunk of the old tree smoking his pipe.

'And good day to *you, Monsieur le Colonel,*' said Bates.

The Colonel withdrew his pipe from his lips. 'Good day, Mister Bates,' he said. 'I apologise for being brusque with you earlier.'

'No need for apology.'

The Frenchman nodded, and sipped again at the stem of his pipe.

'The weather is fine today,' said Bates.

Larroche looked at Bates with an expression of amused puzzlement.

'Ah,' said Bates, benignly. 'But my observation is simply the truth. Is it not? The weather is fine. And look around you, sir,' Bates added, sweeping the panorama with his arm as he turned. 'Is it not beautiful? Even yourself, though a foreigner, must accept England to be beautiful.' The landscape was trim green hills swelling to the horizon, like the cheeks of a giant green face, spotted here and there with the white dabs of grazing sheep. Closer to, a herd of sheep plucked the grass, and rolled their white eyes, and chewed as if chewing were the only thought their heads could hold. Bates watched them, and thought of the many biblical verses about sheep: their placidity; their gentleness; their fundamental connection to the earth. God's chosen, said the apostles, and Christ himself. Nor was the gospel example ill-chosen, for there *was* a sort of nobility about the creatures, their unmistakable idiocy notwithstanding. There *was* something honourable in the notion that sheep might safely graze.

'Beautiful,' agreed the Frenchman, without passion.

'Those sheep,' said Bates. Perhaps he had picked up the spirit of garrulity from the Dean. 'Those sheep. Do you not think it significant that our Lord the Christ chose the sheep as his type of the faithful disciple? I have sometimes wondered whether it does not especially signal a divine fondness for England, the *isla angelica*. For England is the great land of sheep, is it not? We have cultivated sheep for a thousand years, and we cultivate more of them than any nation on earth. Our Lord Chancellor sits upon a woolsack, you know, in recognition of the fact.'

The nearest sheep of the flock raised his head and looked at Bates, as if he knew he was being discussed. The head was white-silhouetted against the sky. The flock, Bates thought vaguely, must be grazing in a valley, or a cut-away of the land, to be able to lift their heads apparently above the level of the horizon in that manner. 'Those sheep,' he said again, 'are the essence of God's England, I think. A timeless feature of our landscape.'

'Monsieur,' said the Colonel. 'Not *those* sheep.'

Bates looked again.

He experienced that trembling sense of consciousness, a purely mental shuddery inner sensation, as the perspective of the scene reorganised and its true proportions reasserted themselves. What he had taken for sheep of ordinary size close to him were in fact sheep of gigantic proportion far in the distance. The realisation made him giddy, in a small way. How could he not have seen it straight away?

'I have always found,' the Colonel was saying, 'the *mouton* from the Brobdingnagian animals too coarse. The ...' he paused. 'How you say? Hairs? No, no. I do not know the word.' He looked into the bowl of his pipe, as if the word were hidden inside. 'The, you say, threads? The threads of the meat are too large. Yes?'

'Indeed,' said Bates. 'The fibres of the meat.'

'Ah, very good,' said Larroche. '*The fibres of meat* are thick like my little finger; and inside is very very little taste, little savour.'

'It is for the poor,' said Bates. He was, greatly – disproportionately – unsettled by the fact of his not seeing the gigantic sheep for what they truly were. Now that he watched them, it was impossible to mistake their proportions. One of them moved, its limbs sweeping with bizarre slowness, and digging deep into the clay of the English countryside. The horizon was dotted with similar craters. And what he had taken for grass was, quite obviously, the green bolted-wheat that farmers grew as fodder for the creatures. Some farmers, Bates knew, had tried growing Brobdingnagian grass from British soil, but it drew too much of the goodness from the earth, and rendered fields barren for more than a year afterwards. Besides, the animals grew fatter on a diet of English wheat.

'We must depart,' the Colonel said, rapping his pipe bowl against the trunk of the oak. As he walked back towards the carriages Bates heard him repeating to himself, 'fibres of the meat, fibres of the meat', as if fixing the phrase in his memory.

All that afternoon, as they trundled further along the Great North Road, the Dean was awake, though surly and withdrawn. Bates watched the slowly processing countryside. Farmhouses and inns moved into view and then paraded, stately and slow, past them. They went through villages, along rudimentary high streets and out the other side again. The sun began its declination. A roseate quality tinted the light.

Late in the day, after many successive hours of silence, the Dean suddenly spoke. 'The box they carry in the final carriage, back there,' he said.

'I beg your pardon, Dean?' Bates replied.

'The large box,' said Oldenberg.

'I believe it to be a Calculation Machine.'

Oldenberg grunted his agreement. 'I attempted to examine it before we left.'

'I would imagine you were prevented by the soldiers.'

'Oh,' said the Dean. 'Oh, I was. But I'll have my look in there. I will.' He was silent again.

That evening they stopped in a village a few miles from Cambridge. Bates was to share a room with the Dean. After dining he requested a candle, and argued for fifteen minutes with the landlord over the item. He was charged a shilling for one tallow candle of poor quality. 'A shilling? Robbery. I could buy a dozen such candles for the sum in London.' 'You an't in London now, sir,' said the landlord, a wheezy old man with one eye cataracted the colour of tooth-enamel. 'Besides, the war puts prices up, you know.'

'The war? There's no war hereabouts,' blustered Bates. 'There's no war south of Derby. And I have no need for the whole candle. I only wish to read a little before I sleep.'

'Shillin',' said the landlord, implacably.

'I'll give you sixpence,' said Bates, fumbling in his pocket for change. said the landlord.

'Shillin','

Bates looked at the man. His chops were silvery with stubble. His forehead knobbed and shiny. His one eye, despite its wateriness, fixed Bates with an immovable stare. 'I'll have a word with the French Colonel,' Bates said. 'The gentleman with whom I am travelling. He will have something to say about your profiteering.'

The landlord shrugged.

In the end Bates did not run tattletaling to Larroche. Instead he used his sixpence to buy a glass of hot rum and water, and sat downstairs in the snug trying to read by the firelight. But red light makes the eyes tired if they try close work, and the words soon swam in Bates's mind. So in the end he simply sat with the book in his lap.

'Reading?' said the Dean, loudly.

Bates started.

The other man came through and sat himself in the chair opposite. 'No wish to intrude, my friend,' said Oldenberg, twitching a little. 'Only I could see that you are reading, and not yet asleep, and I thought I'd come to chat with you. I wanted to apologise for being so taciturn in the carriage, you know. Taciturn as Tacitus, and he's dead and gone and in a Roman grave.' He giggled, in his high-pitched way.

'I see that you,' said Bates, 'have refreshed yourself with some more of your snuff.'

'Miraculous stuff,' said Oldenberg, sitting next to him. 'Miraculous snuff. Stuff. Snuff. Snuff-stuff. Invigorating. *En*vigorating. *Un*vigorating. Virile vigour. *Dignum laude virum Musa vetat mori.* What is it you read?'

'Nothing,' said Bates, unaccountably embarrassed at the question. 'Only – some sermons.'

'How devout you are!' said the Dean in what sounded almost like a mocking voice.

'Surely,' said Bates, 'as Dean of York, you—'

'Oh I know, you're perfectly right, pff, pff, pff.' These last three noises were strange ejaculations, beginning with a pout of the lips and an exhalation but ending as a sniffing expulsion of air through the nose, inexpressibly dismissive. 'Forms must be kept up, forms must be kept up. But gentlemen such as *we* are may dispense with the pieties, no? What?' He winked. 'Prayer and hymns and the eucharist? Necessary flimflam for the Lord's flock. But we are not sheep, I think. Are we? No!'

Bates, tired and cross after his experience with the landlord, could not help the petulant tone of voice in which he retorted, over-loud: 'You call it the *eucharist*, sir?'

But Oldenberg merely laughed. 'Lord's Supper, if you will sir. Lord's Supper by all means. Low Church, if you will sir. What do I care? *Panem nostrum quotidianum.*'

'I am, perhaps, sensitive on the subject, sir. There's talk,' said Bates, feeling immediate remorse about his tone and wishing to explain himself. 'There's rumours, you understand, sir, that the French will compel the Protestants of England to adopt the Roman faith. Perhaps I am over-sensitive to Romish ... what shall we say? To Romanish flavours in habits of speech.'

The Dean made his strange nasal noise again. 'Pff, pff, I think not. The old rector at my school would call it *Breaking the Lord's Bread*, no eucharist for him, no such papistry. Bread, papistry, pastry, fine French pastry. A nice cigar after supping. Food, important, eh? Food – ahh – food. I had the most delicious pigeon breasts in cheese sauce this evening. Delicious. One of the most commendable things about our Christianity is that it places good food, good wine – eating, in short – the heart of religion. Don't you think it? What? None of your Indian Brahmin ascetics, none of your Mohammedan fasting, no sir. Good eating. Eating *is* worship for a Christian, sir. No?'

'There were forty days,' replied Bates, inflecting his words with the gentlest of rebuking tones, 'and forty nights in which our Lord did otherwise.'

The Dean, fluttering his hands before his breast, said only: 'No, no. Medieval theology, sir. Fasting? What, and lashing one's flesh? Hair-shirts and making your pilgrimage on your bare knees over sharp rocks, no *no* no. We are more enlightened these days I hope, and we may truly see that Christ himself placed *eating* and the drinking of *good* wines – none of your burnt tuppenny vintage, neither – but eating and *good* wine at the centre of religious observance. The very centre! Health for the body, health for the soul. Snuff too.'

'You surely cannot assert,' Bates interjected, 'that taking snuff is, in any sense, itself *eucharistic*?'

'And now *you* are using the Romanish word!' chuckled Oldenberg. 'My, my, my, but yes.' He paused, coughed, and then, in a rush: 'It seems to me abundantly clear that that-which-we-ingest, the good things of the earth that have been provided for our health and well-being that these are the things upon which Christ built his religion.

To read the Bible is to read, again and again, of images of food – of food – of food – of *wheat* in the field, if-the-grain-die-not – *mouton*, sheep, mutton as the French call it – vines in the vineyard – salt and fish. A fine, healthful diet! Tobacco, and therefore snuff, is not mentioned explicitly, I accept; but I take tobacco to be a form of wheat, one variety amongst many, and in addition snuff is akin to *mustard*, the grains of mustard that are also mentioned in the Novum Testamentum.'

He stopped here and sipped at his drink, and indeed he fell into a sort of reverie, looking at the fire. Silence reclaimed the room, broken only by the intermittent crackling of the wood in the fire. As the silence lengthened, the energy seemed to drain from the mood.

Bates, looking more closely, could see that there were tears in Oldenberg's eyes. This startled him.

'Dean,' he said. 'What is amiss?'

Oldenberg's eyes gleamed like pearls in the firelight. 'Nothing,' he said, his voice pregnant with misery. 'Nothing, nothing. 'Tis not Shakspeare? I think it be Shakspeare who says it in his *Lear*. Nothing nothing.' The plunge from his mania to his melancholia was so sudden it gave Bates – even Bates, with his own long experience of emotional mutability – a sort of vertigo to contemplate it.

'Pray, sir,' he said, leaning forward. 'Do not upset yourself. Do not, sir. What can we have been saying, to upset you so much?'

'My moods,' said the Dean, drawing his thumb over his left eye, and then his right eye, to wipe some of the moisture away, 'are sudden, I know. You despise me, Mr Bates.'

'Not I!' Bates was shocked.

'You do.'

'No, no, I assure you.'

'Or is it,' he said, starting up with an abruptly restored animation, 'or is it *Hamlet*? The rest is Nothing. I misremember. Never, never, never, perhaps that is the phrase. I should know my Shakspeare better.' He was holding his silver snuffbox between forefinger and thumb, and had flipped the little lid with a practised smoothness of gesture. He placed two miniature mounds of white on the back of his hand, and sniffed one into each nostril. Then he put his head back, holding his breath whilst the skin around his nostril's underwent little shudders and quivers. At last he exhaled, a lengthy sound of pure satisfaction. 'Shakspeare!' he said vehemently, as if the word were an oath. 'I would,' he turned to Bates, 'offer some to yourself, as one gentleman to another, but my supply is limited and I am not certain how I shall come by another quantity, I'm sure you understand.' His words were once again being issued helter-skelter, a near-gasping rapidity in his breath.

'Think nothing of it,' said Bates. 'I do not myself take snuff.'

Bates excused himself on grounds of his tiredness and mounted the stairs to the room he was sharing with Oldenberg. But he could not get away from the Dean, whose body now seemed bursting with energy. 'Sleep, sir, *no* sir,' he said, following him up the stairs and snatching at his sleeve's cuff. 'There is much to do, too much to do.'

The landlord had, it seemed, removed himself to bed long before, and Oldenberg – never mind that it amounted to theft – had taken one of the candles from behind his counter and carried it up to the room. This he lit and glued to the windowsill with a drop of spilt wax. It threw a variable brightness through the small room: the uneven plaster, the two rickety beds.

'I must confess to being tired, sir,' said Bates, seating himself on one of the beds.

'Tired? Nonsense.' The Dean sat in the room's single chair opposite, and talked. He talked on and on, as Bates became more and more exhausted. For stretches of the conversation Bates maintained his interest; but midnight passed, and the small hours tolled dimly on the grandfather clock downstairs, and he grew more and more tired. Oldenberg could not, however, be gainsaid.

'Tired sir? No, no. Thought ventilates the brain,' he insisted, 'wakes the spirits, and if you apply your *thoughts*, sir, you will feel fresh, fresh as a new daisy. Day's eye, the word means, the eye of the day. For the flower is thought to represent the sun. Sun of God, ha-ha-ah-ha! Do you see? A miniature sun, but then again, do we not now live in a world of miniatures?'

'Miniatures?' Bates was not following.

'The little people – *people*, but little. No? No?'

His conversation wandered over all terrain, like a vagabond. But a constant was Oldenberg's fascination with the Lilliputians. 'The scale,' he kept saying. 'I'll tell you, the scale is the key.'

'Key to what, sir?' But Bates was so very tired now. It required a continual effort of will to remain awake.

'Why,' said the Dean, his eyes wide with innocent astonishment at

Bates's ignorance. 'The key to all, sir. Pan-solution. *Pansoluo*, I solve all. The key to everything.'

'I confess I don't follow you sir.'

'The scale,' said the Dean, getting off his bed and pacing up and down the length of the room in his excitement, 'is everything. What is the scale? One to one twelfth. One to one twelfth.'

Bates's upper eyelids felt as if they were composed of some lodestone material magnetically attracted to the lower eyelids. It required specific effort to hold the lids apart. 'One to one twelfth,' he repeated.

'Think of the world revealed to us,' said Oldenberg. 'The Lilliputian is one twelfth the size of a man. The Brobdingnagian is twelve times as large. The number is a significant one. Do you agree?'

'I do not doubt you are correct,' said Bates.

The Dean sat down again. 'I shall tell you in what way this number governs the universe,' he said. From his travelling bag he brought out a leather-bound volume, something like an accounts book. 'Do you know,' he said, looking up with sparkling eyes, 'that the Old Testament is exactly twelve times the size of the New?'

'Truly?' said Bates.

'In order to arrive at the correct number, one must,' said Oldenberg, leafing through his ledger, 'include the apocryphal books in the Old Testament, and disregard certain of the less important New Testament books, but the calculation is sound, the *ratio* is sound. Ah!' He bent the covers of his volume back until the spine creaked, and laid it upon the bed beside him.

A yawn grew inside Bates, enormous as a silent scream. He strained like Samson to suppress it, but it shuddered up through his life and wrenched his jaws apart. 'Excuse me,' he said. 'Excuse me?'

Oldenberg did not seem to have noticed. 'My great love amongst the sciences is astronomy. The noble study of the heavens. It is seemly, too, that a vicar of Christ study the heavens, for God has written there in languages of light and darkness for us to read.'

'Indeed,' said Bates.

'At Yorkshire – outside the city of York – I studied the heavens through the large telescope. Excellent astronomical landscape that, excellent for the science of astronomy, looking up, looking at the heavens, you know. Outside York, I studied there.'

Bates interest revived a little. 'Our present destination?'

'Ah, yes. But astronomy was the least of it,' the Dean rattled on.

'The great cannon was constructed, and I was part of the team.'

'I do find this device to be of particular interest ...' Bates started saying. But the Dean, carried along on his own train of words, did not hear him.

'For anybody acquainted with the principles of ballistics, by which is meant the science of free flight, the mechanics of the device are straightforward. Imagine a carriage, built of iron of course, and padded within. Imagine this carriage shaped so as to fly through the medium of the air with the minimum of impediment. Can you visualise such a thing?'

Bates murmured and nodded. He was not sure how the conversation had come round to this matter. Not that it was uninteresting. But he was tired.

'In effect we would travel – I say,' the Dean started up from his bed with his fist clenched together and his eyes alight with enthusiasm, 'I say we *will*, we will travel – with the *speed* of a bullet, in the *manner* of a bullet. Inside a bullet, inside a bullet of magnificent proportions.'

'Travel in the manner of a bullet,' repeated Bates. 'Pardon me, but—'

'Naturally,' said the Dean, seating himself again, and talking as if replying to a completely different comment from Bates, 'the Crown wished the cannon merely as a device for bombarding enemies of Britain, not as a device for *travel*. They themselves insisted that it be oriented as it is – others wanted it oriented towards France. I worked with the great Davidowic. Have you heard of him? A Hebrew sir, but a genius. He died before he could accept the primacy of Christ into his heart, but what genius he had! And Christ was a Jew too, let us not forget. We worked together. Others would say I was his junior, sir, but he treated me with marvellous condescension. And the *Crown* was, at that time, the Crown, sir, was confident of victory over the French. Foolishness! Vanity! Nevertheless, they assumed that victory was imminent, and they looked to a more distant future. Would you believe,' the Dean said, with a giggle in his voice, 'that they thought the conquest of France a certainty, and were already looking forward to the next war? The next war!'

'Against Russia,' Bates prompted.

'Indeed. Whether it was feared that the Russians would attempt to take the East India Company by force, and occupy the Indian lands, or whether the plan was for an English army to proceed into southern Russia, I know not. But at any rate the cannon was orientated in such a way that a shell might be fired to land in that place.'

'Prodigious,' murmured Bates.

'Truly, truly,' agreed the Dean, nodding so violently that his cheeks wobbled. 'A prodigious quantity of gunpowder would be required, and a cannon shell of prodigious size. But it is perfectly possible, the laws of physics permit it. Think of such ordnance! No Russian cavalry charge could capture it – or escape it!'

'Could it be accurate?' Bates asked. 'I hardly believe it could, at such distance.'

'The calculations required are very precise,' Oldenberg agreed. 'Very complex. This is why the French are so desirous of claiming the cannon.'

'Because?'

'Because their machine – their calculating machine – renders such work a matter of seconds, rather than days. Seconds! And the accuracy is much improved.' Oldenberg shook his head. 'They can calculate the trajectory, the force of gunpowder required, in moments. Accordingly they could use the cannon in a way that not even the most optimistic English generals planned ... they could fire half-a-dozen of shells in a minute. They could flatten their enemy from beyond the horizon.' He shook his head again.

'But why should the French desire to attack India? Or Russia?'

'Or Afghanistan neither – you are correct,' said the Dean. 'They have no quarrel with these peoples, no, no. But the gun can be used to fire upon any country along that line, along the line of its orientation, do you see? They could fire upon Germany – Austria-Hungary – Turkey. Perhaps their military ambitions are in that direction? Besides, once they've claimed the device, and seen for themselves how it is constructed, they may build another, and angle it where they choose – they could build hundreds.' Oldenberg shrugged and scratched the top of his head.

'You seem cavalier, sir,' said Bates, trying to stifle another yawn. 'As Englishmen we should be alarmed, surely, at such a development?'

'Perhaps. But I plan to take us far away from this war-plagued little country – far away – far away.' Trembling with excitement, the Dean hopped from his bed and sat next to Bates. 'There is a hollowed shell of the sort I mentioned.'

'There is?' Bates was uncertain what the Dean was talking about.

'Yes. Padded inside, room for four – room for you and me, certainly. And we'll fly to India!'

'To India?'

'I am very good friends with the Archbishop of Bombay. He and I are very good friends. Balliol. Very. And whilst India remains free of French *interference* we can find a sanctuary there. We might escape.'

'Could we not merely take *ship* to India?' asked Bates.

'The French would never allow it, sir! Never allow it! I know too many things. The things inside my head,' and here he smacked his head, flapped the palm of his hand against it with alarming force, 'would bring *tremendous* advantage to any General campaigning against them! In this noddle, sir! In here, sir! I am too important to the French, sir! They'd never permit me to sail away. And if I did go, they'd send a ship to *recover* me. Piracy, a funeral pyre. *Puero maxima debetur reverentia.* No! The cannon is the only way. They'll not catch *that*, once it's in flight! Eh? Eh?'

'But, Dean,' Bates said, rubbing his eyes and desiring sleep very greatly. 'How can it be? The expulsion of such a shell from such a cannon – it would be too violent a shock to a human body. Would it not?'

'Quite so,' said the Dean, his voice a little calmer. 'Quite so – turn a human corpus into porridge.'

'And upon landing the shell would explode – would it not? Even if it did not carry explosives within it, the force of impact would shatter the shell and its occupants into a thousand tatters. Would it not?'

Oldenberg was silent.

'Would it not, Dean?' Bates pressed. 'Pray, tell me, for I do confess a great interest in the device.'

There was no answer. Bates leaned forward in his chair.

Oldenberg was asleep. He had fallen into a slumber whilst sitting up. Carefully, Bates placed a blanket across his lap. From Oldenberg's bed Bates took up his book. Its pages were covered with columns of numbers, nothing more. He shut it, placed it on the floor. Lying himself down on his bed fully clothed, he fell into immediate sleep.

[4]

Bates was woken shortly after dawn by the noise of horses. The Dean, in his chair, was snoring like a rusty axle.

There was no water in the jug beside the washbowl. Bates rubbed his face with dry palms and resolved to have words with the landlord. Outside, the noise of activity was growing distinctly. Bates stood at the window, tiny stained diamonds of glass in a fishnet of lead, to see what was going on outside. Below him he could see dozens of French cavalrymen passing by, two-by-two, moving briskly along the road past the inn and heading north. In a few minutes the room seemed filled with the sound of jingle and trot, and the occasional shivery horse-voice. The troop passed off and it was quiet again.

He dressed as best he could and made his way downstairs. The landlord was not about. Unable to order hot water he was forced to wash himself at the pump in the back yard. Stomping, cold and wet and in poor humour, to the front of the inn he found the French Colonel Larroche smoking his pipe in the misty air.

'Good day, Mister Bates.'

'Colonel, good day.'

They stood together for a while. Bates watched as the half-dozen soldiers from Larroche's platoon made the carriages ready for the day. They were greasing the axles, wiping the sides, stitching the loose flaps of the leather of the tackle. The carriage carrying the Computational Device seemed somehow more solid than the others. Two men stood at attention beside it, the metal spires of their rifles poking over their shoulders.

Bates sat himself on the lip of a stone horse trough. The water inside shuddered with the movement of a great many tadpoles.

'I saw,' said Bates, 'a troop of horse pass by. Saw it from my window.'

Larroche puffed at his pipe, regarding Bates coolly.

'They do not join our party?'

A puff spilled from the corner of the Colonel's mouth and spilled away from him through the air, like foam washed along the top of an invisibly flowing stream. 'No.'

'They are on manoeuvres, perhaps?'

The Colonel said nothing.

'I only wondered. Perhaps there is fighting further north, and they proceed rapidly to join their comrades.'

'Perhaps,' said Larroche, tipping his pipe upside-down and knocking the bowl against the inn wall. 'Perhaps the fighting is not so far north.'

'What do you mean, sir?' But Larroche had walked away.

Bates looked down, and the slimy water in the trough bubbled coldly and slowly with the action of the creatures within it. Hundreds of squirming tadpoles, each with a body as fat as a knucklebone, all of them blank-faced and black-bodied and repulsive.

Mist, the remnants of which were yet to be evaporated from the more distant hills, gave the landscape a laminate appearance: the vividness and fulfilled reality of the near at hand layered upon by two-dimensional shapes made of nothing but blank canvas, and then the slightly stippled white of the further distance which appeared as if in readiness for the painter's touch to add its colours.

Bates got to his feet and approached the carriages. The two in which the party was travelling were parked side by side, but the third carriage – the one containing the mysterious device – was a little apart from its fellows. A large cover or blanket had been thrown over it, and a fire lit not far from it, as if in concerted effort to keep it warm (but why would it matter if a mere machine felt the cold?). A single soldier sat besides the embers of this fire, his rifle horizontal in his lap and his chin resting on his starched collar.

Bates stopped. His heart was shuddering, suddenly, very forcibly in his chest. Did he dare to take this chance?

He looked about him, but apart from the slumbering *soldat* he was alone with the carriage.

He stepped as lightly as he could past the dying fire and lifted the cover. It was of some dense-woven wool or staple cloth and was leaden with dew. Bates grasped the hem of it, felt the weight of water it held, as if it were woven out of the fabric of rainclouds. Lifting a corner revealed the wood of the carriage, and an opening perhaps three feet square. Through this aperture Bates looked upon the blank wooden face of what, surely, must be the device itself. The Computational Device! A small door was set into this wooden flank, with a brass handle set into the top. Without another guilty glance Bates pulled this handle and the door swung down, a flap.

It was evident that this was the aperture through which the little people inside received their food. A long narrow tube was fixed to the inside with a tiny tube at the bottom and a miniature tap-handle; from here they could take their drink. A number of smaller brass boxes arranged in a line against the inside bottom of the flap perhaps contained their dainty food.

Bates hunkered down and peered through the opening. There was a fascia of wire, the outside of an inner cage perhaps, and through it he fancied he saw, in the shadows, movement. In the diffuse light of the early morning it was difficult to be sure.

He put his hand against the mesh: 'twas cold to the touch, the wire strands taut and ungiving. There was space, just, to insert a finger.

The finger went in. He moved it, as much as he could, wiggling it a little. He was considering, in point of fact, how to frame a question to the little folk who – surely! – laboured within. Could he promise to free them? Would that be the wisest course?

But then there was – *ouch!* – a sudden and fierce pain in the end of his finger, a thorn-stab or splinter-bite, as if Bates had pressed his digit firm upon the sharp end of a needle. He barely contained a yelp of pained surprise as he yanked the hand away from the grill – withdrew it so vehemently that he almost lost his balance. He put a foot out backwards to stop himself falling over, and his heel kicked up the ashes of the fire. He let the covering fall from his left hand and it fell, heavily, wetly, immediately, back into position.

The soldier woke with a cough and a cry of '*Parcours!*' Bates, his heart labouring momentously in his chest, turned quickly. 'Good morning,' he said, too hurriedly, putting his hands into his coat pockets. '*Bonjour.*'

The soldier scrabbled at his rifle, and slotting his hand over the trigger. '*Qu'est-ce que vous . . .*' he started. Then he stopped. '*Je ne dormais pas.*' Then, as if realizing that he was not obliged to explain himself to this Englishman, he growled, and sniffed, and said: '*Le mot, c'est bonjour.* Bon*jour.*'

'*Ce que j'ai dit,*' said Bates, taking one step backwards.

'*Vous avez dit* bongjo. *C'est pas ça.* Bongjo, bongjo.'

'*Je dois,*' said Bates, and could not recall the French for '*to leave.*' He smiled, and turned, and hurried back inside the inn.

Inside he examined his hand. There was a scarlet pearl on the very tip of his index finger. He put this to his mouth and sucked the gem away. Had he jagged himself on some internal cog or spur? Or had one of the little people, furious at his probing, stabbed him with a tiny dagger?

After breakfast the party took the road once more. Bates resumed his place inside their coach next to a gloomily introspective Dean of York. Despite several conversational prompts, Oldenberg refused to explain further his fantastical comments from the previous night. Indeed he refused to be drawn into any exchange at all.

Bates stared through the window of the carriage as they jolted along. They crossed through a pair of gates and over a railway line where the road intersected it aslant: for one moment the metal rails flashed perfectly parallel like an artist's perspective lines sketched out to the horizon. The carriage made no bump or rattle over the railway.

The road wound on, and ever on, but Bates saw no people. Many of the fields were empty. Some were occupied with grazing cattle or sheep of European size. Once they passed a paddock in which a horse stared at them, and seemed to bow his head in exaggerated civility as they passed (except that he was only reaching down to drink from his trough). But there were no people tending these animals. This puzzled Bates. Animals must needs be tended. Where were the people?

'*Ar-rêt-ons!*' came the Colonel's voice.

They stopped. 'Watering the horses, I'll be bound,' Bates observed to the Dean. Oldenberg scowled and did not reply.

Everybody clambered out and walked stiffly. When their legs were stretched, Bates, the Colonel and two other French officers stood in a semicircle watching the men affix nosebags.

Bates asked the Colonel about the vacancy of the countryside.

'The people, the *paysans*, they have departed,' was his reply.

'Why?'

'Fighting,' said Larroche. 'The war.'

'Fighting? Recent or long ago?'

'Recent.'

'So far south? I believed the French to have occupied and pacified the whole country to Derby – and further north than that, as well.'

The Colonel shrugged. 'Perhaps there are some *brigands*, some English soldiers who do not fight in the regular manner.'

'Brigands?' Bates felt an uncomfortable sensation trickle upwards along his spine. 'We'll not encounter them?'

The Colonel shrugged again. 'Possible,' he declared.

'Will there be fighting for us?'

The Dean, leaning out of the coach, barked: 'The soldiers, man, the soldiers. Why else would we be travelling with them?'

'Fighting?' Bates said again, plaintively.

'Fighting and killing too,' said the Dean.

Bates felt a lightness at his temples. Had he been broken in two at the waist and the blood drained from him he could not have felt more faint. Sweat shimmered out of him. His breathing was a wren's wingbeat.

He was going to be sick upon the floor.

He was going to fall into a faint. He sidestepped. His legs were losing their ability to brace themselves.

'Monsieur Bates?' the Colonel was saying. 'Monsieur? Are you unwell?'

'I must—' Bates said. 'Sit—'

Oh but this was terrible.

'Monsieur Bates?'

The blackness swooped, swirled around him. The bird that preyed on the souls of men, and carried them off to death. Death falling from the sky, as a comet come down to Earth. He felt the pressure of the earth under his buttocks, against his hands, waiting to swallow him up. It occurred to him only belatedly that he was on the ground. He must have sat down inadvertently.

'Monsieur Bates?' came the Colonel's voice, somehow muffled. 'I am concerned.'

'It will pass,' gasped Bates. 'A small – fit that has come over me. I cannot – perhaps some fever or – I assure you, this is uncharacteristic of me, I am not one given to—' But it was hard to force the words out; the incoming tide, as it were, of panic was too great, probing further inevitably inward and inward.

Behind him a horse coughed.

The noise was like a rifle shot to Bates. He manipulated his face with fingers that were trembling. 'My apologies,' he called, from behind the coach. 'Gentlemen . . . I apologise.'

They were staring at him. But why were they staring so?

'I,' he said, feeling his face heat with shame. 'I fear I am indisposed. I am a little feverish.'

'Monsieur,' said the Colonel.

'It is regrettable,' he said 'But I am sure it is the mildest of fevers—'

The Colonel took a deep breath. He sucked a great lungful of air into his lungs as if preparing to scream, as if about to yell at Bates. The sight was so disconcerting that Bates even moved back half a yard. The Colonel's mouth was open, as if a flock of black birds were about to swarm from the orifice, as if the panic shout of the god Pan himself were to issue from him.

The Colonel bellowed: '*Al*-lons!'

And the soldiers bestirred themselves, unhooked nosebags, trotted back to their positions, while the Dean stomped grumpily back to the carriage. As he passed a trembling Bates the Colonel murmured, not unkindly, 'Monsieur you have a *nose-bleed*. Monsieur you are bleeding *at the nose*.'

Bates brought the end of his finger up to his upper lip, and felt the warm moisture there. He was fumbling to get his handkerchief out of its narrow pocket as he made his way back to the carriage.

Back inside the carriage the Dean regarded him with a distaste so naked that Bates almost cowered. 'I am not in my best health, sir,' he said. The Dean grunted, folded his arms.

'I believe, sir,' said Bates, a growing pressure inside him, 'that a little rest will ah.' He was still dabbing at his nose with the now bloodied handkerchief. 'I am not myself – sir, I, sir, I, ah, ah,' and he sneezed. It was a huge sneeze, the release of some intense cranial tension that sprayed bloodied spittle everywhere.

'Sir!' barked the Dean. He fumbled for a kerchief and dragged it over his waistcoat front.

'Permit me to apologise again,' said Bates again, miserably, searching his pockets for his other kerchief. 'I am ill. I am abject. Please forgive me.'

But in reply the Dean merely leant back against his seat, and in a moment was asleep.

Bates stared through the carriage window as the procession rocked slowly along the road. His eyeballs felt hot as if candles planted on his jawbone were cooking them with insistent flame. His scalp itched. He tried to distract himself with the prospect out of the window, but there was nothing to see. The green hills lay low all the way to the horizon, making the distance seem an easy reach. Stone walls marked horizontals and verticals and slants across the green, dividing up the pasture like lines of stitching in green cloth. A table of green fields. Who had said so? Beautifully trimmed and laid green cloth, bright in the sun. A copse of trees, an irregular oval running up to the peak, gave the impression of a different sort of cloth: darker green, rougher, gathered into numerous little bunches like the tight bubbles of velvet upholstery.

But there was no sign of life.

He contemplated the episode at the watering-stop. He could not think what had happened. He could not think of it at all. Look out of the window.

There was something out of the window for him to see. But not yet.

Slowly the road brought them round the hill, and into a flatter stretch of land. Their way lay past a good-sized cottage, its red roof shining as if the building had been glazed and baked in an oven. The garden gate was open. Onion plants were growing in the kaleyard. Their leaves made elegant arcs over their flowerbed like giant green eyelashes. No smoke came from the chimney, and nobody came to the door to watch the passing of so many carriages and men.

A half an hour later Bates caught sight of a figure on the road ahead of them: a woman, dressed in mourning. She trod the road with the half-hearted step of the weary, and was carrying a small satchel. A baby was cradled in her arms.

At any rate, she was the first foot-traveller Bates had seen for days. He pulled down the carriage window with a crashing noise, and put his head out.

'Madam,' he called. 'Madam!'

She turned. Her face was beautiful: her hair tied back in such a way as to frame, like tethered curtains, the pure artwork of her features. Her eyes were opened, circular, not to startled or comical extremes, but ingenuous and beautiful. The O of her rosebud mouth was exactly the same size as her open eye. This is what first struck Bates: the precise balance of arrangement made by these three separate features in the whole of the visage, eye, eye, mouth. Everything else – the clarity and pallor of her skin, the regularity and sharp delicacy of her features, the manner in which her hair, though dark, seemed to soak up the morning sunlight – all this additional information, expressive of beauty, registered with him only subliminally. Afterwards he would recall the face as beautiful, but at that moment he was struck, with a combined sense of chivalrous alarm and a deeper, more visceral thrill of satisfaction; for he could see that the woman was afraid.

'I did not mean,' he called to her, 'to alarm you, Madam. Madam!'

The coach was bringing him closer to her. Her face, looking backwards over her shoulder, became larger. The fear he had thought he had seen resolved itself, as the picture became clearer and its details more distinct, into a questioning, even querulous expression.

'I only meant to ask a question, Madam! Are you from these parts?'

'I am not, sir,' she called back. Her voice was that of a gentlewoman.

As the coach drew level Bates could see that the quality of cloth in her mourning dress was high, silk pointed with damask. What he had taken for her baby was in fact a shilling loaf of bread, swaddled in a coarser grey cloth, carried like a sleeping being.

'I only ask, Madam,' Bates said, loudly, 'because the land is so deserted. A wilderness! I wondered if the population had fled some calamity – some battle . . .'

They were level with one another.

'I am not from this place,' said the woman, clearly. 'I am fleeing calamities from over to the west,' and she tossed her head in that direction. 'I had taken the emptiness in this country for a sort of safety. Is this the North Road?'

The coach was drawing away now, the woman's form receding. 'Calamities to the west?' asked Bates, his voice piping soprano suddenly.

'War birds,' said the woman. 'Battles, dead. Is this the North Road?'

'I believe so,' said Bates, clearing his throat to restore his manly tone. 'But, Madam, tell me of the battles in the west. Battles between the French and the English?' One of the draw-horses coughed noisily over these last words of Bates's.

'I could not hear you, sir.'

'War birds? Madam, what do you mean?'

But her figure was diminishing, and was soon nothing but a peg-sized mark against the green. Then the carriages rolled around a curve in the road and she vanished from sight.

Bates resumed his seat. His fever seemed to have abated somewhat.

'Woke me,' said the Dean, aiming a gooseberry-sour look at Bates, 'when you opened the damn window. Woke me!'

'My apologies, Dean,' said Bates, absently.

'Woke me,' the Dean muttered.

'I was speaking,' said Bates, a spurt of nausea in his torso, 'to a person upon the road who reported calamities to the west. Battles.'

'Calamities,' scoffed Oldenberg, as if the word were too tame to describe the dark reality of the cosmos, which he particularly understood. 'We are a nation at war, sir.'

'Of course, sir, of course.'

'There has been,' said Dean, 'a persistent comet. It portends no good fortune with it, such a star.'

'Persistent comet?' asked Bates, not paying full attention. His thoughts were on the beautiful young gentlewoman. Should he instruct the driver to turn about, retrieve her? She could travel in the carriage with them. Would the driver listen to a command from him? The Dean was talking.

'Indeed. As if the astronomers had not decided the orbits of cometary bodies fully last century! But this one seems to defy astronomy, sir. So they say. This new comet appears in the skies, and seems to *loiter* there in a manner quite impossible. It bodes no good at all.'

Soon, after applying more of his snuff, the Dean became much more well-mannered, not to say garrulous. He started to explain the nature of cometary orbits, the attractive impulse of the sun that carries them round in ellipses; the marvellous linkage between the angle of the ellipse and the speed of the comet, such that although the body will travel ten thousand miles an hour close to the sun and one thousand far away, yet if the ellipse be plotted and the wedges swept out by the orbit computed they will always be of the same area for the same time elapsed – the section swept out rapidly close to the sun wide and shallow, that one swept out far from the sun narrow but deep. But this new comet seemed to follow different rules, and the astronomers were troubled by the anomaly, for a theory that did not describe accurately *all* phenomena was no theory at all.

But Bates was feeling a new wave of nauseous illness sweep through the ecliptic of his wellbeing. He was not able to pay attention. Humming and nodding and widening his eyes on a random pattern that seemed to satisfy, or at least not to offend, the Dean's gabbling, his own thoughts were dragged inwards, sinking towards the black sun in his belly, a sort of anti-helios, emanating a corrosive, hot terror. He could feel the inevitability of battle, a miasma of pain and death, gathering all around him. It was unbearable, yet there was nothing to do but bear it – nowhere to escape to, no way to meet the terror head-on and defeat it.

[5]

From this point onwards his sense of reality degraded. The relentless, continuing sequence of events acquired a phantasmagoric, hallucinatory feel. It would not be precise to call this succession and supersuccession of imagery *dreamlike*, for Bates was struck on several occasions by how utterly unlike his experience of dreaming it was – how unvaried, how sharp and distinct in places, and yet how muffled about with a fog of exhaustion and unhappiness. Between this time, when the apes came over the hill, until such time as they were free on the North Road and coming into Scarborough, Bates abandoned all pretension to being an active partner in the real world. He became instead a sort of sponge, soaking up the experience as do clothes doused in the washtub, and then shuddering and twisting and agonised as those same clothes are when the washerwoman wrings them out.

Apes attacked. Monsters. Oh!

Then he experienced a snapping, some sort of breakdown, break-up, break*along* for all he could say. He was aware of it as it happened. He could not be unaware of it.

Battalions of apish demons.

His fever manifested itself as a vivid hallucination of gorillas swarming down upon them from the hills. He looked. There were a dozen of the beasts until such time as Bates looked again; and then there were hundreds. Warriors Achilles. A-kill-ease. Millions of them. A killion a million. They wore leather tunics, pleated with horizontal bands of stitching; they wore tall leather caps, not unlike a bishop's headpiece, on their black-hairy and hourglass-shaped heads, and these bonnets were tied under their great chins with buckles. As they galloped over the grass on legs and arms towards the road a great hullabaloo broke out amongst the French soldiers. Shots were fired. Sticks snapping in the heat of an open fire. Bates merely stared. The apes ran by. They planted their knuckles on the ground and swung their bodies and their legs pendulum-like between the two upright pillars made by their mighty arms. The pairs of knuckles hit the ground with a slightly missynchronised *tha-thad, tha-thad*. There were rifles tied to the creatures' backs. Behind them came men on horseback.

One ape lumbered close to the carriage, his great jaw slung low. The creature was displaying all his teeth, hideous embodiment of aggression – those monstrous, shark-sharp incisors, monumental jags of tapering ivory readying themselves to sink into Bates's flesh. Bates flinched. His poor, edible flesh. His suet flesh.

It was all a terrible fever-dream.

Bates pressed his forehead to the glass and closed his eyes tight. He waited for the vision to pass. But the sounds of battle continued to resonate, forcing themselves in at his ear, packing themselves into his tiny ear-canals and injecting their myriad little echoes and resonances into the centre of his head. It was a cacophonous symphony, with a choir of men's yells and shouts, and the timpani batter of guns firing, the violin whinnying of horses *(hhh*uo*hnnhhm)*, the scrape and drag of some counterpointed rhythm, the brassy yells of the apes, the snowbell tinkle of the harnesses, and then a hollow and distant boom, like a wide-chested man in the audience coughing a great consumptive cough.

Pain speckled Bates's face, but he did not open his eyes. He perspired. He felt ill, terribly ill. Make it go, Mamma. Take it off. He felt as if he were dying.

They were in motion. The carriage lurched and swung round to the right. He wished it would not. He wished it would stay still. He wished he were not so hot and ill.

Bates kept his eyes closed.

The Dean was saying something. Bates kept his eyes closed. There was a throb deep inside his head, pain plucking the cord at the very centre of his cranium, and that is where Bates put his attention.

'For the sake of all that is holy,' cried the Dean, gripping at Bates's arm. But there was a bellow of *pssha pssha*! from the coachman, very loud in Bates's ear, and the whole carriage shook and danced into motion. He was pressed back into the seat by the suddenness of the motion.

The Dean released him.

Bates felt the wind upon his face. He tried to absent himself, internally, he yearned for a swoon; but his consciousness clung stubbornly.

Shortly the coachman relented and the horses slowed to a stop.

Bates opened his eyes. The first thing he saw was that the glass in the coach window had been broken all to crumbs and was sprinkled about the seat and the floor. He put his head outside through the gap and saw the Dean standing on the grass, in gabbling conversation with the French coachman, a fellow who spoke no English. To the left was the third carriage, with its mysterious cargo; its two escorts sat on top like kings of the mountain, their rifles held in one hand.

Bates sat back, closed his eyes and tried to compose himself for sleep. He bethought himself of his breathing, which was forced and over-emphatic. By dint of putting his will into his own body he steadied his breathing, and made it regular. Sitting there eyelids shuttered against the world he found a curious pleasure in simply telling off the pulses of his own breathing. His eyeballs felt hot. He could not distinguish between the voices outside and the voices in his waking dream.

He did not know how much time passed.

Eventually he found the strength to clamber out of the carriage on wobbly legs. The woman was there, the same lady they had encountered earlier on the open road. She was standing beside the Dean. She was helping him communicate with the French soldier. She spoke French. A gentlewoman, a woman of quality.

The fresh air revived him a little, but he felt horribly feverish and ill in his head. His chest felt raw. The innards of his chest.

The sky was cloudy. The light was silver-bright.

The sound of the third carriage's approach broke the conversation. All turned to meet it; Larroche on the top and an uncertain sway to the passage of the thing, as if the axle were bent. It was making a surprisingly emphatic noise of grinding and skirling. When it reached them and arreted the reason for this noise became apparent – a dead horse was being dragged behind it on a makeshift sled, a stretch of tarpaulin roped to the back of the carriage; dragged through the dirt and over the stones of the road.

Larroche said something loud and quick in French. Bates's mind was jangled and he could not decipher the *français*. The Frankish. The Colonel was hopping nimbly down from the driver's seat, one of the men from the Computation Device coach hurrying over to him. The Dean, and then the woman, followed. Bates could not imagine why the carriage had been pulling a dead equine over the road in this fashion.

Unsteadily he made his way to the rear of the coach, where the Colonel was, it seemed, bowing to the head of the beast. But it appeared that the horse was not dead, although the many cuts and red chips in its hide, the little flows and spreads of dried blood over its musculature, indicated a creature badly injured.

'*Monsieur le cheval*,' Larroche was saying directly into the beast's ear. 'I can promise you little, but only this: that if you speak I shall do for you the *coup-de-grâce*. Do you understand?'

The horse's fat eyeballs rolled, the white rims of their bulging brown jelly showing like a border. His lips quivered, foamy with spittle, and pulled back to reveal two clumps of teeth, slab-shaped protrusions at the front of the elongated jaw. A tongue, black as a tadpole's tail, large as a boot, moved somewhere inside. The eye rotated and rotated, giving that impression of intense terror or insanity which only a horse's staring eyes can properly convey.

'*Monsieur le cheval*,' Larroche said again.

The tongue moved. 'Wait,' said the creature. Sapient horses were rarities, for they mostly resisted assimilation into the English army, a resistance that thwarted the traditional modes of horsebreaking even unto death. But some had been persuaded to join, for all that. Bates had never seen one before except from a distance. He had never heard one speak English. Their palates were ill suited to the language, and it required a special attention by the listener to understand the words. All was high-pitched and snickery, with vowels trilled upon like grace notes, and consonants formed by smacking the tongue against the side or roof of the mouth. Bates understood 'wait', but could not follow the sentence which followed.

'*Tu parles français?*' Larroche asked.

A meagre spring drizzle was coming down now, out of the grey sky, dotting upon the horse's flank and settling gently all about on the grass. The quality of the light was changing from blue-grey to grey-blue. It was colder.

Bates felt very unsteady upon his feet. He was not well. He was an ill man.

The breath heaved in the creature's vast hooped chest. It steamed out of the giant nostrils once, twice, three times, somewhere between breathing and coughing. 'I smpeak all the yahoo smpeech,' he said. '*Tous les langues.*' Or this is what he seemed to say. It was hard to be sure.

'My friend,' said Larroche. 'I am cavalry officer, and a friend of horse. Understand? I wish to hurt you. No, I wish *not* to hurt you – excuse me. *Parle-moi et la fin sera rapide, comprends?*' The horse said nothing. 'If not, and the soldiers will break your legs, break the four legs, and we will leave you here. Understand?'

The horse wheezed. 'Owing the Engri-i-i-iss no loyalty,' he said. The *t* of the last word was clicked again the beast's teeth by the tongue.

'Of course you do not,' agreed Larroche. He pulled a long-barrelled pistol from his jacket and rested the barrel against the creature's skull, just above the eye. A fat vein wriggled like a worm under its skin near that place. 'What loyalty should you owe *them*? Of course not.'

'The,' the beast said, and then pursed his flexible lips as if reaching for a tuft of grass, '*mmm*achi-i-ine. They seek it. *Il y a une grann-nne force la-bas.*'

'*Une grande force?* To the south?'

'*Oui, oui, oui, oui,*' said the horse. '*Cassez-pas mes jambes, s' it vous mplait.* A large force.' Uh larssh forssh.

'You have seen it?'

'*Ego ipse oculis meis vidi,*' said the horse, labouring over each word.

'They will attack?'

'We were to mdrive you south.'

'Drive us south? *Oui?*'

'*Oui, oui, oui, oui,*' said the horse.

'Then go we must north, *avancer, advancer,*' said Larroche, in a loud voice. 'This is a trap. Turn about the coaches, *rapidement, rapidement.* A trap – a much larger force awaits us to the south, *allons, allons.*'

He stood and pulled out his pistol. Without another word he fired a bullet through the spacious skull of the creature. One shot. Blood glooped up through the hole in a gush. The eyeballs jammed in their movement and were still. The chest ceased its motion. One of Larroche's men was already untying the beast's carcass from the rear of the coach.

Bates was staring at the dead creature. The hole, so much smaller and neater than the many other wounds on the beast's body, seemed insufficient to bring to an end so large a life.

'Back in the coach,' cried the Dean, bustling Bates towards the carriage once more. 'No time to delay my dear fellow.'

But as he stumbled back to the carriage Bates felt his grip on the cosmos loosen. He could barely make his legs work. His mind was full of worms that wriggled and squiggled. The Dean's head swelled like a balloon, and Bates's own hands felt ridiculously distant and absurdly fat.

The carriage bearing the Computational Device was now the second in train; the coach in which Bates sat shivering was the last. 'This makes us more vulnerable, I fear,' said the Dean, although it seemed he was not talking to Bates. It was not clear to whom he was talking. 'Vulnerable to attack,' came his words. They flapped in the air. They were bats. A kill ease. 'Attack from our own side, which is an unpleasant irony.' Bullets of iron, of copper and bronze, of gold and silver. Pigeons flying off to the left in great numbers. The Dean was talking but his words were now nothing but mew-mew and mow-mow.

Bates shuddered with cold. Or heat. He could not distinguish between hot and cold. He could not see properly. Everything swam. His seat, thin leather over wood, seemed to be convulsing, a sheet being shaken out by the washerwoman on a breezy day. Bates could not get comfortable.

'They'll not be able to keep the horses at this pace for long, I fear,' said the Dean.

Another voice spoke. Bates did not think it his own, but he could not be sure.

The wind was insistently pressing against his face. Bates was cold. Cold as a cape-bound whaler. Could they not do something about the wind? The wind was roasting him. Sirocco. A kill ease.

There was a cacophony, a mixture of human voices and the clanging barks of rifles all jumbled against the convulsive bang and thud and jangle of the hurrying carriage. Bates kept his eyes closed. There was a growl close in at his ear, and far behind it he heard the voice of the Dean crying 'Get thee *behind* me *sathanas*!' and another voice squealing. There was a stink of hot breath, doggy, in Bates's nostrils, but he did not open his eyes. The world seemed to rock more violently even than before. The hubbub reached a crescendo, a small sound growing smoothly into a great noise, like the guillotine's weighted blade sliding down its tracks; and then, like the guillotine climax, there was a loud thump. A crack. A howl, falling away and dying somewhere behind them. The wind on his face again. The carriage rocking less violently. A crowing *halloo* from the Dean.

At this moment, of all moments, Bates fell asleep.

A mighty giant, as huge above Brobdingnagian stature as a Brobdingnagian is above humanity, was stretching his arm across the sky. It reached all the way along the horizon. The cloth of his shift was muslin, great billowing white, stained a little purple on the underside. The sky was in danger. The giant was setting a flaming brand to a copse of trees on the western horizon. The whole world would burn. All of us – we insects. Insects!

The chuttery sound of pigeon wings in flight – fire. The world was alight.

The hawk of death dipped down towards him. No!

*

The horizon was not on fire. The sun was setting. Bates could hardly believe that so much had happened within the space of a single day. So much, in such a short space of time. And a war, he knew, was made up of many days, each one as crammed with death and incident as the day they had just experienced. But – then – he was falling asleep again.

When he woke it was to find the world dark. At first he could not decide whether this was due to fog or to the fall of night. The carriage was motionless. He tried to get up but his limbs revolted. Oh but he was thirsty! He was hideously thirsty, the innards of his mouth caked and dry and ridged like a lizard's hide. But he was alone in the coach. He tried to make his mouth function, but there was no co-ordination between his lungs and his tongue.

He was aware of a disjointed succession of *data mentata*. His environment, the infinitude of Lucretian atoms falling from their great height for ever and impinging upon his tender sensorium. People spoke to him but the words made no sense. Peculiar fantasies occupied all his mental energies. He had been elected Khan of China, but the role required him to sleep for a million cycles of the world, never again to wake. A Roc carried him away in its beak. He was converted, like Apuleius's donkey, into one of the sapient horses, and struggled to give voice to his needs. He saw the body of his unborn son dancing under the moon in a city graveyard where the tombstones stood thin as playing cards, his tiny naked body white as bone, skin taut as sinews, great dark eyes. The moon the colour and shape of those lunulae of pale horn at the base of a fingernail. The horns of the moon closed together like a bird's beak snapping shut on its prey. Then he saw desert, a wide red desert, and the red was the rude blush of Adam's flesh, yet the empty space was the kingdom of the moon.

It was a blur in his mind.

He slept again and woke to the foam-grey light of dawn. He fumbled about in the carriage and discovered a military water bottle, placed on the seat beside him – placed there, perhaps, for his own benefit. It was a strange test of his mental abilities to determine how the cap unscrewed, but once it was removed Bates drank messily, greedily, as if this metallic-tasting water were the very nectar of the gods.

He felt a griping in his guts and knew that a flux of the bowels was upon him. It was a task to get the door open, fumbling and panicky as he was, but he managed it and half-stepped, half-slid down to the ground. His breeches came free and he pulled them down just in time before the mess spewed from his rear. He was squatting next to the great wheel of the carriage, and he clasped one of the wooden spokes to steady himself. It was a position compounded of physical discomfort and indignity.

He did not remember finishing this function, or reascending to the carriage again, but he must have done so, for the next thing to loom out of the miasma of his thought was the sight of the Dean – a handkerchief at his mouth – sitting opposite him. The juggling shift of the seat must mean that they were in motion again. Bates tried to say something, but there were no words. There was somebody else in the carriage with them.

Fog again. The light at the open window flared day, muffled itself as night, Bates didn't know one from the other.

The carriage had stopped. Perhaps they were watering the horses.

Once again the flux of the bowels overcame Bates; he hurried outside and clung precariously to the carriage wheel as he squatted to empty himself. It was humiliating. The flow seemed never to come to an end.

He was back in the carriage. He was half asleep, and half awake; but these two halves did not add up to a complete experience.

And then, with a suddenness that surprised him even as he was experiencing it, the miasma cleared, the world resolved itself back into clarity, and Bates discovered himself blinking spasmodically and trying to control with a soggy handkerchief a seemingly ceaseless flow of watery phlegm out of his nose – like the rheum produced by a cold, except much more prodigious and apparently unceasing. He was outside. Larroche was standing in front of him, angling his head, asking a question. Bates had to exert his will deliberately to understand the words.

Where was he now?

He was standing outside, talking to Larroche. He could not remember how he had come to be in this posture.

'Monsieur Bates,' the Frenchman was saying. 'Not long ago you told me the English word for the material inside the meat of an animal, the lines, the threads. Please, tell me again. I regret, I have forgotten it. I am but a poor student, I am afraid.'

'The word?' said Bates, blinking, dabbing at his nose. Dabbing and redabbing.

'The threads, inside the meat. Such that inside Brobdingnagian meat they are large and coarse, and inside a *mouton* of France or England they are fine. Yes?'

'The fibres of the meat,' said Bates, with a sort of stunned slowness. Where was he? He looked about himself; the carriages, scraped, muddied and bullet-pocked, were standing beside a river. Further away men were working energetically at a wooden bridge, breaking planks from the balustrade at the bank's side to repair a gap in the middle of the span.

'Ah!' said the Colonel, his face broadening and smiling. 'Just so! The fibres of the meat.' He turned, and wandered off repeating, with a sort of heroic inconsequentiality, 'The *fibres* of the meat, the *fibres* of the meat.'

'Monsieur,' said Bates, still looking about him as if he had awoken in a strange land. 'I must apologise to you. I must apologise.' Who was he speaking to? To whom was he speaking? Nobody, nobody, nobody, nobody, nobody. He felt his bowels giving way within him and positively ran from the fellow. He zigzagged across a lawn, and jumped over a low loose-stone wall, where he barely got his breeches down in time.

The shame was hard to bear, hard even to acknowledge.

It was a sunny day, bright and fresh. Bates squatted for long minutes, taking in his surroundings.

Most of the dandelions growing in the lawn had lost their heads. A few preserved their spectral globes of smoke-coloured white, but most looked like pencils stabbed into the turf. Green sticks.

The spring sunlight threw sharp, dark shadows from the trees, hedges, and from the low stone wall to Bates's right. He was in a field where a number of cows grazed; one curious beast lumbered over to the wall, a dozen yards from Bates, perhaps to examine what the carriages were up to. Its preposterous head and brown-globe eyes stared with idiot intensity. Then it dropped its muzzle, as if drinking from the pool of shadow below the wall, to clench a mass of grass in its lips and wrench it away. Lips as agile and strong as grasping fingers. Grasping.

*

They were at a farmhouse, and had invoked military privilege to billet themselves there. The farmer, a pockmarked old fellow in a periwig, tolerated their presence with ill grace: but it meant at least that Bates had a bed in which to sleep. A marriage-bed indeed, which he was to share with the Dean.

'I'll trust you,' the Dean was saying, 'not to befoul the sheets in your sickness?'

'Of course,' said Bates, ashamed at himself. 'Naturally not. Of course not. I do apologise.'

'I feel bad for making *her* sleep in a servant's bed,' said the Dean. 'But we'd not have fitted the two of us in that little cot. And it's a more private space, up in the attic.'

'Her?'

'Her, sir?'

'Who, sir?'

'Mrs Burton, of course!'

'Ah,' said Bates, not knowing of whom the Dean was speaking.

The stars above us, the moral law within. Black sky threaded by the paths of stars. Each drew out a spaghetti-strand of light behind it. He could feel the cold, and see his own breath cresting, like wave-foam, bitter *aphros*, against the chill beach of night. Coming out of his mouth spectrally. He was looking up. Where was he? He did not know that, but he knew that the stars were birds, of a sort: for did they not move through the ether of space, pass with their tail-plumes spread behind them through the skies? Which star was the comet about which everybody was talking? He could not tell, unless it was that star there, smudged like a chalk dot upon a blackboard fingered and spread a little. Was that it?

Pigeons in all skies. Hawks chasing them.

Where was he? He did not know where he was.

And now he was conducting a calm and detail-laden conversation with the Dean. He was not sure how it began, or how it could be that this Abraham Bates was sitting opposite the ordained man in a dark space – darker wood, beams, a candle fizzing with light – an inn somewhere? No: he remembered, it was a farmhouse, he remembered. But how was it this Abraham Bates could speak so calmly, could act so normally, in this interlocution, this charade of speech? More puzzling still was the

Dean's ease of manner, as if there had been nothing unusual in Bates's behaviour in the previous however-many days.

'And the fact that a Brobdingnagian be twelve times as big as a man,' the Dean was saying.

'And a Lilliputian,' Bates was replying, nodding, 'one twelfth the size of a human being.'

'We might ask ourselves the significance of this number twelve. Twelve apostles, sir! Twelve pennies in the shilling! Now, attend to this. The Earth is twelve thousand, seven hundred and forty-two kilometres in diameter,' said the Dean. 'Jupiter is 152,904 kilometres in diameter. Do these figures mean nothing to you?'

'Nothing,' Bates conceded.

Oldenberg poufed air between his lips dismissively. 'Multiply 12,742 by twelve,' he said, 'and you will obtain 152,904. You will obtain *exactly* that figure.'

'You are saying that Jupiter is exactly twelve times as big as the Earth?'

'Twelve times the *diameter*,' the Dean stressed. 'Twelve times the diameter. Jupiter is not twelve times the *size*, to speak strictly. It is three hundred and twenty times the mass, two-and-a-half times the gravitational attraction, and so on. *But* there is a factor of twelve, yes-yes. Allow me to report the radius of Saturn, in kilometres.'

'Please do,' said Bates.

'One hundred and fifteen thousand, nine hundred and ninety-two. Multiplied by twelve, this number becomes 1,391,900. Now, the *precise* radius of the sun, our life-giver, is 1,391,900 kilometres. Saturn's radius is precisely one twelfth that of the sun.'

'Remarkable.'

'Is it not? How long does it take the Earth to orbit the sun?'

'A year.'

'And Jupiter? How long for it to orbit the sun?'

Bates turned his hands over to indicate his ignorance. 'Twelve years?' he hazarded.

'Precisely so! Twelve years. Four thousand three hundred and eighty of our days. But a Jupiterian day is nought point three-nine-five times the length of an Earth day ... excuse my use of *le système decimal*. We might say, Jupiter takes but nine and a half hours to turn on its enormous axis.'

'Dizzying,' said Bates.

'Indeed. And what if our year, our year of 365 days, were multiplied by this number, this 0.395? I will tell you: one hundred and forty-four. Twelve times twelve. Three hundred and sixty-five Jupiterian days is 144 earthly days – twelve times twelve! I am convinced that this number is of crucial significance to the cosmos. I am convinced that as I apply myself, I will be able to reduce all cosmic mathematical relations to this one number: twelve. Do you know that twelve is one times two times two times three? Four times three, two and two times three, two and two and two times two, it is the most harmonious of numbers.'

'A Lilliputian,' Bates said, nodding, 'is one twelfth the size of a human being.'

'And a Brobdingnagian twelve times as big as us,' agreed the Dean.

'You hold all these figures in your head, sir? I am most impressed.'

The Dean squinted modestly. But, Bates saw, he had his ledger-book on his lap.

'And *all* relations in our solar system can be understood as multiples of twelve?' Bates asked.

'As for that,' said the Dean, looking a little pained. 'It is hard to say. I trust that it is so; but to date my calculations have found the rule of twelve to apply particularly to the relationships between the sun, the Earth, Jupiter and Saturn. The remaining four planets do not, as yet, fit the pattern. I flatter myself that the sun, the two largest solar bodies and the Earth are, surely, the most important bodies in our system. But I will say more, to you, sir. Sir William Herschel discovered the furthest planet in the solar system fifty years ago, sir. He named it Ouranos. But astronomers insist that there must be yet a more distant body, a planet further out. The astronomers at the French Institute, messieurs Galle, LeVerrier and d'Arrest, peer into the heavens with their telescopes for this new planet. I make a prediction, sir: I say that this planet will be *twenty-four times* as far from the sun as is the Earth. If the distance between the Earth and the sun be taken as *one*, sir, then Jupiter is five and Saturn nine-and-a-half; do you see? Ouranos, it is difficult to measure, it being so very far away, but it seems it is sixteen times as far. The new planet, when it is discovered, will be twenty-four! This will be the last planet to be discovered, it will occupy that orbit around the sun most distant,' he said, with nodding emphasis. 'Of this I am sure. And it will draw a boundary to the dimensions of the cosmos, a boundary determined by the number twelve.'

Mrs Burton was that woman they had passed on the road.

There had been some attempt to ambush the party, presumably to seize the Calculation Device; a feint by a troop of yahoo infantry to drive the Frenchers south into the arms of a much larger army. But, confounding these plans, the Colonel had forced his little convoy north, breaking through the encirclement and pushing the horses almost to their deaths.

And now they hurried on, as if pursued by the very Devil. Larroche was no longer trusting to overnight stops in farmhouses or villages.

A comet ornamented the night sky like a brooch on black satin.

Events were beginning to coalesce in Bates's mind. It was returning health. There was a sensation of coming-together, as if mental fibres were knitting into place and restoring the *textus* of his consciousness. He was able to invoke that faculty that contradistinguishes people from things, memory, and plait together a narrative. They were travelling ever further northward. They had escaped an ambush by bandits – his own countrymen, forces opposing the French occupation. They had sought to seize the Computational Device, deploying forces of fierce yahoos.

He was in conversation with Eleanor. He could remember neither the commencement, nor the topic, of this exchange, except that he almost came to himself (as it were) in the midst of a sentence: 'And this has been my whole life's work, Mrs Burton. The work of my whole life.'

Eleanor waited politely for him to continue, but he was struck with the thought that he did not know *what* he had claimed, just a moment earlier, to be the work of his life. His confusion registered in his face, and after a difficult pause she prompted: 'Please go on, Mr Bates.'

Bates sat back. He looked around him. They were in a room; cedar-floored, oak-walled. The Dean was sitting in the corner, staring straight ahead.

'I beg your pardon?' he said, weakly.

'You were saying that philanthropy has been . . .'

The Dean spoke up. 'Is it not a solecism to call it philanthropy? If the Pacificans be anthropos then the word applies, but if not?'

'I have tried,' said Bates, feeling confused, 'to live a good life.' This sounded to his own ears as a lamentable boast, and he attempted to qualify it. 'I mean to say I have tried to do my duty. But, as with all of us, we must first discover what our duty is – what duty God has laid before us.'

'Very true,' said Eleanor, in a serious voice.

There were gaps in his memory. His health was certainly returning. He was no longer feverish, and no longer deranged in his mind. His body was, at worst, a little weak; but he could feel a fundamental health in his bones and in his blood. He could feel this in part because of the contrast with the way he had been feeling over the previous – days? Weeks? And his thought processes were whole again; his mind ran along its rails of cause–effect, he could think, he had not lost his mind. Once again, he knew this because of the contrast he sensed inside his own head with the spasmodic, heated, furious state he had recently known. He was healthy again, and sane.

Except that – he could not make his memory pull together the various patches of experience into a whole cloth. He could not remember, for instance, how it was that he had come to be sitting in the coach, bouncing and jigging along, with the sky through the little window red (dawn? or sunset?) in the midst of another conversation with Mrs Burton. He could not, indeed, remember at what point he had been introduced to her. And yet, he could see by the ease of exchange between them, her confident familiarity with him, that this was not the first time they had talked. He could see that they *had* been introduced; that they must have had a number of conventional, polite conversations about little; that over time they had become more comfortable with one another; and that now she regarded him as a confidant. But he could not remember any of the stages on this post-road. He smiled, to cover his confusion. He smiled.

'We are in dangerous territory,' said Eleanor. 'I was speaking with the Colonel. He confirms that the coast is *mostly* in the control of the French forces.'

'The coast,' Bates repeated.

'We make for Scarborough. It is a coastal town. It is a spa. For myself I have never travelled further north than Hampstead before in my life!' She laughed, and Bates laughed, in reflex imitation.

'Hampstead,' he said.

'I have been on the Continent, of course.'

'Of course.'

'Naturally,' she said. 'I asked the Colonel why we may not proceed along the coast road. He said that he judged this path safer. From which I deduce that the coast is not *altogether* under the command of *l'armée française..*'

'Scarborough,' said Bates again. He was aware, gazing at her, of her beauty; touched delicately, like a fine watercolour effect, by the ruddy light coming through the window, the pure curve of her jaw, her straight nose, her fine black eyes, her petal lips. Had he never been struck by her beauty before? How could he *not* have been?

'We have been compelled to make a wide detour, I fear,' Eleanor said. 'With many forced stops. It is the long road to the north.'

There was a grunt to Bates's right, a boar-like snuffle loud enough to make him jump in his seat. He had not noticed that the Dean was there also. 'Fie upon it all,' snapped Oldenberg.

'Dean,' chided Eleanor. 'Come now!'

'Fie I say,' he repeated. 'Dick Turpin rode from London, from the Charing Cross itself where he had tethered his horses – rode to *York* in a single *day*. A day!'

'But this was only in story,' said Eleanor.

'Or was it a day and a night? But he rode the whole way, on one horse, and arrived by the next day. And we must dally upon the same road a *week* – or more? And now we go to *Scarborough*? It is monstrous. It is insupportable.'

'It would be quite impossible for a horseman, howsoever determined, to make such a ride in such a space of time,' said Eleanor. 'Unless he were mounted upon Pegasus itself!'

'They assured me that York would be captured! But they have suffered unexpected military reverses, I suppose. Unexpected.'

There was a silence. Bates became more acutely aware of the rattle-chatter of the carriage's wheels upon the road. Beneath that continually percussive noise he could make out a moaning sound, the creaking of the wooden axles distorting under their weight, flexing and giving the weight up again. More distantly audible was the thrum of the horse's hoofs, and the chants and encouragements of the coachman, urging his team onwards.

'We must mount upon a Pegasus of our own,' said the Dean, in a newly sly voice. He leaned forward.

'You refer,' said Mrs Burton, 'to the explosive cannon?' This subject seemed to animate her.

'Of course I do. Your own father's gift to us.'

The fact that Bates remembered something was enough to spur him to speech. He was pleased merely by the fact of remembrance. 'David of each,' he said. 'I remember, Dean, you telling me of your partnership with him.'

There was a silence. It was a moment before Bates realised it was an awkward silence.

'Partnership,' said the Dean. 'Well, well, well. I was honoured, Mrs Burton, honoured to be able to assist your noble father in any respect at all.'

There was silence inside the carriage.

'Mrs Burton,' said Bates, after the silence had lengthened to a painful degree. 'I must confess – Dean. Mrs Burton, Mr Oldenberg. Will you favour me with your attention? Your counsel?'

'You mistake me, sir,' retorted the Dean, sourly.

'Mr Bates, please, please,' said Eleanor, placatingly, with an amused glance at Oldenberg. 'You'll forgive Henry, of course. He has been ill at sorts for these last hours.' The Dean harrumphed. 'If,' Mrs Burton continued, 'there is any way in which we can help, you have only to name it.'

'There are ... intermittencies,' Bates said, shortly. 'In my memory. I cannot recall, for example, how I come to be in the carriage, at this moment.'

'We are travelling north,' said Eleanor.

'Yes. And you ... ?'

'I was a poor exile, a Ruth amongst alien corn, and the Colonel has taken pity upon me. The Dean here very kindly intervened on my behalf. He convinced the Colonel that my facility with the language of France, and my relationship to the great Davidowic, meant that I should be accommodated. But the Colonel does not trust me, I fear. He suspects me of being a spy, perhaps.'

'Spy,' echoed Bates. 'How absurd!'

'Thank you, sir.'

The Dean fell into a slumber from which it did not seem possible to wake him. He snored like a gurgling drainhole. Sweat was on his brow, and his skin felt hot. He was clearly feverish. Perhaps, indeed, had passed into a form of trance. But Bates was more concerned by Eleanor. She sat forward on the bench, and then sat back; she sat forward and sat back. This repeated, almost automatic action, accompanied by the rustling of her dress as she moved, rasped on Bates's consciousness. There were studs of perspiration on her face, a hectic flush in vertical blotches up both her cheeks. Her eyes were filmed over with moisture; they shone like fruit that is waxed, but they did not seem to focus.

'Mrs Burton,' Bates asked. 'Are you quite well? Mrs Burton? Are you feeling in the least out of sorts?'

'Abraham,' she replied, in a choked voice. 'I am ill. I am unwell. I confess it.'

'My dear Mrs Burton,' said Bates, sitting forward and catching up her hand. 'Please be still a moment.' But the rocking went on, pulling away from the hand clenched in Bates's, heaving back in towards it again. The hand felt moist, as hot as lechery, and it slipped from Bates's grip.

'I am unwell, I am unwell,' she said. Then she began moaning, a low noise. To his revulsion, his profound self-disgust, the noise agitated Bates's sense of venery. His skin tingled. His body entered into those familiar and revolting physical alterations, those warm tightnesses underneath the grace of his clothing. How could he respond so at a time like this! To cover his despicable failure of character, he leaned out of the window and bellowed to the coachman to stop. He shouted the word in English. He yelled it in French.

The coach stopped and Bates struggled with the recalcitrant door, pushing and heaving until it gave way and he tumbled outside.

The air felt damp. The light was muted, sifted through several layers of white cloud.

The Colonel, leading the rear coach, was striding towards him. 'What is passing? Why have you called stop? Monsieur, talk to me about this question.'

'Mrs Burton is gravely ill,' said Bates, pulling himself up to his full height.

'Gravely ill?'

Bates nodded, tried to compose himself, and added: 'She's ill at any rate.'

'You yourself were gravely ill. Did this stop the carriage? Mr Bates, do not call such words as *stop* except unless it is an emergency. Do you understand?'

'But we must stop. We must find shelter. Mrs Burton has need of medical expertise.'

Larroche walked briskly to the open door of the carriage and looked inside. He exchanged some words with Eleanor in French, and walked back to Bates. 'She has a little sickness of the head. It is necessary that she remain in the carriage until we are to arrive at our destination. One further night, and one morning, and we will be to arrive at Scarborough. There is no possibility of any other thing.' He hurried to his own carriage. 'Inside, Monsieur, inside, and we must – go – *on!*'

Eleanor seemed to rally. She ceased her rocking, and sat instead wedged into the corner beside the door. Bates made his best effort to keep her spirits up with conversation, but her light was fading. There was a strange admixture of dread and excitement in Bates's heart. He permitted himself the liberty of laying his hand upon her brow once every quarter of an hour. More frequently would have been improper, although more is what he wanted: he was shamefully aware of the urge to sit next to his patient, to press his hand to the skin of her forehead, to take her tapering fingers in his own, to crush her whole body to his chest – a wicked desire made more deplorable by the fact that it seemed quickened by her incapacity. Manly self-restraint was absolutely required. And yet, he told himself, he could not permit his own weakness to result in the omission of any attention at all to Mrs Burton. She would for instance require water (from his water bottle, pressed to the miniature plumped cushions of her lips) despite being too ill to fetch it for herself. And a duty devolved upon him, surely, to check her temperature – in a calm, disinterested manner. Four times an hour would suffice. Less would derogate from his duty; more would stray into – impropriety.

The Dean, dead to the world in the opposite corner, was also sweating. Indeed, an unpleasant smell rose from his body; not the smell of night soil, nor yet of ordinary filth, but nevertheless a reek of some unpleasant decaying savour, perhaps the sweat itself: an off-cabbagey, faintly nauseous odour. Bates checked the fellow's temperature as well, making sure to do so four times an hour, as with Mrs Burton. Perhaps he did not loiter over this second patient quiet so much; but that (he told himself) was because the Dean, a man, could be expected to possess a constitution better able to resist the advance of the fever. Mrs Burton, on the other hand, was a woman. Frailer. Solicitude more needful in her case.

It grew dark. By intermittent moonlight through the broken carriage window Bates watched the progress of his patient. She moaned in her unconsciousness; occasionally she moved her hands, as if making the motions to fend off some too-intimate figure. Bates's own throat was dry. He coughed. He was forced to lick his own lips.

She was, he decided, trying to say something; but her voice was so low, and so broken, that he could not make out the words. But what if it were important? What if this were some crucial communication? It was his duty to – rise, kneel upon the shaking floor of the carriage, place his head close to her mouth. It was his *duty*. Turning his head to present his left ear to her lips, so that his eyes came close to her shoulder, to the line of her neck. Bates's own throat was dry again.

The murmur of her voice, like doves.

Bates could not decipher the—

'There is a *pestilence*!' shrieked the Dean.

Bates was so terrified that he could not hold back an equivalent shriek, a seizure of his own body that lurched him forward, the (delicious horror!) collision of his chest against Eleanor's as he tried, frantically, to stand up, to step away from her. The pressure of his own front against the yielding figure slumped on her seat. He almost leapt as he got to his feet, and he clacked his head against the roof of the carriage. That was a painful lump. 'I stand in for medical assistance,' he cried. 'I seek only to alleviate her suffering – my designs were—'

But the Dean was not addressing him. Moonlight shuddered into the tiny space and Bates could see his eyes were shut. Icicle dribbles of foam were pendant upon his wobbling lower lip. Both his fists were clenched tightly.

'Contagion!' he said, in a smaller voice, and then muttered fiercely and incoherently for long seconds. 'The bolts of Apollo upon the Greek forces at Troy!' he exclaimed. 'We are all suffering the contagion, for does the *Bible*! – the *Bible*! – does the Bible not say that contagion will destroy—' mutter, mutter, silence.

Bates, gingerly, settled himself back into his own seat. His heart was rattling as fast as the horse's hoofs striking the ground outside. His hands were trembling.

After a while he fell asleep himself; an uneasy slumber, the sort in which the sleeper is continually aware of the real world all about his sleeping form, like grit under the eyelid. The noises and movements of the waking world, even as he is immobilised by his own exhaustion. He woke with the window grey with dawn-light and feeling not in the least refreshed.

Matters inside the carriage were much worse. Mrs Burton, deeper in unconsciousness, had lost control of her own body. A stink, most rank and distressing, emanated from her side of the carriage. Bates found himself extraordinarily upset by this development. He was almost unmanned by how upset this simple fact made him. Clearly Mrs Burton was undergoing the same fever that had afflicted him, and was accordingly liable to the same physical lapses that he had experienced. But to think of her, so beautiful, so poised, suffering *such* disgrace touched on a monstrous injustice at the heart of things. Somebody would need to attend to her, clearly. Quite apart from the stench in the carriage there was the consideration of Mrs Burton's own feelings. A nurse, a *mercy-sister* as the Germans styled it, or perhaps some nun or mother, ought to be called at once. Bates could pull the Dean from the carriage and leave this notional saintly female to perform the necessary hygienic ablutions upon poor Eleanor. Was there no village, no town at which Larroche could stop the convoy to recruit such an individual?

Bates stuck his head out of the window, pushing his shoulders out too, and registering at first only the relief from the odour inside. The dawn air was cool, dew-scented, and a brightness was gathering behind the grey eastern clouds, like the pull of a bowstring readying to unleash the first shafts of the day. Sticking his head out was like plunging it in cold water. The road was smooth, and the coach rattled along gently.

Bates rotated his body so as to be facing the rear coach: Larroche was there, all muffled up on the driver's board; one of his men beside him made angler's motions with the reins.

'Colonel!' Bates cried. 'We have need of medical assistance! We must stop – we must find some sister of mercy to attend to Mrs Burton!'

There was no indication that Larroche had heard him. His body jiggled with the motion of the carriage but was otherwise unmoving. He might very well have been asleep behind his padded swathes of cloak and muffler.

Bates decided the matter must be decided at once. He started, awkwardly, rotating his body to bring his face a half-turn about, the better to be able to address the driver of his own coach. '*Monsieur!*' he bellowed. '*Monsieur! Attendez un moment—*'

But no sooner had his face became aligned with the direction of travel than a branch from a roadside hedgerow struck him *thouac!* across his visage. He yelped as if scalded, tried to haul his head back inside the coach, but succeeded only in knocking the back of his skull fiercely against the frame of the window. A second sprig, heavy with dew and evergreen foliage, smote his cheek like a cat-o'-nine-tails. With a second effort he managed to pull himself inside the coach again.

His face sparkled with pain. He sat himself down, and began to explore the damage with his fingers' ends. None of them came away bloody; but his cheeks, his nose and lips, throbbed savagely. There must be weals. He might very well be disfigured! O indignity!

His pain transmuted, following the natural logic of these things, into rage at the coachman for driving the carriage so close to the hedgerow; and then, less obviously, rage at Mrs Burton herself for allowing her own disgrace and so precipitating the entire episode. Bates bethought himself that *he* had at least managed to hold his soil until he could exit the carriage. Why could she not? It was a typical woman's weakness, and he, in a gentlemanly desire to help without disgracing her, had received this punishment for his pains! Well, he concluded, folding his arms and pressing himself into the corner of his seat, she could arrange for her own lavation. He would try no more foolish schemes of that sort. He had learned his lesson.

After a while, however, his rage abated. It was, he found himself thinking, ungentlemanly of him to blame Mrs Burton for something quite outside her power to control – something of which, when she awoke, she would most certainly be mortified and ashamed. He must do something before she awoke. There would be no shame in his helping a lady in such a manner; he would not take any prurient interest in her private corporeality; he would adopt a disinterested and medical frame of mind. And yet, at the mere thought of his intervention, a cockstand manifested itself, and he was aware again of that roiling in his lower gut – not nausea, but excitement; the twinkling and buzzing in his own torso. He was gripped in between the congress of good and evil – the aspirations of his own little soul were continually being defiled by his rattish and verminous body with its revolting folds of pink flesh. The cankerous and grasping flesh. He despised himself.

'The doves of Apollo!' the Dean shouted suddenly. Once again it made Bates twitch. He wished the old fool would stop doing that, yelling suddenly out of the blue. Bates went over to him.

Foam was bubbling in the corner of the Dean's mouth, and the lips were working as if to say something more. There was a series of moans, then some inaudible mutterings, then another cry: 'They spread the poison, the pestilence, the *pesti*poison!' Here – most startlingly of all – the Dean opened his eyes, looked straight ahead, sneezed, and then went back to sleep. Or back into his coma.

'Dean?' Bates asked, tentative. But the man was once again dead to the world.

Bates half-dozed, his head jogging to the rhythm of the carriage's movement. Half-dozed. Three-quarters-dozed. He felt his eyelids rolling down, felt the miniature pressure of their motion upon his eyeball. Eleven-twelfths-dozed.

He woke with a jolt and sat straight up. They were no longer in motion. Larroche must be resting his horses.

Bates tumbled from the carriage and found the first man he could, asking him in poor French for water – a bowl – a towel. He tried to explain Mrs Burton's situation, but the expression was beyond him.

They had stopped in a village, beside a post-house on the high road. The horses were unharnessed: four of them were drinking at a long stone trough and the other two waited, shivering their flanks and fidgeting their heads up and down. Sweat stood up in bands along the creatures' flanks, like strands of tinsel in the morning light. Larroche was there, producing, like a conjuror, enormous balls of smoke from the tiny bowl of his pipe.

'Colonel! I must request from you the implements of washing. Mrs Burton has – suffered an unfortunate consequence of her sickness. There has been a soiling. There is night-soil within the coach.'

Larroche took his pipe from his mouth. 'Indeed?' he asked, with a puzzled expression.

'It is hard to convey to you,' said Bates, feeling his frustration keenly, 'the precise nature of Mrs Burton's accident without bringing obloquy upon her name. I beg you to remember that she is a gentlewoman. I would ask you not to press me on this matter. Can you find a nurse, or some other woman in this village who could be pressed to perform a merciful service for Mrs Burton? Before, I mean to say, she wakes up? She must be washed; preferably washed such that she never discover her physical lapse.'

'A woman?' asked Larroche, still looking puzzled. 'A nurse?'

'Dammit man,' said Bates, boiling over suddenly (for he was not given to swearing), 'can you not understand the delicate situation I am in? It should not be too hard a matter to find some woman in this village capable of performing acts of hygiene for a sister in need!'

'Look about this town, Monsieur,' said Larroche, replacing his pipe.

Bates did as he was bid. The details of the street now impressed themselves upon him as they had not done at first. There was a long façade of housing on the far side of the street, all the dwellings built from suitcase-sized blocks of grey stone and all roofed in slate. Every one of the windows of these houses was cracked, every single pane broken open by star-shaped and maple-leaf-shaped holes. Several of the doors were gone. Chipped indentations and areas of smoke-blackening were visible all the way along. On the near side of the street were a succession of larger, detached houses, including the inn at which they had stopped, and from whose water trough the horses were now slurping. There was similar damage here: inn, town hall, wealthy house, all battered and spotted with damage. A little way further along the street a tangle of nerveless limbs and a sack-like torso. A corpse, like litter, abandoned in a doorway like litter.

Death.

Over his head a bird scurried through the air on its chilly wings. It was gone.

'There has been fighting here,' Bates said, stupidly. The Colonel did not reply. But of course there could be no nurse discovered here. Well then, he must sort it out himself. He felt a draught of resolve pass through him. He must do it now! He would steel himself, carry that cross, and clean the lady up himself. It would be, in its own way, an offer at the altar of her purity.

He took a metal bowl from the back of the front coach, something borrowed from a soldier's pack, and filled it at the trough. With this and his own handkerchief, he clambered back into the carriage.

His first thought was to remove the Dean from the small space, for the practical reason that there was very little elbow-room as it was, and also for the more specific reason of propriety. The old man was unconscious, it was true; but what if he woke up? He had opened his eyes a few hours before. It would make Bates much less uncomfortable if the Dean could be moved outside. But, after placing the brimming bowl on the seat and tucking his handkerchief away, he found it harder to shift the corpulent figure than he had thought it would be. He tried several times to get a point of leverage under the Dean's arms, but without success. Then he dismounted from the carriage, went around to the far side, opened the door, and tried again. He could, he decided, simply pull the old man down, but then he might very well fall upon his head, and – who knew? – injure himself. Better perhaps to leave him where he was. He closed the far door, returned to his side of the carriage and climbed back inside.

On a sudden inspiration he searched the Dean's slow-breathing body for a handkerchief, and, finding one, he placed it carefully over his face. Should his eyes open, as they had before, this screen would prevent even the possibility of him glimpsing anything improper. Prompted by this to another thought, Bates once more climbed out of the carriage and sought out the French soldiers – all standing in a group beside the horses.

'*Tout le monde n'approche pas,*' he instructed them. '*Ne venez pas. Dans la, eh, carriage-là je vais laver une femme, une gentilfemme*' (he paused, unsure that this last was truly a French word, but he could think of none better), '*et je ne veux pas être interrupté. Comprenez?*' The soldiers, as one, looked at him as if he were a crazy man. Piqued, he wished them ill fortune in English, using a mild tone and a smile to disguise the insult.

He returned to the carriage.

He could prevaricate no longer. This thing must be done. He positioned himself opposite Mrs Burton and took a deep breath. The stink came in with the air; but despite this noisome stimulus, and despite his efforts to place his mind in a pure state prior to acting, he felt physical arousal stir between his legs. It was too much!

He needed to get the action over with, finished, complete. With clumsiness born of sheer haste he grasped Mrs Burton's shoulder and pushed her down upon the seat, so that she was lying on her left side, her legs still reaching to the floor of the compartment. Then, trying simultaneously not to look down but also to get his bearings, he raised up her dress to her thighs. A broad mess of brownness ran on the inside of the fabric, from side to side, from the top of the skirt to the hem. At those places where Eleanor's legs had been in contact with this mess the skin was crusted and daubed with the same effluvium. Bates felt the gag in his throat, as if his Adam's-apple had swollen and blocked his airway. Such foulness. He raised the dress further, and found a pair of cotton pantey-shorts, stained and soaked through with the revolting semi-liquid proctal release. The matter had squirted right past the thigh-hems of this garment, and to some degree had oozed through the weave of the fabric itself, like whey draining though cheesecloth. He slid reluctant fingers in at the top of these panteys and tried to manoeuvre them down Mrs Burton's legs. They stuck, they would not slide. He pulled harder, wincing at the slippery feel of their innards, but still they would not move past the place where their wearer was lying against the seat. But they must come off. Off they *must* come. He must, he saw, wash them wholesale in the trough outside. He gave a firmer pull, and at once they ripped and came free, the stitching pulled clean away. Mrs Burton's body shuddered and nearly rolled from the seat – Bates put out his left hand to prevent this, and touched her bosom. He recoiled at once, but there were tears in his eyes, mixed from frustration and revulsion and also from the awareness that this hideous corporeal stink and slipperiness was rousing his manhood to a painful degree. He extracted the slopping undergarment and almost bolted from the carriage with it.

Outside, in the fresh air, he found himself almost gasping. The befouled garment went dunkers into the trough, for the horses had finished their drinking and were now cropping the grass that grew on a patch of land between the inn and the adjacent building. Bates put his hands into the chill water and rubbed the cloth against itself to loosen its dirt, all the time wondering why it was that God had designed his creatures such that a clear application of willpower *could not* override physical manifestations of lust. Wouldn't it be better if the mind could trump the body in this regard? Wouldn't that make the difference between lechers and pure-minded men easier to maintain? Had the Devil wormed his way into the nature of human will itself?

He got a good deal of foul matter off the fabric of the undergarment, and examined it. A brown stain marked the threads in a wide oval. That could not be washed out by mere water. But this was the best Bates could do at this moment. The stitching was all gone from one side, giving the flap of cloth a strange fattened M shape. But perhaps a little needlework would restore that. Worse was the realisation that Mrs Burton would now for know certain her body had been handled in this intimate manner. Of course, Bates considered, she would probably have been able to deduce that anyway. But this made it imperative he prepare himself. What would he tell her? Why not (the idea launched itself in his mind) tell her that they *had indeed* found a nurse, a woman, in this village? A white lie to spare Eleanor's blushes. The nursemaid had ripped the underclothing, which was regrettable; but she had performed the necessary ablutions. Bates (he spun the tale a little) had carried the Dean out of the carriage and waited whilst this saintly woman – this old woman – had performed the necessary ablutions.

Examining the undergarment, Bates realised that he was going to be obliged to remove the whole of Mrs Burton's dress. It could not be cleaned piecemeal. It would have been better had the dress been wholly thrown out and a new one substituted for it. But Eleanor had no luggage. Bates toyed with the idea of searching one or more of the abandoned houses for such a garments, but the practical difficulty of finding a dress of the correct size was forbidding (how could he know what the right size was?). And there were also the moral difficulties: for in effect that would be to steal the dress. Should he then become a thief? Truly? No: better to *remove* the dress, *wash* it, and then dress Eleanor in it again.

Remove and *wash* and—

Cleanness. O–Peal!

He returned to the carriage and positioned himself opposite Miss Burton. It took several deep breaths before he felt steeled enough to proceed.

He began by hauling up the dress as far as he could, bunching it around Mrs Burton's waist, and trying not to stare at the curves of whiteness thus revealed. Then he pulled her body into an upright sitting position, and gathered the far side of the dress too. From here it was a relatively easy matter to pull her sleeves over her arms and tug the whole garment over her head. She was wearing no corset beneath, but she did have on a cotton shift – some small quantity of foul matter brushed from the inside of the dress onto this undergarment, but it was not too bad. A little more had got itself caught up in her hair. He would deal with that in a moment. Her skin was extraordinarily soft.

No.

He bundled the dress into a ball with the dirt inward, and turned his attention to cleaning the soil from Mrs Burton's epidermis. Laying her down carefully on her side once more, he dipped his kerchief in the water bowl and rubbed up and down her thigh. Several times he was forced to change position because the tightness of his membrum virile made his position uncomfortable. He tried not to think of that. He tried to turn his mind elsewhere. He imagined that Mrs Burton was a baby – a giant baby, to be sure; say a Brobdingnagian baby – which had soiled itself and needed changing. But this thought did not quench the intensity, or alleviate the dirty-pleasurable sensation in his own loins. He rinsed the kerchief, wrung it out and went to work again. It was necessary to shift Mrs Burton's body a little, such that her rear quarters be angled in a slightly more upward posture. He closed his eyes. It was too much. With his left hand he touched the globular shape of the left thigh-cheek, and brought his handkerchief-holding right hand to bear on that point. But, in a way, doing this with one's eyes closed was worse than otherwise. It meant that he found himself visualising, imagining, a far more voluptuous process. The thing to do was *not think* of the beauteous smooth curve of the female body, but only to think of the filth he was cleaning from its surface. To think no deeper than the surface. He opened his eyes, rinsed the kerchief again. Turning back he kept his eyes open, but tried with all his might to think only of the filth, not to think of the woman upon which the filth was so lamentably encrusted. To think of a job, to work as an automaton. To think (he stroked the kerchief over the right gluteal muscle) of the filth, not the woman, not her skin. Satin. His cockstand was, if anything, growing more fiercely rigid. But not to think of that. Think only of the dirt – he could not even smell it any more. The smell had acquired innocuousness through ubiquity. He was an automaton, not a man. He was thinking only of the filth. It was necessary to clean that point where Mrs Burton's two naked thighs, pressed close together by her posture, tucked into the crease at the base of her posterior. It was dirty here. This must be cleaned. And, pressing the kerchief home and wiping straight down in a firm motion, Bates felt the twist of his own trowser catch and rub across the head of his deplorable, hateful cockstand and, unable to prevent himself, he cried out in mingled frustration and release as a half-strangled emission burst, a sweet-painful leakage from his loins, a hot and loose phlegm inside his clothes.

He flung himself backwards, and his spine banged noisily against the wooden back of his seat. His eyes were wide. His hand, holding the soiled handkerchief, was trembling violently. His tried to calm his agitated breathing.

He gasped. Fish on the bank. Fish.

Long indrawn breath. His first instinct was to look to Mrs Burton herself – her face, its cheek pressed against the wooden seat, her eyes closed, a globule of saliva bulging from the side of her mouth. She had seen nothing. She had noticed nothing, she was unconscious. He looked at the Dean. The handkerchief on his face quivered slightly, pulled into slight concavity at the mouth and then puffed out as the old man breathed. *He* had seen nothing either. Bates's seed was already clammy against his skin, inside his trowser. Foul. Foulness. He washed and wrung out the handkerchief with jittery hands, the water now quite brown, the cloth irremediably stained. There was nothing for it. He wore no undergarments himself, and he did not want any stain to seep through from the inside. Furtively he unbuttoned the top of his breeches and pushed the kerchief inside to mop up the gluey stuff. How perfectly revolting. How perfectly so. He rebuttoned himself, and washed the handkerchief once more. For some reason his thoughts shrank themselves down wholly to that metal bowl filled with dirty water. Eleanor's wastage, the foul badge of her sickness. Dark. Dark and ill-smelling. His own seminal emission, pale and odourless; the two together mingling in this bowl.

He needed to take control of himself. It was for impulses such as this that medieval ascetics had mortified their own flesh. He understood the impulse to thrash oneself with nettles, or exile oneself to the top of a tall pillar in the desert for decades. But he must get on. He wanted the whole job completed now; he wanted it behind him. He felt nothing but revulsion for the whole process – immerded as he was becoming, with specks and streaks of her filth upon his hands, his sleeves. He wished he had never started. Why could he not have left her to sort herself out? What business had it been of his? *Post emissionem omne animal triste.*

He mopped up the remainder of her right leg as best he could; and then, somewhat roughly, repositioned her, sitting her up and then leaning her against the wall to make her left leg accessible to the handkerchief. Then he decided he had finished. Much of the filth had been cleared away, although he had not been able to remove the sepia-wash of yellow-brown that stained her legs. But he had done as much as he could. That would have to do.

He climbed down from the carriage one final time and carried the bundled dress to the trough. In it went, its upper side seeming to resist the water until Bates pushed it down, held it firmly below the water-level as if he were drowning it. He inverted the dress under the water, and saw granules and flakes of brown detach themselves from the weave. Oh, foul. He shuddered at the thought of his hands touching that disgusting matter. He could never again converse with Mrs Burton.

How could he? How could he look at her face without immediately recalling this shameful scene, this knowledge? He resolved, as soon as he had finished, to beg a place in the forward coach: to swap, if necessary, his inside seat with one of the outdoor places.

When he had finished as far as he judged possible he pulled the massy weight of cloth out from the trough, trailing its splashing tendrils of water. He did his best to wring this onerous mass by hand, but it was hard. Eventually he opened it up and draped it from one of the stone windowsills at the front of the deserted inn. He stood back as another problem presented itself. The air was cool, the spring sun bright but distant. It seemed unlikely that the dress would dry. How long to leave it? If he squeezed Mrs Burton back inside a wet dress, cold and clammy, might she not catch a chill? Added to her current fever this could be a fatal development. Yet she could not be left as she was – nude from the waist down, and with only the flimsiest undergarment protecting her torso.

He stalked off to find the soldiers and Colonel Larroche, to demand that they light a fire at which the dress might more efficiently be dried. Or perhaps they had already kindled a fire for their own purposes? But there was no fire: the *soldats* were behind the third carriage, some asleep on the ground wrapped in their blankets, others sitting and playing cards. Larroche looked up as the Englishman came into view, but Bates could think of no way of explaining his dilemma.

He came back to the dress. His mood was a compound of dark fury, self loathing and a grapeshot hatred of everything – of humanity, especially the female half; of the cosmos; of war and Lilliputians and everything. He fingered the cloth of the dress. It was soaked through and through.

He compared, in his mind, the picture of what he had hoped to achieve with the reality of his present situation. He had thought of Mrs Burton awaking from her fever, as a girl might do from an afternoon nap, to find herself in clean dry clothes, with no knowledge and no need to know of her disgrace. The reality was merely a stained and inadequately cleaned dress, the material filled like a sponge with ice-water. The reality was a gentlewoman stripped and left naked in the carriage. Bates sniffed. Oh he had meant well, but, oh, circumstance had conspired against him.

Suddenly, without warning or comprehension, Bates began to sob.

*

The Colonel found him. 'Monsieur,' he said. 'Weep not. You must not weep. For what is the cause?'

'I do not know, Colonel,' Bates said, struggling with his sobs. 'I feel I have been upon the road these seven years at least. It is a Purgatory. I climb the map of England as a mountain-climber clambers up an endless mountain. It is as though north were truly up into the sky.' He drew a deep breath and pinned back his tears to their internal source. 'I apologise, sir,' he said.

'Ah,' replied the Colonel, with a twinkle in his eye. 'But who may climb into the sky?'

'I do not know,' said Bates.

'Tomorrow, Monsieur Bates,' said Larroche, pronouncing the name beets. 'We shall arrive at Scarborough, where the *Sophrosyne* is anchored. The *Sophrosyne* is a handsome frigate, my sir, with a steam wheel and also with sails. There are many soldiers there, and a barricade across two main roads, in-road, out-road. There is a gun that fires, boum-boum, one hundred blows in a minute.' He grinned.

Bates, as he listened to this, was aware chiefly of the sensation of foolishness for having wept in front of this man.

'Monsieur,' said Bates, his heart suddenly thumping in his chest like a colt's kicking hind leg. 'I discover within myself . . . a tender passion for Mrs Burton.' He surprised himself as he spoke these words, for he had not realised how true they were – or even that they were true at all – until they emerged from his mouth. But once spoken, before a witness, a gentleman and military officer (though French), Bates knew that he had in effect given voice to a contract. He had promised himself; committed his heart.

'So,' said the Colonel, meditatively. 'Therefore you cry?'

'Therefore?'

'You are – *amoureux*. The word in English is?'

'Loving,' said Bates, blushing.

'And therefore you cry?'

'Perhaps so,' said Bates. He rubbed his face with the palms of his cold hands. 'But I must return her dress to her. It is as clean as I can manage. I must re-dress her.'

At this, Larroche looked puzzled. 'Redress?' he asked.

Bates said: 'Place her dress, her garment, upon her again,' and reached out for the garment. But it was icy cold and still wet as seaweed. This would never do. To put such clothing upon Mrs Burton's naked skin would surely chill her – certainly make her ill. Perhaps kill her. This would never do.

Bates thought of her now, suddenly, as his future wife. To marry her, to marry her. This was fated. He saw that only by marrying, and devoting himself to her, would he be enabled to atone for what he had seen – for the indignities that pure woman had been compelled to endure. He would make her his wife.

And it was as he was standing there, next to the placid Colonel, contemplating which of the deserted houses he should first explore with a view to obtaining clean and dry clothing for Eleanor, that the first of several screams sounded from inside the carriage.

Mrs Burton was not to be mollified. She insisted her dress be brought to her, and nothing Bates could say – no matter how abjectly he apologised, or how much he explained how very wet and cold the cloth was – could dissuade her. She opened the carriage door just enough to permit the handing over of this bundle of water logged fabric, and then closed it again. A few moments later she opened the door again and emerged, fully dressed, crimson in face yet shivering vigorously all over her body. 'I shall die,' she said, through the impediment of chattering teeth, 'but perhaps this is the only way to purge my shame.'

Bates tried again to explain. 'Mrs Burton please accept my most sincere ...'

'An outrage, sir!' she exclaimed noisily. 'Colonel! Colonel! Might I oblige you to light a fire?'

The Colonel bowed, without taking the pipe from his mouth.

Bates, however, grovelled like a fawning courtier. 'Mrs Burton, I am more sorry than I can say, I beg of you to hear me when I say I merely wished ...'

'You will favour me,' she snapped, imperiously, 'with your *silence* sir. I have no wish to *hear* you sir. Or to *see* you sir.' Her limbs trembled like a religious Shaker, as if a fit were upon her. 'Colonel!'

She disappeared behind the third carriage. Bates reflected with absolutely misery that she preferred the company of half a dozen common soldiers, of the lowest possible morals, to himself – a gentleman and Englishman.

They were delayed for an hour or more, whilst the soldiers lit a fire, and whilst Eleanor dried herself beside it as best she could. Then, when

Larroche insisted that they could tarry no longer, she remounted the second carriage wrapped in a horseblanket. When Bates stood at the door she closed the door in his face, and through the window instructed him that he might ride postillion – or stay where he was, for all she cared. Never in his life had Bates seen a woman possessed of so overwhelming and so barely contained a fury.

'I shall ride postillion,' he said, in a low and heartfelt voice, 'and cast myself into the river as we pass it to rid the world of my abject person.'

'Good,' replied Eleanor.

And that was that.

Bates himself had no blanket as the carriage rode through the chill spring countryside, and eventually down the hill towards the sea. But he embraced discomfort. Down the hill to the sea. The Northern Sea, grey as fog and flattened under the hammer of Thor to a dimpled and arcing plate. The town of Scarborough lay down the valley towards the sea, and blocked out the north and south upon the seafront. And down they went.

[7]

Here was the seafront at Scarborough. Here he was.

Bates felt as if they had passed halfway round the world, and through every manner of obstacle and hardship, only to arrive at this banal place. A ten-league sickle of sand and sea the colour of cabbage. A wind both chill and penetrating, blowing straight up from the lowest circle of Hell where the gigantic corpus of Satan himself is frozen in ice.

Here was the seafront at Scarborough.

There was at least, he acknowledged, something new in his experience of misery. His usual and familiar despair was contentless, causeless, the simple reflex of his existence. But now his despair possessed a kernel, the scorn of the woman he loved. The more she rebuked him with her eyes, with the turn of her shoulders away from him, with the arctic precision of her politeness towards him, the more hopelessly in love he fell. His usual despair, he reflected, had been an empty stomach compared with this powerful indigestive depression of spirits. This was not a fact that recommended the latter experience to him.

How he loved her! If he could have sacrificed his life to win the merest word of forgiveness – the slightest smile – he would have done so.

It was hopeless, hopeless. He was Young Werther. He bore a Brobdingnagian burden of sorrow within his human-sized breast.

There were many rusty-looking crabs upon the beach, in amongst the shingles and the seaweed and the patches of dirty-looking sand. A seagull slid through the air towards Bates on a line to collide with his face, and Bates flinched. At the last minute the creature wagged its wings and soared up, away behind him.

Very many crabs. The crabs on the beach were performing an elaborate crustacean *dansa flamenco*. Their attention was wholly on one another. The animals went into the ark seven each of cleanly ones and two-by-two of unclean ones. Bates's blood seemed to have quickened, to be moving faster round his body, making him feel distantly drunk. There was an impetuous itch inside his heart.

Little waves on the sea's fringe, rising slowly on the long approach to the shore and then curling over at the last minute as if wincing at the touch of land.

The white-painted wood of a railing, against which Bates leaned. Merely that white painted lattice of wood: but when the sun came from behind a cloud and the light strengthened so powerfully the fence seemed, somehow, naked and splendid. Bates's eye was caught by the lodestone tug of the sky. Blue and white. He stared. Stared. Half an hour passed, or an hour, or more. The last clouds slid away from the sky, apologetic, and the heavens were cerulean blue.

Here were voices, behind him. He turned, and touched his hat as a party of young men and women strolled past. Two men in linen suits and white hats; two women in more elaborate costumes, each carrying a coloured parasol, a green one, a purple one. As if the war were not happening. In their own country, within a few dozen miles of this very place. Bates ducked his head politely, and smiled. In that group they were talking amongst themselves. That group paid him no mind. Facing away from the sea, the sun's warmth lay across Bates's neck. The suddenness of the apparition, people crowding him momently, raised his heartbeat; but soon they were receding, walking further along the promenade. Bates thought to himself, I carry the misery of love inside me, like a baby in my stomach. It will soon come to term.

He watched the woman carrying the green parasol as she strolled away.

The scalloped edge of a green umbrella taking a bite out of the blue sky.

Larroche had billeted his troops in a seafront hotel, a luxurious establishment that was, despite the war, crowded with English pleasure-seekers. A lean Yorkshireman had been ejected from a suite of rooms on the top storey, together with his woolsack-shaped wife and seven squealing piglet children. He had complained forcefully at this eventuality, declared that he would go to law for redress against these occupiers. But the Colonel had stood by impassive, smoking the whole time.

Mrs Burton had been given a small room of her own – a maid's room, the Colonel apologised, but had not the liberty to grant her a larger space. The eight men shared the remaining two rooms. The Dean had been carried and deposited in one of the beds, and there he remained, snoring and feverous hot and never waking. He was fed on milk through a clyster-pipe. Bates slept in the floor beside him wrapped in a quilted blanket from the hotel's store. Two French soldiers slept in the same space. The Colonel and his three remaining men took the other room.

Nothing happened.

Bates disposed of his days merely walking, walking about the town. It surprised him that a human heart could endure so much misery and yet not plain explode. Expire. He felt surprise, a *dull* surprise, on still being alive every morning he awoke. The cardiac muscle was a tougher fabric than he realised, but it was also much more completely provided with tender nervous tissue than he had ever had previous cause to note.

He walked through the days. He watched the crabs tangling with one another on the shore, or inching their way through the seaweed.

By the room's window, tucked away to the left, was a wasp's nest. A wasp's nest. A wasp's nest, a curiously confected habitation. He looked closely at it, where the beasts had chewed up and laid down myriad filigree curls of grey paper, each sheet wrapped with roseate complexity about its inner. The nest was the size of Bates's head. The nest was full of huzzing and thorn-tailed insects, angry-sounding and beady. Bates's own head was filled with wasps, and they gave him no rest, they woke him in the dark hours of the night with pain. *O full of scorpions is my mind dear* – Shakspeare, of course.

He disposed of his days by walking about the town, up on the hill, down by the sea.

He saw a party of four Johnny d'arms patrolling the promenade. Out in the bay a frigate floated at anchor; its sails rolled away into cloth cylinders tucked underneath the spars of its masts, water smacking noisily against its wooden flanks and against the paddles of its half-submerged steam-wheel. The French warship *Sophrosyne*.

He disposed of his days by walking about the town, up on the hill, down by the sea.

Should he destroy himself? Hurl himself into the sea, fashion his own quietus? Thereby to end the chronic sorrow in his heart? To live or not to live?

Shakspeare, of course.

He pondered, and found his only disincentive was fear, and he was fearful only of the wrath of God himself. What if drowning, or jabbing at his own throat with the whetted razor, or taking a pistol to his aching chest – what if this prolonged his agony eternally? Hellfire, and the bitterness of the privation of God's grace. That must feel like this – feel like the privation of the love of Eleanor.

He caught a glimpse of her one afternoon, coming into the hotel as she came out. He swung his steps swiftly to the left and buried his face against the wall, so that she could walk past without needing to avert her furious face from his.

At night a polite commotion ran through the hotel. The comet was visible above, very distinct in the night sky. People hurried from the salon, from the restaurant, out from their rooms, crowding out at the hotel's front, spilling down the wooden steps onto the street. All faces were angled upwards.

Bates went with the throng. He was a little drunk. Bates went with the throng. He had been drinking port wine in the salon with the Colonel. He stumbled to his feet in the excitement at the commotion. 'I have not yet seen the comet,' he told the Colonel, his words blurry with drink. 'Nor I neither,' called the Colonel, separated from him already by several people. 'Nor I neither!'

Outside the sky was a dark purple colour, and seemed to Bates's drink-affected sensibilities almost to throb. A few clouds were laid upon the horizon, dark-grey against the black-purple sky behind. But overhead there was nothing but pure night sky, and four hundred thousand stars like scintillations, and there, in the zenith, the comet itself. People cooed and people gasped as if they were at a display of fireworks, although the comet of course did nothing but lie there, motionless. How cold it looked.

'Was there not,' Larroche asked him, his lips patting on the stem of his pipe, 'such an omen before the invasion of Guilliam of Normandy, and the death of your King Hastings?'

'King Harold,' said Bates, without paying attention.

The comet was preternaturally clear, vivid, a sharp white colour. Its head was tiny, no bigger than any other bright star, but its tail stretched back an impressive distance, a narrow-apexed triangle of misty white. It looked, to Bates's eyes, like an icicle hanging horizontally in the sky.

'Magnificent!' cooed the Colonel. '*Magnifique!*'

But it was hardly that.

The comet, the colour of a blanched summer's-day cloud amongst all that dark, looked stuck. It looked frozen in place. Bates took a step back, his face still up, reeled as his heel struck the stair, and nearly fell. 'Just to sit,' he muttered, to nobody in particular. 'Just sit down for a brief space, you know.' He lowered himself unsteadily into the wooden step. Stuck.

The Colonel walked over to him, comradely, and sat beside him. 'Is it superb?' he said. 'I think it is.' He was extracting his pipe from his tunic pocket.

At the far side of the crowd somebody squealed. Bates watched the Vitus-dance twitching of somebody, their arms up. Who is that? Are they having a fit? The figure jerked, and danced closer. 'A bat!' came a woman's voice. 'Ugh – ugh – ugh!'

'A moth, my dear,' came a gentleman's voice, basso profundo.

'A bat!'

'No!'

'No!'

'No!'

'No,' echoed Bates, so quietly that only he could hear.

'It *was* a bat,' insisted the woman, hurrying now for the stairs as fast as her skirts allowed her. Her shoes hit the wooden boards with a manly clatter. 'There are bats *everywhere*.'

194

Bates looked around, half-expecting to see the night air filled with the creatures, but there was nothing to see. The woman hurried up the stairs and into the hotel, directly past Bates, causing the stair on which he sat to shudder. A moment later the man stomped up the stair, calling after her: 'Miss Laney! Miss Laney!'

Boorish, really. Boorish behaviour.

The crowd, its attention half-distracted, watched the little drama.

'It amazes me,' said Bates, not for the first time, 'that so many holidaygoers could devote their energies to leisure at a time such as this! Wartime, my dear Colonel.' The port wine encouraged him to intimacy.

Larroche shrugged. 'Mr Bates,' he said. 'I fear I am unhealthy. Is this the way?'

'The way?'

'The way of saying it?'

'I do not agree sir, as to your unhealthiness. You are a military man in full command of his physical faculties.'

There was a papery quality to the Colonel's skin. But perhaps that was merely an effect of the lighting. Gas lamps inside the hotel. Papery. The head carefully, the head *delicately* (we might say) fashioned from the busy-bee chewing and chewing of the chewing wasps. If Bates reached up with his fat forefinger, he could push it right through the right cheek, just there: it would collapse, hollow, and with loud dry buzzing out would pour a stream of angry wasps. No, no, no.

'No,' said Bates.

'I do not mean this,' said Larroche. The sweat beads were so tiny on his forehead as to look like the very tips of silver bristles.

'You mean to say you are unwell?'

'I mean to say.'

'That you are unwell?'

'That I am unwell.'

'I am sorry to hear it,' said Bates. 'Is it the flux in the bowels? Perhaps you have caught this from—' He trailed off.

'Unwell,' said Larroche, fixing the word in his vocabulary. 'Unwell, unwell. Unwell.'

'You should go to bed,' said Bates, firmly.

'Unwell, unwell, unwell,' said the Colonel, getting slowly to his feet. 'Unwell, unwell, unwell.'

*

They awaited orders, or so the Colonel told them. Those orders might be to evacuate the town aboard the *Sophrosyne* if the attacking forces came too close, and if it seemed that the calculating machine might fall into enemy hands. But equally those orders might be to press on to York, and deliver the device, and the Dean, to the ordnance located there. The machine was all-in-all important, too important to risk falling into enemy hands. So they were awaiting.

The dilemma was what to do on those few occasions when Bates encountered Mrs Burton. This was a delicate matter. Given the circumstances it was inevitable that, from time to time, they would encounter one another. The first three or four times this happened Bates bowed his unhatted head and looked at the floor to give the lady time to float past without having to acknowledge his existence. How he loved her! Love without hope.

He might have thought that hope was the life's-blood of love, and that a love perfectly drained of hope such as his would be listless and weak. But the contrary was true. The hope had been replaced by quicklime and it burned in the tubules and chambers of his innards. He thought of her at all times. As he walked about the town he wondered what she was doing, with whom she was passing her time.

It was in the nature of his love that he lacked all restraint and composure. In her presence he was too cowed to express himself; but with all other people he met he was immoderate. He confessed his love to the French soldiery in clumsy *fron-say*. Talking to Larroche he found himself close to tears on more than one occasion. Strangers would utter the expected and polite forms required by civilised exchange, and Bates would presume upon this as if it were an intimacy to confess – to confess.

He lacked the ability to control himself.

His shame was insurmountable, woven into his love. The stink of bodily waste aroused him. He settled himself upon the jakes in the morning and voided his own bowels, and the stench of his own matter excited him. He repulsed himself. Yet the stench caused his member to stiffen, and he saw remembered glimpses, projected upon his inner eye, of her softness, her perfect whiteness, the tucked-in curve of a forearm.

Oh!

And then he could no longer gain access to the jakes, because the space was always occupied. The Colonel was in there with the flux in the bowels, or one of this men was there with the same sickness. They had caught it upon the coach ride, presumably; and now they suffered as Bates had himself. He was forced to walk up the steepness of Scarborough town and into the woods, like a peasant or a wild animal. But this humiliation he accepted, because he deserved nothing better. He hid himself away.

The weather was changeable, some days warm and blue, otherwise cloudy and prone to chill. Bates lay in bed, and this was his thought: that he must test himself against the chance of battle. Then, if God were as disgusted with him as he was with himself, he could hand over his life, pay his debt of death, and leave the agony behind.

His choices were two: he could abscond, take one of his daily walks and not turn back, walk on into the countryside until he encountered the English irregulars, and offer himself as a recruit. Or he could ask the Colonel to take him under orders, and fight for the French. His patriotism debated with his understanding.

A sky of mackerel blue. Bates woke and his dream was—

The Dean is awake; bellowing. The ship has gone. The soldiers are dying. The sound of artillery. The sound of artillery.

The sound—

In the room behind him the Dean had fallen quiet. He pulled himself upright in the bed, and called for water. 'The jug and glass are beside you,' said Bates without looking round.

'Damnable thirst.'

'Can you not hear the sound of cannon?'

'Perhaps it is the last trump,' rasped the Dean. 'Where is my snuff?'

'I do not know.'

'My snuff!' barked the Dean.

Bates's mind was not on the Dean. He had to reach Mrs Burton, but of course it was out of the question that he approach her. She was in her room, on the top floor of the hotel; and this is where she had stayed, and would stay. He stood in the hall in his breeches, his shirt untucked, and tried to fight the urge to hurry up the stairs to her. It was, he told himself, to make sure that she was alright; but she would not thank him for it. The—

BOUM!

—the Colonel, perhaps, could approach her. But now that the town was under bombardment from cannon it must be time to evacuate, to leave, *partir*, upon the *Sophrosyne*. Surely?

He hurried down the stairs. He saw nobody else, as if the hotel were deserted. But of course it was not deserted. It was filled with soldiers, citizens; most rooms were occupied by two or three people. So where were they all? Had none of them heard the great drumbeats of gunfire?

He tripped on the landing, and recovered his footing. Here was the place, and he fell to beating with his knuckles on the Colonel's door. Through a small window the sky was visible, blue as innocence itself. But there was no mistaking the sound of the cannonade. It did not match the —

He rapped his knuckles once, twice, and then, exactly consonant with the third,

BOUM!

—as if he were a mighty devil from Milton's Hell hammering upon a door ten leagues high. Bates raised his fist to his face, at the ridiculousness of it. But there was no time to waste! The Colonel was not answering. Mrs Burton was in danger. He turned the handle, and discovered the door unlocked.

Inside was a drawn-curtain dimness, and an unpleasantly yeasty smell, behind which pressed an ungainly combination of rotten fruit and tobacco. It took a moment for the reflex of the eye to adjust to the levels of light, and then Bates saw the Colonel in bed: lying on his back and smoking his pipe. His pipe stood perfectly vertical, just as Larroche's body lay perfectly horizontal, and both were as motionless as if mortise-and-tenoned out of wood.

'Colonel!' Bates called, from the door. And then, because the sepulchral feel of the darkened room made such volume seem impertinent, he spoke again in a lower tone: 'Colonel! Can you not hear the sound of the cannons? They are shelling the town. It is, I suppose, the English, and they are shelling the town.'

He stood waiting for the military man's reply. A single sheet of sunlight, thin as paper but broad and tall and slant from the edge of the curtain down upon the floor, picked out the atoms of dust in the air of the room. The Colonel lay perfectly contemplative.

There was a squeal, almost musical, and then another *BOUM!*

'Colonel,' urged Bates, starting forward and rather afraid of the sangfroid of a man who could lie quietly in bed whilst gunpowder and metal poured down from the sky all around him. 'We must ensure the safety of Mrs Burton.'

He reached the edge of Larroche's bed, and stood for a moment. It was apparent now – it had been apparent since he opened the door, although he had not absorbed the reality – that the Colonel was dead. He lay as if carved. Even the lines and tucks of the sheet, tucked over his chest and under his arms, possessed a sculptural solidity. Standing over him, Bates looked down blankly at the expression on his face: a taut open-eyed tension, made more alarming by the fact that the lips were pulled back and his teeth, biting so tightly on the stem of the pipe that they dented the ivory of the mouthpiece, seemed picked out, every tooth, in preternatural detail.

Bates moved his gaze to the table beside the bed. On it rested a glass, half-empty and with a skein of dust lying on the circular surface of the water. Beside this was a Bible, in French, and a leather pouch around which many threads of tobacco, like brown lint, were scattered.

For a time Bates simply stared at this scene. Then there was another detonation (*BOUM!*), louder and so closer, and he gave a little yelp and hurried from the scene.

Outside, on the landing again, Bates looked upon a scene completely changed from what he had seen only moments before. French soldiers rushed up and down the carpeted stairs; somebody was screaming orders in French, and all the doors were open: scared or bewildered civilian faces peered out. A (*BOUM!*) petty officer pushed past Bates and into Larroche's room, only to emerge moments later in a disordered state, calling something in French in a high-pitched voice.

Bates slunk up the stairway towards his room. Inside the Dean – for the first time in more than a week – was on his feet. He had been (*BOUM!*) brought to the window by the sounds of cannonfire. No, he was at the window because that was where the chest of drawers was, and he was rifling energetically through the drawers, muttering: 'It must be in here, unless 'tis stolen.'

'Dean,' said Bates. 'The town is under attack!'

He did not look around.

'Dean, I have just come from the Colonel's room,' Bates added, 'and he is dead. I am sorry to say it, he is dead.'

'Thieving Frenchmen!' cried the Dean, pulling the top-drawer out entire so that it crashed upon the floor.

*

But there was nothing to do. Bates went among the hurrying French and attempted to report the death of Larroche. Eventually he found an officer who seemed to be the senior man in the town's established garrison, but he spoke little English, and Bates could not be certain that he had conveyed the information.

A troop of a dozen soldiers jogged in formation up the main street. In the opposite direction came three carts, one horse-drawn, the others dragged by weary-looking men – old men, woollen-tunicked and exhausted. On these carts were piled furniture and belongings and children in apparent jumble. All the well-dressed holidaymen and holidaywomen of Scarborough were on the streets too, watching this toing and froing. The sound of cannonades continued, less frequently, and seemingly without effect.

In the bay the *Sophrosyne* squirted white smoke from its square portholes, one, then another. The sound of the cannon came a moment later, and corresponded with a piglet's squeal through the air over Bates's head. He felt a panic, a rush in his breast, and started back towards the hotel. There was singing. He heard high-pitched singing, but the chatter in the streets and the chomp of soldier's boots on the cobbles and the knocks and crashes of cannonades swallowed most of the words. But it was hymn singing:

> *—that with this tincture for thy sake*
> *does not grow—*

and behind the carts was a long line of children, herded down the street by a Dame, and singing hymns. Bates thought: I must reach Eleanor. His mind was wholly taken by that thought. I must reach Eleanor.

[8]

The Dean's lack of snuff drove him wild, and for a day and a night he could not be tamed. His room was wrecked.

The cannonade did not last into the night; and the following day dawned quiet – save only that the streets outside were now busy with people, driven from the outskirts of the town to the seafront by fighting. They camped along the pavements, and tried to beg food from any passing figure. Bates was too alarmed to leave the hotel.

But the following day the street was cleared by a battalion of French soldiery, the citizens hurried along the seafront and south. It was quiet once again. Indeed, the hotel was so quiet that Bates found it disconcerting. An unsatisfactory conversation with a French soldier revealed the fact that all the English guests had been ejected from the place – all save the Dean, Eleanor and himself. Bates assumed that this was to provide space to billet the French soldiers, but none had yet been moved into the house.

Bates spent the day sitting downstairs in the salon and reading – idly, agitatedly, his attention not wholly on the words – through the selection of books.

Eleanor stood in the doorway.

Bates stood up hurriedly. 'Mrs Burton!' he said. 'How glad I am to see you well!'

She looked at him, and her look made no concealment of her repulsion. 'Mr Bates,' she said, tipping her head forward a fraction. She turned and left.

Bates's heart thundered and chugged.

Something very shameful had happened to Bates, something so revolting that he barely admitted it to himself. He became strenuously and urgently aroused, carnally aroused, at the smell of faecal matter. To sit in the water closet and unloose his bowels brought him a cockstand so tight it was painful. To walk the streets and take in his nose the odour of filth – from the gutter, or an alley; from horses or humans, it mattered not – brought his membrum virile to attention. And at the same time there flashed upon his inner eye, which is the taunt of conscience, an image of Eleanor. Her face so pure, so beautiful, her virtue so unmistakable! How could it be connected in his revolting imagination with the stench of foulness, so? It was the devil, the devil, it was the devil; and not the grand Devil of Milton and St John, not the mighty Brobdingnagian beast wielding a trident the size of a Norway pine; but a foul devil, a petty devil, a devil of dirt and degradation.

A short, black-bearded French officer – Bates was unsure of his rank, or name – came in upon him in the salon. He was attended by several figures; his bearing was of a man of importance.

'There are battles to the west,' he said, without preliminary, speaking even as Bates got to his feet. 'We must remove yourself, and the others.'

'Yes,' said Bates, his coward's heart speeding.

'Colonel Larroche's orders are my responsibility now,' said the officer. 'But I must care also for my men. I do not know the disposition of you English – you three.'

'I am Abraham Bates, said Bates. 'I am—'

'We are to put you upon the *Sophrosyne*, a ship,' said the officer. 'That is my decision. Yourself, and the lady ...'

'Mrs Eleanor Burton.'

'She. You, her, and also her husband.'

'She is a widow.'

'Her,' said the officer, 'fiancé.'

'No, sir, you misunderstand. I call her Mrs, as you would say Madame, but her husband is dead, *mort*. She has no fiancé.'

'He must be accommodated also,' said the officer, with a blank expression.

'You have misunderstood ...' said Bates again, but the officer continued talking.

'But there is a problem with the *Sophrosyne*,' he announced.

'Problem?'

'Certainly. The *Sophrosyne* refuses to take you.'

'Refuses?'

'Certainly. They have orders to take you. They have the highest orders.'

'Why, then,' asked Bates, 'do they refuse?'

The officer made a great Gallic flourish with his right hand, as if tracing out a hieroglyph. 'They are fearful of the pest,' he said, in a scornful voice.

'Pest? What is the pest?'

'Forgive me. The contagion. The contagion.'

'It claimed,' said Bates, with a flurry of fear and thrill in his belly, 'the life of Colonel Larroche.'

'And many more,' said the officer. 'They maintain quarantine, aboard the *Sophrosyne*. But we shall move you and the lady and her husband aboard, and the *Sophrosyne* shall take you far from here. These are my orders.'

'Thank you, sir,' said Bates, feeling an unbecoming rush of gratitude. 'But the lady has no husband.'

'Husband in the future,' said the officer, turning his back and leading his aides-de-camp out of the salon.

The misunderstanding piqued Bates, because – and he possessed enough self-knowledge to realise this – it gave voice to his own secret yearning. He was a gentleman. Despite everything that had happened to him, and all that he had done, he remained a gentleman. Mrs Burton was a gentlewoman, respectably widowed. What stood in the way of their marriage? One unfortunate incident, in which Bates had – stupidly, foolishly, absurdly – attempted to act as nursemaid. But once Eleanor forgave him that – as she *must* forgive him that for she must come to see that he had been acting in the interest of her decency – then what else could prevent their union?

He loved her.

He dreamed of her, he loved her.

He got onto his knees every night, like a schoolboy, and prayed to God to deliver Eleanor to him as his wife.

And some days he began to believe that his prayer was being answered. She might exchange a few words with him in an almost friendly manner. And other days she was chilly and distant, as if he revolted her. As well he might!

The following day was Sunday, and there was a renewal of bombardment, although it lasted only a half-hour. In the afternoon, Bates walked along the promenade. Along the sweep of the coast, to the south, he could see that many of the ordinary people, expelled from the centre of town, had set up a gypsy community further along the beach. Seagulls swooped and dived over the sheeted carts and squatting folk. French soldiers patrolled the promenade.

Bates watched as a longboat rowed out to the *Sophrosyne*. A dozen Johnny d'arms sat in rank of three inside the boat, and the black-bearded officer at the helm. The boat pulled alongside, but no ladder was lowered to it. The officer conducted a long exchange with somebody on deck; distance and breeze obscured the words, but Bates could guess at them. The boat lowered its oars again and rowed back to the shore, having embarked none of its passengers.

Bates wandered to the quay, but guards did not permit him to come close enough to greet the bearded officer. Instead he watched as the fellow bustled up the stone flags and away across the street, surrounded by his men. His face was bright red with rage. Bates was struck by how very red the skin above his beard was. He looked, in fact, as if he were suffering from a scarlet fever.

The Dean, having exhausted his supply of snuff, and unable to obtain a resupply, sulked in his room. He could not be talked with. Bates spent most of his time in the salon.

'Good morning, Mrs Burton,' he said, as they met at the foot of the stairs.

'Good morning,' she replied, coldly.

They were supplied with military bread and watered wine for breakfast and luncheon; and they dined in the early evening in the mess with French officers.

'Mrs Burton,' said Bates, summoning all his courage. 'There is something I must communicate to you.'

'I beg you to permit me to go out, Mr Bates', she replied. 'We must hold over your conversation to another time.'

'Of course,' he murmured.

She left. He wondered: How to begin? How to reach her? But he could not find an answer in his own restless soul.

And then, miraculously, there came a day when Eleanor smiled upon him. His heart leapt up. It was afternoon, and a bright day. 'Shall we walk together, Mr Bates? Shall we look upon the sea?'

'Yes,' he said. 'Yes!'

Prayers are sometimes answered, you know.

And so they walked. The sunlight tapped brightly at every wave-peak, and nuggets of brilliance were broadcast over a wide stretch of sea. The sky! That sky!

'We are prisoners,' said Eleanor.

'And yet,' said Bates, 'we may use our time profitably, perhaps.'

She did not look at him, but her voice was not unkind. 'How have you been using your time, sir?'

'I have been considering questions of what Aristotle calls *ethics*,' he said. It was his way of stepping slyly up to the reason for the breach that had occurred between them.

'How so, sir?'

Bates asked Eleanor: 'Do you consider that there are atoms *of morality*, as there are physical atoms, atoms of materiality? I speak of elemental *units* of moral behaviour or belief? Perhaps some great immoral act – as, say, murder – is composed of many small immoral acts, accumulated perhaps over time, such that this small act of neglect to another human, or this act of positive cruelty to an insect, cat or horse, with myriad other similars, might not eventually add to a great sin?'

'I had not considered it by that light, sir,' she replied.

'My thoughts,' he said, 'have been perhaps preoccupied with this matter. But I do not wish to tire you with my reflections.'

'Moral philosophy could never bore or tire me, sir,' she said, and she appeared to speak earnestly, truly. 'Please: continue with what you were saying.'

His heart stood straight up. In his wishes they were already married, and were walking husband and wife. 'Because, you see,' he said, eagerly, 'I cannot otherwise understand why one act may be better or worse than another. Without some form of atomism, surely all sins are the same sins, venal and mortal together?'

'It may be,' she said in a low voice, as if this too were a matter she had pondered long, 'that thus it appears to God, *sub specie eternitus.*'

He did not correct her Latin. It was good enough woman's Latin. 'Indeed,' he said, instead. 'Indeed, there are theologians who consider it such. For a child to steal an apple from an orchard is wrong, and the boy should be beaten to teach him that theft cannot be countenanced. But it is common sense that to steal an apple is not so severe a sin as to murder a man. Or a thousand men. To murder a thousand must be worse than to murder one, and to murder one must be worse than stealing an apple. To hang a man for murder is just; but to send a boy to his death for stealing an apple would be unjust.'

She nodded. She was, he was flattered to see, paying very close attention to his words.

'And yet,' he continued, 'it was for the theft of an apple that the human race entire was sent to its death. For this is what the infallible Bible tells us.'

'It is a mystery,' she said. And then, at once: 'I do not mean the term in its trivial sense.'

'*Mysterium tremendum,*' he said, nodding. How exactly their thoughts fitted together! How alike they were! And his heart swept his blood through his limbs and chest and head with a faster thrum. Oh, he loved her. That word, that *amor*, so soiled with use, so readily found in every mouth, was intarnishable. More, more, *amor*. It shone anew in his heart, the truth of it, the force of it. How well suited they would have been! If only – if only—

They were returning now, along the deserted promenade and towards the hotel. They did not walk arm-in-arm, but neither did they walk at too great a remove from one another. Eleanor was genuinely interested in what Bates had to say; indeed, had he realised how profoundly it might well have jangled Bates's nerves. It was the subject. The subject involved her.

'Yet it would be insupportable,' she said, 'for morality to be established on a merely aleatory basis – as if it were mere chance that determined whether a thing be good or bad. Who could bear to live in such a cosmos?'

'I have so often thought so!' he urged. 'This must be so. In the Arabian Nights, which – have you read the Arabian Nights, Mrs Bates?'

'I have not much savour for romances,' she said.

'And I neither, Madam. But I remember reading as a child and being very struck by one tale.'

They mounted the steps of the hotel and passed into the entrance hall, the sudden gloom framing his tale; from heat and light and into shadow. From the sight-devouring brightness of the desert, and onto the narrow streets of some Eastern city, under the arch, into the shade. 'A merchant, pausing on his road to Medina,' he said, 'stopped by a well to eat dates. He devoured each date and threw the stone down into the well. And then a monstrous genie arose from the well, crying that he *must kill* the merchant, for one of the date-stones had put out the eye of that same genie's son. Did the merchant deserve the genie's wrath? And I believe that this tale touches a profound human fear, that punishment and reward, that goodness and sin – the very bedrock of sentient human life – might be as ... random as this. To throw a date-stone down a well, a death sentence!'

'But this from the East,' said Eleanor. 'Can we take lessons in morality from the East? A pasha might murder his sons and be praised for it. A woman might be condemned to death for walking with her head uncovered.'

They took two seats in the hotel's empty salon: tall-backed leather chairs with two great lapels rising on each side, and curled to inset balls of wood upon which the hands naturally came to rest. The tall alcove windows gleamed with day's brightness, deepening the gloom of the rest of the room. It was wholly empty. It smelt vaguely of the previous night's tobacco.

They sat in silence for a moment, and then Bates spoke again.

'My belief, Mrs Burton,' he said, sonorously, putting the palms of his hands together in front of his face as if in prayer, 'is that some manner of *moral atomism* must be at the heart of God's cosmos. Perhaps acts of carelessness or omission, like casting aside a date-stone, as the *components* of acts of larger commission, such as murder.'

She went very quiet at this. He felt a rush of recklessness, like a blush, pass up his chest and neck. Without giving himself time to reconsider he plunged on.

'If you'll permit me to explain my own circumstances, Mrs Burton, and without in the least wishing to stray into impropriety – although – although it might be said that sin is by its very nature a matter of impropriety.' She had stiffened in her chair, and her face looked blank. But what now? Did he dare unclothe his soul? 'But I have *tried*,' he said, ashamed of the tentativeness in his own voice, 'tried to *do good* in the world. And if I have tried, Madam, I say this through no desire to vaunt myself, but out of the understanding that the desire to do good in the world is the very least duty to which all Christians must subscribe. I have tried, for instance, to help the enslaved Pacificans: the Lilliputian and Brobdingnagian creatures, out of a conviction that slavery is immoral. But many of my best intentions have gone astray, Mrs Burton. And perhaps, I now think, such small smuts or grits of sin, as my own selfishness, my weakness of purpose, or my ... my ...' he was thinking of his fleshly indiscretion with Mary the tobacconist's daughter, but of course it was impossible to mention such a thing to Mrs Burton. Impossible even to approach the whole sordid, terrible topic of such liaisons. Why did that thought even come to him, at *this* time? What perversity was there in his soul? 'My weaknesses of the flesh ...' he said, vaguely, and was assaulted suddenly with the fear that she would think this an oblique reference to the unmentionableness that had passed between them, in the coach, her nakedness uncovered to his unworthy unworthy eyes, so he blurted: 'I do not refer to any *particular* act or, or, or *action*. I take it to be self-evident that impure thoughts are as great a danger to the soul as impure deeds. One flake of soot can dirty a pure cup of water, after all.' He was sweating now. His heart was trilling like a songbird, and there was an unpleasant constriction in his temples.

But she said, leaning forward and even bringing her hand forward as if to rest it on his; although of course she did no such thing. But the surge of gratitude he felt towards her for this minuscule action was colossal, disproportionate.

'I tried with all my heart to do good – to wage the Lord's war *against* slavery – and in consequence of that, with no consciousness of trying to do any further harm against my country, which God knows I love, which anyone who knows me, Mrs Burton, will tell you I love with all my heart. But in consequence of that, in consequence,' what was he trying to say? 'In consequence only of devoting myself to the struggle against slavery I find I have wandered into treason against . . .' And the word was out without him realising, without him planning to say it. He was so shocked at his own words that he stopped dead. He was so shocked at what he had said – treason! – that he felt his eyeballs prickle and a blush spread. It was as if he had uttered an obscenity. But of course he had not. Mrs Burton was still regarding him with the careful appearance of attention to his words, waiting to hear how his sentiment would end.

He tried to gather himself. Treason. It was the secret he had been keeping from himself; the shout that resounded though the crypt of his soul that he had not allowed himself to hear above ground. It was the chord to which his buried life resonated. Terrible!

'Mrs Burton,' he said. 'I am sorry; for there is—'

She was on her feet. 'I am sorry, Abraham, but I must go.' And she swept from the room, so rapidly that he was still sitting there stunned, thinking *addressed by my first name!* as she passed through the door.

'Eleanor!' he cried.

He hurried to the foot of the stairs, and saw the hems of her skirts disappearing round the turn above him.

'Eleanor,' he called again.

He took three-step strides and flew up the stairs; but before he could reach the uppermost level he was intercepted by the bearded French officer. 'Mr Bates,' he said, holding out his arm. 'Mr Bates.'

'Sir,' said Bates, 'I implore you—'

'One moment, Mr Bates,' said the officer. Bates looked him full in the face and, for the first time, saw his skin. It was blistered from hairline to neck; the skin boiling with pustules. The Frenchman blinked and Bates saw blisters upon his eyelids. The black hairs of his beard sprouted from little raw-looking divots of skin.

Bates recoiled.

'We must depart this town,' said the officer. 'We cannot board the *Sophrosyne*, but the English army to the west has pulled back its assault – I do not know why they have, but,' his voice was cracked and dry, 'we can move to the south and round. My orders—'

Bates could not bear to be near him. He ducked to the left and pushed past, running up the stairs. His heart was running faster and harder than he could ever remember it. There was a sensation of ache and tingle in his bowels.

He knocked loud on Mrs Burton's door. 'Eleanor! Eleanor!'

There was no reply. He tried the handle, and – in his agitated state, not caring how improperly he was acting – he opened the door.

Eleanor was sitting on her narrow bed. She looked almost demure, with her hands in her lap and her gaze down. Bates stumbled in, and stopped. 'Eleanor,' he said.

Without looking at him, she replied: 'Close the door, Mr Bates, for there is something I must say to you.'

He closed the door.

'Eleanor,' he said again, stepping towards her, one step, two, 'I cannot contain my – it is love, love for you, and—'

She did not look up. 'Abraham,' she said. 'Please listen to what I say. It is quite impossible.'

'These are strange days, Eleanor,' he urged, stepping closer again. 'My prospects are – but even to talk of prospects seems foolish, in these strange days. Let me, then, talk of love—'

Her head moved back, and Bates could see her face. Her expression was one of anger. She stood, to face him. 'You dare, sir, to come in here with such words?'

'Eleanor,' he cried, in an agony.

'Listen to me now, sir. It cannot be. The Dean has proposed marriage and I have accepted.'

It was quite impossible for Bates to understand these words. Or, rather, he could hear them and comprehend them, there was understanding at that facile level, but they were so completely at odds with his heart's racing that they might as well have been a sentence in Sanskrit.

'The Dean?'

'We are to be married. I am espoused to another. Do you see, therefore, how monstrously you are now acting?'

'I had no idea ... but the *Dean*?' He meant: of all the men upon God's earth, *he*?

'The Dean is a gentleman.'

'So much *older* than you.'

'And you are young,' said Mrs Burton, in a violent voice. 'And you are handsome. And you expect me to fall giggling at your feet for that?

'Eleanor!' This was pleadingly said.

'You, sir,' said Mrs Burton, drawing herself up to her full height, 'you, sir, revolt me! You revolt me! Think back, sir, at the indignity you made me suffer – or have *you forgotten*, sir?'

'But,' he said, 'but I love—'

'To *speak* so!' And her voice grew even more intemperate. 'To *speak* such words to a woman affianced to another?'

Bates felt the urge to run weeping from the room, as a child might. He stifled that, and tried to still his face – his wobbling lips, his hot eyes – but then was almost overwhelmed by the urge to grab Mrs Burton – to throttle her. It was intolerable. The thought flashed upon him of the bearded French officer's hideous and blistered face. Bates felt his chest grow molten. He felt trapped and tormented. He felt a roar, a lion's roar, grow in his chest. But when he opened his mouth all that emerged was the noise of a ridiculous mouse. *Squeee*!

His mouth was open.

'The Dean has proposed marriage to me and I have accepted,' Eleanor was saying, as if she were perfectly calm, and as if this were the most straightforward sentence in the lexicon of English expressions. Then she flared: 'But even if he had not – can you believe that a creature such as yourself, a snivelling *gutter* creature such as *yourself*, could capture *my* heart?'

Miserably, yet eagerly Bates replied: 'No, no, of course not—'

'You worm! You are—'

'I am,' he agreed, miserable and excited. 'Oh I am!'

'How I *despise* you!'

Suddenly they were embracing. Afterwards Bates tried to relive the moment, to separate out who clasped whom; but in the moment it seemed to happen without premeditation on either side. They were simply together. Bates held her hard, even fiercely, and felt the stiffness of her starched dress-body against his own breast. She dug with her nails into the fabric of his shirt. She thrust her face up against his and chewed at his mouth, biting his lips, and – startlingly, repulsive –

excitingly – pushing her tongue into his mouth like a wet nurse feeding pap to a baby. He pressed against her and the two of them fell backwards upon the bed. She was making small sobbing noises. Or he was making the noises; it was difficult to tell. She was hurting him, but he cared not. She was drawing blood from his lips, and then she moved her hands from his shoulders to his head and took handfuls of his hair and yanked as if trying to pull the hair out. The pain thrilled him. They struggled. They acted out their dumbshow life-or-death fight, there, upon the bed.

He pulled his face away from hers to breathe, and she grabbed at his ears and pushed him further away. He fell off her, to the left, and she lifted herself and spat upon him – spat in his face. He felt the spittle land on his cheek. Warm, and frothed. 'Your trowsers,' she sneered. 'Your trowsers! Your *trowsers!*' He did not know what she meant. He understood the scorn in her voice, but he did not follow her meaning in the words. 'Take them *off*,' she hissed – and, with agitated, febrile fingers he unbuttoned his fly and pushed the garment down his legs. He was lying on his back now, and Eleanor was on her left side, propped on an arm and looking down upon him. His cockstand was flat against his stomach. He sat up a little way, so as to be able to pull his trowsers over his boots and remove them entirely, and his cockstand wagged forward. Eleanor gasped in disgust. 'Oh, *there*,' she whispered. 'Oh, *foul*.'

No other words could have excited Bates as did these statements of revulsion.

She reached a hand tentatively towards the organ, as if about to touch it, but at the last moment she instead cuffed it – slapped it. It bounced comically under the force of her blow. This stung, but exquisitely. She slapped it again. She leant her face towards it, and spat at it. This time the saliva missed its target, landing upon his thigh. Then she was on her feet, rummaging under her skirts and removing her knickers. Some part of Bates's mind crowed, yet he could not believe what was happening. He shivered. She lay back upon the bed, and Bates clambered upon her, his whole body trembling as if an ague were in him. He pushed her skirts up and lay in her lap, as Hamlet with Ophelia, but as his cockstand pressed blindly on towards her cut she grabbed a chunk of his hair and twisted it violently. The pain was enough to distract him.

'Not *inside*,' she said. 'You comprehend?'

'Yes,' he said. 'Yes. Yes. Yes.'

And it hardly mattered anyway – the snout of his member pressed up against her Organ of Venus and almost at once he jerked in the little death, and his seed squirted out. The expression of her disgust was loud in his ears, *Euh! Euh! Euh!*, so much so that the moment of pleasure was muddied by a fear that her cries might bring other people to her door. But she was wriggling in a kind of fury, pressing the mound of her female Organ against the ledge of his pelvis, pushing and pushing and then, abruptly, she was still. A long sigh breathed from her lips. She went limp beneath him.

He was panting. Sweat itched on his scalp. He did not know what to say.

Outside the window: birdsong.

Light from the sky, and reflected off the sea, and both lights mingled in the glass of the window.

He did not know what to say. The larger picture reoccurred to his mind, and he found himself afraid. She had told him she was to marry the Dean! But, he thought, now – now she must marry me. And the fear was now perfectly knotted up with his hope.

Should he apologise? He had hardly acted as a gentleman. Eleanor! Forgive me! But he did not say anything.

She spoke first: 'Get off me.'

He rolled to one side.

She sat up and adjusted her dress. She pulled a handkerchief from her sleeve and reached underneath the skirts to wipe herself.

'Eleanor,' he said. His voice was scratchy. He sat up, suddenly and uncomfortably aware of his nakedness, and he scrabbled on the floor to recover his trowsers. They had become inverted and strangely tangled, and in his agitated state he could not seem to make them right. He sat on the bed, leaning forward to cover his private organs, and fumbled with the cloth of them.

'It seems,' said Eleanor, in a calm voice, 'that we share a shameful inability to restrain our baser passions.'

'I love you,' he said, without looking at her. 'I love you. Permit me only to promise you this: that when we are married—'

'We shall not marry,' said Eleanor.

He thought about this. He gripped the ankle hem of the left leg of his trowser and pulled the tube of cloth through itself.

'I shall marry the Dean,' said Eleanor.

He did not contest this statement directly. It was not in his soul to deny her anything at all. 'Shall I challenge him to a duel?' he asked.

He had meant the phrase seriously, as his sole way of articulating once again his love for her. But she laughed at it, a low, clucking laugh, the very first time that Bates had ever heard her make such a sound. And at the laughter he smiled – he had, he decided, intended it as a joke all along. He had been trying to make her laugh.

The trowsers went over his boots with difficulty, and he was compelled to lift his hips and struggle a little, which caused his member to jiggle. When the trowsers were up to his knees Eleanor stopped him.

'Wait,' she said, with an almost childlike earnestness. 'Sit for a moment.' So he sat on the bed, and she leant forward to bring a scientific curiosity to bear upon his *membrum virile*. Her lips pursed, as if it were distasteful to her, and yet her eyes were bright with fascination. She reached out and touched the thing, picking it up with thumb and forefinger and letting it drop. It began, again, to stiffen. 'How ugly it is!' she said, in an innocent voice. 'Chicken-skin. Yet the texture of the flesh itself is . . .' she searched for a word.

'It is a shameful thing,' he agreed.

'I don't mean that,' she said. 'I mean, in a scientific sense. The texture of the flesh differs from that of any part of the body. It feels granular; a softer manner of – I know not. A softer manner of gristle perhaps.'

'It is no longer soft,' he observed, as it stretched itself and grew hard under her hand. Once again she laughed, releasing the organ from her right hand and lifting her left to cover her mouth. 'How funny!' she said.

'Do not blame *me* I pray you,' he replied, smiling in turn. 'It has a mind of its own!'

'How funny,' she said again.

'Eleanor I love you,' he said. 'I love you, Eleanor.'

She sat upright again. 'Pull your clothes on, Mr Bates.'

He began doing so at once. 'Eleanor, what are we to do? What are we ever to do?'

'I shall marry the Dean.'

He thought about this. There seemed to be nothing to say except 'Yes.'

'He is a man of means. We cannot pretend money does not matter.'

'Will you put me from you?' he asked. And in that moment his whole life teetered on the hinge of her answer. She looked at him, bringing him under the same dispassionate inquiry she had just been bestowing on his organ.

'No,' she said. 'I don't think so.'

And a shaft of light shone bright through Bates's soul. He beamed. He could have embraced her, there and then. He did not consider this a shabby second-best; it was, he knew, exactly what he deserved. Which is to say, he knew he deserved no more. Though, of course, he could hope.

'What must we do?' he asked her. He was the Red Cross Knight, and she was Gloriana. He was ready to take her commands.

'We must get away from this town. We must determine,' she said, 'which force is more likely to prevail in the war, and make ourselves useful to them. We must, at least, survive.'

'Yes.'

'If the English are now beating the French in battle, then we must seize the Computational Device and drive it to them.'

'Yes.'

'But if the French are destined to rule this land, as once they did, then we must deliver the Computational Device to the garrison at York, as was the mission of this party.'

'And you are familiar about the mission?'

'Henry has told me everything. We are,' and she smiled, 'to be married, after all, he and I.'

'Yes,' said Bates.

'But above all, we must leave this town.'

'Quite apart from anything else,' said Bates, 'there is the matter of the pestilence.'

'The plague,' she said, nodding. 'It is a concern.'

[9]

Soon afterwards Bates met again with the Dean. He felt he ought to be anxious about this meeting, but he was not. He was not, despite his act of betrayal with the Dean's affianced. Betrayal *was* the word for it. Sin was the word, also. Disgrace, debasement, dishonour, these were the words. Yet merely to think of his encounter sent bubbles of excitement cascading upwards through his torso. Its secrecy, as much as its intimacy, was its thrill. The hiddenness of it bound Eleanor and he together. The fact that she was to marry the old, corpulent Dean – that was something he put from his mind. It would be no true marriage, he thought. The true marriage belonged to him. He had not realised before what power there is in secrecy.

Eleanor led him through to the Dean's room – for now the hotel had been emptied there were plenty of spare rooms – and they sat together to discuss plans. The Dean, deprived of his specialist snuff, was surly and withdrawn, and snorted air in at his nose from time to time, making thereby a very disagreeable noise. 'Henry!' Eleanor scolded mildly.

'We must decide. The French army will no longer escort us to York, that is clear,' Bates said.

'And yet it is to York we must go,' growled the Dean.

'Then we must make our own way there,' Eleanor said briskly. How Bates loved her force of will! How perfectly were manly self-assurance and womanly beauty combined in her! 'If we could take the Computational Device, it would act as passport through any English sentry – passport into any general's tent.'

'It is well guarded,' the Dean snapped.

'The plague is running through the soldiery here like fire through autumn stubble,' said Eleanor, leaning forward.

The Dean snorted, a weird camel-like sound that almost made Bates laugh.

'Henry!' rebuked Eleanor.

The Dean stood. 'I'll not be scolded like a schoolboy!' he said querulously. 'I'll not *stand for it* from a woman! You care nothing for my sufferings! My sinuses are like tar! Like molten lead!'

'Sit down, Henry,' said Eleanor, sharply.

The Dean sat again with a pained expression on his face. There was silence between them. Then the Dean said, in a small voice: 'Salt water.'

'I can't hear this mumbling,' said Eleanor.

The Dean set his lips together more tightly. Then: 'Salt water,' more loudly.

'You'll ask for it with proper courtesy,' said Eleanor.

The Dean's face clenched, and settled. Bates found a queer elation in sitting there, spectator to this squabble. He felt, perhaps for the first time in his life, what it was to be *powerful*.

'Salt water,' said the Dean, 'please.'

Eleanor swept herself to her feet. How proud and fine she was! 'Abraham and I shall fetch you some, my love,' she announced. Then she waited. The Dean was staring at the carpet. Bates stood, but Eleanor waited. Eventually, speaking as if the words were being pulled from him by pliers, the Dean said: 'Thank you.'

Eleanor walked from the room, and Bates followed. He followed her down one flight of stairs, and on the half-landing there he asked: 'Why does he desire salt water?'

'He will sniff it up through his nose and spew it from his mouth,' Eleanor replied, matter-of-factly. 'He believes it eases the pains in his sinuses. Here,' and she pushed open the door on the half-landing to reveal an empty room. 'Find a bowl.'

'A bowl.'

'To carry it from the sea.'

'But whose room is this?'

'Does it matter? I suppose it is some Frenchy's.'

'And what if he returns?'

'Am I surrounded by cowards?' she said and stepped into the room. Bates followed. There was a single narrow bed, and a table beside it with a wide wooden bowl upon it. As Eleanor took it and turned, Bates – moved and overwhelmed by her beauty, and moved more, in truth, by her very *presence*, her *accessibility* – put his face up to kiss her cheek.

She slapped him. It was a cuff on the side of his head. It was not a painful blow, but he leapt backwards with the shock of it and almost fell. 'Take this to the shore and fill it,' she said matter-of-factly, holding out the bowl.

And yet sometimes she would be affectionate with him. It puzzled him, and also acted as a charm upon him. It drew him tighter into the web of her. Once, as they passed along the hallway to the Dean's room, Eleanor turned to him and demanded, in a quiet voice: 'Show me it.' He did not understand what she was asking, yet as she repeated the request he realised that of course he knew what *it* was. 'Show it me!'

'Now? Here?'

'Yes – immediately.'

'Shall we go back to your room?' he asked. But she pushed a fist in his chest so that he stepped backwards and against the wall. There, in that public space, he fumbled his buttons and drew out his member. The blank outrageousness of what he was doing pressed fear into his heart – for what if somebody came up the stairs? Or emerged from a room? What if the *Dean himself* came out and saw this base display? But this same fear prickled as excitement in his solar plexus. His membrum grew harder. 'Your hand is obscuring my sight of it,' said Eleanor in a brisk voice, and he moved his fingers and held it at the base.

'Be quick,' he said, glancing left and right. 'Oh!'

She dropped down and settled on her haunches, brought her face close to the exposed organ. She stared at it, close. There was something of the child in her gaze, the naïf quality of a child's curiosity. For long seconds she stared at it, moving her head from the left to the right. She seemed to sigh. 'How ugly it is!' she exclaimed.

'Yes,' he said. 'Yes. But hurry.'

'Hush! Oh, but it is *foul.*'

'Somebody might come!'

'To be burdened with such an ass's tail,' she said 'Ugh, the *colour!* The colour at the *end*, there!'

Then she was standing upright again, and walking away, and Bates must fumble away his shame and hobble after her. But the more she scorned his *membrum* – quite properly so, of course – the more aroused Bates became.

Night fell, and they took their supper in the hotel's kitchens with various French officers – none of whom Bates recognised – and afterwards made their way to their rooms. Bates sat in his, listening to the stamp of soldier's boots on the cobbles outside, and the shouts of command, and he wondered what to do. He *yearned* for Eleanor, like a dog. His very soul itched for her. And were they not, in a sense, linked? Had they not undertaken their sinful, secret version of marriage? Yet he had no idea whether he should go along now, in the dark, to her room and knock at the door. Would she welcome him in? Or rebuke him and send him away? Fear of the latter balanced desire for the former.

When he could stand it no longer he left his room and crept along the darkened corridor. There was a gleam far below, a lighted room spilling light onto the foot of the stairway. Distantly could be heard the sound of a man sobbing, or moaning. Bates placed his steps carefully, as if the slightest floorboard groan might rouse the Dean. He knocked gently at Eleanor's door, and knocked again.

Eventually: 'Who is there?'

'I, Abraham.'

'Who?'

Louder: 'Abraham.'

A pause. 'What do you want?'

This took him aback. After a moment he hissed: 'I am concerned at your solitude.'

'I cannot *hear* what you are saying.'

Louder, though the wood of the door: 'Are you alright?'

'Of course.'

'I was concerned.'

'For me?'

'Yes. May I come in?'

A lengthy silence. The sound of the man sobbing, far below them in the cavernous building, slowed, and ceased. The silence it revealed had an eerie quality. 'You may not,' came Eleanor's voice, clearly articulated.

Bates felt a lurch in his heart; sadness welled from the ceaseless spring inside him. But nothing was too demeaning for him now, and even abasement contained its dark joy for him. 'Please!' he urged. 'I beg of you!'

'Go away,' she said. 'Tonight – no, not tonight.'

This was a straw at which he might clutch. 'Tomorrow night, perhaps?'

'Go away.'

He retraced the steps to his room.

He was awoken by a voice in his ear, which he took – his heart thundering suddenly in his breast – to be Eleanor's. The voice said 'Awake! O!' A small voice, that seemed therefore tender. 'Rejoice not against me! O mine enemy —'

It was the thought that it was Eleanor, crept into his room like the Song of Solomon, that saved Bates's life. He was wound so tight with erotic expectation, so thrilled by the possible anticipation, that he almost *leapt* from the bed – which is to say, he sat up abruptly, and felt, as he moved, a fierce pain at the side of his skull, a little above his ear.

This woke him fully.

Blood was coming out. 'Eleanor!' he roared. But she, of course, was not in the room. He was alone, save for the voice – and looking down he saw, beside his dented pillow, a Lilliputian, carrying a miniature pikestaff, the hook and bladed end of which held up a crunk of folded skin, several hairs, all bundled into a parcel with bright bead of blood.

Bates might have screamed, except that he was too surprised, and that the pain had fined his nerves. He hurled himself off the bed, slapping his hands upon the bedside table to lever himself, vault-like, away. He landed on the soles of his bare feet. 'What?' he cried? 'What-what?'

The Lilliputian was running now, lengthways along the bed. It was clear (Bates realised this a little later, when he had time to determine what the course of events must have been) that the little being had made his way from the windowsill, along the ledge of the dado and onto the bedside table, positioning himself on the bed ready to thrust his pike through the corner of Bates's eye and into his brain. But now that route of escape had been cut off by Bates's leap, and the creature was dashing as fast as it could for the far corner of the bed, hoping perhaps to clamber down the sheeting and across the floor. Like a mouse.

Without the least deliberation Bates grabbed the Bible from his bedside table and threw the book. Had he gauged and weighted the shot he surely would have missed, for he was no pitch-and-tosser; but from his instinctive throw the volume flew true. The spine of it squashed the Lilliputian hard against the mattress; the book bounced up; it fell hard upon the floor.

Bates, in a state of excitement that drowned out the higher functions of rational thought, hurried round the bed and plucked the Bible from the floor. On the bed the Lilliputian was endeavouring to rouse himself. Bates's throw had struck his back, and appeared to have marred his ability to stand upright. Bates lifted the Bible and brought it hard down upon the little man. The book bounced on the mattress. Underneath the Lilliputian lay, now, motionless. Bates used the edge of the book's front cover to lever the little creature from the bed, as he might have done a spider, and to flick him upon the wooden floor. He raised the book over his fallen foe, and readied himself for the coup de grâce – flinched, steeled himself and heaved down. The book banged a single thundercrack.

His heart beat, and beat again, and beat. The blood seemed to pass hard through his chest.

When Bates lifted the Bible again it was to reveal a starburst pattern of red on the floor's planks. The Lilliputian lay face-down, his little limbs arranged in a swastika pattern.

Bates took in a long breath.

Another.

He felt round at the back of his head: had he not jolted his head upwards the pike would have been plunged through his eye. He could feel a scratch running, like the mark left by an acid teardrop, from the edge of his eye, along the side of his temple and ending in a gouge above his ear. Blood was sticky there, becoming granular.

He was trembling now, and he sat himself down upon the bed. His eye was drawn to the hieroglyph of death, written in flesh and blood, upon the floor. Now that the sharper fear was resolving itself into a trembly sense of alarm Bates felt guilt intruding. He, the friend of the Lilliputians! It rushed upon him that he should pray, straight away, with the blood of this little creature upon his hands, hot for forgiveness from the Father of all things. Bates allowed one thought to pass: Is this how soldiers feel when they take a life? Then his gaze lifted, and he saw the windowsill.

Two more Lilliputians were standing there, beside them an aeronautical toy. One of the Lilliputians was labouring at the leather strap, twisting it to build up motor power once again by leaning repeatedly on a wooden spar. The other stood, with that unearthly stillness the little folk were capable of, staring directly at Bates.

Bates stood up. His soul was poised precisely between a desire to abase himself before this miniature embodiment of conscience, and a rage at the monstrous race of all of these creatures. Attack *him* whilst he slept? The devils! He still clutched the bloodied Bible in his right hand, and he lifted this so that it crossed over his breast.

The standing Lilliputian raised a spear; but the distance between him and his man-target was far too great to cross with an arm's-throw. Then everything happened very quickly. The end of the spear gave out a puff of smoke, and at precisely the moment that Bates realised it was a miniature rifle he was struck on the left cheek with a tiny pellet. It was a bee-sting sensation, and made him flinch and recoil, and then in the same motion, made him step towards the window. But the rifleman hopped into the cockpit of the aero-device, and the other one pushed the nose of the toy to face the world outside and jumped in too. The propeller whirred and the little machine drifted unsteadily into the air and dropped. Bates was the window in a second, but could only watch as the device banked and flew a lolloping rise-and-fall trajectory along the length of the street and turned the corner.

Bates examined his face in the hand mirror. His cheek still smarted where the Lilliputian bullet had entered. A red spot right in the centre of his cheek, exactly like a carbuncle save only that the border of this redness was a tiny ring of scorched and blackened skin. Probing the inside of his cheek with his tongue he could feel the peppercorn bullet itself, embedded in the flesh of his face. Resting the mirror against the angle of table and wall, Bates put both hands to his face and tried to squeeze the projectile out through the hole it had made, like evacuating a blackhead; but it was a sharply painful process, and the bullet seemed to have travelled laterally through the flesh of his cheek. He gave up.

He dressed and hurried from his room. And only at this point did it occur to him to wonder why the Lilliputians had mounted this attack up him. Audacious, in fact! Was it a general rising? Had he ended the life of some Lilliputian Spartacus?

Outside his door on the upper landing the silence of the hotel intruded upon his consciousness. Why so quiet? And there, right there halfway along the landing, was a body.

It was sitting, legs out, back against the wall, arms loose at its side, in a French military uniform. And the skin of its face was reddened and blistered above its beard – it was the French officer, slain by the pestilence. Evidently slain by the pestilence and not by Lilliputians at all.

With the instinctive fear of a man faced with a diseased body, Bates squeezed past, and fell to knocking lustily upon Eleanor's door. There was no reply, but the Dean's door opened and the Dean himself – nightshirted – emerged. 'What the devil? What – oh,' catching sight of the Frenchman's corpse. 'Oh!'

Bates was agitated enough to gabble. 'A Lilliputian warrior has tried to murder me!' he squealed. 'This very minute, as I slept. It is merest chance that I am alive to speak to you now! It is chance – or' (for this thought was just occurring to him) 'God's will that I survived! There may be a general attack!'

The Dean stepped forward, covered half the distance between himself and the corpse, and stopped. 'Oh!' he repeated. 'But this is most unhygienic! How could this be permitted . . .'

'Dean,' said Bates. 'Do you not attend to my words? I say that we are attacked, surrounded by enemies! We must preserve ourselves, we must escape, and save the life of Mrs Burton—'

Eleanor emerged, fully dressed and severe-faced, from the Dean's room. 'What clamour disturbs our breakfast?' she declaimed, the-atrically. 'My affianced and myself?'

'Eleanor!'

'Now!' barked the Dean. 'We dress, we depart. We shall *seize* the Calculator and drive it to York. The time has come.'

But it took Oldenberg half an hour to dress himself and gather what he called 'necessaries'. Bates sat in a chair in his room and told the story of the assault upon him, repeated it several times. Eleanor, her manner cold, peered at his face and tutted at the wound in his cheek. But otherwise neither of them seemed very interested in his adventures.

The silence of the hotel remained perfectly unbroken. From the Dean's window, which gave out upon a side-alley, the view straight down revealed a number of motionless French bodies. There was no other motion; and no sound beyond the calling of the gulls and the hush of surf. 'Perhaps,' Bates said, 'the pestilence has destroyed the French army.'

'The whole army!' said the Dean.

'Perhaps,' said Eleanor, her eyes flashing. 'Yet it spared us.'

'Providence,' rumbled the Dean, seated on the bed. 'Help me with my boots, Bates! I'm not so supple that I can stretch down to my own *heels*, sir!'

Bates knelt at the bed. 'Divine Providence,' he said. 'It must be! For we three fell sick and have been spared, whereas these French invaders ...'

'Tush!' snapped the Dean. 'You pinch at my calf! Pay attention there!'

They hauled their luggage, all three, down the stairs. At the bottom, animated by the sense of escape, Eleanor took charge. 'Henry, go out and look in the coachyard. See what life, if any, remains there: but above all see what carriage, and what horse, we can obtain to speed our escape.'

'And the Calculator,' announced Oldenberg. 'I'll look for that. Will you come?'

'Bates and I shall go to the kitchens and take what food we can find there.'

'Quite right! Quite right! Let us not starve upon the road! Fetch bread and cheese and anything else ...' He seemed happier than at any time since their arrival in Scarborough. Perhaps he hoped, in returning to the British forces, to obtain again some of his exotic snuff.

But it did not matter. Eleanor swept off and down the servants' stair to the kitchen. Not a soul was about. A long central table had been scrubbed and cleaned and left bare. Most of the cupboard doors were open. Somebody had been there before them.

'The parlour,' said Eleanor. There was a powerful gleam of excitement in her eyes, and Bates could not contain himself. Despite all that had happened to him since awakening, he felt desire overmastering every other consideration.

'How happy you look, my darling!' he said.

'Happy to be leaving this place,' she said. 'To be on the move!' She pulled the door of the parlour and stepped inside. The space inside was dim, illuminated by a single grilled window high up. The shelves were mostly empty, although there were several jars containing dried fruit, a large wrap of lard and a Hessian-load of potatoes.

Eleanor passed these out to Bates, who placed them on the counter. Then he stood, shivering with half-suppressed desire, at the doorway.

'Come,' said Eleanor, hurriedly, and pulled him inside. With the door shut behind them the space was cramped, and the light low. Bates was pressed up against her, aware of the stiffness of the fabric of her dress against his own chest. She was breathing quickly. 'He is outside now,' she whispered in his ear. 'Perhaps,' and she gestured with her hand, 'only *inches* away, on the far side of that *grill*.'

'Eleanor!' gasped Bates.

'Sss! My future *husband* – do you understand?'

He nodded.

'That *holy* estate, that Godly estate. He a man of *God*. He is my betrothed, and you are nothing. He is a gentleman and you are nothing. He treats me with respect and you treat me with such – contempt. I am no gentlewoman in *your* eyes. You see me in terms of the merest harlot. Shame on you! And you – you —'

And of course Bates wanted to deny these shameful words; he wanted to insist upon the purity and wholeness of his love for her, but he knew that it was not his place to speak. Eleanor did not wish him to speak. His speaking was not the point of this encounter. She was rustling at her own skirt with one hand, and grasping Bates's right wrist with the other. 'He is inches away, you *devil*.' She thrust his hand between her legs. She wore no undergarments there. 'He is a man of *God*! And you – you—'

Her eyes rolled white in her head. It took all Bates's self-restraint to prevent himself shouting out in excitement. He put his face over her shoulder, in at the space of an empty shelf. He stuck his tongue out as far as it could go, and bit at the base of it. With his right hand he was tickling her between her legs, fumbling at the smoothly wet membrane, at its enclosure of hairy skin. He needed, desperately, to touch himself. He tried to force his free hand in at the waistband of his own breeches, but there was not enough space. He tried undoing his buttons, but left thumb and fingers stumbled at the task. He strained to reach his own organ.

Eleanor breathed out hard and clenched her thighs together on his hand. She stiffened, and finally he got the top of his trousers unbuttoned. The tip of his membrum, all hard as mahogany, protruded, and he pressed the palm of his left hand over it, pressed and pressed and *out* it came in a gush, phlegmy and warm onto his wrist; and he was clasping Eleanor closer to him, tight as a child clings. But even in this moment she was pushing him away, and rearranging her dress, and squeezing past him to open the parlour door again.

'All!' he said. One syllable to express both release and disgust.

He took a sheet of ancient newspaper, lining the bottom shelf, and wiped himself as clean as he could. But, coming into the kitchen he saw that there was a stain on the front of his trowsers. Rubbing with the paper only spread the stain wider. 'See!' he said to her. 'This is but dirty work.'

'We have tarried too long already,' she said, matter-of-factly. She pulled an empty basket from under the table and pushed into it the food they had found.

They came back up to the lobby and out to the front of the hotel again, and were faced with a scene of perfect desolation. Eleanor, the basket over the crook of her arm, came down the steps and crossed the road to stand at the seafront, and Bates followed her. The sun low in the sky still morning-white, and the mist visible far out at sea draping the horizon in gauze. The waves, nearer at hand, endlessly rubbing and grinding at the shore with a Lady-Macbeth intensity. Several men – soldiers – were sleeping on the beach nearby. But, no: for clearly they were not *sleeping*. One lay on his front with one arm flung out. His hand, visible, was rouge and black and puffed-up, like a clutch of carrots gone bad. The other lay on his back and his face seemed scaled like a fish's.

Bates turned, and glimpsed a pile of bodies further down the street; but here was the Dean, bustling up with a cross visage. 'I have found the Calculator,' he gasped, trotting up to them. 'Found the Calculator and its door is wide.'

'Wide?'

'It's empty.'

Eleanor spoke decisively: 'Show me.'

A road led up the side of the hotel to the coachyard. There were more bodies here; one still standing up, or rather leaning in at the coign of a stall and, by some freak of balance, not fallen over in death. This one's face was puffed and very white, the eyes buried in the bulge of check and brow like a Chinaman's. These others were sprawled on the floor. One of these still clutched an unopened bottle of wine.

The Dean took them to the far corner of the yard. Here a sentry sat on a stool, slumped forward and propped on his rifle. What looked like tendrils growing from his downward-pointing face were the dried and scummed remains of drool – from mouth, nose, and eyes, black and dark green. The stool and the ground beneath it were covered in a spread of foulness, like cow-flop. This man had been guarding a stall and had died at his post, yet Bates found nothing but a thrilling revulsion in contemplating his end.

His sentry keeping had been in vain, for the stall door was now open. The Calculator was there, but as Oldenberg had said its hinged side was wide and its Lilliputian occupants long gone.

'Is it not interesting, though?' Eleanor said, peering into the workings of the device. 'These little hutches! These tumblers, and cogs – and what is *that*?' Her eyes had brightened.

'You are as little like a natural female,' growled the Dean, 'as an abacus is like a lily.'

'This,' she snapped, 'will still be valuable to the army, to our army, sir. It is true that the little people have vacated it, but the working alone will surely be of interest to our generals.'

'Yes, perhaps,' Bates put in, 'perhaps Lilliputians loyal to the Crown could be trained to take the positions of . . .'

The Dean scoffed noisily. 'Lilliputians loyal to the Crown! They have no loyalty, save to the Devil.' And he squinnied at Eleanor, as if daring her to express offence at his vulgar expression.

Eleanor only ignored him. 'We must harness a horse to the Calculator,' she said, running a hand along the spar at the front of the device. 'Let us ride it west until we discover the English forces.'

'There are no horses, Ma'am,' said the Dean. 'Look around you!'

'None in the whole town?'

'What d'ye think? Do ye *hear* the whinny of a horse? Can ye hear such a thing in this great silence?'

Eleanor fixed her eye upon the Dean. 'Your tone, sir. It is unhelpful, sir. If we cannot find a *horse* then I suggest that you two gentlemen—'

No!' interjected the Dean. 'I'll not haul a carriage about like a beast of burden! I am Dean of York! A gentleman, I!'

'Perhaps,' Bates put in, eager to act as peacemaker, 'we might secrete the Calculator hereabouts – lock it away, and take the *key* to the English forces, with our knowledge as to how and where to find it?'

Eleanor and the Dean both looked at Bates. 'An idea,' Eleanor conceded. 'A good idea.'

The door closed again, and could be secured by a padlock through the two metal hoops – closed, but not locked. 'We must find the key,' said Eleanor; but this proved no easy matter. It was Bates's opinion that the key must have been in the possession of the beard-faced Frenchie officer, for he had evidently been in command. Voicing this opinion was tantamount, it seemed, to volunteering to go and pick this corpse's pocket; and no quantity of bluster or complaint on Bates's part shifted this duty from his shoulders. 'Go,' said Eleanor. 'We have no time to waste.' Then she turned to the Dean, who was grinning like a schoolboy, and commanded him to search the servants' rooms for another padlock and key.

Bates walked again up the silent stairwell. A ghostly silence: it incommoded his manly self-possession. He found himself glancing over his own shoulder. The whole building creaked like a ship at sea. The sound of the surf could be heard as a mocking thing. And there, on the topmost landing, slouched the body of the Frenchman. Bates tried to steel himself, but it was hard. He hunkered down and gingerly prodded the pockets of the man's uniform greatcoat. He lifted one side of this, a heavy flap of cloth, and tried to insinuate his finger into the waistcoat pocket. But the stomach was pushing hard against the fabric. His flesh felt taut as a drumskin. Cold drum. In at the corner of his eye Bates was aware of the proximity of his face, the ruined and blistered face, the eyes rolled up as white as cataract. Bates's gorge rose. He tasted a thin sourness in the throat.

It was no good.

He thudded back down the stairs gasping. It was no good. It was no good. Eleanor would be displeased. She had set him a task and he had failed. But the rotting flesh! The decay! And yet, as he ran, he was aware of a stiffening inside at the top of his breeches. Oh, how he revolted himself!

Eleanor would be displeased.

'This morning I was awoken by an assassin,' he said to himself as he jogged down. 'Death!' And the remembered terror, the remembered thrill, roiled in his mind with the general sense of agitation. Of arousal.

A half-hour passed before they abandoned the search. 'We cannot waste the entire day,' grumbled the Dean. 'And I have yet to break my fast! I cannot ransack any more of this hotel's rooms! There are bodies everywhere – it is an uncleanness. We should leave, and get ourselves into the cleaner air of the countryside.'

'We must think ahead, husband-to-be,' said Eleanor prissily. 'Let us be more than mere refugees.'

'Perhaps you are worried at becoming a pauper?' scoffed the Dean. 'Well, and you might. For you have *nothing*, madam. But I have much – and once you accept my authority as husband   '

'Here is the key,' exclaimed Bates. It was trodden into the dirt of the stable-yard floor, not three yards from the door. ''Twas here all the while!'

He picked it up and pulled a strand of muddied straw from its shaft: a brass key, nothing more. But Eleanor was at his side, and her fingers had closed about the shaft of it. 'Now,' she announced. 'Let us go!'

'I have yet to break my fast, Ma'am!'

They set out on their journey after one further bickering. Oh, they were like children. 'If we are to walk,' Bates said, 'then I shall leave my valise here.' And he ported it and tucked it into a cupboard beneath the main staircase, thinking at some later date to return and reclaim it.

'Good,' said the Dean, wheezily. 'Your hands are free to carry my cases instead.'

'I shall not!' said Bates. He spoke, perhaps, more sharply than he was wont; but then again, his nerves had been jangled fierce enough by the morning's events. The Dean opened his mouth very wide, and then closed it. His face was dark.

'You forget yourself, sir,' he said. 'You were brought on this journey as my assistant!'

'The nature of the journey has changed, sir!'

'I am *Dean* of *York*!' the Dean bellowed. 'I'll not carry my own *bags*!'

Bates glanced over at Eleanor, but she seemed amused by this altercation.

'I'll not carry them either, sir,' Bates said, emboldened by the expression on Eleanor's face.

'You'll do as I *tell* you, sir!'

'I am not your flunkey, sir!'

'I am Dean of York!' the Dean screeched. And then, abruptly, tears slid from his eyes and made his pink cheek to shine in the sunlight. 'I'm Dean of York,' he repeated, in quite another tone of voice. 'I'm an old man! Too old and infirm to carry such baggage – it may be that I'll not endure the walking . . .'

'Come come,' said Eleanor, putting her arm about him and drawing his tubby body into an embrace, as a mother might with a mewling child. 'Come come. You are in the prime of your maturity. Aeneas was your age when he stepped out to leave Troy – if not older.'

'Older,' said the Dean, in a small voice.

'Come, come, my hero.'

Eventually they stowed the Dean's cases in the same cupboard as Bates's, and set off carrying nothing but the basket with its ill assortment of food.

There were bodies everywhere, so much so that they quickly became accustomed to the fact of death all about them. They ate as they walked through the town, chewing leathery strips of dried apple from one of two glass jars; but it was unsatisfying food. They grew thirsty, and although the road out of town, up the hill, ran alongside a chuckling stream, none of them felt secure that the water was potable. There were bodies everywhere, and some lay in the stream, and who knew how many more clogged the path of the water further up. 'We should have found a pump – we should fill a jar from a well,' grumbled the Dean.

'We will find clean water in the countryside,' said Eleanor.

And they walked on.

Soon enough they reached the top of the rise and were able to look down upon the town and the sea. It was perfectly still. Not a single thread of smoke escaped any of the chimneys. The great blue fray-edged blanket of the sea was tucked up close. The *Sophrosyne* looked like a toy. 'How peaceful it looks,' said Bates.

'It is the peace of death,' said the Dean.

They walked on for an hour or more, and then sat themselves down in the lee of a stone wall to eat. The Dean plucked twigs from a hedge, like feathers from a goose, and piled them. 'Let us set a fire,' he said, 'and bake some of these potatoes.'

'Do you have flint?' asked Bates in, he thought, a mild voice.

'Hold your tongue!' retorted the Dean, his face red. 'Look to *yourself* sir!' he barked 'Must *I* think of everything? Why have *you* not a flint, sir? Why not?' Bates's nerves were already jangled. 'Because sir,' he retorted, with more heat than was customary for him, 'I do not smoke. Unlike you sir!'

'I smoke? I? I do not smoke!'

'Your snuff, sir —'

'*Snuff*,' screamed the Dean, his face scarlet, 'is *not smoking!*'

The wind sobbed distantly, but otherwise there was no sound. Eleanor had her face down as she looked through the basket. Bates avoided the Dean's eye, but when he glanced up he saw the fellow struggling to calm his temper.

'Gentlemen,' said Eleanor, softly. 'I beg of you not to fight.'

'Quite right, Ma'am,' said the Dean, at once. 'Quite right.'

'If we cannot light the fire then we must eat the potatoes raw.'

'Quite right.'

They sat in silence. The Dean, who possessed a small folding knife, passed it to Eleanor, who used it to scrape the skin from her potato. The Dean, and then Bates, followed suit. The silence was broken with the melancholy sound of three people crunching their tubers, without great gusto. 'It sits,' said the Dean, in a low voice, 'ill on my stomach.'

'Perhaps we will chance upon a finer repast,' said Eleanor.

'My stomach dislikes it,' the Dean said. Then he said: 'Fetch me some of the dried fruit, Eleanor, to sweeten my guts a peck.'

Eleanor, though Bates noticed her flinch, did as she was bid. 'We must husband this fruit,' she warned as she opened the jar. But she passed a piece to both men and took one herself. 'Or it will all be gone.'

Bates stared across the field, with the hedge running in a trembly line away to his left and the ground all overgrown with weeds. The reality of his situation began to bear itself upon his mind. 'These are terrible times for England,' he said.

'Terrible times,' agreed the Dean.

'Pestilence and war – God's displeasure.'

After a pause, Bates said: 'Yet I wonder why did that Lilliputian assassin attack me this morn? What would it benefit them my death, I mean?'

'Perhaps they planned to murder us all in our beds,' said Eleanor.

They walked on for some few hours more. They followed a road, but it seemed to lead to nowhere but to an empty field. Crossing this folded clogs and bulges of mud about their feet and made walking harder. On the far side was a wood, and they stopped here for a while. It took them an unconscionable time to scrape the mud from their shoes, the Dean complaining shrilly all the while.

They passed through the trees and out the far side and at once came upon a large grave-ditch dug into a field. It was a hundred yards long, though no more than six feet across: a trench, too narrow for a Brobdingnagian. But there was no mystery here: for a line of dead bodies – forty or more – lay on the far side of the trench, ready to be given into the soil and covered over. The bodies lay all on their backs, daring with their white-open eyes the open sky to blink. But the burial had been interrupted; the gravediggers dead themselves, perhaps, or scared away by battle.

'Let us hurry on,' said Eleanor, distressed at this sight.

They skirted the trench and made their way to a metalled road. There was enough mud on the base of Bates's shoes to glue the small stones of this thoroughfare to his feet. He crunched on with the rest of them. The sky began to cloud.

As night began to draw itself around them they looked for some place to spend it; but the only building they encountered was a single-room hut, some peasant's cot; and at the doorway of this place they found themselves repelled by a fierce stench from inside. 'Death,' cried the Dean, dashing backwards. 'Death!'

There were several bodies on the floor. They walked on, and eventually found a barn – a structure as old as Chaucer, probably, made of planks of black wood so brittle and dry with age that they resembled stale bread. Moss had grown across the floor inside, and this, though not wholly dry, was soft enough to lie down upon. They peeled and ate another raw potato each, and then a piece of leathery fruit. The uncooked potato sat very ill in Bates's stomach. 'My future wife – my betrothed and I,' the Dean announced, pompously, 'shall sleep here. There's nothing improper in that.'

'Of course,' said Bates, a little too hastily.

'There is a leaning board. You might want to sleep there.'

'Outside?'

'Under the board. I saw it, before. That's a perfectly well-sheltered space.'

'I shall sleep in here, Dean,' said Bates, 'with you.'

'It is hardly appropriate!'

'Come come,' said Bates, trying for a reasonable tone. 'These are extraordinary times. You'd not deny me shelter. Think of your Christian duty.'

'My duty?' barked the Dean.

'Be quiet, you growling dogs,' said Eleanor. But there was a smile on her face. It did not help take away the rankle from Bates's mood.

'Yes sir,' he said, more aggressively. 'Thrust me out of doors? Whilst you are cosy within? What if it rains?'

'You dare *preach* to me, sir? Dare tell *me* my *Christian* duty, sir?'

'It is because you are Dean of York, sir, that I would expect you ...'

'Do such words come from *your* mouth, sir?'

'And why not? I'll stay under this roof. It's humble enough, and you'll not push me out into the storm like King Lear.'

The Dean's eyes popped, but he held his tongue. Eleanor looked from the one to the other, with sparkling eyes.

'My stomach,' said the Dean, looking at neither of them, 'does not like this food of unboiled potato. It's a poor sort of supper. It gives me mal de stomach.'

Bates adopted a conciliatory voice. 'We are all of us finding this enforced vagrancy a trial, sir. I sympathise.'

But this, for some reason, riled the Dean up again. 'You sir,' he cried. 'Be still, be quiet, do not speak. You are a hypocrite! A whited sepulchre! I despise – I *despise* ...' He had gone red.

'Henry,' said Eleanor, coming over. 'I fear for your health when you allow yourself to be so angered.'

'This sneaking serpent,' spluttered the Dean, pointing a trembling finger at Bates.

'You might suffer an apoplexy,' said Eleanor.

'I fail to see,' said Bates, with some pomposity, 'what harm I have done to merit such calumnious speech.'

'Do you think I have not observed you, sir? Do you think I have not seen with my eye – you, you.'

'Me, me? What, sir? Me, me, what?'

'Matthew chapter five,' said the Dean.

It took a moment for the point of the Dean's words to register with Bates. He scoffed, and fluttered his fingers in the air, but even as he did so his heart was studding in his chest. 'Thou shalt not commit,' said the Dean, in a towering voice, 'adultery.'

'I have done no such thing!' squealed Bates. 'How dare you, sir, a man of God, how dare you accuse—'

'But I say unto you, That whosoever looketh on a woman to lust after her hath committed adultery with her already in his heart!'

'I know the scripture, sir—'

'If thy right eye offend thee, pluck it out, and cast *it* from thee.'

'Henry!' said Eleanor sharply.

'You *look* at her – she is betrothed to—'

'Henry!' said Eleanor, a second time.

But the Dean seemed to have worked himself into some sort of frenzy. Spittle was upon his lips. His large head waggled. 'For I shall not be able to bear my shame, and thou shalt be as one of the fools in Israel: but rather speak to the king, and he will not deny me to thee,' he gabbled.

'Henry!'

'And Absalom her brother said to her: Hath thy brother Amnon lain with thee? but now, sister, hold thy peace, he is thy brother: and afflict not thy heart for this thing. But Absalom spoke not to Amnon neither good nor evil: for Absalom hated Amnon because he had ravished his sister Thamar.'

'Henry!'

The Dean rolled over onto his side and clutched at his stomach with cries of 'Oh! Oh! Oh!' Bates was panting. Eleanor went over to the Dean and lay down beside him, putting her arms about his shoulder. Bates took the corner further from them, set his face to the wall and tried to sleep. It was a lengthy time before sleep came.

The morning came wearing a pearl-coloured veil. Bates had slept poorly and his limbs ached, his neck and shoulders especially, but it was a sort of relief to rise, to stretch himself and walk about.

Behind the hut was a small copse, and a trickly stream flowing down through it, where Bates was able to end his thirst. Several varieties of mushroom were growing there, but on the subject of mushrooms Bates knew not the poisonous from the edible, so he let them alone. He went round the side of this little wooden hillock and found a secluded spot to empty his bowels. When he returned to the hut the Dean was standing at the door.

'Good morning, Mr Bates,' he said.

'Good morning, Dean.' And nothing more was said of the previous night.

Soon enough they started on their way again, walking. They walked a path away from the rising sun, hoping to find a larger road, a turnpike, or some other travellers of whom they could ask directions to York.

They saw nobody at all. They were walking through an emptied land. 'Has everybody died of the plague?' asked the Dean. 'Is this the world picked clean?'

'We survived the fever, we three,' Eleanor observed.

'That is true.'

'If we survived then others have survived.'

'I have a fear in my breast,' said Bates. 'Rather, a *suspicion*.' He waited for the others to ask him what it was, but they trudged on in silence. 'It is,' he said, eventually, 'that the Lilliputians have brought this plague with them from the Pacific hemisphere. I fear that they . . .'

'Humbug,' snapped the Dean.

They walked on in silence.

The sun rose through the sky. The three travellers saw a farmhouse further along the road, and their stride picked up at the thought either of begging hospitality from it, or, if it happened to be deserted (as well it might be), of breaking in and taking what they found. It was a two-storey house, long, stone-built under a slate roof. Behind it was piled a towering haystack, which suggested if not plenty then at least a well-managed farm. 'Come! said Eleanor. 'There must at least be a stove within. To me a baked potato would be as good as a Fortunatus' feast.'

'Aye,' said the Dean.

But as they approached the haystack moved, and a great face reared up, like a parody of sunrise, over the line of the roof. The giant grinned his great grin, teeth like a row of crusader shields, his brown flesh folding and creasing with audible noise.

The three of them stopped; but there was no hiding place, and no benefit to be had from running.

'I,' said Bates. 'I have had converse with these creatures. Have you, Dean?'

'These monsters? Not I.'

'Then let me – let me address it.' He forced his legs onwards and approached the being. It had been lying its length in the field, behind the farmhouse, and now had raised itself on its elbow and turned to face them.

'Hello!' cried Bates, and his voice wobbled. Try as he might to control himself, it wobbled. 'We are travellers!'

'Travellers,' rumbled the enormous mouth.

'Are you under orders from the military forces?' Bates shouted, pointing to the great studded leather jerkin the being wore across his chest.

'I cannot hear you.'

'Shall I elevate myself? Might you position your great ear, Sir Giant?'

'I cannot hear you.'

Laboriously, Bates went to the side of the house and clambered up the unevenly sloping chimney stack, until he could settle himself on the roof. Straddling the centre tiles like a jockey, he tried again.

'Are you under military orders?'

'Aye,' said the giant, meditatively. 'I am of the French.'

'We have met before, sir!' cried Bates, with great excitement. 'We have met once before – in London!'

'Met before?'

'Yes, sir, do you remember? Can you remember?'

'Forgive me,' rumbled the giant. 'You tiny people are not easy to distinguish. Forgive me.' He exhaled a long sigh, and the bushes trembled.

The Dean and Eleanor had come over to the house. 'Is it a friendly giant?' called up the Dean.

'More,' rumbled the being, 'travellers.'

'You and I sat together on the banks of the Thames – do you remember, sir?' urged Bates. 'You were mournful at the destruction of the city.' The giant, by turning his head so that his ear was receptive to Bates's words, appeared to be staring at the horizon.

'Tell it,' shouted the Dean. 'That we are eminences in the French army. It can help us! It could carry us to York with seven-league strides!'

This had been in Bates's mind too. 'We, sir, have important business at York. Important business. If you help us, you would be handsomely rewarded.'

'Rewarded,' rumbled the giant.

'What is it you need? You helped me once – don't you remember? You carried me along the river, and placed me at the Tower. What do you need?'

'I am,' said the giant, his voice like a mighty boulder rolling, 'hungry.'

'Food! There are great supplies of food in York.'

'I have eaten all there is to eat,' said the giant, 'in this place.'

Bates looked down. So intent upon the Brobdingnagian had he been that he'd not until this moment noticed the disarray in which the yard and fields of the farm lay. A hedgerow was sooted with fire. Many trees from a small wood six hundred yards distant had been uprooted and stripped of branches. The carcasses of half a dozen cows, in various states of having been eaten, were spatchcocked upon the trunks of trees, and now lay scattered on the turf. It looked as though a battle had been fought; merely a snack for this giant.

'There were people,' he said. 'They ran.'

'No matter! No matter!' said Bates, excitedly. 'If you help us, we can repay you! Take us to York! Do you know York?'

The enormous head moved, with a tidal slowness, left, right: a shake.

'No matter! Put us on your shoulders and we can spy out the way! It is not far; a few strides for you.'

The giant turned his head to look at Bates, perched on the roof like a cockerel. Then he looked down at the Dean and Eleanor on the ground. Despite himself, the Dean flinched.

'I was with the army,' said the giant, in the most mournful drawn-out basso profundo. 'But the soldiers sickened and died. Many died, and the others went away, afeared of the sickness.'

'I understand!' bellowed Bates. 'You have no orders! But we are eminences in—'

'This is a land of death,' said the giant.

'No matter!' shouted Bates.

'I wish that I had never come to this land,' said the giant.

The impact of the being's melancholy was like a natural force, a great pressure. Bates could not think what to say in the teeth of such enormity of grief.

'Giant!' shouted the Dean. 'Giant!' And for once the Dean was equal to the task. He *projected* himself. 'Giant! GIANT!'

The Brobdingnagian angled his big head.

'Are you a *Christian*?' bellowed the Dean. 'Have you accepted Christ into your *heart*?'

'I have,' said the creature, sounding almost surprised.

'I am Dean of York. Do you know what that means? I am a man of God!'

'God,' said the giant. 'Is bigger even than I.'

'God is bigger than all,' said the Dean. 'And I am a vicar of God! Do you understand?'

'Of God,' said the giant. 'The God died, but he was bigger than death.'

'Yes! You must help us – you must help *me*.'

'Yes,' rumbled the giant.

'For the sake of God!'

'Yes.'

'Carry us to York!'

'For,' the giant said, with his enormous slowness, 'the sake of God.'

'Carry myself, and carry this lady – she is my betrothed. But not this other man.'

'Dean!' shrieked Bates. The word came out much more high-pitched than he intended. 'What? Dean – no!'

'Yes,' said the giant.

Bates hauled himself to the chimney stack and began, ungainly, to clamber down. 'Dean, what are you doing? The fellow can easily carry us three.' His foot slipped and he half-fell, half-dragged down to the turf at the bottom. 'Dean!'

The giant was unfolding himself. He got to his feet with vast unhurried motion; then, again slowly, he bent down to squat on his immense haunches.

'Dean,' said Bates, breathlessly, hurrying over to Oldenberg. 'Of course I must travel with you to York.'

'You, sir?' said the Dean, not meeting his eye. 'You viper!'

Bates was startled out of speech. 'Are you jesting, sir? Are you joking?'

'No sir. Our paths diverge at this point.'

'But – but, Eleanor!' he appealed. 'You must tell him!'

'You must tell him yourself, Mr Bates,' said Eleanor, demurely. 'He is my future husband.'

'Eleanor!' Bates felt a panic rise within him. 'Say – not this! Do not abandon me here!'

'My advice,' said the Dean, in a deep voice, 'would be to walk south, return to London.' And then, in his excitement, his voice resumed its more usual higher pitch. 'I have nothing more to say to *you*, sir.' And he hurried forward. 'Sir Giant!' he bellowed. 'Myself and this lady – to York, sir! To York!'

'Eleanor!' cried Bates, once more.

She stepped to him. 'Do not despair,' she murmured close to his face. 'And do not think I love him, for I do not. But – he has wealth, and position, and these things ...'

'Eleanor,' he urged. 'I love you! You know this, that I love you.'

'If I had a free choice,' she said, making a pretence of buttoning her jacket to her neck. 'If my choice were free – then of my two husbands, you know which I would choose. But, choice is not given to everybody, dear Abraham—'

'Eleanor!' barked Oldenberg. 'Why dally with that man?'

'Bidding him farewell, my dear,' she said.

'Eleanor,' Bates said, in a low and urgent voice. 'We have shared – we have shared a thing that—'

'I know it,' she returned. 'But our choices are not often free. Let us say we shall meet again soon, and perhaps ...' And she lifted her hand. Feeling the biggest fool in Christendom, Bates kissed it. And then she trotted over to where the giant was already scooping up the Dean.

Bates started running towards the enormous hand. 'Take me too!' he cried. 'Take me too, Sir Giant!'

'Don't listen to him, Sir Giant,' bellowed the Dean, already fifteen feet in the air. 'Take the lady, but *not* that other one.'

'Wait!'

But it was already too late, and the giant was stretching himself to his full height. And then Bates could do nothing but stand and watch as the great figure strode away to the west, stepping over hedgerows and sending the birds bickering into the air all around him.

FOUR

GUGGLERUM AND LITTLEBIG

❁

[1]

Let the giant plunge on with his giant stride. Let him step over rivers as if they were runnels of mercury upon a green floor. Let his head graze underbellies of clouds.

The Dean clung to the creature's shoulder. He plunged his hands in amongst the giant strands of the creature's woollen vest and clasped one of the ropes inside. He was saddled upon the shoulder-strap of leather – three inches thick – that linked the front of the Brobdingnagian's protective jerkin to the back, and gripping at the network of interwoven ropes of wool, he clung on. Mrs Burton was cradled in the creature's left hand. But Oldenberg wanted to *see*. He wanted the aerial seat, like Euripides on his cloud, to look down on mortal vanity. And this seat he had, save only that it jiggled and swung, and that he must focus most of his energy in simply hanging on, or face a seventy-foot drop to the ground.

'Are you alright, Eleanor?' he called, but she could not hear him over the whooshing of the air. And he was elated. They mounted a hill and the prospect from the top was of Yorkshire all to the west, and the spire of York Minster – was it? – visible pricking the horizon, and villages and copses, but the trees looked like broccoli florettes, and the sky was filled with rainclouds, taller even than he. Great mountain-peaking clouds with grape-coloured bases. With what certainty they promised rain. The deluge! Lave the world clean! 'York city!' cried the Dean. 'I can *see* it, Sir Giant! The horizon – the Minster, proud – make for—' but the rest of his words were swallowed by thunder. A great Brobdingnagian rumble of thunder, like a boulder

as massy as the moon rolling down the mahogany grooves of the sky.
On strode the giant.

[2]

Bates surprised himself. He expected to be stricken and downed by the fact of his abandonment. He might never see her again – never, never – and here he was marooned in the middle of a desert county, a land picked clean like the Black Death. And yet, his heart, like a hot coal – elation. She had said: *If my choice were free – then of my two husbands, you know which I would choose*. He would see her again. The Dean was an old man, old and ill with his snuff, and corpulent. He was rickety after the fever. Death had curled a bone-finger through his buttonhole. But Bates was young, and would prevail. Young and, people said, handsome. Eleanor had been a widow before, and would be a widow again, and then – and then – and then.

Dear Abraham, she had said.

He must follow them to York, of course. He could not walk to London, and the thought of returning to the coast was repugnant to him. He would walk west, and make his way to York. He would present himself to the English forces – he would style himself as a man with important knowledge of the French – or . . . he knew not what he would do. But he would follow her. She was the star that guided his life now.

First he must address his hunger. He made his way to the pile of cattle carcasses that the Brobdingnagian had left, for there was meat still on the bodies, and cooked too. He pulled some chunks from one and, chewing, he made his way to the cottage and inside. His cheek ached mildly when he moved his jaw. The skin of the side of his face, punctured by the tiny bullet, stung when stretched. No matter.

It was dark, for the shutters were still closed. But the kitchen had not been looted, and Bates found first a large knife with a bone handle and – better than that – a heel of bread. It was moulded over with blue fur, but he pared this away easily enough to fashion a cube of bread unspoiled, if a little stale. At the back of the kitchen was an annex that led, round the corner, to a covered outhouse, and here there was a well. Bates dropped the bucket and hauled it up, and drank until his stomach creaked. Then he moved from room to room chewing on the cube of bread, exploring the rest of the house. It was quite empty, though the bed – which was on a broad shelf overlooking the main chamber – was ruffled, as if somebody had but recently arisen from it. Bates did not care. The combination of a full stomach, and his poor sleep the night before, spurred him. He climbed the ladder and fell on the bed. *Dear Abraham*, she had said. He was asleep almost at once.

Upon awaking he found the pain in his cheek much more severely disagreeable. The carbuncle, where the Lilliputian warrior had shot him with his miniature rifle, felt hot under his finger. It ached now as a toothache aches, a continuous and distracting quantity of pain. The pellet was still embedded in his flesh. Bates could feel it, like a pea under a quilt; but no matter how he manipulated his cheek with his fingers he could not unloose it.

Annoyed by the ache of it, Bates found his mood slipping. He recalled himself to his resolution – to follow the giant's footsteps, and hurry to York as fast as his own feet could take him. 'Rouse yourself, Abraham,' he said aloud. 'What? Indolent? In a stranger's house?'

His slogan must be: *Eleanor*!

So he climbed down the ladder and searched rapidly through the house for items to carry with him. He found little enough, but he did chance upon a Hessian-cloth satchel, and into this he put his knife, some leeks from the larder (they were starting to bolt, but he took them anyway) and a stoppered jug which he filled at the well. Then he went outside and carved some more pieces from the scorched carcasses of the cattle. He thought of salting it, but there was no salt to be had. He felt quite the pilgrim, to be thinking in such terms. He, who until a few months ago ate only what others cooked for him, servants or the chef at his club. Now here he was, like a questing knight, attending quite to his own needs!

The sun was past the zenith, and the sky was busy with corpulent white clouds, each of them edged with blue like the mouldy bread in the kitchen. A storm might be coming. Bates debated with himself whether he should spend another night in the farmhouse, and set out the following day. But no! he told himself. I have delayed long enough! I must get on. To Eleanor! And so he set off, walking west.

At first he made good progress, crossed three fields and found a road; unmetalled, but made of solid dirt and with a hedgy strip of grass growing along the middle. He walked with long strides. The sun shone warmly, but with the warmth of a friend bidding farewell. Soon enough, the sky became covered entire with cloud. A wind got up. It grew colder.

Nevertheless, in his heart: *Dear Abraham.*

It began to rain, mildly at first, and then more heavily. There was no shelter, and nothing to do but press on, but Bates found his resolve melting and shivering out of him. Turn back, advised his inner voice. Go back to the farmhouse. 'No!' he said to himself, aloud. 'Be a man, Abraham. Eleanor! Eleanor!' And that word was his tocsin. He put his head down and marched on.

The rain wet his clothes. Soon enough it got through to his skin, and started to run down the crease of his back. His stockings became clogged with water inside his shoes, and chafed at his heels. His shirt adhered coldly to his back. It was much darker now, and blackening more every moment.

Thunder crumpled the sky over his head.

Flickers in the corner of his eye, and the rain was illuminated, momently, as a million wriggling threads. After the flash the night was darker than before.

The road passed a house. It was a farm, with a cart in its yard, and a duckpond. With a cry of thanks to merciful God Bates dashed over the muddy yard and pushed open the door.

The inside was too murky to be able to see. But the smell was offensive: merde-ish, redolent of corruption, and Bates hesitated on the threshold. But tush, he told himself. His need for shelter outweighed his dainty repulsion. He stepped forward.

Round the corner from the entrance there was a glow. It was a candle, lit in the corner. One individual, or perhaps two, lay on a heap of rags by the wall. He, or they, were not moving. 'Good day,' said Bates. 'I of course must apologise for entering uninvited, but—'

He felt a painful crack on his shoulder, *ah!*, and he spun about. Someone had struck him! An old beggarman in filthy clothes, rheum flowing from his eyes, he had bustled up from the other corner and had struck him with a staff. Struck him! And now he was raising his staff for a second blow.

'Sir!' cried Bates, holding his hands before him. 'Please sir! I ask only shelter for a short space until the storm—'

The staff landed *thwack!* on Bates's forearm and made him shout in pain. He danced backwards. 'I assure you,' he said, in a higher-pitched voice.

'Get away o' my house,' cried the old man.

'Sir, I am begging shelter . . .'

'Get away and *out*!'

'The storm outside – it is not weather to cast a stranger—'

'Get *out*!'

'The Bible, sir. Think of the *Samaritan*, he—'

The stick swung again and caught Bates hard on the side of his head. This was a severe knock. Bates spun about and stumbled, but did not fall. His head resounded with pain; it *rang* with pain like a gong. He staggered sideward and collided heavily with the wall. His vision was jarred double. To prevent himself from sliding to the floor he reached up, grasped at the wall, and a piece of plaster the size and shape of an ear came away in his hand. There were flashes of light inside his eye, like miniature inner lightning.

He heard a swish, and, stunned though he was, Bates understood that the staff had been wielded once more and had missed his ear by a fraction. He needed no further persuasion. He lurched, he stumbled and ran, loomed left, hauled himself right, fumbled at the front door and in moments was outside again in the rain. An ache gripped at his skull where it had been hit. The rainwater dribbled and stung on his skin.

Behind him the door shut with a thud.

He stood for a moment in the downpour gathering his wits, and then, despite everything, he returned to the front door. 'Let me in sir, I pray you!' he called through the wood. 'Sir!' and knocking, 'Sir! I beg you!' and knocking again. He shouted that he would pay for lodgings, that he had money, although he had none. But the air outside was silvery dark, and very cold, and he had nowhere else to go. The rain was falling enormously all around.

He had, he realised, lost his sack inside the house. 'Sir! Please allow me at least to retrieve my satchel! It is all I have to eat!'

But there was no reply. The yard was slithered over with a covering of water. The rain made glassy stubble all across the face of the duck-pond. It hissed like a huge serpent over the slate roof. There was no helping it. Anger came up inside him, and he picked pebbles from the side of the pond and hurled them at the flank of the house. But he fast became tired of this, and the anger was soon washed away by the inundation. Bates clutched his head and stumbled away.

'Eleanor,' he shouted aloud into the teeth of the storm, trying to spur his spirits. 'Eleanor!' But it was very hard to feel anything except sorry for himself in this freezing and soaked universe.

It was purple-and-black night now, completely wet, completely cold, with the occasional bone-coloured flicker from lightning that projected momentariness upon the shivering grass. A great surf-crash of thunder followed hard upon each flicker. In all the universe now Bates was aware of only two things: the sensation of the cold and constant pressure from the rainfall; and the enormous *sound* of it – the mocking applause of it, as if the cosmos were a cynical audience rejoicing in his suffering. He stumbled through the mud and back onto the road. His muscles twit ched and juggled with chills. Oh, but he was freezing to death. He was soaked in ice-water and pummelled with blows from above.

His sufferings stretched the time out; swelled each minute to pro-digious proportions. It seemed to him that he had walked on for hours, though it was not so long. The road he followed turned right but he could not see the turn in the darkness with his head down, and so he stepped into the ditch. The trench was a foot deep with water. And there he stood, shivering, up to his shins in it. This was the lowest point of his journey – of what, afterwards, he would call his great odyssey of discovery. Naturally, such grandeur of self-characterisation bespoke that one (of the two) Abraham Bateses who possessed energy and the higher spirits. The heartened and not the depressed Abraham. When, in later life, his blue devils afflicted his spirit (as naturally they did, for they were a part of that same soul they attacked) he would recall to himself the rain, the terrible cold and *hopelessness* of this moment – standing, in the dark, in the ditchwater, and every scrap or atom of life purged from him. He would recall it to remind himself that even the most terrible sufferings have a finite duration.

He stood there for long minutes. Only the completeness of his prostration of mind prevented him taking such action as, for instance, throwing himself forward and drowning himself there – or of ripping his sodden clothes from his body, like Lear on the heath, and raving. But he did not do these things. He was as perfect a physical emblem of passivity as could be imagined.

And then, as if remembering something he had forgotten, he said the word aloud: 'Eleanor!' It was a mumble. He said it again, speaking more distinctly.

There was a glimmer of light, away to his right.

'Eleanor!' he cried.

With some difficulty in the dark, he clambered out of the ditch and lurched off towards the gleam. A house, with people inside. A light in the dark. He would beg shelter – he would sleep, like Joseph and Mary, in the stable, yea in the pigsty if needs be, but he would get himself out of the flood.

The light was small, and Bates lost view of it several times. He had to leave the road and walk, with mud-clogged feet, directly across a field, and start up a slope before he found from whence it was issuing.

It was a cave, set into an escarpment where the hill rose more steeply and lost its covering of grass. Bates stopped at the entrance. The light inside did not flicker, as a candle or fire would; which could only mean it was gas. A lamp! It showed the entrance to the cave as a rough a-shaped hole in black and glistening rock; but it showed, also, that blocks had been laid at the floor of this entrance to smooth the path in, and that therefore this was more than a mere wild hole-in-the-hill. This was a place used by humanity. Shepherds, perhaps, might shelter here. Bates stepped in under the roof, ducking his head a little, and called out.

'Helloa,' he cried.

He had entered that place which would for ever be associated in his mind with Knowledge, as if it were Plato the Philosopher's cave, or a cavern from Fairy Romance that led through to an otherworld that gave the hero glimpses of a Truth hidden from ordinary eyes in our ordinary world. He would find out soon enough. 'Hello,' he cried again, stepped forward, and wiping the wet from his face with his right hand. 'Do not refuse me shelter on this night, friends! I saw your light and came to it! A poor traveller, caught in the storm—'

And the light went out.

[3]

The giant strode easily through the rainstorm. Rain came in myriad lines and bars, like an artist's shading of blue-grey on some mighty sketch. It filled the Dean's boots and soaked into the Dean's clothes. In mere moments he was wet through. Oh! He had not felt such elation since his supply of white snuff had been exhausted. 'On! On!' he cried.

But the giant stopped his striding, and turned his back to the wind. Leaning forward to give his tiny passengers some shelter, he caught them up in his hands, his great paws big as the hand of God, and he brought them both up to his face. The pores in his nose loomed like whirlpools. 'On! On! On!' squealed the Dean.

'You,' said the giant, with his infuriating and penetrating slowness, 'are wet. Shall I place you in my,' each word a boulder dropped slowly from his great cracked pink lips, 'pocket?'

'Yes,' called Eleanor. Her dress was wet and clung to her form. Oh, it reproduced the lines of her body, as a sculpture working in finest Valaprozzi marble might carve a dryad and capture the wrinkles and folds of cloth so perfectly that the form appeared naked! 'Place me there, Sir Giant!'

It was in the Dean's heart to demand a saddle on the creature's shoulder – or the crown of his head! To sing *Laudamus cum spirito in exulto* at the very topmost of his voice as his steed strode at forty miles an hour towards York – the rain and wind slapping his face and the elements themselves joining his joy! But he checked himself. The prospect of being in a pocket with his fiancée was appealing too. To be in *a pocket* with a handsome young woman! Tucked up together in a pocket, truly.

'I shall put you,' said the giant, 'inside.'

'Me too, Sir Giant!' cried the Dean, raising his arm. *'Adsum! Adsum!'*

Carefully the giant placed his hands, first the left then the right, in at his large pocket and deposited his charges. He folded the pocket-flap over the top and it was dark. A bouncing motion told that the fellow had resumed his onwards march.

'My dear!' squealed the Dean, trying to settle himself, to brace himself against the fat fibres of the cloth so as to counter the upset of the motion, 'my dear! Who would have thought that you and I, engaged to be married, should find ourselves the pocket-pets of such a creature.' His eyesight, dimmed at first, was beginning to resolve a faint image from the darkness. The fabric, spun of Brobdingnagian wool, seemed woven of soft cables, and light made its way very faintly in at the edges of this grid. Eleanor, bless her beauty, Eleanor had steadied herself with one leg out and the other curled underneath her.

As the giant moved the ropes that were interlaced to make his coat rubbed and groaned, like a ship's at sea. The noise of the storm outside rushed, rushed upon the ear. It was a regimental assault, and roar, and the ordnance of thunder.

And the Dean thought to himself with a kind of glee: I have the Calculating Machine in my pocket, or at any rate its key! His elation bubbled into a fantasy of the future. Received in York as a national hero. Marriage to Eleanor in the Minster. Preferment – a family! Eleanor with sons and daughters about her. He in a large house in the town, working his investigations into publishable form. His investigations unlocking the mysteries of the cosmos. The Garter, a permanent place at court. A statue in a London square. Eleanor gazing up at him with pure love, a love prompted by admiration.

'My dear,' he called, raising his voice. 'We shall soon be there!'

'Indeed.'

He scrambled a little closer to her. 'I have decided that we shall marry in York Minster, my dear,' he called.

'A grand prospect,' she said.

'I shall be a hero of the patria! We shall have the most magnificent of ceremonies.'

'Very good, my dear.'

Her calmness punctured his mood a little. He felt the edges of irritation. If only he had some of his snuff! Lacking that, he reverted to a desire to provoke some reaction from his fiancée, for good or ill.

'Come,' he said. 'We must embrace. 'Twill make our passage in the pocket easier to York.'

'Sir,' she replied, and the Dean was gratified to hear a tone of annoyance in her voice. 'It will be *easier* to remain as we are. If we were to do as you say we would roll about like a coin.'

'Nonsense, woman,' he declared. 'I am to be the husband, and can hardly need recite to you what the Novum Testamentum says about the husband! Wives go *back* to your husbands, slaves *go back* to your masters!'

'You intend that I be your slave?' flared Eleanor. 'What manner of oriental vision is this? Do you see marriage in such terms?'

'Come come!' declared the Dean, strangely pleased by her anger. 'I mean no such thing! Why twist my words, when all I do is quote scripture? I intend for you to be the partner of my life. But the woman to the man is a relation of the lesser to the greater. Surely you do not contest that?' And yet, the thought of her *enslaved*! The thought of himself the potentate and she his vassal!

Eleanor was not looking at him. It was hard, in the dimness, to make out her face. 'I can hardly hear your words over the sound of the storm,' she said.

'It is loud,' he conceded.

'We can talk of this another time.'

'Another time,' said the Dean. He shuffled closer again. 'A kiss, my sweet,' he said.

Eleanor did not move. They rolled and jiggled. They moved onward. Slowly she turned her face towards him, pushed with one arm to move her head closer. His lips brushed her cheek, and a bump pushed his face firmly against hers. 'I am the happiest of men,' he said.

'A wife,' she replied, turning her face away again, 'should indeed make a husband happy.'

It was possible for both of them to lie flat along the bottom of the pocket. It was not comfortable, for a seam, thick as the bough of a tree, ran along the base; but it was more agreeable than trying to remain upright. The Dean dozed rather than slept. The darkness inside the pocket intensified.

A lack of motion woke him.

His first thought: 'We have arrived! We are at York!' He got, with some difficulty, to his feet and began shouting. 'Sir Giant! Sir Giant! Take us from this pocket, that we may talk with the garrison of the town!'

'He cannot hear you, sir,' said the still supine Eleanor.

'Sir Giant! Sir Giant!'

'Your voice is small to him at the best of times,' she said. 'Muffled within his pocket you must be inaudible.'

'I demand to be released!' said the Dean. He leapt, as high as his portly body would manage it, attempting to grasp onto the fabric, to pull his head to the top of the pocket. But the manoeuvre was quite impossible for him. He was frustrated. 'Sir Giant!' he cried.

'Hush!' said Eleanor.

'Giant, *release* us! Let us out of here!'

'Be quiet,' said Eleanor, more sharply. 'Listen.'

The Dean stopped bobbing and fell silent. 'What am I listening *for*?' he asked.

'The giant is talking.'

Quiet: Oldenberg could hear it, a low rumbling, like the lowest drone of a mighty church organ, broken into portions and cadenced slightly up, slightly down. Then silence. Then it would start again.

'To whom,' the Dean asked, 'is he communicating?'

'Another giant,' said Eleanor.

'How so?'

'Can you not hear the difference in timbre, the two voices?'

'Not I.'

'You have no ear, then, for music.'

They were silent. The conversation seemed to continue for a very long time. 'What are they saying?' the Dean demanded several times. '*What?*'

'I do not know. Even if I could pick out the occasional word here and there, they are not speaking English.'

'Heathens,' said the Dean.

But there was nothing to do save wait.

Other voices: human voices, somewhere down below them. Shouting. Who was this? French people! The French were here! The French had come!

And then, with a rustling and a rush of cold air from above, the flap to the pocket was lifted, and the great hand of the Brobdingnagian came down and clasped them both. They were lifted into the night; half-sitting, half-lying on the cupped Brobdingnagian palm. The sky had cleared of cloud, and the moonlight was so bright that it actually hurt the eyes. It was almost as bright as day.

The Dean was excited, and a little scared, and dug his nails into the horny skin to keep from falling. 'Giant!' he cried 'Giant, why have you stopped? Are we at York?' They were lifted past the huge face and brought up to the ear, and Dean repeated himself.

'With whom have you been talking?' cried Eleanor.

The giant lowered his hand again, nodding with tremendous slowness. 'With my friend Brulbug,' he said. There was another giant, tall as a tower, standing thirty feet away. He had achieved that improbable invisibility of the very large, so big that the eye had not at first registered him. But there he was, in plain trowsers and jerkin, with a great shaggy head of hair. There was a forest a little way off, behind him.

'What good is that?' cried the Dean, furious. 'We must get on! Have you forgot our conversation?'

'I cannot go now to the city,' said the giant.

'Cannot?'

'To York town, to York town, I cannot go.'

'You promised!' shrieked the Dean. 'Well, well, betrayal, is it? Place us on the ground, sir, at once, sir. Put us *down* and we shall walk, arm-in-arm, the rest of the way ourselves – and no thanks to you sir – and God will not be pleased with *you*, sir.'

The giant angled his great head, as if trying to catch at this stream of words.

Then Eleanor's vision resolved itself. She had been confused, for a second, by her unusual vantage point – raised so very high. The sky was *there*, she saw, and there a fiercely bright moon, and the giant's face. But the stars were orange and seemed to have fallen to the floor of the world, for the space above her was empty of their light and the space below glittered with a receding vision of light.

She looked again. 'Dean,' she said.

She looked again and saw more clearly: the lights below were camp-fires, perhaps a thousand of them. A very great number.

The forest that she had thought she saw was not composed of trees, but of hundreds of Brobdingnagian giants, all equipped in a livery of blue. 'The army of France,' she cried. 'Dean!'

'We are in the champaign before York,' the Dean shouted, extraordinarily excited. 'We are before York, and the French have invested the city!'

'Two armies,' said the giant, and with his free hand he reached out two dozen yards and gestured. The moonlight really was intensely bright, giving the whole scene a curiously oneiric vividness. Eleanor could see very clearly, etched in silver and black and illuminated by a thousand orange nests of fire, the myriad tents of the French. The field running down a slope. A river dividing them. And, on the far side, the Union Flag; the tents and fires of the British.

'In the plains before York town! A great battle,' cried the Dean. 'In the *heart* of Britain – for heart, in the human corpus, *is* upperwards, and towards the neck, and so I say the *heart* of Britain is northward, at York.' He was childishly excited.

'Two armies,' said Eleanor. 'But the Brobdingnagians are all on the French side.'

'Not all, surely,' said Oldenberg. 'Some must have stayed loyal. Sir Giant! Sir Giant! Is it not true? There are some who have not betrayed their loyalty?'

She had never seen moonlight like it before. Never had moonlight been so bright.

'But the moon,' said Eleanor, in a wondering voice, 'the moon.'

'What do you say, Madam?' asked the Dean. 'Sir Giant! Have you talked to your giant friends? Is there to be battle here in the morning?'

'The moon, moon, moon,' said Eleanor, pointing. She sounded like a child. The sight of it had reduced her to inarticulacy.

'War!' said the Dean. 'You giant fellows always complain how you hate it, and yet here you all are, lined up and ready. War!'

'The moon is *not* full,' Eleanor cried, pointing again at the steel-coloured sliver hanging over the horizon, like a clipped slice of thumbnail. 'The moonlight is not – it is not from the moon that – not the *moon*, not the *moon* —'

'What are you saying, my lady?' said the Dean.

'Look how bright the moonlight,' said Eleanor. 'And look how *thin the moon!*'

'What is the nonsense of—'

'*Look!*'

Immediately below them there was motion, as of insects. And it was the French soldiery moving about the shins of the giant. The horizon eastward was starting to thaw and gleam with incipient dawn. But this only made the shaped moon seem paler. And yet the silver light washed over everything.

'Bright the moonlight,' Eleanor repeated. 'And not from the *moon.*'

'Light,' said the giant. 'Look up!'

Of course they looked up.

'He has come again,' cried the Brobdingnagian.

'Who has come again?'

'The man bigger than any. Mitras, mitras. The *Christ* man. And only look up, to see his coming.'

Eleanor and Dean looked up before the giant could get to the end of this last, rumbling, slow sentence. There was the comet, much larger than it had been before. Much larger than the moon ever was. A great teardrop of light in the purple and the black, overwhelming the sky. And silver light poured from it.

'He has come again,' said the giant. And somebody was crying aloud, in Latin, somebody below them on the ground crying in good ecclesiastical Latin though with a French accent, *ante paucos annos*

propinquus uester Christus nobilitatem patriciam nomine sonans nonne specu
Mitrae et omnia portentuosa simulacra . . .

[4]

Bates stumbled in the cave, regained his feet with difficulty. The darkness was total. 'Do not extinguish your light!' he called into the black.
'I pray you!' Then he bethought himself of bandits and robbers, not
shepherds but desperadoes, and he was filled with despairing terror.
'Who's there?' he querulled. 'Is anybody there? Who is it? Who's there?'

It was perfectly black. He could only orient himself by putting the
sound of the torrenting rain behind him, and shuffling forward slowly
with outreached arms.

'Don't torment me, sirs!' cried Bates, feeling his self-control slip
towards weeping. 'If you be robbers, then know that I have nothing on
my person – nothing worth murdering me for. But I am a gentleman!
And in this fearful night, when I have been cudgelled already, and near
drowned in a ditch, and chased from stump to stump by the lightning,
I—'

There was a squeaking sound, and then Bates's thoughts of banditry
were replaced by thoughts of rats. 'Ugh! Ugh!' he called. 'But whose
light was that?'

'Stand still,' said the squeaking.

And then with sudden recognition, Bates understood. 'O Lilliputian
sir!' he called into the darkness. 'Oh, reignite your lamp, I pray you! I
mean you no harm. I am a friend of the little folk – I have devoted my
life to—'

'Stand still,' said the voice again. Bates obeyed.

There was a pause.

'I am shivering, sir,' he said. 'I mean you no harm.'

The little voice sounded nearer. 'You misunderstand, for the balance
of consummation lies upon the other side.'

'I,' said Bates, his teeth chittering, 'I do not understand, good little
sir.'

'The slowness of wits of the big folk,' said the little voice, as if
reciting a proverb, 'is like the motion of glaciers.'

And then there was light.

Bates's eyes flinched, and he rubbed them. The illumination came from a lamp of a style he had not before seen: a block, black, and on top a bright globe pouring out light with unflickering intensity. This light showed the walls of the cave, ribbed like the roof of a man's mouth, black and yellow and glistening. On the floor rested one of the toy aero-fliers of the sort that Lilliputians flew. It had room in its slim central carriage for two pilots. A flying machine. But only one Lilliputian stood next to it, handsome in a yellow uniform. He was holding one of the tiny muskets, and this was aimed at Bates's face. But he held this weapon with one hand only; in the other he had a tiny brass-coloured megaphone, and this he lifted to his lips.

'You are no Dean of York.'

'Not I!' said Bates, startled. 'Do you know of the Dean?' Then, with realisation: 'Did you fly after us in yon flying machine?'

'Sit yourself, Sir Giant,' said the Lilliputian, through the little trumpet. 'Sit cross on the floor.'

'Sit cross?' Bates asked. But he lowered his shivering body to the floor, and of course he knew that the Lilliputian meant cross-legged. He arranged himself. 'I am cold, sir,' he said, hugging himself.

'That cannot be helped.'

'Are there no supplies in this cavern? The entrance has been laid with stones – people sometimes—'

'Nothing.'

Bates rubbed himself, sending spray into the air. 'I must make the best of things, then,' he said. 'I am Abraham Bates, sir.' He felt terrible *ill*. Terrible ill. His head throbbed, and his nose ran. He *was* ill. A fever. Another fever, or a recurrence of the former.

'Not being the Dean,' said the little fellow, 'I deduced as much.' He laid his rifle along the top of his flying machine, with the muzzle resting near one of the sycamore-seed-shaped propeller blades; and he sat himself on one of the wings. This left his hands free, although he was within easy reach of the trigger.

'You know of us, clearly,' said Bates.

'Until this killing rainstorm,' said the little fellow, 'I followed you. I followed you when the sky was clear. But we are not so brutish as the big folk, to be able to withstand the falling of the sky.'

'And so you were compelled to seek shelter,' said Bates, hugging himself, 'or have your head stove in by these raindrops, I see, I see. Sir, little sir, I sympathise – for it is a fierce rainfall, I agree. I suppose the rain is thinner in your homeland.'

'You suppose as a fool supposes,' said the Lilliputian. He kept his eyes unwaveringly upon Bates. 'Rain falls the same size the world across.'

'But of course it does,' said Bates. His physical discomfort was making it hard for him to think clearly. As the immediate misery of the freezing rain began, slowly, to reduce, he became aware of the throb and grind inside his skull: a headache where he had been smitten by the peasant with the staff, and a burning pain in his cheek where he had been shot the morning before. Oh, his poor head! Battered and shot! He looked again at the toy plane.

'You, Sir Lilliputian, you – aaa—' A sneeze vulgarly interrupted the sentence. When he recomposed himself, Bates asked: 'What is your name, sir?'

'My name is Gu'glrem.'

'Good little Sir Gugglerum,' said Bates. 'Methinks I recognise your craft – and recognise *you* sir, too.'

'So you should, Abraham Bates.'

Bates looked around. He did not feel threatened by the little fellow, for all his popgun weapon. Very like he was too tired and cold to feel the fear. Besides, the mouth of the cave was fifteen yards behind him, and a quick sprint into the rain would save him, whatever befell. Then he thought: this creature has just told me that he would be *smashed* by the force of the raindrops, where I can walk through the deluge with my head high. And who, then, is the weaker? Except that he, Bates, was ill. The fever was inside his bones, and he felt tired, tired.

'Your comrade tried to kill me, I think,' Bates said, attempting to keep his wits about him. 'To lance out my brains as I slept.'

'Not that.'

'Yesterday morn. You stood on the windowsill and looked on. You and another – the third of you crept up to my pillow as I slept and tried to stab me.'

'He tried only to scratch you.'

'And so he did!'

'He was successful in his mission,' agreed the Lilliputian.

'Psh! He tried to kill me – 'twas no scratch. Were it not for my quick reflexes I would not have been saved!'

'I watched,' said the little fellow. 'I know what passed. He scratched you, but you killed him.'

'In self-defence!'

'I watched,' said the little fellow, and then: 'You killed him. He was a great warrior, but luck was not with him. You killed him with a book the size of a building. You dropped a house on him. No warrior, no matter how great, could survive such assault.'

'A warrior great in Lilliputia.'

'I am Blefuscudan.'

'Blefuscan!'

'Blefuscudan, and so was he, and so was A'gglem.'

'The third there present?'

'He was.'

'What happened to that third fellow? Is he here? He should step forth, and not hide in the shadows—' and Bates felt a spurt of anxiety: for whilst this one little man kept him talking, who was to say that the other wasn't creeping up with some weapon or thorn-prick or other horrid scorpion surprise?

'Dead,' said the Blefuscan. 'He is dead. They are both of them dead. I fly this plane alone.'

'And how did *he* die? This Haggleman?' Bates asked, hugging himself again, and trying to squeeze the shivers out of his torso. 'Is his death on my conscience as well? I mislike killing, little sir. Did I kill him? I'm sorry if so.'

'I killed him,' said Gugglerum. 'I killed him with my hands.'

'*You* killed him?'

'I fly the plane alone.'

'But why did you kill him?'

'With these hands,' said the little man.

'No – *why* – why did you kill him?'

'I heard your question. Did you think I did not hear your question? My ears are young, and your voice booms.'

A silence fell between them.

Bates clung to himself, and tried to calm his shivers. The pains in his body intensified and calmed, grew and diminished, in time to his pulse. There was a dizziness in his head which gave the tiny creature's words a weird, prophetic, John-of-Gaunt quality. The cave itself seemed to throb around him. He put a finger to his cheek, and the carbuncle that marked the place where the musket-ball had struck him felt hot as a struck Lucifer head. 'You,' he said, trying to focus on the little man. 'You followed us.'

'We had orders. We are at war.'

'You aid the French—'

'Indeed no,' said Gugglerum. 'The Fronssai are as greatly our enemy as the English. We have declared war upon all of the big folk.'

'You might have done us the courtesy to have informed us of this declaration,' said Bates.

'Such would advantage you.'

'It is the honourable way.'

'This is a big-person religion,' said Gugglerum. 'Honour.' He said the word blandly, without scorn, but as an empty thing, as he might have said *dust* or *straw*.

'Why were you following us?' said Bates. 'Before you were compelled to take shelter in this place?' And then, his mind distracted by his own pain, he lost the thread of what he was asking. 'And does it happen in your own country, that when the rain comes you run and hide your heads? Or die? Can that be so?' He was shivering prodigiously.

'It is so.'

'How,' said Bates, 'inconvenient.'

'In Blefuscu,' he said, 'we have shelters on all the turnpikes, and we have many public halls in every city. The rain is sometimes small enough to do nothing but soak us, but often there come what we call *p'grerum*, which is rain in which the drops are the size of a man's fist, or his head, and they fall with great vehemence and will break your bones, or flatten you and drown you. We see the clouds that bear such rain from afar and take shelter.'

'But are you never surprised by the rain?'

'Some die in rain. And we execute criminals by tying them to posts in the storm.'

'And hailstorms!' said Bates. 'They must sure break your roofs! Imagine,' he said, 'hailstones the size of cats and dogs.' The shivers, he thought to himself. These shivers are feverish, and not from the cold. Or were they the cold?

'We have no such weather in Blefuscu,' said Gugglerum. 'Though I have seen it here in England.'

Shiverish.

'I must sleep,' said Bates, feeling his weariness very heavily within him. Oh, he had suffered so much! 'Can you let me sleep?'

'Sleep,' said the tiny man.

'You'll not harm me in the night? But what answer can you give? Honour is a void to you.'

'I shall not harm you,' said the man. 'Sleep.'

'I'm too ill and worn to care,' said Bates, with a queer flicker of liberation in his breast. 'I do not seek death, but I am too worn and exhausted to care.'

'I shall not harm you.'

'I would not blame you. For I killed one of your comrades.'

'You killed one, and I killed the other,' said Gugglerum. 'With these hands.'

Bates got to his feet, slow and creakingly, and removed his coat. He was shivering. A few steps towards the cave mouth and he wrung it, as best as his trembling hands could manage, to rid it of some of its water. He took off his boots and poured trickles from them. His stockings were black, wet as dishcloths. He wrung them out too, and then – because he could think of nothing else to do with them – he drew the cold cloth back over his toes. Then he laid himself full-length on the floor of the cave, and drew his coat over him. He was shivering fiercely. He tucked his arm under his head.

'Sir Gugglerum,' he said. 'I am not well.'

'I know this,' said the tiny man.

'I shiver. I shiver with more than the cold.'

'I see you doing so.'

'I may die of an ague or a fit in this very night,' said Bates.

'Everything dies.'

'That is less comfort,' said Bates, 'than it ought, perhaps, to be. But if I die I pray that Jesus Christ take my spirit into his hands.'

'Jesus Christ is big-people religion.'

'No, no,' said Bates, urgently but in a gravel voice, his eyes closing, 'no, no. He came to save *all* the creatures of God's world. Many Lilliputians have converted to the religion of the true saviour – you too, my little friend, could welcome him into your heart, into your heart. For souls are the same size, though the bodies differ.'

He may, or may not, have finished this sentence, before he fell asleep. But he was ill, and he slid into sleep, and he slept the uneasy sleep of the feverish. Consciousness of the throbbing walls of the cave leering up over him did not entirely leave him, and his own body tormented him, bringing him almost awake with pain. Almost. He sat up, and felt a great gout of phlegm leave his body from his nose. He was lying down again, and the tiny man was close up against his face. He could not rouse himself, tho' the creature was at his eye, at his *eye*, and it was

256

holding a tiny knife in its tiny hand. Bates tried to give voice to the Lord's Prayer, but the tongue would not work. He dozed, or half-dozed, or quarter-dozed. He shivered. The pain never *quite* withdrew itself from him. Time passed, or re-passed, unaccountably.

'Fear not,' said the tiny being. 'It was for your sake I killed my fellow.'

For my sake? But the words would not come.

'We are at war with you. We were ordered to follow you and slay you. We were to slay you, because you survived the pestilence. But I foresee a greater danger, for us all, and so with my own hands I have killed my friend.'

Your friend!

Then Eleanor was somewhere about, near at hand but out of sight. Bates wanted to turn but could not. And whilst he knew that this was because he was lying upon the stone floor, he also thought he was standing, and Eleanor was behind him, and he tried to turn. Eleanor! Eleanor! Think of Democritus. The Continental calculator and man of science, Leibniz. He, like Democritus, believed atoms to be the basement of the real world. But what if they were *wrong*? O Eleanor!

A deeper sleep swelled, neaptide-like, and Bates sank down.

It was light outside. The rain had stopped and a bright sunshine filled the cave mouth.

Bates sat up, slowly. It was not that he felt refreshed by his sleep, for the night had been desperate and uneasy. But he was no longer shivering. His clothes were drier, although not entirely dry. He put a finger to his face, and the lump in it was gone.

A fire was burning. A thread of smoke stretched to the ceiling and rolled away into the depths of the cave. Bates shuffled forward towards the heat and warmed himself at the low flame. There was the little fellow's tiny plane, and there was the fellow himself.

'I brought in wood and straw,' said Gugglerum.

'For a fire?' said Bates, with a croaky voice. 'But it will be wet.'

'At dawn, when the rain stopped, I flew in my craft to a great barn. There were many mighty beasts there, and some big men. The big men were alive, or dead, I know nothing of that; but whilst they lay I gathered wood and straw and tied it and flew in my craft here.'

'Thank you.'

'I have cut away the musketball.'

'Cut away?'

'Out of your face.'

Bates felt his cheek again. 'I do not understand.'

'I did it when you slept, though you slept ill.'

'Did I not wake when you cut me?'

'No,' said the little man. 'My knife is true Blefuscudan make, and finer than any of yours. It parts the skin so sly, so fine, that your nerves hardly know it. Afterwards I threaded the wound with thread.'

'You carry thread? And a needle?'

'No needle. But I pricked and fed the thread through the holes in your skin.'

'With your fingers?'

'My fingers are fine,' he said.

Bates did not know what to think of this. 'Thank you,' said Bates.

'It was poisonous to you,' Gugglerum said. 'It was putting poison in your blood.'

'I believe it *had* become inflamed,' said Bates.

'You would have died.' The little man was perfectly matter-of-fact.

'It is true,' said Bates. 'I was not well,' conceded.

'I shot a bird.'

'A bird?'

'It will be an easy matter for your strength and size.'

'What will be an easy matter?'

'The unfeathering of the bird. Do you have a knife?'

'I lost my knife,' said Bates, remembering the mad old man who had beaten him with a stick. The nightmarish night of storm and cold and pain.

'That is poor news, for with my knife it would be great labour to fillet the bird. Can you cook?'

'I am a gentleman,' said Bates. When it became clear that this did not supply Gugglerum with an answer to his question, he added: 'It has not been my custom to cook. Rather, I employ others. To cook for me.'

'This is poor behaviour,' said the little man. 'You must follow instruction from me.'

Bates recovered the dead bird − a sparrow, or something of that sort − from the mouth of the cave where Gugglerum had shot it. He sat upon the floor like a country wife and pulled its feathers out, one after the other. Tiny fleas, white as rice grains, crawled onto his fingers, and he flicked them away. When the bird's carcass was denuded

Gugglerum told him to coat it in mud, of which the night's deluge had generated a great supply outside the cave. Bates, under instruction from the Blefuscan, then carried this ball to the fire and dropped it into the midst. From a pile of dry sticks and straw – and surely the tiny man had made more than one journey with his craft, to accumulate so large a pile – Bates built the fire up. They sat for a while as it cracked and chuckled.

'You have done Christian acts today, sir,' Bates said, 'though perhaps you do not recognise them as such. But Christ knows what you have done, sir. He will not forget.'

Gugglerum said nothing.

'Christ tells us,' Bates explained, 'to turn the cheek. If our adversary strikes us on one cheek we should turn the other to receive another blow. I killed your comrade, sir, though it was in self-defence. But you have returned that act with kindness. You have saved my life. Thank you.'

He turned his back to the fire to warm his coat. A thin steam was coming from his clothes now.

'You had survived the pestilence,' said Gugglerum.

'I was truly sick,' said Bates. 'But God, in his wisdom, spared me.'

'Our allies said, we must send in reinforcements.'

'Your allies?'

Gugglerum stared at the fire.

'Your allies – you talk of the French?'

'No.'

'Then – who?'

'Your enemy,' said Gugglerum. 'This is the army *you* are fighting.'

'You must mean the French, then? Our enemy is the French.'

'No. You and the French are one man, one form.' He thought for a moment, then said. 'You share dimensions with the French. These are *your* allies.'

'The animosity between the Fran and the Anglo-Saxon races has a long history,' Bates said.

'Nevertheless. Your enemy will slay you and the Fronssai both. Your land will be strewn with the bodies of your kind. You fight this enemy and you do not even realise it.'

'You speak,' said Bates, turning to face the fire again, 'of your own kind, I fear. The Lilliputians.'

'Not they.'

'Your people, of Blefuscu.'

'Not we.'

'The Lord know you have good reason to be angry. We have treated you in ways that shame any Christian nation. But peace, peace between our peoples. Peace is possible. Look how we sit and talk! We two!'

'The bird.'

'The bird?'

'Take the bird from the fire.'

'How? I shall burn my hands.'

'Find a stick outside.'

Bates went out of the cave into the sharp, clean air. The sunlight fell upon his skin like a blessing. The view was across green Yorkshire dales and hills, laved by the rain and shiny in the morning, gleaming as if newly made. He found a stick, and came back inside. Using the cleft of the stick he levered the mudball from the fire. The stick hissed as the flames touched it. Once he rolled the baked mudball on the cave floor, he used the end of the stick to crack it open. Inside the flesh of the bird was cooked.

He and Gugglerum ate in proportion to their size. The little man filled his belly. His quantity was a snack for Bates, though savoury and reviving.

'My people believe this alliance to be in our interest,' said Gugglerum. 'But I see they are wrong. My friend A'gglem was furious to kill you, and complete what the pestilence should have done. But I see the truth, that you must live. Not for your sake, or your people, but for the sake of *my* kind. We quarrelled, A'gglem and I fought. I killed him.'

'It is the pestilence,' said Bates. 'Yes? It is the pestilence. When you talk of this great enemy that will destroy both French and English? You refer to—'

'Yes.'

'And are you immune to the infection?'

'Of course. There is no such thing in my land.'

'No disease?'

'There is no plague amongst us.'

'But you cannot mean that the *very* concept of . . .'

'There is no such thing as plague among us.'

Bates nodded slowly. 'So it was with the anthropophagi of North America,' he said. 'Or so I have read – another great wrong of my people, we brought diseases unknown to these people and smallpox and typhus destroyed many of them. I am sorry again, my little friend. Sorry that we have introduced such a thing to your world.'

'We cannot become ill with such disease,' said Gugglerum.

The truth came to Bates. 'You are immune?'

'They do not exist in my land.'

'They do not? Diseases do not?'

'There is no such thing.'

Bates was amazed. 'But,' he said, shortly, 'they exist in *my* land.'

'Nevertheless, they do not afflict us.'

'You must have your own forms of sickness! You must have some manner of fever?'

'These are big-people afflictions. These are unknown to us. They cannot afflict us.'

'Providence has made you immune,' said Bates, wonderingly. 'It must have its purpose in doing so. Perhaps – and I have often thought along these lines – some manner of *universal* justice applies. For you are so vulnerable to the greater size of our kind that Nature has given you this compensation.'

Gugglerum looked at him with his unnervingly unwavering stare.

'You brought this pestilence from the Pacific islands,' said Bates. 'I suspected it. You have somehow brought it hither, and use it now as a weapon of war.'

'We did not bring it.'

'Do you mean that it is *we* that brought it? That our sailors brought it back with them?'

'No.'

'No? You are cryptic, sir. But how – in what manner have you used it as a weapon of war? Tell me that, tell me only that.'

'The Dean of York,' said the little man. 'He is great amongst your kind?'

'The Dean? He – how do you mean?'

'He is a great man of God. I had hoped to find him. But I have found you.'

'You confuse me sir.'

'You must speak to the King.'

'The King of England?'

'Aye.'

'Sir! I cannot merely stroll into the Court and demand an audience with the King!'

Gugglerum seemed to revolve this sentence in his mind. Then he said: 'But the Dean of York may?'

'I suppose – I do not know, in truth. He is no Archbishop, I know that. But perhaps he has affairs that take him into the Court.'

'Then we must follow after the Dean.'

'He,' said Bates, with a pang (for the memory had been obscured in his heart whilst he broke fast with this little man), 'persuaded one of the giants – one of the giants to us, you know – to carry him and ... another person. To carry them to York city.'

'Then we must go there.'

'To give the Dean some message that he, in turn, must carry to the King?'

'Yes.'

'But what message?'

'Words to save your kind.'

'To save our kind? What can you mean? How can that be? Do you mean,' Bates said, 'that you have a *cure* for the pestilence?'

'I have understanding.'

'You veil your meaning, sir.'

'I have the way to a cure. The Dean has such a way. You have. Come,' said Gugglerum, leaping to his little feet. 'We must not delay.'

'But you can fly to York in your device, can you not? It will take me the Devil's own time to walk there.'

'You are the Dean's friend.'

'I,' Bates began. But he could think of nothing to say beyond this word.

'He would not listen to a sole Blefuscan warrior. He would try to swat me like an insect. *You* must introduce us.'

'I,' said Bates again.

'We must leave now, for there is no time to lose.'

[5]

The light of the stars was dampened by the splatch of brightness. The cries of the French militia below them, Oldenberg and Eleanor stared skyward at the comet. It was a circle of light, large as the shield of Satan of which Milton speaks.

The giant lowered them slowly to the ground and they stepped off.

The Dean, adjusting himself to his new situation, was ready. '*Mes chers citoyens*,' he cried, advancing towards the French soldiery. 'Allies! I bring news from the coast, from the command of Colonel Larroche and the frigate, the frigate *Sophrosyne*. Allies, my friends! Allies.'

But Eleanor was not happy to leave the Brobdingnagian. 'Sir Giant!' she cried, even as she was dropped onto the ground and the huge creature unfolded upright again. 'Sir Giant! The light in the sky – the light in the sky—'

The giant seemed to sway against the paling sky.

'What is that great globe of light?'

He was swaying away.

Three French soldiers stood in a row with their rifles lowered, but from behind them stepped an officer. He spoke, in fluent and unaccented English: 'Good morning to you, good morning to you both.'

'Ah!' exclaimed the Dean, shaking this officer by the hand. 'Splendid. I am the Dean of York. I have come from the coast . . .'

'Riding an unusual sort of horse,' said the officer. 'Leave him, Madame, the giant I mean. He goes to confer with his fellows.'

And indeed the giant was raising his leg and placing it down again and moving like a stormcloud away to stand alongside his fellow Brobdingnagian.

'They are sturdy lads,' said the Dean. 'Strong arms for the army of France.'

'They are no good,' said the officer.

'No good?'

'They mislike killing people,' said the officer, with disgust in his voice.

'They mislike?'

'It is good English?'

'Indeed, sir,' said the Dean, half-bowing, 'your English is as good as any native's.'

'My English mother,' said the man. 'But my blood is French.'

'Of course!'

'I am unused to speaking it, though I spoke it often as a lad. English. English. They mislike the killing, the giants. They are good for smashing buildings, and for breaking cannons. They will march about with their clubs and break houses. But they are squeamish. They are *squeamish*.'

'Permit me to introduce myself, sir,' said the Dean. 'I am the Dean of York. That,' he swept his right arm in a semicircle, 'is in a sense *my* town.'

'You gesture to the south,' said the French officer, dryly.

'Ah!'

'To the west is York, and to the morrow is a battle. This day now dawning. The sun intimates its coming by painting the walls of the eastern horizon with orange and yellow. And the battle is *here*, sir.'

'Ah!'

'You were travelling to the city.' This was not a question.

'Indeed. But the military needs—'

'Mr Dean of York,' said this French officer of military. 'Am I to take it you are by way of an *advance* party?'

'Advance?' repeated the Dean, a little confused.

You have ridden your giant horse—' and here, as if reminded of the existence of the Brobdingnagians, the Frenchman shook his head and t't-t'ted. '*Such* poor allies. So great their strength, and yet they can only with the greatest effort be persuaded to use it against human life! They are peaceable. Quakers in spirit if not in name, sir.'

'I do not believe you have honoured me with you name, sir,' said Oldenberg.

'And this light in the sky has distracted them further,' said the Frenchman, talking as if the Dean had not spoken. 'My men are – how do we say it in English – spooked by the light as well. My captains are having a devil's job of keeping their minds on the coming battle. They take it as an omen, sir.'

The Dean looked up. The sky was now pearl, the eastern stars swallowed up in the pre-dawn, the western stars shrivelled and greyed. The sliver of the moon looked as insubstantial as a magic-lantern projection against the pale screen of the atmosphere. But the great white circle still shone, like a silver sun, or a great globe of glass suspended in the heavens and lit from within. For the first time the sheer strangeness of this apparition penetrated the Dean's resolute self-absorption. 'It is queer,' he said. 'What is it? It is an oddity. It is a comet. We saw a comet in Scarborough – has it come so close to the world?'

'Of course,' said the French – Colonel, General, whoever he was. 'What else?'

'It has swung perilous close to the world,' said the Dean.

'You observed its approach?'

'I – did not,' said the Dean, reluctant to add that he had been *inside a pocket*, for fear that it would paint him in a ridiculous light. He had a great fear, as do most pompous men, of appearing to others as ridiculous.

'No?' said the Frenchman. 'It was a curious thing. There was rain, a mighty deal of rain. But then, of a sudden, as if it had veered rapidly in, the light of the comet was apparent behind the clouds. Understand this: the clouds were black, black in themselves and black in the night. Thick clouds, like blankets, and rain pouring from them. But nevertheless the light became visible, first a smudge, and then a blot of brightness. Then the clouds thinned and parted, as if driven away by the light. As a breath of hot air may drive away cold fog. And they boiled and separated and in the middle was black sky and the great circle of light. It swelled. It swelled and grew. My men – we were all looking up, and some cried aloud in grief and some threw themselves down and prayed, for it looked as though the comet was to collide into the earth. To crash into our heads.'

'Good lord,' said the Dean, weakly.

'It is fortunate that we have discipline in the Army French, fortunate. I ordered the troops from their tents and to form lines. A soldier feels more comfortable facing death if he is in an orderly line, with his comrades on either side. So we lined up. And the light grew and grew and – stopped. It is an unaccountable comet. It may have become tangled in the rigging of the sky, or perhaps it is spinning, or perhaps the explanation is some other thing. But it is coming no closer.'

'I've never heard of such a thing,' said the Dean.

'Indeed. But we are soldiers, and we have the job before us. The sun is coming up, and in no more than an hour we shall go to battle. The English are arrayed before York town, and we must attack.'

'Attack?' said the Dean, half-comprehendingly.

'Indeed. What else are soldiers *for*?'

'There was a comet presaging disaster before Hastings,' said the Dean, his head back. 'The tapestry-maker at Bayeux stitched it into his fabric. Made of dabs of fabric rather than dabs of light. Though that one did not come so close, at Hastings, yet they are both cometary. Cometary. A comet, and then King Harold goes to battle against the French at Hastings . . .'

'Ten and sixty-six,' said the French commander. 'It presaged disaster, but only for the English. Not for the *French*.' He smiled broadly. 'And I have told my troops so.'

'I cannot tear my eyes from the sight,' said the Dean in a desolate voice, still looking up.

'You,' said the French commander. 'You have come from Monsieur le Colonel Larroche.'

'I – we have.'

'You are, in other words, by way of an advance guard?'

'I fear I do not . . .' started the Dean. His eyes were constantly pulled upwards towards the light in the sky.

'Sir you are slow,' said the French commander, for the first time appearing to lose a little of his temper. 'Larroche is *my* man. I know what his mission is. Why he would send someone as unmilitary as yourself I know *not* – unless it be that only a man of the Church could persuade the Brobdingnagian giant to carry them – for of course they are as superstitious and religious in their minds as they are stubborn and peaceable in their habits. So: is it thus? Larroche sent you because the giant would carry none other? But he sent *you* to inform *me* that he is marching hard over the countryside to join us? Is this your message?'

The Dean looked at the French commander with wide-opened eyes. 'It is to say,' he started, and paused. 'It is to say,' he tried again. With a knot of resolution he pushed the lie through: 'You hit it exactly, *Monsieur le Commandant*. This is exactly the situation. Colonel Larroche is force-marching to . . .'

'Colonel Larroche and a force of . . .?'

But the Dean was unused to lying, and poor at thinking on his feet. 'I am,' he began, 'which is to say, I am *unsure* as to the numbers of men . . .'

'Surely the Colonel would not send you on such a mission without this information? It is vital that I know.'

'But of course,' said the Dean, looking at the ground. The light was strong enough now to etch each of the blades of grass dark blue and green in the sward by his boots. Nearby was the dint pressed flat, as big as the keel of a great ship, by the giant's foot; and beyond it the impressions of other feet. 'The Colonel leads a force of,' he plucked a number from the air, 'four hundred men.'

'So many?'

'We were reinforced from the sea,' said the Dean. He twirled his right hand.

'It matters not. How far are they? For our hostilities will commence very soon, and the sooner they arrive the better.'

'A few hours' march, no more.'

'A few?'

'Two.'

'Two hours?'

'Just so.'

'Good, very good, but tell me, Monsieur,' said the Frenchman. 'This is not the true purpose of the Colonel's mission. He has the device? Yes?'

And here the Dean had no need to lie. 'He has,' he said.

'He brings it?'

'It is well guarded,' he said, 'and brought hither drawn by horses. Yes he brings it.' It occurred to him to add *And I have the key to it in my pocket*, but he restrained himself. He had no idea where these lies were taking him. Indeed, he did not know quite what he was doing, or why he had said what he had said, except that he felt it prudent to ingratiate himself with this unnamed commander. But the full import of what he had been told began to sink through his mental slowness. A battle was about to commence!

'Monsieur,' he said, starting forward and laying a hand on the sleeve of the Frenchman's uniform. 'The battle is almost upon us. This lady . . .' and he gestured towards Eleanor.

'I confess I am surprised that Larroche would send a gentlewoman upon such a mission.'

As Walter Scott wrote, it is a horribly entangling business when one first essays deception. How to explain her presence? 'It is unusual, I grant,' he said. 'The lady is my fiancée.' Should he have said *wife*? It was too late. 'She was disinclined to be separated from me.'

'So, so, and thus you have brought her to a very dangerous place,' said the Frenchman.

'Is there no haven, so safe place in which she could shelter?'

'Look about you, sir,' said the Frenchman.

It was now plain day. To the east the sun, molten orange and coldly bright, lay upon the high horizon as if it had been balanced there. Its illumination combined with the white light from above to light in pale yellow the whole of their surroundings. Oldenberg could see that they were on a broad sloping hill, pasture all the way up, westward, to a distant line of trees. Below them, away to the east, was a broad and shallow valley, a twisting river, the tessellated parallelograms and strips of fields marked out by stone walls. Closer at hand lay a host of pyramidal blue tents and the black asterists of numerous dead campfires; and there, being mustered by their mounted officers, many thousands of blue-uniformed troops. And beyond this scene, on the far side of the little river, toy multitudes of English soldiers, likewise forming ranks. The officers, likewise mounted, were conspicuous in their red coats; the ordinary soldiers milled and formed up. The red looked like some thousand flames in amongst the dark green. On both sides of the river units were wheeling; men were readying their rifles and fussing about the cannon.

'You see there is no shelter,' said the Frenchman. 'I should say to your fiancée to remain behind the lines; but when the artillery begins this will be no guarantee of security. You should not have brought her.'

'Eleanor,' the Dean cried, turning, and turning about to find her. 'Eleanor!'

He could not see her. She had gone.

He looked again, and saw her rushing towards the legs of the two distant giants. It occurred to the Dean (and as he thought it he thought to himself how strange that this had not occurred to him before) how very large and easy a target the giants must make to the cannonaders. 'Eleanor!' he cried. That was no safe place, where she was going. He took two steps towards her, and stopped. 'Eleanor, where are you going? Not there! Not there!'

Then things happened very suddenly, although in a distinct sequence and without ever losing a sense of perfect clarity. Eleanor was running towards the giants; or if not running exactly then proceeding rapidly, walking at the briskest of paces. The light hung in the sky. Then it suddenly increased in intensity, like a lucifer's flare or a candle about to gutter. There was an unreal vividness in the very air; every one of the French commander's wrinkles and pores, every untrimmed stalk of bristle on his chin and lip, leapt out at Oldenberg. An abrupt stench of scorched hair, or something very like it. The Dean turned to face the direction of this flare of light, and was dazzled, whiteness, blankness, and then the bleached-out vision of startled eyes, in which the sight of things returns to the senses but with a hollowed-out quality. He blinked, and blinked again. The air was burly around him. There was a wind blowing, a sudden and violent wind; it made the grass struggle frantically below and it flapped the tails of his coat with great force. Then, strong as it was, the wind grew sharply in intensity, and the Dean felt it shove at his body, such that he lost his footing and fell backwards.

He climbed to his feet again, and the air was still. The comet was still large in the sky above him. The two giants, who had been standing a few hundred yards away, had vanished. And so had Eleanor.

[6]

Conviction lent speed to his heels, but the going was not easy. Gugglerum flew in his craft, tracing carrion-bird circles up above, and Bates pressed on as fast as he could. But he was not a man in prime physical condition, and his sufferings over the previous days had drained him further. He struggled along the York road, but was compelled frequently to rest. He sat on the grass bank with his legs out straight, and the angle between them no greater than thirty degrees. The buzzing of the flying device distracted him. Memories of nightmare, the bird of prey, the pigeonhawk swooping on the pigeon, death coming from above, these thoughts assaulted his mind. It was a plague of fantasy. He told himself: But this Lilliputian is my friend! Yet it had a hollow sound. Though little, his escort possessed the sky, while Bates was confined to the trudgy ground, and each step felt like the step towards his own death. He went slow. Gugglerum would fly off, swoop higher, swing low, and land bouncing and wobbly on the grass beside him.

'We must move more quickly.'

'I am exhausted.'

'This is as nothing. Your tiredness does not signify.'

Bates shook his head, as a dog shakes himself dry. 'I shall try to gather myself. But my head is light, and my limbs weary. If we had a machine-for-flying of an appropriate size,' he added, 'then we might progress more rapidly.'

'You are too big.'

'I fear so.'

'On! On!'

Bates got to his feet.

The road went downhill and alongside a river. The waters were plump and rapid with the previous day's heavy rain. Where there were submerged obstacles – boulders, say – the flow cast humps and arcs of clear glass from the fluid medium. It sounded continually in his ears.

Above him, in the morning sky, the comet was so prominent that it was clearly visible now by day. It was a disc, clearly defined against the blue but gleaming and bright with silver light. From time to time Bates would find his eye drawn up to it. His expertise in astronomical affairs was limited, but he could think of no comet in history that had approached so close to the Earth as this one. In the daytime its tail was invisible, but it was as large as the moon, and brighter – self-luminous, compared with reflected light of that satellite. Bates, as he jogged along, tried to reason it out: it had swept up to the world so rapidly, surely it must speed on with equal celerity, must hurtle past and away into interplanetary space. And then he must perforce stop again and regain his breath, leaning over his own stomach with his arms braced on his legs.

The landscape through which Bates moved, though green, was a desert. Each cottage or hut he passed was empty. In some of the yards animals lay motionless, and death blew its great bubble into their guts. And ever and above the buzzing of the Blefuscudan's flying toy. The chirruping of death. Pigeonhawk, pigeon, pigeonhawk.

Around the corner the road ran through a copse, the leaves dark, the tree stems tall. There were human bodies here: one man face-down in the middle of the road, two more lying on their backs with their boots on the path. Bates peered into the shadow and saw more corpses. There was a smell. He hurried through. The sound of rushing water was continually in his ears, as if all the noise of the night's storm had been distilled into the nearby stream. It seemed to be hushing him, mockingly. Hush, hush, hush. Why do you strive? Hush and be still.

Eleanor!

Out of the wood and into the sunlight and Bates hurried through a village. It was perfectly deserted.

The comet in the day sky was an ill omen. It shone with an ill light.

He knocked on doors and peered inside windows, but there was the stench of decay in the air and he dared probe no further. Here was a public house, the Duke of Cumberland, its pendulous inn sign gleaming in the sunshine as if recently painted. Stepping cautiously through the door, Bates found a fat man sitting in a chair beside a cold and sooty grate, his head tilted back. He was dead. There was, as yet, no smell, so the death must be recent. Upon the bar stood some bottles, but all had been opened. Bates peered at the contents of one of these, debating whether to taste or leave it be, until his thirst overcame his squeamishness and he drank the beer. Behind the bar was a door and a larder-room in which a ham dangled like a hanged man. There were flies on it, and a green tint to the flesh, but he pulled the meat apart with his fingers and dug chunks from inside.

He went through to the inn yard hoping to find a stabled horse upon which he could ride the rest of the way. He found instead a horrid sight: the bodies of many people, men and women both, piled in an unruly heap with faggots stuffed in between them. Somebody, perhaps the fat man inside, had intended to immolate them. Perhaps the wet weather had prevented it. This holocaust had a foul smell upon it. Bates felt the food rise in his gorge, and hurried out onto the main road. The sound of the river was still there, hushing, hushing.

'We must move on,' said Gugglerum. The little one had landed his plane in the middle of the main street, and had disembarked. He was speaking through his cone. 'These continual stoppings, stoppings, we shall never reach our destination.'

'I'm sorry,' gasped Bates.

'You have within you,' Gugglerum chirruped, 'what is necessary to *save your people*. Without it your people will die. The battle that was fought in your body was fought when that army knew not what enemy it would face.'

'What's that? What?'

'*They* learnt from you, as your army learnt from them.'

'What do you mean, my army?'

'*Your* army was victorious. It has fought more battles than you know. It fought again after we had scratched you and was victorious. It is an army experienced against our enemy.'

'I do not understand what you mean.'

'But our enemy has learnt from its experience. With *these others*,' said Gugglerum, but he made no gesture. Bates did not know what he meant. 'With these others it overcomes its objectives quickly, and deadly.'

'Sir Gugglerum,' said Bates. 'You must explain to me what ...'

A shout resounded. From the end of the road. Bates looked up. It was a man. It was a soldier. A scarlet-uniformed soldier. 'Man!' this individual bellowed. 'Man!' An English soldier.

'Holloa!' cried Bates, ridiculously grateful to have encountered a living being in this deathly village. He put up his arm and waved.

The soldier seemed, for a moment, to be falling forward; but he was merely launching into a jog-trot along the road and towards Bates. Gugglerum was back in his little flying machine. Its engine started, pudda-pudda-putudda, and the thing rolled wobbly along the road.

The soldier was running faster now. 'Hey! Hey!'

'I am *English*,' cried Bates, waving both his arms. 'An English *gentleman!*'

The plane was in the air now, on an upward line, and it started to bank and turn. The soldier skidded to a halt and dropped to one knee, simultaneously pulling his rifle from where it was slung upon his back. Bates saw then what he was about. 'No!' he cried, and started forward. 'No! No!'

But the man had levelled his weapon, and was aiming it at Gugglerum's flying craft. He swung the barrel carefully, following his target. He, *ptang!*, fired. The noise bashed against Bates's ears, it was so very loud, so very at odds with the hush, hush of the river and the silence of the streets. Smoke poured promiscuously from the end of the barrel.

He had missed his aim. Gugglerum continued to climb in his toy craft, higher and higher, a hundred feet or more. But the soldier took a second aim, and fired once more, and this time, this time his aim was true. *Ptang!—thd.* Bates watched as the flying device folded in its middle and broke in two. The chatter of its engine ceased. Shards tumbled and separated and it fell as rubbish from the sky, away behind the houses.

The soldier was at Bates's side. 'Lucky for you,' he said, his voice tinged with London, 'that I'm the sharpshooter that I am. They're buggers, them littlers.'

'He was,' said Bates, still trying to understand what had happened.

'I'm with the Seventeenth Buffs, up on that hill,' said the soldier, swinging his rifle back onto his back. 'Charlie Cheeks, my name. Yourn?'

'Abraham Bates,' said Bates, automatically. 'He was my ally.'

'Ally?'

'That Blefuscan.'

'That be-what-un?'

'That Lilliputian fellow. You just killed him.'

'They're tricky buggers,' said Cheeks, nodding, as if Bates were confirming what he had said 'Caused us some real problems. But lucky enough they abn't hard to kill, once'n you've located them. Their size makes 'em vulnerable.'

'He was,' said Bates, fixing the soldier with his eye, 'he was telling me something. He was in the very process of telling me something of the very greatest significance.'

Cheeks was nodding again. 'Them flying devices,' he said. 'They'bn the trickiest of all. In them, see, they can fly off like regular birds. They get in the sky above you – we had a flock of them. No lie, a reg'lar flock. They were shitting out incendries, excuse the expression I pray you but that's what it was.'

'This one,' said Bates again, feeling the admixture of hopelessness in his frustration, 'was our *ally*. An ally of the English cause. He was helping me. He and I were on our way to York.'

'It's good,' said Cheeks, 'to see another living soul, and I can say *so*. They're all dead roundabouts, all these Yorkshiremen and York-shirewomen. We've been sore taken with the plague oursel, to be truthful.'

'The plague,' said Bates.

'Come along, you'll have to talk to my Captain. He's not well himself, to be truthful – up here.' He took Bates's elbow. 'End of the street and up the hill. Like I say, it's a fortunate thing that they're easy enough to kill.'

And so they marched off together, along the road of the dead village, and up the hill to the encampment of English soldiery. Bates was still stunned. And here were the Seventeenth Buffs, three tents and a campfire. And here was the Captain, on a stretcher, looking poorly and like to die; pale as wax and shivery, shivery. And here a dozen soldiers in the scarlet uniforms with the tan facings, no more than seventeen left alive. 'We've buried a number,' Cheeks was saying. 'And a large number at that. We were to flank – there's a battle brewing, over yonder, York way. We were to make our way about and stab the Frenchies in the kidneys. We and many other battalions, though it's only us left. We started with four score and now we're twelve fighting-fit and five more in a poor way. Wonder what good we can do now. Though wondering is for captains. And the Captain, as you can see, is not well.'

And during the whole of this speech Bates, still stunned, was trying to make sense of the last thing Gugglerum had said, as if it were the secret and the mystery and the key that would explain everything and make everything come right.

7

Eleanor had wanted only to ask the giant about the nature of the light in the sky, for it seemed to her a *scientific* mystery, and one of the very greatest importance. It went without saying that, as such, it must be reducible to a coherent scientific account. But no sooner had she reached his hut-like boot, big as a cabin of leather, than there was a mighty sensation of applied force. Force directed fully upon her, like a blow from every direction at once. There was a dazzle of light, too much for her eyes to deal with. She knew, of course, that the eye has a tiny orifice of muscle – that the pupil of an eyeball, which seems so solid, is in fact an absence, opening or closing like a mouth to draw in more or less light. She knew that in the presence of a great phosphoric stimulus the pupil shrinks to a moue. She thought all this with a slow, rational mentation, even as the gravity vanished and her stomach clenched and she rose into the air. Her ears were filled with the noise of surf, or rushing wind. Reaching forward she encountered something solid but yielding, a curving shield of leather, a great shoe. The next thing: she made body-contact with the shoe, as if she had stumbled forward upon it. But there was no ground over which she might stumble.

The rushing noise withdrew from her ears, leaving a single pure soprano note. She swallowed, and swallowed again, and the noise disappeared.

Everything was white.

The great shoe shifted beneath her, and she cried out, but although her diaphragm worked underneath her ribs no voice emerged. This peculiar detail was the first to alarm her. She tried again: forced air through her throat in as hefty a shout as she could utter. Nothing, again, nothing. She must have been deafened, she was deaf. Oh unfortunate!

But, no: she could hear her own bloodstream gushing and pulsing. She paid attention: she could hear her own heartbeat too. But she could not hear herself speak. And yet, when she spoke she felt her throat vibrate, and sound is of course nothing more than the vibrations of such surfaces in air.

The ground shifted again, and lifted. She felt the tug of gravity again, for she was conscious of being swung high, and then lowered again. She tried to shout out in alarm, but there was no sound.

Then the giant heel impacted silently upon a floor. Eleanor fell from the curve of the great boot and jarred her hindquarters upon a floor. Perfectly white, perfectly smooth, like the finest and most flawless polished white marble reaching in every direction around her as far as her eyes could see. If a comet be made of light, only, then this is what it would be to exist inside such a medium. The giant towered above her, his head lost in dazzle and blanch. His great foot lifted and swept through the air and away.

It disappeared into the dazzling fog of white.

Eleanor got to her feet.

Her eyes were already beginning to adjust to her new environment: a vastly spacious hall, larger than the sky, like a canvas painted by John Martin, like an opium-eater's vision. It was a space clearly lit, but not as white as Eleanor had at first thought, for in the air were colourfield stretches of blue, and pink. She could see him now, the Brobdingnagian upon whose boot she had travelled, a little way off, but in motion: walking away from her, with his great head upwards. Eleanor craned her own head, followed the direction he was looking, and saw the object of his scrutiny. It was a shape, like a stormcloud. It hovered in the space, a diffuse and floating vastness. But, as she looked, she saw other shapes: great columns, shattered and leaning, as from a ruined temple worthy of Pandaemonium; such that the idea occurred briefly to her as to whether she were not now dead and transported to some other realm. But then, with a tickling sensation in her abdomen, of the sort that often accompanied mental insight or inspiration, she comprehended. These vast and disparate shapes were all part of one shape, and that was proportioned as a man. A being so much larger than the Brobdingnagians that they were like unto specks.

Giants upon giants.

She stumbled upon nothing. Even though she took no step she stumbled, and fell backwards to sit hard down on the white floor. Her mouth was open. The more she looked the more she could comprehend. There were several of the larger variety of giants in this space: two, three, four. They were in various poses: one standing, one sitting, one leaning forward over some unseen object of attention. The standing one was larger than a mountain. He was a feature of the landscape rather than any living object. The Brobdingnagian took a few more dwarfish steps and then stood. His voice rumbled out and was swallowed in the enormous space. But, Eleanor said to herself, there was a rational likelihood here. It was something, she said to herself, the possibility of which ought to have occurred to her: if there be Lilliputians and humans and Brobdingnagians, then why not continue the scale upwards? And – who knew? Perhaps there were creatures, somewhere in the cosmos, to whom these colossal creatures were but toys – Hyper-*hyper*-gigantos. Why not, indeed? Why *not* supercolossi?

She felt a strange queasiness coming upon her, and she lay down supine upon the floor. On her back. Then on her side, which brought this surface closer to her eyes. And perhaps it was a better object for her contemplation than these world-sized beings, carrying shields as large as the moon and spears larger than the trunk of the world-tree itself. The floor. The floor appeared perfectly smooth, a white substance not unlike marble but slightly more pliable. It was warm to the touch.

Her eyes closed. She felt dizzy. Did she sleep?

A rumbling. If she had been asleep then this noise woke her. If not it merely caught her attention.

Feeling, abruptly, exposed and vulnerable Eleanor got quickly to her feet. Her head swooned. She pressed her temples and tried to pull herself together.

The Brobdingnagian was sitting cross-legged before her. 'Little lady,' he rumbled.

'Sir Giant.'

'How did you come here?' It took, as always with the giants, a great length of time for the sentence to roll itself out.

'I was upon your shoe,' she said.

'Speak louder, little one.'

'Your shoe! I was upon your shoe!'

'Ahhh.' He nodded, a gesture as slow and solid as the tides in an ocean.

'Where are we?'

'With the great folk. This is their house.'

'Their house?'

'I have spoken to them. They are—'

'Who are they? Where is their house? Is it the light in the sky? Have we climbed into the sky? Have they *lifted* us into the sky?'

'Little lady,' grumbled the giant. 'Please, you should speak more slowly.'

'I am sorry, Sir Giant.'

'I have spoken to the man.'

'Man?'

'He has a name.'

'What is his name?

'His name,' said the giant, ponderously, 'is called Littlebig.'

'Littlebig?'

'He says . . .' but here, shaking his head, the giant reached down with the palm of his hand and slapped the floor. Eleanor braced herself, expecting there to be some tremor passed through the material to where she stood, but this did not happen. Instead a pool opened at her feet, a great lake-sized stretch of clarity in the white floor. It took a moment for her to realise that the floor had disappeared. She was falling through the air like Mulciber to dash herself to death on the ground far below. She cried out, hugged herself, and her feet skittered and danced, but the floor had *not* disappeared. Though she felt the terror of one about to fall, she did not fall. The floor had acquired a transparency of unusual limpidity, but there was still a floor.

'Watch,' said the giant, and he ground his palm against the floor.

Below – for, of course, they were indeed suspended in mid-air – Eleanor could see the Yorkshire landscape. Then the image shivered and resolved itself again. Eleanor had again the sensation of plum- meting – her viscera contracted within her – and she gasped again: but she had not moved. The image had become magnified, as with the Leeuwenhoek microscopic technologies, except on an unimaginable scale and with an extraordinary facility. She saw the two armies, French and English, distributed about the green hills and green valleys: thou- sands of troops, all tiny as toy soldiers.

'I was there,' she cried, excited.

She could see the trickling movement of men along a valley; and, there, men passing into a trench cut into the hill, where shadow hid them. And, there, three dozen: shapes – cannons. And now whiteness squirted from the barrels of these guns. And now florettes of grey sprouted on the green. Like splatches of boiled water scattered in an ant's nest these florettes caused great commotion amongst the men. Some scurried, others jerked left and right and lay still. There was a sudden surge forward of a great many scarlet-coloured men. Ranks of giants stood perfectly motionless, like colossal Egyptian statues, as the smoke and commotion swirled around them. It was all perfectly silent.

'Monsieur Littlebig is intrigued,' boomed the Brobdingnagian.

'It is war.'

'It is.'

'My fiancé is there.'

'The Dean of York. A powerful man-in-Christ.'

'He is in danger! Can we not snatch him up to this vantage, as I was snatched?'

'You rode,' said the giant, 'my *boot*.'

He paddled on the floor with his enormous forefinger and again the image shimmered and changed scale. At that moment Eleanor understood. 'You pressed upon the floor to – knock away its shutters,' she said, excited. The giant looked at her, as giants often do: the slow, contemplative look that often precedes their speech. It was a long time before Eleanor realised that this giant was not about to speak.

'To make the floor glassy, to create *transparency*,' she urged. 'How did you do it?'

'It is a device,' rumbled the giant. 'Like the clockwork of watches, though more subtle.'

'I see that,' said Eleanor, a fire lit up inside her.

'Press the hand upon it, and twist.'

'But will it work for ... oh no matter, let me *experiment*.' She pulled off her glove and laid her hand flat. But nothing happened, nothing happened, and she slid her palm left and right and up and down and nothing happened, and then, suddenly – as if she had chanced upon some secret switch, the floor started to whiten and the vision to disappear. By rotating her hand first one way and then another she was able to clear the floor or fill it with opacity. It was a simple matter, then, for a person of Eleanor's systematic and rapid wits, to determine the gestures that controlled the telescopic magnification. She *pulled* the image, as it were, towards her – until individual men became discernible and even recognisable.

A kind of joy filled her heart. Not her heart of course, for that was mere conventional speech. It was a joy of the mind. But her heart did scurry, and a warmth did spill through her belly and her loins. Machinery, but so superb a piece of machinery – so cunningly worked, elegantly constructed. Like a combination telescope–microscope. The gods of Homerus, seated upon their clouds, must have examined the battlefield before Troy with precision like this.

She permitted her vision to swoop and dart like a peregrine. When she lifted her *point de vue* high in the sky the two armies became two wriggling masses, like two stretches of caviar spread over the green, except moving and twitching. Like, perhaps, tadpoles twitching on a green board. But sweep down, and the dots resolved into grubs, and then into individual toy soldiers. And with a firm spin of her palm a single soldier swelled to fill her vision. She saw him from above, but the glass possessed the curious property of rendering him in a plastic and sculptural manner: not *quite*, but *almost as if* height and depth and breadth were included in the vision. Eleanor could see his face, exhausted-looking, as he rested, using his rifle as a crutch. The blue weave of his uniform. She could see the black dots of uncropped beard upon his chin and cheeks. The bar of his brow over small, blue eyes. And then (the image staying perfectly centred) he lurched back, and pulled his rifle up, and wrestled with it to aim. There was a puff of dust or smoke, silver-grey, and he stood straight up, very straight, the rifle-butt still at his shoulder. Eleanor could not, at first, see what had happened. She inched the image back, to get a fuller view. Her man was there, blue-clad, standing straight up. His rifle had shattered. Had it blown to shards when he attempted to fire it? Or had it been struck by a musket ball from the enemy? She inched in again. His right hand held the shattered stock, his finger still hooked in the trigger guard, but bloody and dripping. The barrel was gone. The stock was in splinters. His face was bleeding. Needles of wood had embedded themselves therein. All from a mere puff of dust! But, of course, the artificial silence of these images belied the violence. She waited for him to fall, but he did not, he stood still.

She pulled her artificial eye back a little way. There was a mess of action around her randomly chosen figure. Soldiers scurried. But, here and there, people stopped to – to what? It was unclear to Eleanor. But, in the heat of battle, surely they must bestir themselves – but there! One was kneeling and emetically voiding the contents of his stomach. In the middle of the battlefield! As musket balls and shells flew about them —

But of course they were sickening. Eleanor had too sharp a memory of exactly what the sickness involved. She looked at the field with a new sense of what effort must be involved in this physical labour. Were *all* the soldiers ill? Yet (withdrawing her view to a more aerial perspective) with what cumulative vigour did they push forward! Eleanor pulled back further and saw the whole battlefield: the sweep of the landscape up and down, the myriad forms twitching and flowing over it, like gnats in a cloud, or a mist of flocking starlings folding over and in upon themselves as they gather for migration. The left flank of the French poured up a hill, to where the English, in thready lines, fired their many muskets. The lines spilled squirts and puffs of smoke. More smoke jetted from the cannons – many many cannons. And this grey gunsmoke poured over the whole of the battlefield like a coastal bore.

And then, on the right flank, Eleanor saw the reactive movement of an English counterattack. There were horses, but no more than a score – sapient horses, perhaps – and they were surrounded, seemingly embedded, in a mass of foot soldiery that rushed the length of a field. The French generated their own grey dusty smoke from ranked muskets and cannons. The seething mass of the English was like a red foam pushed forward by the seawave. As it rolled on many of the bubbles in the foam popped and disappeared. Or, Eleanor thought, with a delicious and perfect detachment, the entire battle was like an organism. It was an organism that had come together for this morning, assembled out of a million constituent parts like cells and given temporary life by the two interlocked powers-of-will of the commanding officers. And now the organism was slowly turning about, as the French pushed the English back on the left and the reverse action happened on the right.

The thought of her fiancé popped into her head, accompanied by a twitch of guilt that her thoughts had been distracted. How was he faring? Was he caught up in the battle? She had been lucky, she realised, to have been plucked from the field immediately before the fighting began. With an increasingly sure touch of her hand upon the miraculous floor, she spun the image about, swept along it, darted in and in, pulling out face after face contorted in rage or pain or drained by illness or fear. And – there! Henry, on a hilltop, away behind the main bank of French cannon. Oh, he was terrified. He had scurried behind a French cart and was trying to wrap his arms about his head. She peered closer at him through the magical glass, and could see how tremulous he was, how blanched and fearful.

She was at that moment aware of two distinct, opposite and yet intimately connected emotions. One was a sort of sudden glory in herself, an inner triumphing – for she was aerially projected, secure and potent as a god, and he was suffering and vulnerable. But, at the same time, she felt a genuine pang of compassion. How strange it is that compassion can strike with a pang like physical pain! She became aware of a new quality in her emotions, something that had been steadily cultivating itself inside her without her even being aware of the growth. She became aware of shame.

She must help him.

She leapt to her feet and ran towards the Brobdingnagian. 'Sir Giant! Sir Giant!'

With his infinite and infuriating slowness, the giant brought his head round and leant down. 'Child,' he boomed. 'I am speaking to the king of this craft.'

'We must help them! Tell the King – tell the King – that just as he lifted *you* to safety, he must bring up here my fiancé and ... tell him that!'

'The King,' said the giant, shaking his head, 'is not concerned with such little things.'

Eleanor took this immediately in her stride. 'He must use his powers to end this battle – he surely has the power to end this battle. Tell him!'

But the giant's head was still shaking. 'He has not come to talk with you,' he said, 'and I am sorry.'

'Sorry?'

'I am sorry for you. But it is not your world any longer. He talks with us about it – he and his kind.'

'He and his kind?'

'There are one hundred and forty-four of his kind, in their various craft, all coming to this world. And why should they consider you? It is not *your* world to cede to them. It is a kindness,' said the giant, in an enormously sorrowful voice, as if this were a kindness that pained him acutely, 'that he speaks even to *me*.'

'Wait!' cried Eleanor. 'What is your meaning? Why do you talk of ceding the world? Wait! Wait!' But it was no good, for the giant was straightening himself and standing upright, and that was the end of his conversation with Eleanor Burton.

[8]

Bates dipped a mug into a metal canister of coffee suspended over a campfire. He was so thirsty that he bolted the boiling fluid. The life of this little knot of soldiers pressed upon him, after days of solitude. The English chatter, after so long amongst Frenchmen, sounded almost alien to him. And if they were to discover that he was a registered *Ami de France*! It would mean his death, surely. And here was the Captain, on his stretcher; brought out from his tent, by his own orders, so that he could see the morning star Hesperus once more before he died.

'It is, sir,' the Captain was saying. 'It is always a pleasure to meet an English gentleman. I am like to die, sir. But I am glad to know you, before I do.'

'Surely not to die, sir,' said Bates, reflexively.

'I have made my peace with God,' said the Captain, in a weak and wretched voice. 'He has spared me longer than many – I have seen men sicken and fall down on the spot never to regain their consciousnesses. I have seen men, hale and strong in their youth, standing one minute – spitting phlegm and weeping the next – dead the next. It is a plague. It came upon us, and in less than a week it has devastated, it has devastated the civilised ... well, well, perhaps it *is* the end-times.'

'End-times.'

'Revelation speaks of plague, and the star Wormwood coming down to Earth. You have seen it? It grew and grew in the sky and last night it swelled overhead.'

And there it was, huge in the sky, much larger than the moon and still clearly visible in the late afternoon sky. The two men looked at it in silence for a while. It seemed to look back at them, this cataracted great eye, bone-white in the sky. *That* made Bates uncomfortable. He spoke up:

'I could see little last night for the storm.'

The Captain coughed. 'The storm was great,' he conceded, 'and then it passed. This Wormwood-star swept it away, I think. It was brighter than an argent torch. Still, if it be the end-times then I am selfish enough to be grateful that this sickness will carry me off soon. For if it be the end-times, then terrible things are before us.'

Bates hid his face behind the tin mug, and took another swig. But all he could think was: Once on a time I would have thought that way myself. Once I would have been eager to project my own sufferings onto the cosmos as a whole. What had changed? And then he bethought himself of little Sir Gugglerum, who had slain his own kind to protect humanity. Who had saved Bates's life for some great purpose – Bates knew not what – only to be shot like a quail in the sky. So arbitrary a dying, a randomness. Though he had been little, yet there was exactly as much life in him to be lost as in Bates himself. It was a bitter turn-about. The sorrow smote Bates's soul. He had learned, perhaps, to feel another's suffering as more acute than his own. And that, perhaps, was something, in a universe created by a deity of Compassion.

'What would your men do,' he asked, 'if you were to pass away?'

'They are a dozen. I have promoted one Corporal, and he shall lead them on a roundabout path to York. We cannot join battle now. Our numbers are too few. Some of those alive are sickening themselves.' He shook his head. 'End-times, sir, end-times.'

'Perhaps not. Perhaps it is merely a regular cometary body. Perhaps it is an astronomical rather than a theological object.'

'Look about you, sir,' the Captain gasped. 'The northlands are laid waste by pestilence. I would despair of our ability to fight the French, were it not that I feel sure their army is as afflicted as is ours.'

'It is,' said Bates, at once, with feeling, remembering Scarborough. 'Believe me sir, it is.'

'But it hardly matters. These are puny matters, these human quarrels, in the face of the Great Day of His Wrath, which is to come. Wormwood is His avenging angel.'

'And what chance,' said Bates, 'do we stand, squeezed between Pestilence from below and Force from above?'

What chance indeed? But his thoughts were not on what he said. His mind reverted again to Gugglerum. Why had the little creature sought to help Bates at all? He had been about to reveal a great secret, and had been prevented. But what secret? Whilst he did not ratiocinate it in precisely such terms, yet was Bates's mind caught between a sense that the world was arbitrary and abrupt – a concept against which all his yearnings revolted – and a sense that everything happened for a purpose. On the one hand was the chill perception that such was indeed life, a cold and vasty chaos. To think that brave Gugglerum, who had sacrificed so much, could be snuffed out like an insect as he was on the very edge of revealing the profoundest mystery that could save a whole nation, a whole world. And on the other hand was Bates's inner infant, the naked newborn portion of his soul, who *knew* the universe to be ordered. Who knew in his heart that not a sparrow fell but had a place in the grander plan. Greater minds than his had pondered this dilemma, of course, and come to no stronger solution. But Bates felt that there was *something*, just below the oceanic surface of his mind; something that dabbed a fin into the air before diving again. There *was something*.

What had Gugglerum been about to tell him?

'I do not know your name, sir,' the Captain was saying.

'What's that?'

'I do not know your name.'

'Abraham Bates, at your service.'

'John Longley, at yours.'

Bates held out his hand.

Captain Longley uttered a half-cough, half-laugh, and shook his head. 'I would advise you, sir, to forgo the formality. I have seen the pestilence pass from person to person by as little a contact as two hands shaking.'

'What matters it?' Bates said, with a curious inner sensation of mental shifting, as if something within him were on the point of collapsing – or, strangely, of *assembling* itself, like the temple erected in moments by Solomon's magical key. The sensation caused tingles up and down his backbone. His stomach thrummed. There was a smell – bread, or something else, in Bates's nostril. He was on the precipice of comprehension, a half-inch from understanding everything.

'Sir?'

'Oh, I only meant, what matters it if the light in the sky is truly Wormwood, as you say? If the world is ending then catching pestilence from your hand is the least of the things I should be worrying on.'

The Captain angled his head and looked at Bates, and then laughed. 'Truly said, sir.'

He grasped his hand, and the two men shook.

'You are not afraid, sir,' said Longley. 'I admire that in any man, sir, soldier or civilian.'

'My trust is with Jesus Christ, sir,' said Bates, 'though I am as miserable a sinner as any, and worse than most.'

'I too,' said the Captain.

'And besides,' said Bates, as an afterthought, 'I have suffered through the plague once and recovered. I do not believe it can afflict me again.'

'You've recovered?' said Longley, nodding. 'Bravo, sir. Bravo. I could wish I had a constitution as robust as yours.'

A chink.

Everything tumbled and collapsed in Bates's head, a scree slope of falling pieces; and then with a noise of wind, and the thundering passage of blood through the vessels of his body, past his inner ear and into his brain. And the tumbling and collapsing reversed itself, and everything swept up in a pillar of wind and a pillar of light. Everything suddenly made sense.

There it is.

For this Gugglerum saved him, and died. For this! Bates had reached into the calculating device and been pricked upon the thumb—

'This disease is a malign thing,' Longley was saying. 'My brother is a physician. I used to talk with him about the great debate as to whether sickness is passed by a miasma that moves through the air, as an odour may; or whether there is some other agency. I inclined to the former explanation. As a soldier, you see, I know that illness is always accompanied by bad odour.' Bates was too stunned by his revelation to interrupt the man's chatter. 'But my brother,' Longley continued, 'insists that the new technologies of microscopy have brought to view a whole universe of animalcules and specks and germs, and that these tiny beasts are what sicken us. As the Lilliputian devils are to us, so there are creatures smaller than they who—'

'Your brother is correct sir,' Bates burst out. 'This is what Gugglerum was trying to tell me. Of course! Of course! Your brother is correct, Captain, for science has known for some years now that infection is caused by the action of these animalcules. But what we should have known – what we did not know, but should have known, is that *Mind* is a universal principle . . .'

'You speak too rapidly, Mr Bates,' said Longley.

'But the principle of mind – no *atom*, but that thinks and feels and – and why, for who was it, sir, that claimed there were no atoms, only a continually refined and infinitely refinable flow? Was it a Greek, sir?' He stopped himself, drew himself. 'I apologise for my outburst, Longley,' he said, frankly. 'But I have, just this moment, experienced a profound revelation. And what is more, I think I see how this sickness may be cured. I see it.'

The Captain shook his head. 'It has baffled greater healers than you, sir. Better to accept God's will. If I am to die here, then I am. Into his hands I commend my spirit.'

'But you need not die! I too have been sick with this fever – my body had been the battleground. But . . . I think I see. The Lilliputians made an alliance with the animalcules. This is what Gugglerum spoke of. And I can see, also, why he was uneasy at what his kind had done – for once the animalcules had killed off the human beings, who is to say that they would not go further? Lilliputians have been immune to illness, and perhaps the animalcules are creatures too coarse to infiltrate and devastate Lilliputian bodies – but – but—' the insight was sudden and complete, 'who can say that there are not animalcules to whom animalcules are like men? That there are not sub-animalcules with whom the animalcules might not treat and parley, and turn them against the bodies of the Lilliputians? It is a dangerous balance to upset, Gugglerum was right. Oh, he was wise to oppose the alliance. He was a wise creature.'

'I pray you leave me,' said the Captain. 'To be frank, your chatter wearies me. I am on the threshold of death, sir, and I must sleep.'

'But I can cure you!'

At this the Captain looked disgusted. 'You are the Lord Saviour to touch the lepers and heal them, are you? Such talk approaches blasphemy, sir, I repudiate it. I ask you to leave, sir.'

Bates gaped at the Captain. The revelation had been so sudden, and so complete, he doubted his ability to convey it to this person in any comprehensible way. But he saw, now. He had reached inside the Computational Device, that dawn many weeks before, and his finger had been pricked. The sharpness of the wound, the little bite – was that where the animalcules had been introduced to his body? And they had fought with his own cells. But why had he not died, as had so many? Was it that the invading army was, at that point, inexperienced in the war it waged? Bates's own body, and then the body of Eleanor, and then the body of the Dean, each had possessed – or acquired – the skills to defeat the invaders. But the invaders had at the same time grown more expert in their strategy. As some of them had passed from person to person, swept over in the phlegm or unspeakable matter that the sick expelled, they had taken their expertise with them. And with each new battle they had grown more expert. And soon they knew how to storm the citadels of the world with unpreventable force.

Is that what the Lilliputians had been doing, three mornings before in Scarborough? Had they scratched Bates with some new type or variety of animalcules, hoping to infect and destroy him? But his own defences had learned the ways of the invaders. They were experts now, like Sir Balian defending Jerusalem. They knew what they were doing.

'It is a deal to explain to you, sir,' said Bates, urgently. 'I would ask you, ask you as one gentleman to another, to trust me. I *can* heal you.'

'Step away, sir,' said Longley, waving his hand weakly. 'Leave me in peace.'

'It is a life-and-death question.'

'I know of what it is a question.'

'But will you not permit me? I can heal you – your men too.'

'You are a crazy man,' said the Captain. 'A deluded man. You are a –

I *mistook* you, sir, when I thought you a kindred spirit. Leave me in peace.'

'Why do you doubt me? You do not know the experiences I have lived through.'

'Nor do you know mine.'

'I ask humbly and in Christ's name—'

'Enough blasphemy, sir. Consider that I am about to meet my maker. Do you think I want to do so with the odour of impiety about me? Show some compassion.'

'Captain—'

'Cheeks!' rasped the Captain, in an approximation of a shout. 'Corpo*ral*, come here! Come here!'

Bates looked and saw the Corporal, by the fire, turn his face in their direction. 'Sir!' he barked, and got to his feet.

There was no time.

Bates acted on the spur. He could think of no other way of communicating his immunity to the dying man. It was, he reflected afterwards, uncharacteristic of him; but circumstances had altered many of his characteristics.

He pressed forward and grasped the Captain's head between his hands. The sick man opened his eyes very wide, and wailed feebly. He scrabbled at Bates's arms, but feebly. Bates pressed his lips to the Captain's mouth, and kissed him as hard as he could. He tried to push his tongue into the man's mouth, and to force as much spittle as possible. He was aware of the ungainly texture of stubble upon the fellow's chin and lip, and the sour decay-y tang of his breath. He felt the man's wasted muscles twitch and flip as he struggled. Then Bates felt stronger arms clasp him from behind, and he was wrenched away from the Captain and hurled to the ground by a growling soldier. 'Enough of that,' said Charlie Cheeks, standing over him, and behind the Captain rasped and coughed. Bates wanted to say, *No don't spit it out, it will save your life!* But another soldier had hurried over and contributed to the moment by planting his boot on Bates's midriff.

[9]

The Dean cowered. A French officer came by, and the Dean leapt out at him and grasped at his sleeve. His mouth was working, his eyes wild, pleading. Eleanor twiddled her fingers and the image shrank beneath her. She swung it about. The giant members of the army – two dozen, all in French uniforms – stood motionless as the statues of Aegyptian Memnon. French officers rode around their legs, shooting off pistols, their mouths working furiously. 'Is there no way to capture the sound of these events?' Eleanor wondered.

The Brobdingnagian had sat himself down crosslegged, and leant forward to bring his enormous face close to her. 'I don't know.'

'They are seeking to persuade the giants to fight,' Eleanor said. 'To no effect, evidently. They do not wish to fight,'

'The big fellow is come,' said the Brobdingnagian. 'The Christ man, the Mithras man. Wherefore should we fight?'

'They call you cowards, I daresay,' said Eleanor. 'Your kind, I mean.'

The huge face was impassive.

'But, look: the English have a brigade of yahoos. I have seen them in action before.' She paddled her hand on the floor, and swept the view like a bird's flight to the west. A twisting cord-line of apes was running down the hill and splashing into the river, roaring and contorting as bullets clattered through them. How ferocious they looked! Leather jerkins and hourglass-shaped helmets. Fangs and wild gesticulations.

'West,' said the giant.

'The English camp.'

'Further west.'

It occurred to Eleanor that she had not tested the limits of this visualisation enabler. She pressed her palm on the floor and slid it and the point of view swept, faster than the wind, westwards. Her view flew over the ranks of the English and along a road where the camp followers had parked their carts and caravans. On she went. Fields and cottages, and a sole horseman galloping. Flecks of wet dirt scattered from the beast's hoofs.

'It has taken me beyond the horizon,' said Eleanor, wonderingly. 'It is a marvellous machine. It is the device from the French novel – I forget the name of the novel, but it has the devil in the title. And sticks. Sticks.'

She swept past the horseman. The outskirts of York came into sight: houses numerous enough now to line the road. An inn, and a stableyard. A broad low building. There were people here, in the streets; some in motion, others standing and looking east. Eleanor lifted her hand, fiddled on the floor with her fingers' ends. A dozen people, scattered about on the street, all standing and looking east. They were listening, Eleanor realised, to the noise of battle over the horizon. She moved her viewpoint about the streets, and in towards the centre of the town. There were few enough people out or about; they had, she supposed, vacated the town when news of battle had reached them. She made a rapid dart westwards, swept over the ornate block of the Minster's tower, over the river flat and bright as a swordblade, and along the west road. And, yes, here was a line of carriages and handcarts, and a hundred people, or two hundred, making their way in that direction that was opposite to the noise of war. She stopped for a moment, and examined them, as dispassionately as any myrmecologist ever peered down a brass tube at insects. Some of them were well dressed, others were poorly clad or ragged; but one man pushing a handcart was wearing a new blue suit in three pieces and a hat; whereas one of the men seated in a high brougham, urging his horse on with repeated flourishes of the reins, like an angler – *he* was wearing only one boot and had holes in his trousers. Why was he in the carriage and the other man on the ground?

But there were no more than a few hundred of these fleeing citizens, and Eleanor wondered what had happened to the rest of the inhabitants. Had they already gone? Had they elected to remain? She pulled her view back eastward to the town, and spent some minutes flying birdlike along the routes of roads. The medieval clutter of rooftops and the rickety jigs and twists of the ancient passages. And here she saw another reason for the emptiness of the town: in a house's back yard a sheet, with six people laid out on it, like cutlery in a drawer, head beside feet beside head beside feet. The plague.

She was surprised she had been so unobservant as not to have noticed it before. Everywhere she looked in the city were corpses; laid out in open spaces, or beside half-dug and abandoned graves, or on pallets before houses. There were many people sleeping in the precincts of the Minster; except when she moved her magical eye closer and closer, and saw the flies itching their way across stubbled and unresponsive faces, she understood that they were not sleeping.

'A little north,' boomed the giant.

She was so entirely captivated by her powers of seeing that she knew not how much time had passed. She moved her *point de vue* north, over rooftops of grey and carrot and brown. Housing thinned. The ground became more uppy-downy. Over a field and there – she saw what the giant had been directing her towards. Lying along the westward flank of a hill, like the gigantic Python Apollo slew, lay the straight fat pipe of the cannon. Her father's cannon. Its base was buried in a group of wide brick buildings, surrounded by a circular wall. And along the road leading to the gate in this wall came hurrying the horseman, the same one Eleanor had seen earlier galloping away from the battle. He thundered right up to the gate, and men busied themselves in hauling the metal doors apart so that he could enter.

'My father's cannon,' she said. And then, because she had spoken in a hushed voice, she said again, loud and enunciated, for the giant to hear. 'My father's cannon. He built that great device.'

'The plates.'

She saw what he meant. Running her magical eye along the straight enormity of the barrel towards its elevated end she saw the two house-high metal plates positioned thirty yards apart on either side of the mouth.

'They are charged with electrical power,' she said, and then she said it again in a louder, slower voice. When the giant's puzzled expression did not change she added: 'The shell is given a quantity of magnetic potency, and these plates can be charged with a positive or antagonistic electrical power to influence the direction in which it flies. It is not, they say, precisely accurate method. But since the cannon is too large to be moved or aimed . . .'

She looked again. There was a scurry of activity in the yards and spaces at the base of the cannon. A shell, long as two tall men, shaped like the pinnace of a metal church spire, was being borne from a warehouse; on a railcart along its twin lines all crowded about with soldiers.

'They are loading the gun,' observed the giant.

'But why. At whom do they intend to fire? That horseman rode in with orders, perhaps – but what?'

But she knew at whom they intended to fire. 'If they fire cannonballs at the French army,' she said, starting up from the floor, 'They could very well strike this comet, this comet, this cometary craft!'

'It is that they intend,' said the giant, with his mournful and apparently endless voice.

Bates was manacled and kept in a tent. He sat on the floor with his arms behind him, and he waited. The light through the fabric of the tent faded, and still Bates sat. He passed through stages of fear, indignation, resignation and finally boredom. A trooper flung the flap back and kicked a metal bowl into the tent, and Bates caught a glimpse of an apricot-coloured sky and trees inked black on the horizon, and closer at hand two men building up a campfire for the coming night. Then the flap was closed again, and he was alone in the dark of the tent.

As nobody unlocked his manacles, he was forced to lean over the bowl and devour its contents as a dog might do. Then, since he was prone, he rolled to his side and slept. He woke with the pain in his shoulders, altered his position, and slept again.

'Come on,' said a voice. 'Up you get.' It was dawn, and Bates's arms were numb and spangled with pain. Arms lifted him upright and hurried him, blinking, through the tent flap and outside into a cold, clear light. The sun was not up and the moon was setting, but the comet – larger than ever – shone with its eerie silver brilliance. 'My arms,' he moaned. 'My shoulders.'

One trooper held him, and another went behind to unlock the manacles. Bates had time, momently, to absorb his surroundings; the dark-blue completeness of the sky; the green lacework of distant trees; the grass, marked here and there with chinks of mud, whispering and whispering and spreading itself ready to receive the sunlight. It was vivid, in the core sense of the word; it was alive, alive. Every needle-thin strand of grass, alive. Every atom of tumbling air was alive. When his wrists were freed he chafed feeling back into his arms. He was led over to the smouldering campfire, where half a dozen soldiers stood, rubbing and squeezing their hands against the cold. A trooper brought Bates a tin mug of hot coffee *negra*. With the drink his power of speech returned to him.

'I might think about becoming angry,' he said, in as genial a tone as he could manage. His voice croaked, and he had to clear his throat several times. 'I come, an English gentleman, and try to heal your Captain – and I am treated as a criminal.'

'The Captain,' said a trooper, shaking his head. It was Cheeks.

'Aye, your Captain.'

'He's most fiercely angry with *you*, sir,' said Cheeks, grinning. 'Assaulting him like that? In front of his men? Who'd blame him for his rage?'

'I most certainly did not assault him.'

'Neither do *we* blame you, sir,' said Cheeks.

'Handsome man, the Captain,' said one of the other troopers, and a laugh guttered round the group.

'You misunderstand—' said Bates.

'Truth is, we're waiting on the Captain. If he, God forbid it . . .' and Cheeks paused instead of saying the word '. . . then command moves along and it'll be Harrison's business. But even if he lives, it's a dilemma. If you're a French spy—'

'The idea!' exclaimed Bates, too loudly.

'Then we'll have to shoot you. Spies is shot, everyone knows that.'

'It's preposterous.'

'Shoot you, leave you at the side of the road,' said one of the troopers.

'But,' said Cheeks, holding up his hand, 'but, but, if you's a *loyal* Englishman—'

'I am!'

'Then the Captain says he'd consider you one of his troop. All Englishmen have to pull together to defeat the enemy, you know.'

'And any way in which I can help . . .' Bates offered.

'Then he'd shoot you for assaulting a superior officer.'

Bates stared. 'I see,' he said.

'It could go either way,' said Cheeks.

'Right.'

A breeze started. The sun was coming up. The flank of a loosely strung tent bellied and flapped like a sail. The light filled out, gleamed. In the face of such immanence of vitality the prospect of his own death was beyond his comprehension. Whatever language Death speaks is not ours; and most of us spend no time acquiring the complex grammar, in which every verb is irregular and only the past tense obtains, until it is too late.

'Should the Captain recover,' Bates said, 'it will surely be on account of my intervention. I would never, of course, seek to exploit any sense of obligation that he might feel . . . except that, and to speaking of ethics, saving a man's life is . . .'

'If I w's you,' said Cheeks, 'I'd hope the Captain passes. Harrison would probably take you back to York for trial. I'd say he'd not want the burden of orderin' you straight death. But the *Captain*, now ...'

'Oh the Captain,' agreed another soldier, nodding.

Bates drank the remainder of his coffee. He was handcuffed again, but this time with his hands in front of him. He was given no instruction, so he sat himself down, crosslegged, by the remains of the fire and watched the comings and the goings. It was impossible to avoid staring at the Captain's tent. Soldiers lifted the flap and stepped inside. The flap would twitch and rise, apparently by itself, and a man would emerge. The weave of the tent fabric changed hue, delicately but noticeably, as the sun moved into the sky. Bates contemplated his new-found gnosis. He had dedicated so great a portion of his life to the Lilliputian cause itself that his natural curiosity about the universe in which they were located had atrophied. It was *his* universe too, his, Abraham Bates's. But it made deep sense. Not a leaf fell but that divine Providence marked its passing; and what other name for that force than Intellect, the divine principle itself? Thought; sentience; will. Not an atom moved in the void but it loved and hated, it thought and dreamt. Lilliputians below Lilliputians, and beings a scale smaller than they. Brobdingnagian towering over Brobdingnagian, and beings a scale larger too. Where was the foundation to it all? At what point did it all converge? And what if this were a world in which there was no fundament? Atoms composed of miniature atoms, and they in turn – or giants for whom the entire cosmos was but one component cell, they themselves but specks in the eye of something unimaginably colossal. And so on, and so on.

The coffee was no breakfast. He felt it swell in his bladder across the course of a half-hour, until he needed to void the processed fluid. But no soldier would answer his hail, and in the end, with some shame, he crouched by the fire and fumbled at his trowser with bound hands and unspooled an unbroken thread of urine from his loins. After this he lay on his back and stared at the sky, like a child. Hunger polished the inside of his empty stomach, and made his head giddy. It gave heft to speculations that he would otherwise have dismissed as gossamer. Larger and larger beings, smaller and smaller, and the principle of Mind operating at every level. But Bates's heart revolted at the idea that this sequence continued without end, into the infinite: as the schoolyard rhyme put it, fleas with tiny fleas on their backs, and fleas on those, and so on. That couldn't be. There had to be a ground, against which everything could be measured. This was God. But at which *end*? Was God the ultimate principle of Magnitude, the biggest of the big? A child would think so. But could it not also be that God might be the smallest of the small, the fundamental particle or spiritual building-block, out of which the variegated enormity of the universe is constructed? Bates wanted to believe that the very largest scale and the very smallest curled round upon one another, and became the same thing. That God the Giant and God the *particule élémentaire* were the same God. But this, he saw, had more to do with his own mind's preference for neatness than with reality. Who was to say that the cosmos was determined by a principle of neatness?

He sat up. Such arid speculating, and he was on the very edge of his own bloodied death. The urge to find a final resting point was the urge to locate a *unity* in this multiplicity of atom-people, Lilliputians, humans, Brobdingnagians, over-giants and the rest. But the unity was there, of course, not in what grounded them, or in the sum of the scale-series they represented, but in what they all shared. That the universe hummed and found plenitude in Mind. And what was God, if not Mind?

'Bates,' said a voice. The silhouette had the winter sun behind it, and for a moment Bates couldn't see who it was. But, of course, it was the Captain.

'Feeling better, Captain? Up and about? I'm very pleased to see it.'

'Despite your unnatural assault upon me,' the Captain said. He was leaning on a walking stick, and looked thin. But he did look better.

'*Because* of it,' countered Bates, quickly.

'I've a mind to order the men to shoot you now,' said the Captain, calmly. 'We're moving camp, heading back towards York. I sent Harsent out on horseback and he's reported that battle is joined. It's the major battle. It's the Blenheim of our days, and I want to be involved. And we can't have civilians, or spies, drifting about in the furnace of war.'

'I can shift for myself, sir,' said Bates.

'Nonsense. If you're a spy you must be shot. If an Englishman you'll want to pick up a rifle and join the fight. There's no middle ground.'

'Then give me a rifle.'

'Give you a weapon,' said the Captain, 'for you to aim it at me and lodge a ball in my skull? No, no. I think it's safer, for the cause of the war, to perform the extermination.'

'Sir,' said Bates, getting to his feet. 'As one gentleman to another I appeal to you. On my word of honour I am no spy.'

'Your word of honour?' asked the Captain. 'Or your *parole d'honneur*?'

'Let me ask you, sir, why you think a spy would be wandering the Yorkshire countryside? Why a spy would save the life of an English army Captain?'

'Wandering,' agreed Longley. 'But in the company of a Lilliputian. Come from London are you, sir? London, where the French rule?'

'I travelled north as the assistant of the Dean of York – surely you don't consider *him* to be a spy?'

'The Dean of York,' mused Longley. 'And where *is* the Dean?'

'Captain Longley,' said Bates. 'I'll not lie. The Dean and I became separated. I met with the Lilliputian, the same killed by your Corporal. He, it is true, was once an enemy of ours. But he had repented of his ways. He begged me to take him to the Dean, to impart the secret of curing the plague, and I ...'

'Cheeks,' called the Captain, and in a moment the Corporal was there.

'The Corporal has already,' Bates began to say. But Longley spoke across him.

'Cheeks, execute this man, and leave his body behind when we move camp. There's no need for a burial party in his case.'

'No!' Bates could not help the exclamation.

'We'll be having those manacles back, then,' said Cheeks, reaching for his keys. 'Wouldn't want to leave an adornment of such fine iron on a corpse, now, would we?'

The Captain was walking slowly away, putting weight on his walking stick. 'Captain!' Bates called after him. 'Wait! You have sick men! They'll die – but what if I were to cure them? Would you believe me then?'

'Hsh now,' said Cheeks. 'Hssh. There's a good gentleman.'

'Captain! I can do it, I swear!'

The Captain stopped. Then, without turning, he said. 'A rescission, Cheeks. Keep him chained, but put him on the cart with the sick men. If he's cured them by tomorrow—' and he closed the sentence with a cough.

Cheeks looked, grinning, into Bates's face. 'Looks like you'll keep your fancy bracelets, my lady,' he said.

*

Camp was struck, the tents and other paraphernalia gathered and stacked onto the cart, and all with startling rapidity. Cheeks pulled Bates over to a covered cart, drawn by one sluggish-looking horse. Inside lay eight men, all of them ill. The stench was severe.

Bates clambered into the cart and eyed the shadowy space, counting the bodies and trying to determine which of these men were the sickest.

'I'll be on yer carridge behind,' said Cheeks, 'with my rifle in my lap like I was cradling a little baby. You'd best sit here, in the light where I can see yer, and where I can shoot yer if you try to go leapin' and runnin' away over the moors.'

'That man,' said Bates, indignantly, 'is already dead. That one there! You'll not be expecting me to cure the dead, surely?'

Cheeks peered in. 'He'll have to tarry the burying,' he said. 'For we're going presently and not pausing to dig soldiers' graves.'

'But I want it officially logged! There are seven sick men in here. If I cure seven men, and not the eighth, I want it officially noted that this was because the eighth was dead when I first encountered him!'

'Chuck chuck,' said the trooper, grinning. 'Chuck chuck chuck.'

And within minutes the whole troop was on the road; Bates in his cart, Cheeks riding next to the driver of the large carriage that followed behind – containing, perhaps, the Captain himself. The cart he was in had a deformed axle, like a farm truck, and swung high and low, high and low, with a juddery and lurching unsteadiness, as it moved. Cheeks kept his smile aimed at Bates, and ran his hand lovingly up and down the barrel-shaft of his rifle.

There was little Bates could do, but that little required him to swallow his disgust. He made his way, shuffling on crouching legs, from man to man. The floor of the cart was slippery, the wooden slats painted with filth, and it was human filth, and even as Bates's gorge rose, and his throat constricted, he found himself thinking of *her* – of Eleanor. His membrum virile twitched and thickened. Oh, he revolted himself. Oh. He did. Sweet Eleanor, and her skin, the softness of her skin, that he might roll her plump flesh through his fingers, as soft and yielding as materia faecalus. That so pure a face, so angelic a body, should be tethered to such filth. He deserved the filth. He deserved it. He moved through it now, and it was his proper medium.

Some of the men were very far gone; faces rimed with dried filth, blood and phlegm mixed. Most had sores about their mouths, like bubbles of blown glass. Their hair was all matted together into one mass. Their breath, as Bates leaned over each in turn, was corpsey. But he kissed each man, drawing together what little spittle he had in his dry mouth, and holding down his bulging stomach contents by an act of will. Each soldier received the kiss slightly differently, some moaning, some lying motionless, one muttering, another clasping clumsily at Bates's head as if to draw him in. Bates could not stop his heart quickening at this, and he almost forgot himself entire. Eleanor was strong in his thoughts, and he almost blew out a mess of his own seed then and there. Oh, foul! He disentangled himself and shuffled to the back of the cart, and daylight, and fresh air, and could contain himself no longer. He put his chest on the lurching lip of the cart's end and vomited up a pocketful of burning slime. When it was all out, he sat back. Corporal Cheeks was watching him. He had raised and aimed his rifle, and his finger was on the trigger.

'Have you any water?' Bates called with a raw voice. 'For the love of Christ himself! Water!'

Cheeks, still smiling, placed his rifle back on his lap. But he said nothing in reply, and did nothing but watch Bates.

The afternoon drew onward. Despite his physical discomfort Bates seemed to float, or bounce, in a kind of visionary moment or ec-stasis. Eleanor. Her face, her face. *Elle*, as the French said. *Elle-même*. And *or* was French for gold. The gold of her soul. His thirst grew worse, and was scratchily ever-present in his throat. Eventually he picked up one of the sick soldiers' canteens with his shackled hands, and debated with himself whether it would be hygienic to drink its contents. In the end the thirst overcame the caution, and he took long swigs. The water was warm, but tasted sweet.

Then, with only his griping hunger to contend with, he sat and watched the countryside pass. The fields were seamed together with greystone walls of an apparently immense antiquity. Irregular stones, packed without cement into structures, and those laid like veins and nerve-lines that stretched from hill to hill, forms that seemed to have been naturally grown by the environment rather than constructed by men. Sheep arranged themselves in the fields on the principle of the nine queens of the famous chessboard conundrum. The sky greyed and greyed, as if seeking newer and more varied hues of grey and silver-blue, until finally the sun laid its severed head upon the horizon rail. But over and above everything, the blank white eye of the comet glowered down upon everything. Bates contemplated how quickly he had become accustomed to seeing that new object in the heavens; although it was as malign and deathly-looking as ever it had been.

The carts were drawn up at the side of the road, and troopers ran back and forth with their rifles to scout, establish guards, and build another campfire. A soldier, not Cheeks but a man who introduced himself as Green, helped the still handcuffed Bates from the cart. 'Grub,' he said. 'Grub.'

'What of the sick?' asked Bates, slightly dizzy and with pains in his legs where they had been folded beneath him.

'They've their canteens, water. If they're well enough they'll drink from them. If they're not well enough to drink from their own canteen they're beyond help anyway.'

'But food . . .'

'They don't keep the food down. Come o'er,' and he led Bates to the fireside, where the flames coated the wood like the eagerest strands of grass wriggling in the most tart of breezes, and sparks swirled and danced like fairy lights. A leg of meat – perhaps cow, or perhaps Brobdingnagian hare – was being coated in tar prior to being tossed into the flames. A jar of colourless liquid, or at the least a liquid that wholly absorbed the colour of the firelight, was passed from man to man. Bates took his turn and swigged an acidic and bright-tasting mouthful.

'The comet seems very low,' he observed. 'Low and large.'

'Low and large,' echoed somebody.

'It's elbowed out the moon,' said Captain Longley, standing without the assistance of his walking stick and looking strong. The sun was over the horizon but the sky was still bright. Bates peered again.

'Luna yonder,' shouted a soldier, pointing with his whole arm, straight as a rifle from his shoulder. And there, yes, was the C-shaped moon.

'It's larger now, there's no doubting it,' said somebody.

'The British army will not suffer it to come any lower in our sky, lad,' declared the Captain. 'Not much longer, lads. Not much longer.' Bates filled his lungs with fragrant air, and breathed it out. The outward breath took a tremendously long span of time to complete itself.

'Listen,' said somebody.

'Listen,' said the Captain, almost simultaneously.

The men fell silent. At first the most noticeable sound was the snap-crack irregular drumming of sticks burning in the fire. As Bates's ear became habituated to that sound he made out the distant cold grace-notes of night birds. And then, softer and almost melodic, Bates began to hear another sound: a male choir, very distant; or a series of woodland creatures rustling in a hedgerow. But not rustlings – a rapidly folded together quantity of pops, a fabric of high-pitched booms and clicks. The noise you make when you fold fingers into fingers and stretch, forcing the joints to pop. That noise, repeated in unison ten thousand times. And then the vocalic moaning, or cooing, or humming, but unmistakably human voices, unmistakably male voices, and listening more carefully still, beyond all the other sonic interference, the texture of that sound could be discerned, some very distant yells, and then again some very distant shrieks; some martial cries, and some shouts of pain.

'The battle,' said Bates, in a tone of awe.

'Over that wide hill,' said the Captain, 'and a little further. They have been fighting a half-day, I'd think. Neither side having the advantage, according to my scout.'

A boom cracked across the sky, like the very fabric of the heavens buckling; and a banshee screamed over their heads and whistled away to the east.

Everybody stood, silent.

The chatter of sticks breaking in the fire.

'What?' Bates started to ask again. Before he could finish the question the sky was rent again: a boom, a scream, and an enormous sound of detonation. Instantly the silver circle had grown a tuft of orange-yellow hair, which spread further out and then dissolved into brown-black smoke. It took a moment for the assembled men to understand what had happened, but when they did an uneven cheer rose from the whole group. There was another explosion, loud enough to fill all the skies of Yorkshire, and another flare of orange light marked the side of the silver circle. Bates tried to say 'What mighty cannonade ... ?' but his voice was squashed by another enormous crash, and another flow of sparks and smoke high above them. And besides, he knew which mighty cannon had created the fusillade: the same device to which they had been travelling, of course. The same the Dean had hoped to use to propel himself to freedom in India (insanity!). The same the French hoped to capture, and then use the calculating engine to orient it, to unloose its enormous explosive power.

Another shell boomed and shrieked, and passed by over to the east. A minute passed, in silence. Another detonation. In between the crashes the sound of distant cheering could distinctly be heard. Who was cheering? Was it the English army, away over the hill? Was it both armies?

The shelling ceased. Looking up, all eyes scanned the great silver circle – twice the size of the moon, three times. Its flawless silver surface was now cratered, but in irregular oval patterns that revealed a strange network of lines.

There was a long pause, as everybody there waited for further noise. The silence flowed slowly around them,

'Food, food, food,' said the Captain, jollily. 'Harrison, if you'd be so kind as to locate a fork with a suitably long handle?'

They ate, but the chatter was sparse. Afterwards Green took Bates back to the cart, unlocked one wrist from the handcuffs and fixed the empty ring to the axle. Bates, alone, manoeuvred himself underneath the cart for cover and tried to sleep. But something unspeakable, foul-smelling as liquefying flesh, dripped between the planks of the cart above and soiled his clothes and hair. He rolled out under the night sky and tried to sleep there instead, under the baleful silver eye of the scarred circle. It took a long time.

He started to dream, or rather hovered on the very edge of a dream, as if all his consciousness were a dam-wall bulging under the cataract pressure of – something, some fluid waiting to burst through and flood, when—

He was startled awake. The bombardment had started again: a screaming across the sky from west to east, another, another, and then a great detonation seemingly right overhead. A firework throwing fiery confetti onto the world below. Frosty snowflakes of fire scattering from the flank of the great circle. Bates scrabbled beneath the shelter of the cart; a puny enough haven, to be sure, but better to have something over one. Peering out, he watched the circle. Another shriek and whoop filled the sky and another explosive crash. A long silence, and then another. For an hour or more it went on, screaming *tutti crescendi* all leading to the same conclusion of wrenching and sparking crashes. Bates started counting at five, and had reached twenty-one before there was any pause. By then the whole camp had come out of their tents and were standing around watching the barrage.

The dust cleared, blown like moonclouds from the face of the great circle. There were more scratches and patches upon the silver purity now, but not many.

'Shelling the moon itself,' shouted somebody. Somebody else began singing:

> *Cannonade-balls of old England*
> *And oh! for old England's great balls—*

The silence had just enough time to settle, like dirt in a cup of clear water, when the firing began again. Bates watched and watched. For every seven shots, one went wide, howling away to the east to land who knew where – in the sea, perhaps. Or on some village trying to sleep, who knew?

Cheeks coughed next to him. Bates started. 'You scared me!'

'Those explodings don't scare you, but my cough do? What a powerful cough I must have, to be sure.'

'I didn't realise you had come behind me.'

'Mesmerised,' he said, in a chiding voice. 'By a great light in the sky?'

'It is indeed a—' and the rest of the sentence was squashed by the squeal and the crash. As the reverberations died away, Cheeks was saying:

'— and everything about it. Eh? Why do you think they're doing it?'

'Doing it?'

'Shootin' at it, like it's a great grou-ou-ouse?'

'I've no notion.'

Woe-oe-oe, screamed the sky. Woe-oe-oe *CRACK*.

'—from London myself, and bitterly sorry the city's in French hands,' Cheeks was saying, when the noise died. 'You're a Londoner, no? So how you get out? That's the question. What deal did you strike with the Frenchies to *get out*? That's what we all want to know—'

Another cannon shell hurtled with steamwhistle vehemence and crashed explosively into the *Fausse-lune*. Bates's earnest denials, 'No, nothing, I swear, I am a true patriotic Englishman' were inaudible.

'And why shoot at *it*?' boomed Cheeks.

'Why?'

'And why *shoot* at it?'

'Why?'

'It's the enemy, that's why. Why else? That's why.'

Another shell scraped through the air with its appalling friction, and this one hit its target. Fiery confetti fell away. The thunder quietened once more.

'I reckon, the Lieutenant reckons, e'en the Captain reckoneth,' said Cheeks, gaily, 'that you know more about that there monster,' jabbing the point of his rifle up at the sky, 'than you – are – let – tin' – *on*.'

'Nothing! I swear it!' Bates said, oppressed by the noise in the sky and the apocalyptic fire above him, and by the presence of Cheeks so close by him, with Cheeks's rifle and its bloodthirsty little mouth. Was this the moment? Were they to kill him now? 'I beg of you – I beg of you—' His heart was swooning.

But Cheeks did not shoot him. Instead he left him alone, and Bates lay down again under the cart with his face behind the great wooden wheel and closed his eyes. He was so tired that he repeatedly drifted towards sleep, only to be repeatedly jarred awake again by the expected-unexpected horror of the cannonade.

Finally he did sleep. He woke again with the silence, and dozed further; and then woke once more with the cold, but curled up as best he could and slept again. Finally it was daylight that woke him. The great silver shape was still there, scratched and scuffed on its leftmost side but as implacable and apparently unmovable as the moon itself. The bombardment, clearly, had not dislodged it from the sky.

The soldiers were scowling as they built up the fire to cook their breakfast. Bates tried to rub life and warmth back into his limbs with his free hand, and sat with his back to the cartwheel. For a while he simply stared at the object in the sky. He tried to determine whether it was a naturally occurring celestial manifestation (as it might be, an asteroidal or planetary thing) or some artificial or constructed device, like a great balloon. If it were the former then the most pressing question, or the question with the most alarming implications, was: How did it come to be *suspended* in the sky by some freak of electrical or gravitational vortex, sitting as a tennis ball might do upon a jet of air except on a much larger scale? Perhaps it rested upon a tourbillion of unknown energy. For there was a great deal that science had yet to uncover. But if it were a manner of balloon or other aërial device – then who had constructed it? To what purpose? Was it perhaps a French machine of war? Or from some other nation – Chinee, Aztec, which?

Bates wondered: could it truly be the comet? He could piece in his mind the comet small in the sky, then larger, then here; but he could not relinquish the idea that there might be some disconnection between the two phenomena. Was this truly the comet? Had it come visiting? Wormwood, Wormwood, and the ending of the world.

'Did you see the green light?' asked the Captain.

'Green light? No.'

'*Vous avez vu la lumière verte?*' he said, with a facetious expression on his face.

'Captain,' said Bates, getting to his feet, or as close to an upright posture as his left hand permitted him.

'Unhook him from that cart,' Longley ordered. 'We don't want to be dragging him along behind us when we go, after all.'

'You speak of a green light?'

'Before dawn, there was a great wash of green light. It was like unto an aurora.'

'Sickly,' said Cheeks, slotting the key into the padlock of Bates's manacle and pulling it out from the cartwheel. 'Hup hup, stick your wrist in here then.' The handcuffs were linked together again, linking his wrists before his belly.

'I saw no light. Though I slept fitfully.'

'Some new devilish French trick, I'll wager. There's been no noise of war this morning. Nothing from over the hill at all.'

'They're all abed, and its nigh on eight o'clock,' said a man in a lieutenant's uniform; presumably Harrison.

'Cinderella,' said Cheeks. 'Or is that the wrong'un?'

'Gentlemen,' said Bates. 'I ask you: is it truly needful to keep me shackled in this fashion?' He held up his two chained wrists before him, as if to say *Am I Not A Man And A Brother?*

'I have checked your handiwork, sir,' said the Captain.

'The men?'

'My men.'

'You seem well enough yourself, Captain.'

'I'm much recovered, thankee. *Much* recovered.'

'Yet yesterday you claimed you were certain to die.'

'The Almighty still has His uses for me in this world, I suppose.'

'That makes *me* the instrument of the Almighty,' Bates said.

'The men you tended in the cart,' said the Captain. 'They are better.'

'Better?'

'Healed. Or on the way to being healed.'

Bates felt his heart rise. 'You see! It is as I said – the sickness is ...'

'I have decided to execute you,' the Captain said.

Bates was silent.

Longley turned and shouted some orders. His men stamped out the last of the fire, began gathering their kit and harnessing the horses to the two carts. 'Captain,' Bates cried. 'Did I mishear you?'

But the Captain was otherwise occupied. Cheeks stood, with a mild-looking smile on his face. The thought crashed into Bates's mind to run – to make as rapid a dash for it as possible. He looked around: what if he could make it to that low stone wall, and leap over it? But Cheeks would overtake him easily and finish him. Then where was sanctuary? Those filigree trees, void of foliage, on the horizon? How could he possibly make it to that destination? That *hill*? But on the far side of it the battle was even now readying itself to recommence.

The circle in the sky was white as a spirit-eye. Death was about to swoop upon him. The pigeonhawk of death.

The cart behind him lurched and pulled away. Bates felt the scrape of the wheel against his back, and turned, for his shirt was tugged, the tail caught in the axle. The act of turning about freed it, and Bates watched the conveyance dwindle, with faces staring from the back of it. Yesterday those faces had been oblivious and on the edge of dying; now they looked fresher and recovering. One of them winked at him.

He turned back. His skin was crawling. 'Captain. Captain. I don't understand.'

'The queerest thing I ever saw,' Cheeks announced, apropos of nothing. 'That greeny-greeny light. Like something from a poem I did once read.'

'Captain!' called Bates.

But he understood that this was the place he was to die. They were going to murder him here, and leave his body in the grass at the roadside. The rush of imminent mortality quickened his heart. 'Explain to me your *reasons*, Captain! At least that!' Sweat upon his brow. He thought: Eleanor! Never to see you again.

'One man,' Cheeks was saying, 'shouted *Green! Green light!*, like a fool.' He balanced his rifle by laying the centre of its gravity across his forearm. 'And you know? Private Green started up with, *What? What?* We might have laughed,' he concluded, 'save that the light itself was too foul a thing.'

'Foul.'

'Diabolic.'

'You do not intend to murder me, I hope,' Bates tried.

'I?' said Cheeks, with all the appearance of innocence. 'I's a soldier,' he said (or did he say 'as a soldier'?). Then, with a grin, 'My intent don't enter into it.' And he flipped up the rifle and aimed his sightline along the barrel, and straight at Bates's heart.

'Oh!' Bates half-cried, half-shouted, to think his whole life had come down to this sordid moment. He shut his eyes. But, as it happened, it was not to happen just then. It was not to happen for another full minute. The Captain wanted to have a word first.

The Captain was, it seemed, much recovered from his previously sickened state. He was well enough to ride again. 'For which I'm grateful to the gods of good health,' he announced, pleased, as one of the men led his horse over. He patted its nose. They were alone now: Bates, Cheeks, the Captain, his horse, and the man holding the beast's bridle. The other soldiers had gone off down the road with the two carriages. Bates thought of the possibilities. To start running now – just to run. At least to have that rush of air on his face before the thud of a rifled ball opened up the flesh of his back and pushed him, face forward, into the dirt that was his true medium. But he did not move. Cheeks was aiming his rifle. The Captain carried a long-barrelled pistolette in his belt holster. He was a dead man. And he would never see Eleanor again.

'One last thing,' said the Captain, and with a *hough!* and a heave he pulled himself into the saddle. 'It *was* the French you were spying for?'

'I cured you and your men,' said Bates, speaking quickly. 'I could cure more. How many more English soldiers are sick with the plague? How many will die? I could save those lives. For my country.'

'As you explained it,' the Captain said, '*I* could save those men myself.' He laughed. 'And not only myself – but any of the men in that cart.'

'For Christ's mercy and love,' Bates said. His mind was dry. He had the feeling that he was missing something obvious, some form of words that would hold off this monstrous and offhand sentence of death.

'The French, then?' the Captain asked again. 'Your treachery?'

Bates could feel the very pressure of his death upon his back. The predatory raptor-claws in his flesh. It was a real pressure, as if the medieval sketches that showed angels and devils upon men's shoulders and whispering in their ears were given literal life. The tiny devil hissed

Run! Run! in his ear. It was so real Bates fancied he could even hear it. But to run and be shot in the back – it was too terrible a thought.

'This disease is a weapon of war,' said Captain Longley. 'You said so yourself. Ergo the French concocted it. The fact that you know so much about it,' he shook his head. 'That very fact condemns you as a spy, my dear fellow. Cheeks —' And pursuant to his commanding officer's orders Cheeks raised his rifle again, and sighted down the barrel at Bates's chest. And this time he was not playing. Bates, trying to think of something to say, as if thinking of something to say were the most important thing in the world, could think of nothing. Nothing at all. And the finger squeezed the trigger.

[11]

The sky was amber, streaked with purples and blues. Eleanor watched a great seizure in the English lines. Horseman prancing ho and ho, up and down the lines, and men gathering their weapons and trotting back up the hill. The French charged down the middle, but were repulsed by cannonfire and an unyielding phalanx of red. But as the French jarred back and withdrew this same phalanx retreated too, in order. The central ground of the battle was emptied, and as the French regrouped the English cannon began laying out rows of feathery smoke, and churning up the turf and steaming gouts out of the river.

'The assault heroic,' said the giant, in a mournful voice.

'I do not understand,' said Eleanor. 'Are the inhabitants of this airship here merely to observe this battle? Why did they pluck *you* from the field?'

'And you with me.'

'Did they intend to take me?'

'I mediate.' The Brobdingnagian gestured by slowly uncoiling an immense finger. 'Those—'

In the bleary and white distances of this huge space Eleanor could make out the huge figures; three, or maybe more of them – for, strange to say, their very size, and the very fact of there being nothing but clear air between her and them, somehow obscured their details. They were too large for the brain to apprehend them. Great round-bellowed giants, but somehow *not*.

'They are the masters of this craft,' said Eleanor.

'Not they.'

'No?'

'*They* are beings twelve times my size,' said the Giant. 'But the master of this craft is greater, far, than that. Twenty thousand and more.'

'Did you say *thousand*?'

'Twenty thousand.'

'Where is he?'

'We are upon him. This is the suit of clothes he wears. This is the manner of his giant steps about the cosmos. He is an explorer. I can speak to those great beings, and they can speak to him. Or so I surmise.'

After a moment, Eleanor said: 'It is hard to comprehend the existence of so large a being.'

The giant said nothing.

She was hungry, and roamed about the white floor for some time. And, to her surprise, she found food: long stems of white grass growing upon a fold or ridge of the floor. They smelt sweet, in a distant way, and when Eleanor tried one she was surprised how well they tasted. She explored her immediate area, climbed the strange hillocks, peered into the vast white distances all around. Plain fluid ran in perfectly straight lines, eight such lines in parallel rows. She tested the fluid; it was water, or something very like. It attended to her thirst, at any rate, although after she drank she felt a little elated, or heady.

The giant was stretched out on his back and seemed to be sleeping.

Then the sky rang like a low gong, and Eleanor felt a tremor pass through her feet. She dropped where she was and tried to summon up an image on the floor; but this portion of the strange space did not seem to function after that manner. So she ran over the pliant whiteness to where the giant lay. 'Sir Giant!' she cried. 'Sir Giant!'

There was another shudder.

Here, where she had been before, she pressed her palm into the floor and the image coalesced in the magic substance. She scanned the land below. The image that first greeted her was of thousands of faces – English soldiers looking up, directly at her. Then, with perfect co-ordination, they all cheered: mouths flying open and eyes widening, some of them raising arms and fists.

There was another shudder.

She moved her godlike eye through the air. There, briefly, she saw a flash on the horizon; and caught the briefest glimpse of a blot, flying faster through the air than any bird. The cannonball.

'They have begun an assault upon *this* place!' she exclaimed. There was none to answer her, or to heed her words.

All around her the life inside this bizarre place seemed unconcerned. Although each detonation brought palpable shudders through the whole structure, none of the strange inhabitants seemed perturbed. She leapt to her feet and climbed a nearby eminence and observed. As she became more accustomed to the scale of her surroundings, she found herself able to make out more and more detail. The space curved up and round, and what she had first taken for uniform whiteness revealed itself, on closer examination, to be a patchwork of creams and pales. In addition to the hyper-giants, lumbering round-bodied types, were a dozen or so Brobdingnagians; some lying, and some standing about with puzzled expressions. But then, with a physical jolt, she saw that what she had taken for fields of waving grasses were in fact hordes – crowds of human-sized albino people flowing hither and thither on who knew what strange purpose.

The cannonade seemed to have finished.

Eleanor ate some more of the sweet grasses and refreshed herself at one of the queerly regular streams. The water, she noted, flowed out from a lip a hundred yards away, ran straight without the benefit of grooves or runnels, and disappeared into a sort of mesh several hundred yards further away.

The Brobdingnagian – her Brobdingnagian, as she thought of him – was sitting up; his head like a watchtower, his shoulders like buttresses. She went over to him.

'Sir Giant,' she asked. 'This craft has travelled between the very planets themselves?'

'And more,' he grumbled.

'Why does it not move now? Why does its pilot permit it to be shot upon?'

The giant said nothing.

'Sir Giant,' said Eleanor, her voice trembling. 'I am afraid I will never again reach my home. Can I disembark? How can I leave this place? Am I prisoned here for ever?' She felt a welling up inside her, and tears started to come. Tears.

In sympathetic convulsion, the whole craft began to shudder once again.

'They bombard again,' said the giant.

Time seemed to flow differently here. She could not say how, exactly, except that there was some pulsing quality, some sluggishness to her heartbeat and her breathing. Some otherness to the light. No, not her heart, nor her breathing; but the hourglass sifting of the granules of her thought. The throb of memory succeeding memory. Her father, white as this world, and breathing out. Her mother. Christmas cards strung on a smiling thread. The popgun percussion of a cab rattling down Poland street. A man's face, smiling, and smiling at her. Which man? A water-blue sky, clouds of paint-daub white.

Eleanor slept, briefly, but woke again. Something troubled her sleeping mind, and when she woke she cried out, for she was in clear space and falling into the night amongst stars. But it was the floor, transparenced again, although not by her hand.

She leapt to her feet, fell, clambered up again. A vast expanse of ground had been made glassy, a huge oval of blackness cutting into the white surround. It was her Brobdingnagian: his huge hand, pressed flat against the floor, summoning the vista of the battlefield below. 'They withdrew their fighting men,' he grumbled. 'They hoped to bring Littlebig crashing down upon their enemies.'

'To destroy the entire French army in one action,' said Eleanor. 'I see – I see the tactical advantage of it, I mean.'

'Now they sleep under their fabrics and, some of them, in the open air,' said the giant. He hummed, hoomed, and moved his hand slightly to bring the view out and round.

'It is night. The sky eastward is paling,' said Eleanor, more to herself than to the giant. 'Is war truly conducted after this manner? Like office business? Sleep the night, wake together, ready oneself and begin again the fighting?'

'They will not wake again,' said the giant, sorrowful. It was not clear whether he had heard what Eleanor said.

She felt the chill in her viscera. It did not so much as occur to her to doubt what the giant said.

'So many men ...' she started to say. And, with an afterthought, 'and the Dean too!'

The whole ground below them lit up with a firework shine of green. The shadows became ivy and *vert-noir*, the prominences vermilion and spring-green. The colour held. The weird illumination, like a cheap trick of stage-lighting except for its staggering scale and size, burned for many long seconds. Then it slowly faded. It flickered, for a time briefer than an eyelid-blink, a deep red and then it vanished. The ground was dark again.

'That?' Eleanor breathed. And again, louder for the benefit of her companion, 'What was that?'

'An antivitalic,' said the giant, sonorously.

Eleanor digested this fact, and sat down. Then, surprising herself utterly, she embarked upon a great series of wailing sobs, each hurrying so fast after the previous as to tread upon its heels, and all, like winter-storm waves hammering a supine shore, expressive of a desolation so profound it passed beyond, or beneath, all words. She had not known she had it in her. Her tears wet her face and her neck. Her tears came and came and felt to her as if they would never stop.

[12]

One thought, and only that, crossed Bates's mind as Cheeks pulled his trigger. We perhaps think of thought as something that requires an extensive stretch of time in which to make itself manifest. But Bates was conscious of this thought all as a whole, an infolded rose-bloom of thought fully apprehensible in an instant: the same instant that Cheek's finger curled in on itself and the ignition-cap sparked a hushing hiss of gunpowder inside the weapon. The thought had to do with infuriation and meaninglessness. It was, in effect: To have lived through so much – to have survived the plague that had killed so many, to have effected that profound connection with the one woman he would ever truly love, to be so close to a profound moment of consummation: to be *there*, in that place, almost in that place, and *then* to have it all severed. It was the roughness of it; the unpolished and irregular ugliness of it. Of all things death, surely, ought to *mean*. It ought to be the knot into which all life's threads are bound. But it was wrong for those threads to be severed so random with a random sabre's stroke.

The rifle's snap.

Run! Run! cried the voice of death, small in his ear. Run where? Run out of this life and into the next. To discovery. The land of death, under its permanent cap of seventy-mile-thick ice. Into the tiniest, or the largest, of coffins. What running could *he* do?

He opened his eyes.

'Run! Go now!' called the voice.

There was a commotion. Several voices were shouting. Cheeks was lying on his back and his face was all blooded. Blood flowed over his skin and over his uniform and laid its redness upon the green. His rifle lay in shreds of wood and metal at his side. Stupidly Bates stared, and stared. He turned, slowly, and looked up at the Captain, mounted on his horse. The Captain had his pistol out and was aiming directly at Bates.

'Run!' Oh, it was a real voice. It was a voice in his ears.

Then Bates took a step forward, stupidly, moving towards the Captain's weapon. Then, the excitement bayoneting into his soul, he leapt back, and turned, and started to run. That pressure upon his shoulders was more than conscience.

Run.

Behind him he heard the pistol's discharge, and hard upon the noise a woman's scream, and he flinched in the expectation of the great blow of a pistol ball between his shoulder blades. But there was nothing, and he half-turned his head, still running staggeredly onwards, to glance back. The Captain sat on the ground, holding out his right hand towards Bates's retreat, as if accusing. The Captain's hand was gloved in blood. A glistening clump. His horse was cantering away in the opposite direction. The Captain was pointing at Bates with his stump – 'After him! – After him!'

Cheeks was lying on his back, very particularly not looking at the sky.

The one remaining soldier looked over at his commanding officer with dismay – at his wound, or at the order, it wasn't possible to say – and then launched into a rapid stride after Bates. He covered the ground alarmingly quickly. Bates put his face forward and reached as hard with his stride as he could.

'Run!' He felt the weight of his conscience shift upon his shoulders.

'But where?'

'On!'

'I am glad,' Bates panted, exhausted already, 'that you are alive after all.'

'Save your breath for *running*,' said Gugglerum.

Bates ran. But the soldier was yelling at him, and the yells were coming rapidly closer. Bates panted. Why did his pursuer not fire his own weapon? Was it that he now had reason not to trust guns? They had malfunctioned, or been sabotaged. But this soldier would have a knife. And he would have crushing hands, capable of wringing Bates's neck.

And there! The fellow was upon him, grabbing both of Bates's shoulders at once and pulling him back so that Bates's legs kicked forwards in a way that would, were it not a matter of life and death, comical. Bates almost fell, struggled, kicked out again. And then there was a *crac!* and a *crac!*, and from where the fellow least expected it – from Bates's own hair – two pellets shot out. The man reeled away screeching, palms to his eyes, and Bates wasted no time in picking himself up and running on. He ran towards the false moon, which now seemed larger than ever it had. Up the slope, and further up, and still the curving base of this celestial apparition did not come free from the land.

He mounted the hill and got halfway up before he stopped. Each breath was wrested with intense effort from the air. But he was alive. The breath boomed in his chest.

He felt Gugglerum shift across his left shoulder, coming from behind the curtain of hair and hauling himself round. 'Come,' he said, directly into Bates's ear. 'There is no time to waste here.'

With effort Bates pulled himself to his feet. 'Your flying craft?'

'Destroyed.'

'Yet you survived?'

'Yes.'

'You blocked the rifle-barrel of . . .'

'Yes.'

'The Captain's pistol?'

'Yes, yes, of course. Mud and sorrowwort wrapped around a stone, with a little heat from the day, of course. Now, on!'

Bates started into an uneven stride. 'Are we to run to *that* . . .?' he gasped. He did not need to be more specific. Naught but the *mendax luna* could be called *that* in such a tone of voice. Now that he was over the top of the hill Bates could see how large a portion of the morning sky was occupied by the circle of it. It had come much closer to the

Earth now. Morning light coming at it horizontally from the east gave it a weird almost convexity, rendered more optically disorientating by the odd scuffs and rents made by the previous night's bombardments.

'Why do I run?' he gasped, stopping to lean forward and stay his hands on his knees. 'They are not, are not chasing . . .'

'We have lost much time,' said the Blefuscan.

'I cured the,' said Bates, sucking in big breaths, 'I *listened* to your words, my friend. And from your words I learned the truth. I cured the sick soldiers.'

'I have been attending,' said Gugglerum in his singsong voice. 'I hid by the cart and watched you.'

'And why do we hurry?'

They were almost at the peak of the hill.

'The comet the comet the comet,' said Gugglerum.

'You were talking,' Bates said, hauling his right foot up and planting it saggily on the turf, pulling his left foot and planting it similarly, ratcheting his unfamiliar way up the hill, 'of the people who are Lilliputians to your Lilliputians . . .'

'Much smaller,' he said. 'You misunderstand the logarithmus.'

'The?'

'The scale.'

'Not a twelfth? Not a twelfth your size?'

But they were at the top of the rise, and a terrible panorama had raised itself before their eyes in the valley below. The field of battle spread before them, but there were corpses, lying face-down, face-up, grasping at air with dead fingers, stretching their limbs out straight or curled like babbies, even, some of them, sitting – corpses everywhere. They were not bloodied, most of them. They were not blackened or scarred, not, most of them, even dirtied. They looked as if asleep.

'Grief,' said Bates, in a reduced voice. 'Lord. What has happened here?'

Gugglerum clambered to stand on Bates's shoulder, steadying himself with his hand on the back of his head.

'They are dead. Are they all dead?'

'They are all dead,' said the little man.

'How?'

'I do not know.'

'But—' said Bates, starting forward, and then, in a risible fear of infection – worked into him by his recent experience, but out of place here – starting back. 'But how are they all fallen? Is it the result of the battle, or ...?'

'I do not know.'

Bates, overcoming his waverly timidity again, strode forward, hurried to the nearest of the corpses and knelt down. 'No blood, no blood upon them,' he said. 'Did the life strength simply evaporate out of them. Is it that?' and he put his face up to look at the great, scabbed circle of white over their heads. It dominated the sky completely. It dwarfed the moon, supplanting its right to come more near the Earth than it was wont and make men – nor Blefuscans—

'Gugglerum!' Bates urged. 'Tell me.'

'I do not know.'

'Is there some malign being in that giant circle? Is there a – man in that false moon?'

'I do not know.'

'But if there are beings *smaller* by each factor of twelve, or twelve-dozen, then why not larger? Why not giants to whom the Brobdingnagians are toys? Could one of them be living in that great circle, and breathing ... contagion, or other death, upon the people beneath him like ... like a terrible being of ... is it so?'

'It is possible. I do not know.'

'Why do you not know?' Bates cried, leaping to his feet. The miniature hands clasped in his hair for balance.

'Why should *I* know?' squealed the little man. 'Why should I know any more than you? I know *my* business, the business of regular-sized people. This thing in the sky – it is big-person business. My business is with the pyndoonemel, the little creatures who swarmed through your blood, but were defeated by your own pyndoonemel. I must talk to the monarch of your people ...' He said some other things too, but the voice became too squeaky for Bates, in his own agitated state, to follow.

The sky yawned above. How tired must the sky be, after so many wearying shifts? The circle shimmered, and rolled a ways left. The sense of it as a giant plate, or something of that nature, poised precariously over Bates's head, was so marked that when it moved like this he quailed and whimpered, throwing his arms over his head and running for some dozen yards in a bootless attempt to flee, like the chicken in the fairy tale who believed the sky to be falling.

He stumbled over a body, and fell. Looking up it was clear that the *mendax luna* was not falling after all. Rather it had rolled a little way through the sky, and the small craters or ragged spots upon its surface had been rotated away.

Getting to his feet Bates saw another person standing amongst all the supine bodies. As he saw this other man, the other man saw him; two pairs of eyes meeting across a field of dead human bodies.

'*Buongiorno!*' boomed this fellow.

'Hullo!' There was a mania in Bates's manner now. He was running, hulloing, leaping over the boulders and blockages in his path that used to be human beings, towards this fellow living man, whose blue coat marked him as enemy, or friend, or anything at all, beneath this baleful silver wash of cometary malediction.

[13]

Eleanor had passed from being the person she was and had become a newer person, perhaps better, but then again newer and better have rarely been synonyms. She wandered. The grief in her heart was larger than the heart that was – she supposed – engineered to contain it. The grief in her heart swelled and became bigger. An antivitalic it had been; and her husband down there, again. Husband, weddingband, herband, *ta foi conjugale ô l'Espouse!* The whirlwind, the delirium, the gospel terror of watching, of being the *audience*. Observing from above, whilst the savagery and cruelty flew into new eddies and intensities. Whilst a new Nero arose and cried aloud *If only all Rome had but one neck* – the fold of the skin, under the chin. Her own neck white and plump, as perfect a neck as any in the world. If the whole world possessed but one neck, one mighty neck ballooned like a goitre. She had been taught, as a virtuous woman, the holy truth of the gospels, and the suffering of God when He had slid himself, effortlessly, tightly, into the pain-aware envelope of flesh. God had made Himself vulnerable, and had been stabbed and hammered and His wounds washed in a sal volatile mixture of vinegar and antivitalic. It had been so monstrous a legend that her mind had revolted. She had directed her attentions to the study of the natural sciences, where the licence of her mind had room to move. Not that claustrophobia of human sufferings. But now, she understood, now she *thought* she understood. Now she finally had a glimmer of what understanding might mean. Imagine God watching, from His soaring –

this *soared* – throne; eternally looking down, and observing the misery of His creatures. Imagine! How could it *fail* to be a relief to swoop down, like the hawk of compassion, like the shrike, to enter into the midst of the pain? The whippings and the metal pinioning wrists and shins to wood, the weeping agony, it must have been a relief in its very *focus* to the endless spectating of the sufferings of others. The auto-messianic apparition; to save God from His own sense of impotence in the misery of others. It is and has always been, and it will always be easier to suffer oneself than to watch the people you love suffer. And if you cannot alleviate this latter condition, then the very least you can do – for the relief of your own tormentuous consciousness – is join them.

Time seemed to flow differently here.

Eleanor lost a portion of her time. Days, and, and. She was not sure how long she strolled. When she was hungry she devoured the sugar grass, which was as white as a bridal gown. She closed her eyes and attempted, with every appearance of a sincere effort of will, to summon the wraith of her dead father. *Guide me, Papa!* But there was nothing. She stumbled up a broad hill or rise of perfect whiteness, its texture not unlike baked earth although not dusty. At the top she looked down into a channel thronged with strange figures, all hurrying from her left to her right, or else hurrying from her right to her left. She turned her head and it was gone.

The angels held crystal wands in their hands that could, with a flick of expanding fire, cleanse the whole sky from east to west; could scorch away every living being. Yet God had chosen instead not to immolate the suffering but rather to plunge into it. Purity of self-sacrifice, or desperate prophylactic medical treatment of his own isolation? For even if He purged the world of future suffering, the pressure of past horror would be lodged in His Divine plenum, under the Holy breastbone, unrelieved. The spear that wounded Him shall also cure. Did not the Homeric gods hurl themselves, like suicides, from the highest high into the unresting surge of human warring down human? Was this the same urge?

She saw an arctic fox scurrying from one bank of white grass to another. Even its glistening nose was white. Its eyes too: not albino pink, but white as paper.

Feeling the abandon very acutely in her soul, Eleanor hurried down the slope and threw herself amongst the bustle of this strange crowd.

The individuals were a little above human height, but thinner and more wraithlike. They were clothed, but in shifts of such loose weave that their skin – white as ivory – was perfectly visible. The men walked with loose sleeves or flappy folds of white flesh, like untucked kerchiefs, where their membrum virile might be expected to perpend. The women were bushy with white hair. Their large almond-shaped eyes carried the slightest of blue tints, which caused them to stand sharply out from their white faces; faces shaped like two cupped hands.

'Friends!' cried Eleanor. 'Enemies! Help me, I beg of you!'

Most of the white folk ignored her, and continued with their myriad tasks, their hurryings and comings and goings. But a dozen or so clustered around her, broadening their mouths and speaking: a *wei-lala wal-lala* babble, a bass-flute warble, quite pleasant.

'I do not speak your language! O friends, help me!'

They babbled: *wal-lala wei-lei-lala.* They seemed very interested in her clothing, and peered at her with a disconcerting candour. Others moved past this little knot of interruptants, jostling, but without, it seemed, rancour.

'I have come to cry you mercy,' Eleanor tried, hoping to chance upon some piece of universal vocabulary. 'Love!' she tried. 'God! Truth! One!' There was an odour about these people, not unpleasant but remarkable: the scent of new rag-paper, or of something growing, something dry yet alive. And soon enough they seemed to lose interest in Eleanor and went about their business.

She used her elbows to make a way out of the pressure of white folk, and wandered some more. A tiredness oppressed her and she lay down and fell at once into a despairing, hopeless, total sleep. She awoke with no sense of time passed, for it was the same mild white lightness all around her. She could see the ceaseless traffic of pale folk along the straight road a little below her. To her right was a stone circle, a dark Stonehenge against the whiteness. But it was nothing of the sort; it was half a dozen Brobdingnagians sitting, still as the centre of their own spun worlds. Her giant, the fellow upon whose foot she had ridden, did not seem to be amongst them; but she made her way over to them anyway.

'Can you help me?'

She danced and cried to them, but they seemed to have entered a trance state; their eyes open but rolled up white. She wondered briefly if they were dead, but the geologic but certain slowness of their chests moving in, out, in, disabused her of such a notion. There was nothing she could do to attract their attention.

Yet it was peaceful, perhaps strangely so, simply to sit amongst these figures and be silent. She ate some more of the white grass, which tasted less sugary to her now. She drank from one of the improbably linear streams. It began to occur to her that, or she began to become aware of the process of wondering whether, she might be dead; and this strange place heaven. But as she looked about her the whiteness had lost its brute quality. She could almost, loosening her focus and simply letting her eyeballs sit in her skull, begin to see varieties of colour in the bright blur. Palenesses to begin with: creams; the suggestions of tan; low-intensity turquoises like the gleams that lurk in a pigeon's feather.

This was no heaven; or heaven was only a material and physical place. Those white people she had seen, hurrying along their pathways, were only the crew of a giant flying vessel, sent by their commanding officers on ordinary missions to make the great steam-engine, or crystal, or stellar fire machine operate.

And there – was – *her* giant. Disappearing over one of the pale golden hilltops, marching purposefully. A long spar in his right hand that, she could see, was his iron weapon, his huge *fusil*.

She leapt to her feet and pulled up the dirtied and fraying hem of her ample skirt and began to run. 'Sir Giant!' she called out. 'Sir Giant! Wait! Wait!'

He was too fast for her, of course. And as she laboured up the hill she wondered if it had indeed been him, for her eyes seemed tricksy and unreliable in this strange place. But of course it was.

She ran and ran, stems of grass whipping thin as silver thread against her legs as she moved through. Into the valley and up again, breathing hard, unused to the exercise. And at the top there she could see him: sitting in a hollow, nursing whatever giant metal tube he was carrying in his lap. 'Sir Giant!' she called, running and tumbling down the hill. 'It is I!'

When she got closer he looked up, with his vast head, and nodded.

She reached his legs, crossed and massy, and rested there. It took her several minutes to recover her breath.

'Sir Giant,' she called, loud as she could. '*What* is your name?'

'It is Splancknunck,' he said.

'Sir Splancknunck,' she cried. 'I have missed you!'

'Littlebig does not speak to me now.' The words rolled out with the slowness of seven sunrises. Eleanor clung to the cords of his trowser-fabric, held tight as if he represented her salvation.

'You intend some dire action with that gun,' she shouted.

He looked at the fusil in his lap: a cannon, bolted with mighty shafts to a barndoor for a stock. 'There is little enough damage I can do with this weapon,' he said.

'We must forgive! I understand now the impulse of the divine sacrifice – forgiveness not as an end in itself, but as the opening up of the mortal level, for without forgiveness the divine cannot enter in; cannot partake of *our* pain; and it is cruelty to God to exclude Him.' But he cannot have heard much of this, for she spoke rapidly and indistinctly.

'There is,' said Splancknunck, 'no harm I can do Littlebig with so small a weapon.' And he laid it on the white lawn.

'How can we harm him who is so great?' Eleanor agreed.

'He intends *us* no harm.' But the giant, saying this, bethought himself, and looked down at his tiny companion. 'I mean my kind,' he clarified. 'He is content to truce with us. But you – your kind—' and the great head shook left, shook right.

'It is the end of our world,' said Eleanor, to herself. She repeated the sentiment at a louder volume for the benefit of the giant's slower, greater ears: 'It is the end of our world.'

With tremendous sorrow he ducked his great head down, raised it, ducked it down again, raised it, ducked it down.

Things were silent for a long time. Eleanor smelt the breeze that blew without vehemence over and around her: a pale cinnamon, a light autumnal fragrance.

'I mistook him,' said the giant, after a while.

'How so?'

'I thought him the Christ man, of whom I had been taught by your people. But he has nothing to do with them. He had nothing to do with such a God.'

Eleanor tried to digest this thought. She thought of her own heart, like a globe of that cheese for which the Swiss are famous, containing bubbles of air throughout its mass. She thought of mountains and goats, clouds resting their weariness like enormous canvas sacks of water. Goitre is common amongst the mountain herders. She had read that in a book on European medical disarrangements. She had been thinking about goitre a little earlier, but she could not remember when, or why. Everything was dislocated within her. She felt tears swirl within the empty globe of her cranium like snow under the influence of a tremendous gale.

'I have been involved for years,' the giant said slowly – which is to say, slowly even for a Brobdingnagian – 'in such fighting and killing as has wounded my soul very sore. I have been full of sorrow for many years; and there is more room in me for sorrow than in you.' He said this without reproach.

'We must *forgive*,' urged Eleanor, who was starting to understand the direction his words were taking him. 'Even unto forgiving *ourselves* . . .'

'It is hard and contrary to Brobdingnag to perform such killing. In my country murderers are unheaded. And all killing *is* a murder.'

'But you cannot abandon me here,' Eleanor urged, with an extraordinary urgency and force of will-to-life flaring in her breast. She struggled and clambered up until she was standing on the being's leg, a footstep away from where his knee triangulated outwards.

'I have tried to serve the Christ-man,' said Splancknunck, 'even unto crushing my own soul. But it has been in vain.'

'Do not,' cried Eleanor, tears flowing easily now and spattering downwards, 'do not compel me to *watch*, sir! Do not do that!'

The giant hand moved slowly but with irresistible force, and lifted the giant pistol. 'There is no compulsion in my heart,' he rumbled. He lifted the gun. 'My name is Splancknunck,' he said.

Eleanor had enough self-possession, even with her trembling and her eye-fogging weeping, to scramble down from the giant's lap and to run, irregular and desperate, from the enormous figure, and not to look behind her when the cannon made its panic-shout to violate the air.

[14]

The man was called Captain Portioli; and although his men hinted at a grander title even than that (Count Portioli, perhaps even *Prince* Portioli) he himself eschewed all manner of flamboyant appurtenance. He was an Italian military man, a mining expert and gentleman, but he had been stricken with the pestilence and had been laid in a farmhouse with some other senior officers likewise afflicted. Hence he had, it seems, avoided the devastating and fatal effects of the strange green light that had flowed – it was assumed – down from the *mendax luna* and had slain all the fighting men *and all their officers*; all French, all English, with the unseemly swiftness of a great tidal bore, flushing everyone instantly at once. He was still sick, but not so ill that he could not walk about.

Portioli was a tall, thin man with a very dark skin. From a distance he looked bruised all over his body, as if the plague had taken some terrible hold upon him. But this was Bates's agitated mind, of course, and not the reality of the figure. As he came closer, and spoke words of greeting, Bates saw that this dark brown tone was the actual colour of the man's skin. He spoke a rapid and fluent English. 'I was staying in a farmhouse, where a great many French men were laying.'

Bates, jangled from his recent experiences, could only repeat certain words from the Italian's speechifying. 'Laying?'

'Very sick with the fever. The fever has gone very quickly through this part of the world, I say. I'm certain that the many English are sick with it, precisely as many as the French. Yet the officers pushed many sick people into battle despite their malady. On both sides, I have no doubt. They did this on both sides.'

'On both sides.'

'Not me. I am an expert in mines and sieges, and seconded from the Army of the Separate Imperial Kingdom of Italia. From your face I can see that you don't a-believe in the separation of kingdoms between Italy and France, but there is a great amount of independence, truly, truly, in the running of affairs in Italy.'

Bates nodded dumbly.

'So I came out, and found all these people dead. There are many people dead in the farmhouse too, but dead of the fever. There were soldiers assigned to dig trenches.'

'Trenches.'

'To dig trenches to dispose of the bodies, and many bodies were going into this trench. But then the diggers got sick with the fever and they have stopped digging.'

Bates's exhausted and jittered mind latched onto this. 'I can cure it,' he said.

'Sir doctor,' said Portioli, bowing. 'I am glad to hear it. I am glad to hear it because I have felt the first unsettlements of fever in my own blood.'

'I have cured,' said Bates, looking around himself in some agitation, and keen not to overstate his achievements, 'six or seven men.'

'I have seen the course of the fever,' said Portioli, bowing again, 'seen it take that course many times: and any treatment seems to me to be preferable to that fate.'

'I must kiss you.'

'Kiss me?'

'It is the cure.'

Portioli stepped back. 'You seem, sir doctor,' he said, smoothly, 'to be a little – ah – as the French say, *distrait*.'

'Distracted,' said Bates, turning, slapping his own shoulders and chest, turning again. 'Distracted. Distracted.'

'If there is a way in which I can be of assistance to . . .'

'It is a question of the portage of a Lilliputian, or rather Blefuscudan, fellow,' said Bates. 'He was on my shoulder. He was on my hair. He was keen I hurry to the King himself. But he seems to have fallen from me . . .'

'Perhaps,' Portioli offered, 'when you stumbled, earlier? Forgive me, but I saw you trip over one of the many bodies with which we are . . .'

'Still, still, still,' said Bates.

'Come,' said Portioli. 'I have been searching for supplies amongst these bodies, and have enough *biscuits militaires* and wind-dried meat to make a good meal. Come back to the farmhouse and share it with me. I would be glad of your assistance, and perhaps your arm to lean upon, for I am not well. I am not well, sir. Perhaps, too, you might tell me more about this cure?'

They picked their way across the endless litter of bodies, with Bates trying to piece together his shattered consciousness. Oh, he was aware of his disintegration of soul, although it was his very awareness that was so jangled. There was no paradox or mystery there. He ranged through the disorienting rush of events of the previous few weeks in search of some fixed point, *pou sto*, by which to reorient himself. It came to him at once, of course: Eleanor. His slogan. His love for her, the one fixed point in an ocean of chaos. So much, such a flux, so many folds and involutions: to fall sick with the fever, because the Lilliputians had – what? Negotiated with the atoms who existed beneath them in the scale of things? But being one of the earliest of those assaulted in this manner had probably saved him; the soldiers who has swarmed invisible into his body had been unused to fighting the forces – whatever they were – that defended bodies such as Bates's. But the myriad insect-like peoples of Lilliputia ... he lurched forward, and grabbed Portioli's elbow.

'The little people,' he urged, 'those of Lilliputia – they have declared war against all mankind. Not only against the French, or the English. Against us all.'

But Portioli smiled, and was calm, and this in turn helped calm Bates. He did not flinch, but placed his own hand on Bates's hand. 'I have sworn an oath to the army of France,' he said, 'and the army of France has no love for those little things.'

'No,' said Bates. 'No, and the army of England neither.'

'Not to be trusted.'

'And yet,' said Bates, folding his brow upon itself, 'the one of which I spoke, Gugglerum, he saved my life, not once but *several times* ...'

'Come,' said Portioli. 'We are nearly there.'

They reached the limit of scattered bodies, three-quarters up the flank of a green hill. Looking over his shoulder Bates could see the extent of the catastrophe: bodies filled the declivity, splotches of scarlet and blue blending in the mid-distance to achieve weirdly painterly effects, as if each destroyed life were nothing more than a brushstroke on an unshaped canvas.

'It will be,' said Portioli sadly, 'pestilential in only a few days.'

'Yet there are no carrion birds ...'

'There are some. The birds were killed when the people were killed. All were killed at once with this stroke from that malign – object – above. But other birds have begun to fly in. In days this terrible sight will grow more terrible still.'

Bates's heart convulsed. 'Eleanor! Sir Portioli, is there a woman ... I am searching for a woman ...'

'A woman has no place on a battlefield,' said Portioli.

'She was carried away by a Brobdingnagian, she and – a man.'

'Aha, the giant people, *they* were here. The army of France has sworn in many of these. Yet they are reluctant to fight. It is a cowardice, say some, in their great hearts. Others say it is a moral choice, as with the holy men of India or the farthest East.'

'Perhaps the giant man brought her to this place?'

'Was he coming here?'

'He was going to York. He may have passed through this place.'

'But look, my friend,' said Portioli. 'Look back across the field of many dead. There are no giant corpses. They were here, ready to join the battle. But they have vanished – who knows where?' Bates scanned the field, but it was clear that Portioli was correct, for it would not have been possible to hide even one Brobdingnagian corpse in the mess of human bodies.

'She is not here,' he said, with a sigh. 'I am relieved of a great pressure of anxiety. But, Mr Portioli, I cannot go with you. I must find her. I must go *on*, perhaps to York city itself. She has gone there, I do not doubt, with the Dean.'

'Dean?'

'The Dean of York.'

'But I have this Dean!'

'You *have* him?'

'In the farmhouse. He is there, come, come.'

'I can scarcely believe . . .' But he went on; and soon enough the low broad shape of the farmhouse was visible, with a dozen or more French soldiers sitting along the wall outside taking as much heat as they could from the winter sun. And through the low-lintelled door, there indeed was Henry Oldenberg, sitting in a rocking chair with a blanket over his knees for all the world like an old woman.

'You!' he exclaimed upon seeing Bates. 'You!'

Bates ate a little, and slept in a cot at the back of the house. When he woke he felt a little better, although agitated by a dream that he knew to be important, that might disclose some plangent and essential mystery at the heart of things – a dream he chided himself to remember even in the midst of dreaming it – but which fled away on waking, such that after splashing his face with cold water and smoothing back his hair it had gone entirely, leaving only this impression of a great solution lost.

The farmhouse was large, with several outbuildings and a two-storey barn; an arrangement of buildings occupied by three or four dozen French soldiers. A great many more were dead, their bodies laid in the far field behind a stone wall. Most of the French were ill. Bates felt the pincer of guilt upon his heart – that he had attended to his own exhaustion rather than to these his brothers in Christ. He approached Portioli. 'You must forgive me my – former distraction,' he said. 'I have had, as we all have had, a terrible number of weeks. But it does not excuse my behaviour.'

'There is no need to apologise,' said the Italian.

'Will you permit me to cure your men?'

'It is hard for me to think of them as *my* men,' said Portioli, ruefully. 'Although you are correct in so describing them, I think. I am *faute de mieux* the commander here.'

'I must go among them. I hope you trust me to do that?'

'To save them,' said Portioli. 'Of course.'

'You sir,' said Bates, tears of – joy?! – tickling the backs of his eyes. 'You sir are a good man.'

'I am not sure,' said Portioli. 'Show me first how you intend this cure.'

Bates sat down, his head still dizzy, and gathered enough of his wits to be able to explain to the Captain the nature of the fever. Rather than disbelieving, Portioli breathed a great sigh. 'This of course explains! This explains! I understand, my dear Monsieur Bates. And you have suffered this fever and survived?'

'I have.'

'The Dean, also?'

'Him also.'

'Then pass to us your immunity, Englishman.' And he angled his dark face to receive Bates's kiss.

Bates worked his way around the men, explaining to each in turn what he had to do. Some were too ill understand what he said to them; others were resistant but too weak to prevent him, or else accepted his ministrations. Three looked fiercely at him, and brandished their rifles, and them Bates left alone; although – subsequently, when they saw their comrades recover, they altered their opinions. For Bates the hours he spent doing this came to seem to him an act of penance, and it worked a kind of cure upon his own mind even as it passed the expertise to fight over the bodies of the French. It calmed him. Some of the men were handsome despite their sickness; smooth-skinned and fierce-eyed, beautiful with the beauty that the young possess without knowing it. Others were made hideous by their suffering: boils and pustules upon their faces and around their mouths, slime in their mouths and the stench of death everywhere about them. With these Bates bethought himself of Christ and the lepers, and said a whispered prayer to the

Lord before embracing them. Had Christ felt revulsion when touching such foulness? Had He needed to conquer his own inner fear of defilement? And there was a profound sort of liberation, a freeing of the spirit, in this abasement. It gave him some understanding of what, had anybody asked him prior to these times, he would have dismissed as Romish impostures; the mortification of the flesh, nuns who kiss the sores of beggars, priests who deathify their flesh. For it became, with the ninth man, a ritual: an embracement of the essence of flesh, which is that, like fire, it is continually in the process of wearing itself out. Corruption and decay were not unfortunate side-effects of the incarnation of human spirits in this world; they were the very ground of all spiritual possibilities; and Bates discovered a strength in overcoming his own squeamishness that he had not found through all his previous prayer and church-devotions.

The self-sacrifice was given sharpness by the fact that Bates longed to talk with the Dean about Eleanor's whereabouts. He wanted the conversation eagerly, and yet he feared it; for what if the Dean had only bad news about her? The agony of uncertainty was so acute that it was palpable pain in his own body. And, nevertheless, he embraced even that. His own suffering gave strength to him. It was petty enough, he knew, when compared to the sufferings of the world around him; but it was his. For a small man, Divine Providence provided an appropriate suffering, perhaps: for the Blefuscan Bates had killed in the hotel room, striking him with the Bible, had experienced but a small blow, yet it had surely been a great suffering proportionately. And so it was for Bates.

When he was finished he washed his face and drank some water, and then he ate a circle of stale bread from Portioli's supply. And finally he sat down on the Dean's left hand, with Portioli on the right.

'Henry,' he said, in a gentle voice. 'I must ask after Eleanor.'

The Dean looked at him with one watery eye. 'She is *my* fiancée,' he said.

'I know that.'

'I have *seen* the way you look at her.'

'I respect God's commandments,' said Bates. 'Believe that I do. She had her choice, and she chose you.'

This seemed to mollify Oldenberg a little. 'They're all dead,' he said, grumpily, sweeping his arm at the wall. 'Ten thousand, perhaps. More than a thousand, at any rate. All slain. All,' he added, with a spurt of vehemence, 'save this blackamoor ...'

'Dean!' Bates said. 'Do not forget your manners, I pray you.'

'He claims to be Italian,' Oldenberg continued. 'But his mother is Abyssinian.'

'I apologise,' said Bates; but there was a calm expression on Portioli's face.

'There is no need,' he said. 'I have often found such hostility amongst the English.'

'Black as the Devil,' grumbled the Dean, drawing the blanket around him as if it might shield him from the whole world. 'His mother an Abyssinian maid! Born, I daresay, amongst the very foothills of Mount Abora.'

'In Genoa,' said Portioli, gently.

'He asked after the giants,' said Oldenberg. 'But I'll not talk to *him*. Have ye any snuff, my dear fellow?' he added, darting a claw from the blanket to grasp Bates's arm. 'Any of my snuff? Have ye chanced upon any, on your travels here?'

'I'm afraid not, Dean,' said Bates.

Oldenberg's gloomy countenance reasserted itself and he sat back in the chair. 'Of course not. Neither has this blackface. Neither he, although he comes from the land of opium itself.'

'Genoa,' said Portioli, again, giving his head the mildest of shakes.

'Dean,' Bates prompted. 'Eleanor?'

For a minute, or more, it seemed as though Oldenberg was not going to say anything. But eventually he spoke. 'She was taken up.'

'Taken up?'

'With that treacherous giant. She ran to him and he was swept into that Satan's sphere – all the giants were; all at once.'

Bates looked at Portioli, but he only said: 'I did not see it. I was here the whole time of the battle. The most I saw was the light of the green colour that flickered over the lip of the hill, there, and that filled the valley.'

'That death light,' cried the Dean. 'The comet, you see. It was the comet and it has swooped down upon the world as its master intended.'

'Its master?'

'The Devil, of course. The Devil. Who else? The Devil. Diabolus. Bolus means sphere, and this is the Devil's throne, and that's where Eleanor is.' And with that he threw the blanket over his own head, like a grieving woman, and would say nothing more.

Bates and Portioli walked to the lip of the hill and watched the mendax luna for a half hour. 'It is lower in the sky,' Portioli said. 'Every day it comes a little lower. I can only believe that eventually it will rest itself upon the ground.'

'Yet it can be damaged,' said Bates, scrutinising the scuffs made upon its surface by the English bombardment.

'That was a fierce cannonade,' said the Italian. 'But it has torn some rents in the surface of the thing.'

'If it can be damaged,' said Bates, 'then it can be destroyed.'

'Possibly so, my friend. But it would require a thousand mighty cannons bringing their fire upon it over many nights to break it up. So many cannon shells, and mighty ones, from the great cannon at York that the English captured last week. So many, and all that has resulted are some nips and tears in the outer skin of it.'

'It is a machine,' said Bates. 'I think.'

'I think so too. *Deus ex machina*.'

'Yet no *deus*, I think.'

'Your friend the Dean thinketh it a devil?'

'And I have met soldiers who think it is Wormwood, the day of judgment. But I think it a machine, and inside it a giant.'

'Brobdingnagian?' Portioli asked, but immediately answered himself: 'But you mean a giant to whom the Brobdingnagians are but shrimps and mice. No? And why could it not be so? If there are miniature people to whom e'en the Lilliputians are giants – then why not extend the scale up?'

'Perchance there are giants to whom even that creature,' and Bates waved his right thumb at the sphere, 'is but an atom. Perchance every world that moves through the aether interstellatum is but an atom in the body of some super-gigantos.'

'Dizzying speculation.'

'We cannot lose ourselves in such speculation. We must attend to the matter in hand. If Eleanor is inside that sphere then inside that sphere is where I must go.'

'To rescue another man's wife?'

'She is not married to him,' Bates said, sharply. But he rebuked himself. 'She is not yet married to him, although they are, it is true, affianced, it is true. They are. But it is possible to love another's wife with a pure heart, to love all life with that human love that exists in a ratio inferior to the love of God himself. As Sir Lancelot loved Guinevere, although she was married to his King and best friend.'

'Sir Lancelotta,' said Portioli. 'An Italian man.'

'I had thought French,' said Bates. 'Lancelot du Lac.'

'So styled in the French *romances, bien sûr*. But at first he was Lancelotta di Laca, from the Laca region of Piedmont.'

'If you are correct about the sphere lowering itself, day by day, until it rests on the Earth, then perhaps there will be the chance to enter it through one of the rents caused by the bombardment.'

'Possibly. But it is a huge space; a world-in-little. Would one say worldkin?'

'One might.'

'Would one say worldicule?'

'A word formed on the analogy of ridicule, perhaps?'

'I thought, on the analogy of animalcule.'

'I see. But I would search it even if it were the whole world itself.' And as he said it he believed it, as if the spirit of the *romances des chevaliers* had entered, to some degree, into his timid blood. 'Search the whole world and retrieve her.'

The following day the men were showing signs of returning health. The Dean, however, had withdrawn into a miserable state; he only left his rocking chair to attend to his bodily functions; and he spoke to nobody. The day after, as Bates sat nearby staring at the stone wall and trying to think through his situation, Oldenberg spoke up.

'I'm sorry,' he said.

'You have no need to be sorry,' said Bates.

With a little gunpowder flash of his old anger he retorted: 'Do not tell me what I *need*, sir! Nor what I *need not*, neither! A gentleman never apologises or explains, and I am a – I am a gentleman. But nevertheless, nevertheless, it might be said. I might say. I do say. I should not have abandoned you. When Eleanor and I climbed aboard our giant, I should not have left you behind. It was not the action of a Christian.'

'I forgive you,' said Bates.

This seemed not to anger the Dean. 'Truly?' he asked, in a small voice.

'Of course. We are brothers in Christ, sir.'

'Perhaps I have misjudged you, Bates.' He mused for a while, and chewed on the edge of his blanket.

'I am not the man I was,' said Bates. And he felt it in his heart to be true.

They were, it seemed, merely waiting. For what? 'The news has gone back,' said Portioli, 'to your people and to mine. Two mighty armies were sent here to clash, and they have both been swept away into death. Whichever nation can raise a new army, or bring up new forces, will claim the field. They need only march here. As to which will come *first*, I do not know. That is in God's hands.'

'The English hold York?'

'The French had not yet taken it. But I do not believe the city well-garrisoned it. I do not believe they needed to: many of the citizens had fled before the French, and those few who remained, being English, would not need a force to subdue them. But the French hold the coast.'

'They have suffered at the hands of the plague,' said Bates.

'The English too.'

'How long must we wait?'

'It is in God's hands. But should the English come first, then we,' and he gestured to his men, 'will become your prisoners.'

'And if the French, then the Dean and I will become yours.'

Bates discussed this latter possibility with the Dean, seizing an opportunity when the two men were alone in the farmhouse one afternoon. 'If the French come here they will imprison us.'

'*Amis de France*,' grumbled the Dean.

'But we have the *key*,' said Bates in a lowered voice. 'We can barter the *key* for our freedom – and if the English come first, and are hostile to us because they have heard, somehow, of our collaboration – then the key to the Computational Device will free us!'

'I do not have it,' said the Dean, dolefully. 'I do not have it. Eleanor wore it about her neck, and she has been taken away from me. My comfort in my old age! Like David and Bathsheba, but the Lord has taken her.'

'I shall retrieve her,' said Bates. 'I shall recover her. I shall rescue her.'

The following day the *mendax luna* was lower again in the sky; and again neither French nor English armies came marching to claim the field. Bates went out with Portioli and two French soldiers – now fully recovered – to glean such provisions from the fallen men as was possible.

An unmistakable stench was gathering, like a miasma of evil, in the valley. Its odour was in the farmhouse too, of course; and familiarity with it reduced its offence; but to walk amongst the dead was to steep oneself in it. Portioli and the Frenchmen were as pale as bones, and all of them stopped at one point or another to vomit. Bates misliked the stench of it, of course, but he also welcomed it, the mortification of its rasp in his lungs; and below it all an odour of immerding that thrilled his body. They gathered such packs and pouches as were not too badly defiled and carried them back to the house.

'We cannot stay here for much longer,' Portioli opined. 'Two more days, I think, and we should abandon the field.'

'And go where?'

'This great sphere descends. It has slain countless of our people and your people. Do you think it bodes us well?'

'No.'

Portioli shook his sage head sadly. 'Mankind is in a dreadful place, at a dreadful time. The plague is a terrible affliction. But this great visitor from above the sky is worse. And we are caught between the two, squashed like a flea between two thumbnails. All of mankind is but a flea to him, perhaps.'

'Humankind is dying,' grumbled the Dean. 'We are all dying. Every soul on this stony earth, every child, every man, every—' he choked. He began, feebly, to weep.

'The prospects are not good, I agree,' said Bates, energetically; 'but we must not despair. Despair is a sin, my friends. If humankind must assemble a thousand giant cannons to destroy this machine, then assemble a thousand cannons we shall!'

'The great Davidowic is dead,' said the Dean. 'Who can build another? I knew him, and though a Jew he was the greatest of men. The greatest man I ever knew.' The tears came again, rheumy and thin, and he continued speaking though his voice warbled. 'But he died of the consumption of the lungs. And if we had a thousand Davidowices, it would take a lifetime to assemble so many great guns. And all the time our people dying of the plague.'

'Come,' said Bates. 'This giant-of-giants, though he is huge, is slow. When the English bombarded him he moved his craft – but a day after the cannonade began. He has taken a week to lower his craft to the ground. He is slow, and we are quick!'

*

The following morning, as dawn was smoothing the fields with rose-gold palms, the English soldiers came. But not an army. It was the same troop of English soldiers that had earlier taken Bates into its custody. Eleven men. Captain Longley, Cheeks and the other man were in the cart: the last of these with a bandage around his eyes. Longley himself looked iller than he had done when Bates first met him: as white as ice, trembling slightly. 'He's lost a peck o' blood,' said one of the men – a bearish, brown-red, pock-faced private called Dartford. 'We had to tar up his stump. We had to fetch the tar from the field.'

'Field?'

With a sour expression, as if Bates were being deliberately obtuse. 'Battlefield; from one of the guns.'

'They use tar on cannons?'

'On steam cannons they do.'

'They do?'

'Barrels need caulking. Or the water'd leak away.'

'Water,' said Bates, 'for the cannons.'

'By the time we got back he was near dead, 'cept the scorching of the wound had sealed some of it.'

Bates felt a queer pressure of guilt about the loss of Longley's hand, although God knew it had little enough to do with him. He had not wished it, or worked for it, had raised no cleaver to his wrist. But, after the Captain was carried, moaning softly, into the farmhouse, Bates sat beside him and attempted such ablutions as seemed appropriate: brow-wiping, sheet-adjusting and so on. He sat with him for some hours and attempted questions, but all Longley did was mutter and keen and fall silent. 'Should we change the dressing?'

'I know nothing of wounds,' said Portioli. 'You are the doctor, my friend.'

'No doctor, I,' said Bates.

'You healed me,'

'Not I,' said Bates. 'The animalcules inside me, educated by martial experience in the ways of their incomprehensible wars, and carrying that knowledge with them into other bodies.'

'And I suppose,' said Portioli, leaning over the Captain, 'that a similar war is being fought in this poor soul's body now. His own forces fighting a war against – what?'

'Animalcules in the air – the bad air,' said Bates, 'from the field of death over the hill.'

'The breach in his skin,' agreed Portioli.

It transpired that Dartford, who had a brother in the navy, had heard of but never actually witnessed the therapeutic tarring of amputated limbs. Portioli reasoned that more than simply coating the stump in tar would be required – the channels and veins of the arm would need to be knotted together. Moreover, as they discussed it further, they agreed that the air on board a ship, salted and washed by continual oceanic laving, was healthier than the air in such a place as they now were for surgical interventions of any sort.

The evening came. Bates slept in the floor space with Portioli and another man. This was the first night they had to soak a cloth in rum and wrap it about their mouths. They tore little plugs of cotton, rolled them and tamped them into their nostrils.

In the morning the Dean complained loudly that Longley's arm was gangrenous. He would not be silenced, nor reasoned with, to grant that the stench now unavoidably filling the farmhouse came from the harvest of corpses over the lip of the hill. 'Take him out of the place,' Oldenberg insisted. 'His flesh is decaying with the gangrene.'

'It is not, Dean, I assure you,' said Bates; but he could not be certain.

They waited another day, but still no armies came, neither English nor French. Another trip to the corpse valley in the late afternoon, with dusk grinding the sky to a fine dark powder and a faint but unsettlingly evident luminescence, pale green, as if mocking the strange light that had slain the men. They went out under the enormous lowering presence of the great white circle, stage scenery on a vast scale, a shield fit for God himself rolled against the sky. They scurried under this: Portioli and Bates and one of Longley's men, called Benfy. All three were muffled. 'Strange to think,' said Benfy, in his boomy London voice, 'that if the Frankies come o'er us first then you and I'll be prisoners, Mr Bates, and this here Italian lord.' He pronounced the word eye-tail-un. 'Whereas if the English come first then you and I will be heroes.'

'I do not believe, Private, that we will be able to stay here for much longer,' was Bates's reply.

The *mendax luna* was much lower in the sky now – its lowest curve perhaps only a hundred feet from the side of the opposite hill. 'It is coming down,' observed Portioli. 'Another day, or two, and it will have made land.'

'It moves so slowly.'

'The slowness of the leviathan,' said Portioli, 'is the same thing as the swiftness of the flea.'

The trip was not so much for food as for tobacco: pipes and pouches retrieved from those who could no longer use their lungs. Back in the farmhouse everybody smoked; and most packed their nostrils with wads of moistened tobacco. It reduced the oppressive foetor. 'How long must we remain in this place,' complained the Dean, as he attempted, onto a handkerchief, to shred pipe tobacco fine enough with his fingers to take it as snuff. 'We should leave in the morning.'

'Abandoning the field,' said Portioli, 'is no military honour.'

'The field,' scoffed the Dean. 'We do not possess the field – what? what? Two dozen Frenchie and one dozen English soldiers? A Pyrrhic sort of victory, ain't it?'

'Naturally one side or the other awaits reinforcement.'

'And what if it come? What if it come? The globe will kill them all anyway. I'm only surprised it hasn't sent its devil death upon us. But I tell you all, it has only omitted to do so because we are so few, we are beneath its notice.'

This sentiment lowered the morale of the farmhouse. There was no denying its truth, although it was of course possible to deplore the tone in which it was uttered. 'It looks bad,' said Benfy, sounding surprisingly undowncast. 'If the plague don't get us, the death will come down from above.'

'They are two invading armies,' said Bates. 'The plague is caused by a vast horde of miniature, invisible, tiny soldiers. The *mendax luna* is crewed by a troop of giants to whom our Brobdingnagians are as Lilliputians. Both wish us ill, or at least wish us disposed of and out of the way.'

A man came running in at the door. 'Captain,' he cried. 'Somebody has leapt from the great circle.'

Scarfed and smoking, a dozen men followed Bates and Portioli to the summit of the little hill. The light was almost gone from the sky, but enough of a blue gleam remained over the western horizon to silhouette the figure of a man. 'A giant! He came from the circle?'

'Yes Captain – he leapt down.'

'Leapt a hundred feet – a mere nothing to him.'

'What should we do?'

'Do? We must signal him, of course. We must light a fire. A fire here, on the hilltop.'

It took minutes to assemble the materials and light them, and soon enough a fire threw an upward shower of flames and sparks into the dark sky. The giant stood still, motionless. Portioli leapt and hallooed, threw his arms around, and several of the men followed him. And then, sure enough, the giant started into its great stride. In moments it had walked down the valley, and stepped over the river, and started looming up towards the light.

'*Mon ami!*' cried Portioli. 'My friend!'

And the figure, red and black in the firelight like a painted savage, came closer, with his great jacket like a bell tent with sleeves, the rope strands of the cloth visible; and his trowsers creasing with audible cracks like the fire itself. 'I recognise you,' shouted Bates, in a sudden ecstasy. The nighttime, the shove of heat given off by the fire on his left hand, the stars shimmying in a dance with the hundreds of aspirant sparks – it all added to a dreamlike quality. 'I recognise *you*!' And with dreamlike rightness, as the giant reached the top, his enormous seamed face made craggier by the underlighting of the blaze, and looked down upon them – lowered himself, and folded his treetrunk legs into a child's posture – and opened the flap of his pocket, Bates heart thrummed and leapt over irregular chiasmuses, and there she was. Of course it was her: for in dreams this is the nature of consummation. All the tedious days of waiting, as the stench grew around him, slipped from his mind. Now there was only this intimate linkage between his wanting her and her appearing.

Men were helping her down from the pocket, and bringing her over to the fire. Her face, as beautiful as ever, looked warm in the blazelight, but also severe, changed by her experience.

'The smell!' she said, holding a hand before her mouth.

'It is terrible, Madame, I know it is,' said Portioli. 'I can but apologise for your offended feminine sensibilities. Permit me to inform you that my name is Portioli.'

'I am Mrs Eleanor Burton,' said Eleanor, looking around. Bates could not move, he was so deeply and terrifyingly thrilled. He could not squeeze enough will into one foot to move it so much as an inch. Her gaze passed from face to face, then alighted on his, and shared no shine of recognition. It passed to another face. And with that a dark hand moved over his heart. 'Eleanor!' he cried.

She looked at him. Looked, and then recognised, and called back: 'Abraham! You're here!'

'Eleanor,' he called back, delirious and careless of his surroundings, 'are you well?'

'Madame,' said Portioli, bowing. 'May I ask – did you come out of that great sphere?'

She looked back, distractedly, and then at the giant. 'My friend,' she said. 'He broke through the skin and leapt down, with me in his pocket. I thought he was going to murder himself, but that – no. That is not the Brobdingnagian way. He used his great pistol – he fired it again and again, for a day. Or a night? He broke through the skin and leapt.'

'But, forgive me,' pressed Portioli. 'I have a particular reason for repeating my question, and avoiding all obscurity: you have been *inside.*'

'Yes,' she said. 'Yes.'

From this moment could be dated the inevitable gathering of force, of collective will; and Bates found himself quite literally turning and turning about, as if spun by the swirling force of hurricane. When the Dean saw Eleanor come walking through the door he barked like a dog, barked and got to his feet, scattering a brown snowfall of tobacco all about him. He was crying. 'I thought you dead!' he wailed repeatedly, childlike, embarrassing, yet touching too. Eleanor was damp-eyed too as she embraced him, and the blanket that had covered him fell to the floor. 'I thought you dead!' he said.

'No, no, my Henry.'

'I thought you dead!'

The mood of celebration infected everybody, even the score-and-a-half of soldiers, French and English, to whom Eleanor was as perfect a stranger as Eve. Such rum as had been gathered from military supplies, and hoarded as an antiodorant in which to douse rags and headscarfs, was brought forth and drunk. There was singing.

Splancknunck (for Eleanor told them his name) sat outside the farmhouse with his head down, silent, motionless, like an Aegyptian statue of a long-passed Pharaoh.

Everybody gathered in the farmhouses – three dozen eager people, to hear Eleanor give a halting and, truth be told, not very coherent account of her time inside the super-gigantos. Portioli questioned her minutely.

She continually broke off her narrative. 'The smell! Oh, forgive me – the smell.'

'Have a pipe, Ma'am,' offered Private Dartford.

'Tobacco? No thank you.'

'Come, Ma'am, it'll mask the smell better than ladylike tea.'

She took a pipe and sucked timidly on the end, letting the smoke leak from her lips.

'Please continue, Ma'am,' pressed Portioli.

She looked around the room, the faces packed so tightly around her they might have been bricks piled upon bricks.

'And the green light – there was a green light – did ye know of that, Ma'am?' asked somebody.

She told them about the antivitalic, and the things that Splancknunck had said.

'Trust a giant?' scoffed Benfy. 'A Frankie giant?'

'He is my brother,' said Eleanor, in a more severe voice. 'He has saved my life, and I love him. I'll not hear him abused. He is my brother.'

There was silence.

When it became clear that Eleanor had no great tale of adventure to relate, merely confused recollections about Hamletian out-of-joint time and a white land, a place where time seeped and dipped instead of marching straight on, people broke away. They sought out the remaining rum and drank it; found their way to the outhouses and slept. But Portioli – and, of course, Bates – stayed with Eleanor.

Bates could see the way Portioli's mind was working. But surely it was a death wish, and nothing more. It gave him glimpses of everything as sickeningly strange, but he could not dispute the logic of it. 'Do you doubt the danger this creature embodies, in his vastness?' Portioli hissed, as they lay on the farmhouse floor in the dark. Eleanor had been given the roof space to herself; and the Dean, Bates, Portioli and two others were rolled in blankets on the floor.

'It is his vastness that renders the prospect impracticable,' whispered Bates.

'Did the animalcules that have slain so many human beings in these lands over the last months think so?'

'The case is hardly comparable.'

But there was a ferocity in the heart of the well-mannered Italian that burnt with an unwavering blue-purple flame. He would not be dissuaded. He was, Bates understood, lying in the darkness on the stone flags, one of those men whose commitment to a chevalier code compelled them to seek out self-sacrifice. The stench that revolted Bates's stomach – even Bates's stomach, and even as he felt revolting desire stir again interfemorally – seemed to spur him on.

'But does it not seem ...' Bates tried, searching to find a means of expressing the range of his disillusionment, the way the tiny crystal of his own sufferings had acted as a lens that revealed deserts of meaninglessness. 'Does it not seem that this super-gigantos, in his airy chariot, is but a man – and that man moves through a space inhabited by beings that seem gigantic to him – and those beings are dwarfed in their turn – does that not seem ...' But there were, it seemed, no words in his store to capture it: 'Does that not seem ...' What did it not seem? Why did the breeze that blew up from the hatch he had opened into the infinite vista chill him to?

'It is – forgive me, my friend,' Portioli said. 'Is it not the thing that all schoolboys do when they are given their copy book? They write in the cover ...'

Bates knew immediately what he meant. 'Yes, they write in the cover,' and he repeated, in a singsong:

Abraham Bates
Year VI
King's School
Canterbury
Kent
England
The United Realm of King George
Europe
The World
The Universe

It was the ease with which a few scratches of a boy's pen could transport him from exactly inside his skin to the grandeur of the universe itself. But at least that was a progression with definite commencement and completion points. If the list indeed kept shifting, step back and step back, Abraham Bates to Gugglerum to animalcule to who knew what ... and if it spooled out, such that the entire universe were a single man in a population of many men, and they themselves dwarfed by something larger and more pitiless still ... it collapsed the mind even to begin to think of it. Was the God Abraham had worshipped the being constituted by the whole universe? Did God himself quail beneath the enormous stride of some God-giant?

'It is,' he whispered, in the dark, turning on his side, 'schoolboy matters, you are right.'

'A man,' whispered Portioli, 'understands that we are not given a place to stand. We must make that for ourselves.'

'I try,' Bates whispered, 'to take comfort in that.'

The birds had returned to the fields now in large numbers, to feast on the dead flesh, and very penetrating and ubiquitous were their multiple ululations. In the dawn they shrieked as if the sunlight scalded them, and flew in great snow-flurries, and fought one another. In the evening they were calmer, satiated, many of them making their way ungainly on two legs over the uneven ground, made uneven by the presence of so much butcher's material.

The great disc of deadly silver dominated the sky. Everything they did was rendered inert and petty beneath its magnitude.

Splancknunck rose to his feet and departed that place, silent except for the thud and the thud his feet made on the moist earth and the bodies of the dead. He spoke to nobody and nobody knew where he went.

In the morning Portioli gathered all the soldiers together outside the farmhouse. Eleanor stood in the doorway, looking out over them.

'Are you soldiers?' he cried. They, muffled to a man, and all with smoking pipes, mumbled and muttered, so he sang out cheerily and huzzah'd them into more of a soldierly state.

'Are you soldiers?'

'Y/y/es-yes. Mmmmm.'

'*Are* you soldiers?'

Louder – 'Yes.'

'Are you soldiers?'

As one, 'Yes!'

'We face an enemy, a terrible enemy. But we are soldiers, and we can fight the enemy.' He attempted to explain the nature of the situation. But the men were disinclined to see it.

So—
So—?
So – we are to fight the . . .

Portioli flashed fire from his eyes. 'Think of this great sphere as a castle. We must capture the castle – for by doing so we defend the world from this invasion. And what else.'

'We shall capture the castle, as an animalcule invades . . . infects . . .'

'This is what I understand,' Portioli said, 'from the esteemed and medically-trained Dr Bates. But I prefer to think of it this way, that we are to capture the castle by *colonising* it, and making it *our* colony, a portion of *our* empire. That this body is to be our America, our new-found land.'

'In which case . . .' shouted one of the soldiers.

There was some commotion.

'In which case we will need women!' yelled a trooper, from the back. 'Women!'

There was much agreement amongst the group of them.

Portioli waited until the clamour had died, and held up his hand. 'But you have not yet grasped it. It is not by a process of *outbreeding* the invader that we shall defeat him. For to do so would take many centuries – and that without certainty of success. But it is not needful. We do not need to outbreed the enemy's population of—' but, here, he could not supply the word to describe them, and after a pause he continued, '—for we have another way. Do you know why? Because breeding generates matter, and inert matter is not the *principle* of the *cosmos*. Do you know what the principle of the cosmos is? It is mind! It is mind! Every atom thinks, the whole cosmos thinks – the whole cosmos is but an atom, and an atom that thinks.'

This was too metaphysical for the men. 'But! But! But!'

'How did the Romans, my ancestors, conquer the world?' shouted Portioli. 'One tiny city against millions? Some they fought, yes, when that was necessary. Some they killed. But most, the majority, they *turned into Romans*.'

He turned his face from person to person.

'Conversion is a better weapon than a rifle. You will storm the castle as a small band, but you will win over those of your enemy you do not kill. And you shall not kill many.'

'But how!'

'With an idea. An idea is more infectious than the most violent plague. The idea of Christ! You shall be missionaries. You shall be Christian soldiers.'

'But how shall we live? What shall we eat?'

'Food? Food is plentiful. We shall be the bearers of good news. *We* will be revered as princes and kings!'

At the end of the talk Portioli led the men to the brow of the hill and had them stand and gaze upon the ghastly spread of dead men, walking amongst them and reminding them: 'These were your comrades – these were your friends – would you not be revenged on him that did this?'

And then he repeated the stories that Eleanor had told them, embellishing them to stress both the feebleness of the crew, or cells, or what-might-they-be of the giant being – whilst also hinting at an unspecified but sizeable wealth that awaited them, like stout Cortez, ready for the plunder. Within the hour the group of men were one cohort, French and English together, united with an eagerness to storm.

Bates felt a sickness in his heart. It took him most of the day to understand that this sickness was hope.

He pincered Portioli's shoulder, and pushed him to the corner of the room. 'We cannot lead Mrs Burton into this assault.'

'Indeed not. She must be escorted – to York, I believe best, as she is English. Although I fear she will find a city mostly deserted.'

'Escorted by whom?'

'By yourself, my friend, for you are no soldier.'

'Indeed not. Myself and the Dean?'

'The Dean?'

'He is affianced to Mrs Burton.'

Portioli's face ticked through several expressions. 'A widow, then,' he said. 'Alas there are many in these days. And January can marry May – my father was Genoese and decennads older than my mother. My beautiful mother. Is it decennads? In English?'

'You mean . . . decades?'

'Ah! Just so. But there is a problem. It is a problem we have. We have need of the Dean.'

'The Dean is no soldier.'

'Come! Friend! He is a soldier of Christ. He is Dean of York.'

'An old man . . .' said Bates, with a sense of desperation in pressing his case that he did not properly understand. The shocking revelation that hope can work in the heart exactly like greed. Even as he spoke the words he understood that he was offering them not in the rhetorical sense, to persuade Portioli; but in the sense that a toy is offered to a cat, that she can *bat it away*.

'Not so old as some,' said Portioli. 'Not so old as he is pretending to be, sitting in that chair all day with the blanket on him.'

'But I do not see . . .' Bates pressed, a voice sounding as strong in his ear as if Gugglerum had made his way out of the mess of carnage and had climbed inside the empty bone globe of it: *Stop! Be rid of him* – and yet he pressed on. Why did he continue? What had he to win by this effort, except, perhaps, to test his manly courage, in the truest way – 'I do not see what good the Dean will do inside that great place. You have seen him, how easily enfeebled he is.'

'My friend,' said Portioli. 'He is your friend, evidently, and you are noble to hope to spare him. But it is his duty. We need him, and for this reason: that he is a man of God, and God will be our weapon. We will neither kill all the inhabitants, nor could we ever outnumber them. We must work as a missionary works.'

Bates said nothing more, but walked outside to stare at the great sphere – now closer than ever to the ground – and at the stars behind it. The valley of dead bodies was gleaming with its greenly nacreous decay. It twitched and wriggled with life – birds, and dogs, come hurrying in from the surroundings to snatch what morsels they could. The still of the nighttime was laid under the occasional raucous dog quarrel, or the occasional niggling and yawping of birds.

The Dean was having none of it. 'Do you take me for a stumparumper? No, sir. I'll not take orders from a black-face man, and an Italian into the bargain, *and* a sapper in the French army, and all of these things in one man – you sir. No sir.'

'Dean, I implore you to put aside mere national differences – you have seen the devastation this Littlebig creates with his antivitalic. Do you wish to see York, or London – or Paris, or Rome – washed over with this terrible light?'

'I'm no *soldier*,' Oldenberg insisted, with an almost unhinged emphasis on the last word.

'Your presence will be by way of missionary work, my dear Dean, as I explained . . .'

'I'm no dear of yours, sir!'

'The greater good of humanity . . .'

'No sir!'

'The calling of Christ himself . . .'

'Do you dare to lecture me on *that* subject?'

'I dare,' said Portioli, becoming stern for the first time in Bates's memory, 'to insist upon a man's duty in the face of . . .'

'I am a man, sir,' shouted the Dean, his face reddening. 'I am a white man, sir. It is not for a white man to take orders from . . .'

'Dean!' said Bates, loudly. 'Hold your tongue, sir. You speak offensive impertinence.'

Oldenberg's glaucous eyes bulged in their sockets, but he kept his silence, shocked, it seemed, at Bates's intervention. His breathing deepened. He might have been having an apoplexy. His skin tone darkened further, to purple, until it was almost the same albedo and contrast, although of course differently hued, as Portioli's.

'Dean,' said this latter, calm again, 'please understand that I command the men, French and English both. The requirements of war are such that I have the power to compel you to accompany us on this mission. Such would be a perfect legality, on my part. But I offer you the free choice.'

The hrrr-haa of the Dean's breathing.

'A free choice.'

There was chatter, and a variety of non-specific activity, as the men arranged their possessions, packed their satchels, readied themselves for the morrow, as soldiers have done on battle's eve for thousands of years. Bates wandered, uncertain. He was on the verge of obtaining his heart's dream, perhaps; a more alarming prospect than the verge of one's own death. For after all death, whatever else it may be when it comes to us, is not going to be a disappointment. 'And why tomorrow?' one man was saying. Another translated the question into French, *Il dit, pourquoi demain*? Because that is when the great circle will touch the Earth, and we can scramble aboard.

– But surely it will rest there, as solid a feature as the White Cliffs Dover-way?

– Oh who knows? Who knows? It could fly straight back up.

– No I hope *not*.

– But who knows?

Somebody else, a rough English voice, picked up the echo of who knows, and sang in a low tone:

Oh who is it knows
For whom the rose blows
The white bloom of Bristol
The red bloom of Cloves?

'Abraham?'

It was her voice, it was as pure as a musical note in this stinking place.

They walked out together in the starlight, she sliding her arm into Bates's, and causing his heart to flipper like a fledgling's wings as he attempts first flight.

'I cannot go back into that great white place,' she said.

And Bates's heart sped faster. 'No, of course, Eleanor, of course. You are to be escorted to York.'

'Escorted by . . .?'

He gulped a fishlike gulp. 'By – but whom would you like to attend you, Eleanor? My—' and he swallowed the word. But then he rebuked himself inwardly, and blurted the word, just as Eleanor began to speak. '—Darling—'

'—I hardly feel,' she stopped, started again, 'that I need any escort at all. I have walked the roads of the country alone before. But if others are going that way . . .'

'The others are storming the castle.' And he gestured with his free arm. 'All the others, save only—'

'Henry will not go,' she said. 'He will not go into the sphere.'

'Indeed he says so,' agreed Bates. 'He says so, although Captain Portioli is adamant that a man of God is essential to the success of . . .'

He felt as if the things they had to say kept bumping in at one another, although there were as many empty spaces as there were words between them. There was one now. Bates found his stomach curling and its content pressing against his gorge. The caprice of the cosmos: a starlit promenade arm in arm with the woman he loved – but accompanied by the stench of putridity.

He, she, silence. Then – he and she together: 'I have thought of you constantly —'

'I am changed from the woman I was before I—'

Silence again.

She took up the chain of conversation. Each of the links was heavy

344

in her hands. 'I am not the woman I used to be,' she said. Bates heard this, and weighed it, before it was able to fire the hope higher inside him. Did she mean that she could now be —

'I witnessed the destruction from on high,' she said. 'Inside the sky-ship of this Littlebig giant.' She waited for the next words to gather enough momentum to leave her: 'Never again can I sit aside and spectate.'

'I think I understand.'

'Everything in my life,' she said, slowly, 'has been wrong.'

'But your future . . .' he urged.

'Everything I have seen,' she said, 'connects me now to the sufferings of others.'

And in a perfect moment there was, for Bates, a vision of himself and herself married, missionaries together to the suffering poor, to the sick and the godless, devoting themselves to others and which other had greater claim on him than her, or on her than him? Human being, believe it, for you find perfect happiness only in others.

'I love you Mrs Burton,' he hurried. 'I love you Eleanor. Eleanor.'

And she stopped and clasped his hands in hers, such that they faced one another, and she said: 'You must know that I love you also, Abraham,' in an earnest, almost pleading voice; and he knew with that, just that arrangement of her body, that pressure of her cold hands, the emphasis of her voice, that she would not marry him. That even if circumstances removed the Dean, then she would not marry him. It struck out his heart, of course. It was the blocked barrel down which he had fired his charge, and its retorting explosion had excavated the cavity of his chest; but the wound in such cases does not smart, nor even necessarily disable, the warrior.

'You know that I must ask you to marry me.'

'I shall marry Henry,' she said.

He was silent for a while. The great and oppressive circle was a lid ready to clap shut over the entire sky. It was death to him, and death to his hopes, and it was readying itself to stifle his love. He must go into it, in Oldenberg's place, and she must go with her affianced husband to York. He did not will the words, but nevertheless his mouth was saying: 'I have always understood this.'

They stood in silence, and he added: 'You said before, after the intimacy we shared . . .'

'Do not think,' she interrupted, 'that it was meaningless to me.'

'No.'

'Do not think that.'

'You said once that you wished you could take two husbands.'

'I could fashion that wish within me again. But you understand why I must marry Henry?'

'He can escort you to York,' said Bates.'

'You may come with us, if you wish it.' Almost coyly.

'Though not a man of God,' said Bates, 'in a doctrinal or official capacity, yet have I worked to spread what I took to be God's message. In the days before the French came I took the news of the importance of the freedom of the Lilliputians' (a shiver across his mind, a fleeting memory of Gugglerum) 'to many meetings, to people susceptible to the message and to those hostile. I can carry the message that Portioli needs me to carry. I can teach the soldiers to carry that message too.'

'You will go inside . . .'

'I will. I will go inside. I have bethought me: on my journey here, from London, I fell into a fever twice, and each time it might have been my death. Once in the carriage —'

'I could hardly forget that,' said Eleanor.

'And once again in a cave some miles to the west of here. That first time I survived, as you did, because my vital energy, or the vitalist intellect of my body's components, defeated an enemy inexperienced in attacking humanity. The second time I was saved by a Blefuscan. But this time, this third time, *I* shall be the illness. I shall be the scourge. For too long I have wallowed and been passive. For now I *seize* the doom.'

'You are brave.'

'My love,' he said. 'Forgive me for using such words with you, but it is the truth, my love. I shall love you always and with a pure and unsullied devotion, as a knight-at-arms would love an inaccessible maiden in—'

But there was something wrong with Eleanor, a choking in her throat. He started forward, concerned, and then immediately understood that she was laughing. Laughing! 'My darling,' he said, in a wounded voice. 'Pray do not mock me.'

'Mock you!' she repeated. 'Oh I apologise my love, but,' and the laugh poured from her again in a series of arpeggio vocal striations.

'What is so funny?'

'Your self-fashioning, my dear! And now the pomp in your voice! Oh the pulpit tone of it! *Purity!*'

A din of self-righteous wrath and injured amour-propre skittered through his thoughts, and took only a single second to flow straight out again, and he joined in with her laughing. 'You're right! What a fool I am! Oh, it is my curse, this foolish self-theatrics!'

'The purity of your love for me,' said Eleanor.

'Or yours for *me!*'

'Don't,' she added, growing serious again, 'misunderstand what I am saying. I am not denying the strength of it.'

'The strength of the love.'

'It is a force, and real, this emotion. It is realer than any I have felt before. But hardly *pure.*'

'Pure,' said Bates, the words popping into his head from some unpremeditated place and surprising him as he spoke them with the sudden realised truth of the sentiment they expressed, 'is a kind of lie, most especially where love is concerned. How could there be such thing as a pure love?'

'It is for the impurity that I love you,' she agreed. 'It is the impure humanity in you.'

'I am your jakes,' he said. They both started laughing again, Bates feeling a freedom in his chest that he could not remember having experienced for a very long time. And perhaps never. His cockstand was as rigid as ever he had known it. His eyes were brighter; the sheer liberty of being able to say to this beautiful woman, whom he loved, and who had saved him from the terrifying consummation entailed by the disappointment of actuality – to say to her what he truly felt.

She was laughing hard and pressing her hand to her mouth. 'Then,' she managed eventually to get out, 'then Jake shall be my name for you.'

'A private name.'

'A *private* name.'

'A name for the privates.'

And more laughter. But noises behind them, over by the farmhouse – a cough, the chutter of subdued male voices in conversation – stoppered up the laughter. They grew serious, and stood arm in arm. The stench of death was still there, still all about them, in the stillness. 'And yet,' he said, in a low voice, attempting what he knew, in the attempt, would be the unsuccessful and last throw of words, 'you will not marry me.'

'And yet,' she said.

'Is your marriage to be your pure love?' It was not a rebuke.

'In the eyes of the Church,' she said, plainly. 'For I shall marry a Churchman.'

'And there may be something to be said,' he mused, 'For keeping these things all separated off from one another.'

She kissed him and then, without a word and with a haste that – had he not known better – he might have thought unseemly she turned and hurried inside the farmhouse again.

Bates went to Portioli and explained to him that he, Abraham Bates, would be accompanying the party into the sphere, and that Henry Oldenberg would be escorting Mrs Burton to York. 'I have,' he assured the Italian, 'experience of missionary work. A kind of experience. I shall take the Dean's place.'

'Then the Dean,' said Portioli, 'must be ready to escort Captain Longley as well as his affianced.'

The night was interrupted by the moaning of Longley. An inflammation had taken hold upon the raw burnt-up stump of his hand. The fingers were all gone, all save the littlest, and the body of the hand itself was bright red, like the painted face of a savage, and swollen to twice its size. He cried in the night, but there was nothing to be done. 'It looks poorly for him,' said Portioli, in a low tone. Some time before dawn Longley fell into a deep sleep.

'And I suppose,' complained the Dean, 'that I'll be expected to nursemaid this fellow on my journey? I am no nursemaid!'

In the predawn Portioli was busy, rousing the men. The cart on which Longley's men had brought him in was now being loaded with military necessaries. 'We must enter the sphere with equal force to persuade and compel,' said the Italian.

'Hence the gunpowder,' said Bates, watching anxiously as a French trooper and the English private Dartford hauled a small barrel whilst smoking pipes the entire, time.

'Precisely,' said Portioli.

'But perhaps it would be better not to smoke whilst handling the ...'

'Psssh,' said the Frenchman.

'But I mean to say,' winced Bates.

Dartford moved his pipe to the left side of his mouth without using his hands. 'Don't you fret,' he said, in his raspy voice, 'none, fret none, sir. I've rolled a thousand barrels of the powder in my time.' A faahsand bah-wwls. 'And ne'er a slip.'

'But a naked flame so close to the—'

'Don't,' said Dartford, interspersing the words with grunts as he and the Frenchman hoisted the barrel into the back of the cart, 'uuHH, you, uuHH, fret.' And afterwards, 'Mercy, my old 'ammy, mercy,' to his comrade.

'The sphere has touched the ground!' crowed Portioli. 'Our duty awakes!' And he marched off, with the two others behind him, calling a reveille to all the men. Away to the east the dawn was starting to pour its chilly apricot along the undulating line of the horizon. The wind was tart and shivery. Bates, buttoned up as he was, stamped his feet and gave his hands a rub. The cart was filled with instruments of death, and he stood at the lip looking into it, half-wondering whether he should take for himself a pistol, perhaps; and half-thinking that the boards of the cart were still thick with the excremental residue of the sick men it had once transported: dried and hardened, to be sure, but offensive for all that. A pistol might be the thing. Still standing on the ground, he leaned a little way forward into the cart itself, the lip of wood pressing against his loins. That disgusting smell, almost indistinguishable against the wider stench of decay in all the air, was starting to work its hideous effect upon him.

'Still,' said the voice.

Bates began to straighten up, and the voice said fiercely: 'Be still! Do not move!'

'Gugglerum.'

'Turn your large head to the left.'

Bates looked. The tiny man was there, seated upon the barrel of gunpowder, and holding in his right hand a small tar-brand alight with flame at one end.

'My friend,' said Bates, carefully. 'I feared I had lost you amongst the dead bodies on the battlefield.'

'Understand this,' said Gugglerum. 'If you displease me with anything you do I shall plunge this flame into this deadly powder.'

Bates could see that the fat stopper was out of the barrel. How the little fellow had managed to remove so toughly inserted a cork was beyond Bates to imagine. But that was not the pressing issue.

'It will destroy you,' Bates said, slowly. 'If you do that.'

'And you also. Our lives are short, and our spirits rejoice in victory.'

'Do not set the powder alight, my friend.'

'You betrayed me.' Such a squeaky, grasshoppery little voice. Yet it was *plein* with death, and Will, and with a ferocious kind of strength.

'By no means,' said Bates, levelly.

'You abandoned me to a landscape of decay. You promised to take me to the King. I saved your life.' There were several more sentences like this, but they were spoken so rapidly and at such a pitch that Bates could not quite follow what was being said.

'I apologise,' said Bates.

'Do you think the pyndoonemel will abate? I have *listened* to the conversations you have had, and you intend to go into that large circle in the sky. To go there! To *go* there!'

'You have seen, I think, the power to make death it possesses?'

'But the pyndoonemel are as deadly! You must come with me ...'

'Listen, Gugglerum, my friend, listen to me, I beg of you, I pray you.' As he was speaking there was a chill that began to penetrate. 'Inside the house is Eleanor.' He thought of adding *the woman I love*, but sensed something in his miniature companion that would be liable to the vacuum collapse of irrational rage if *love* were brought into the question. 'The Dean is there, the Dean of York, the very man you were seeking when you found *me*. The Dean of York will escort the lady to York town – and you can go with them. He is an intimate of royalty. He will serve your purpose much better than ever I could.'

The Blefuscan moved the flaming stick closer to the circular hole in the top of the barrel.

'Don't!' cried Bates, in an anguish that channelled a sudden realisation that Gugglerum was not here to negotiate. At once, with whole vision, Bates saw how slender was the thread spun from Portioli's passionate adventurousness: if Gugglerum slew him, and the others; here in this place, then who else would have the knowledge – or the position – to attempt the assault heroic upon the Littlebig castle? What supplies would they take with them? Who else would do the necessary missionary work?

'Eleanor and the Dean have survived the plague,' he said, 'just as I have. They can *pass their strength* to others, as I have done.'

The little man stood astride the hole and held the little brand before him.

'You can go with the Dean! He will take you to royalty.'

'I can no longer trust anything *you* say,' said Gugglerum.

'But you saved my life,' said Bates.

'*You* are thinking,' squeaked Gugglerum, his amber-coloured face indecipherable, 'whether you could move your fist fast, whether your reach could grab me, or this flame, before it fell to the powder below.'

'I am thinking only of talking with you,' Bates lied.

'*You* are thinking of whether your heavy legs could run fast enough to outpace the flames that will burst from this detonation. But you could not.'

'I beg you – no. You saved my life. That means that you have taken on a responsibility.'

'Such is another,' said Gugglerum, 'incomprehensible big-person belief.' He held the matchstick-sized brand, with its gleaming cowl of flame, directly over the hole.

Bates thought: Perhaps the powder is damp, and will not explode. He thought: Perhaps the barrel is hooped, and will contain all, or even some, of the explosion. He thought: Perhaps I will survive the explosion with only scars, or burns, but well enough to go on. He thought: Perhaps I will die, but it will not matter, for the others will live, and the assault heroic will be accomplished. In every direction he looked he saw hope, and if he probed into the hope he found only further complications of hope, and opening of possibilities. It is the tyranny of hope that it cannot be construed in any except its single, linear mode. It is a one-size-fits-all-clients, and a one-dimensional thing. The powder itself was four hundred thousand dots of blackness each of which would oxidise with an instinct close to instantaneity, and the outrush of superhot material would burst over him no matter how he tried to run. For, like hope, an explosion knows only one direction, and the same direction at that – outwards.

There was another voice: the bearish, brown-red, potchy voice of Private Dartford. 'What's this?' It was only Dartford's head; resting its chin on the side planks of the cart, and close to the little fellow. Were he a lizard, Bates thought (but why? apropos of what?), he could have whipped him with his tongue.

'I just *loa*ded that barrel. Don't you go disarrangin' it.'

Gugglerum was undismayed. 'Do as I say, you both, or you both will die at once. Fetchez-vous the Captain Portioli.'

'He wants Portioli here to murder him,' said Bates. 'I would beg you to refuse his request.'

'I have no intentions of murder,' said the little man.

A shadow passed over the cart; the smaller of clouds, high in the zenith, interrupting the light of the sun.

'Murder him?' Dartford said coolly. 'Why would 'e want 'at?'

'If you move towards me I shall drop the flame.'

A shadow passed again. But this could not be the same cloud, for clouds do not pass and repass the same spot. This circling, and recircling, and revolving the same spot on the ground beneath. And then, a flurry of wings; and Bates experienced epiphanically, the bluetopia of London, the bird of Apollo, they bickered noise, light, light and shadow in riffling alternation. The action of wings. The chilly noises. Dartford's head was back, his mouth loose and open. He raised his hand in salute. But he was not saluting, he was shielding his eyes against the glare of the sun. And he was looking up into the sky. Bates moved his own head, and looked too. And there, a blot against the great wash of light, he saw the shrinking sight of a bird, carrying its cargo in bronze-coloured talons. An owl, perhaps, or kite; or – but, no, it was not possible to see distinctly what manner of bird had plucked the little man from the cart and carried him away.

Away.

FIVE

THE GIFT

✳

It is a year, or a little more than a year, after the events previously related. It is London, the great city of Empire, somewhat reduced in material prosperity, with a noticeably thinner flow of humanity along its streets, but the same city for all that. Establishments exist all along Charing Cross Road, spreading west along Oxford Street and south over the river into the streets, spread like the cables of a net through the clogs of housing and manufactories of Southwark and Kennington and the Borough, all promising CURE FOR THE PESTILENCE, or GUARANTEED CURE FOR THE RECENT PLAGUE, *enquire within*, or more ambitiously, **CURES ASSURED for the** LATE PESTILENCE *but also* FOR ALL THE PANDORAICAL AFFLIC-TIONS OF MANKIND, BUBO, AGUE, GOUT, CANKER, INFLUENZA, WATER-SICKNESS AND INFLAMMATION OF THE BONES: *members of royal families and aristocrats from seven nations treated; testimonials upon request; the cost of consultation and treatment guaranteed not to exceed one guinea.* The French flag still flies from one broad marble building abutting the Thames, but the Union Flag flies from St Paul's breast-shaped dome – rebuilt, after the recent war, using the newest concretised materials by Brobdingnagian craftsmen. The joint committee for governance has recently renegotiated the terms of its Royal Charter, and British-born representatives for the first time sit in the majority, although since constitutional change required a two-thirds vote the French-born delegates were still a powerful *bloc*. The King, who had spent the war and the subsequent tribulations in an estate upon Anglesey, with a boat crewed and ready to depart for Ireland at a minute's notice, has returned to the capital only weeks before.

And here is an old friend: Abraham Bates, in a purple velvet suit. He is sitting at a café with the paper folded on the table before him, and a glass of sugared coffee half drunk, and he is watching the pigeons. He is watching the pigeons and they are watching him.

It was not for wealth or position or status that she married the Dean, or at least not *only* for those things. Not primarily for those things. He understands this now, although arriving at the full appreciation of it has taken him many months, and he had no easy time of it during those months. He fought the demons jealousy and rage, entities small enough to live inside him yet large enough to rampage and rail like giants. But the battle has brought him a sort of inner peace, at last, a way of treating with his own allergy to contentment without giving way, as he always had been used, to the blue wraiths of dread melancholy. He feels he is now able to hold the ideal of spiritual and sensual love at exactly the correct distance from his life: neither overwhelmingly intimate nor inaccessibly remote. The fact that her marriage to the Dean was entered into for precisely this reason on her part too gave him a warmth in his soul which was amongst the most prized of his non-material possessions. This a point of connection.

And here she comes now.

In the space of a year he had been redeemed in the official eye. Once a despised *Ami de France*, now a hero of Great Britain redivivus. The Littlebig downed and slain. The enormous aerial circle had lost its rigidity, and was now bowed and belled over the Yorkshire countryside, half submerged in the great foul effluvium that had gushed, extraordinarily copious, from the rents in the side of the structure. Like human diarrhoea except on an incomparably greater scale, and with certain other peculiar properties. It had, for instance, remained in a fluid, or semifluid, state for many days: and even now – nine months after its emission – it had not precisely *hardened*. There had been enough of it to fill the entire valley. It covered the great mass of decaying soldiery in many plumblines' depth of dirt. Portioli, Bates and the other men who had survived had been obliged to build boats, like Phoenicians, from such materials as they could find – binding together sheaves, cutting and strapping. And on these unlovely constructions they had oared their way across the valley through a faecal sea, until they broached clean turf and could disembark. By that time the Littlebig was dead, or dying. It is now dead. Unless it is still dying. It is difficult to be sure.

And here's the strangest thing of all: out of this fertiliser, most fully concentrated in the valley but spread over a great many acres where it had spilled along the river's path, were being created wholly new and unseen crops. Wheat grew in new hues and new florettes; great marrows and strange bone-shaped trees, and single leaves larger than any Brobdingnagian growth. Whether these were new metamorphoses of Earthly plants, or plant seeds born through the aether from a distant world, nobody is in agreement. The army has built a camp on the edge of the outflow. But the Littlebig, his craft or himself, whichever it is, is dead. Perhaps he is dying.

And here she comes now. She looks eye-smitingly beautiful, her dress a cantilevered arrangement of dark and light green in strips of silk and ribbon over the bell-dome of its skirt, and a sheen-filled upper portion and tight sleeves. Her hair is bound up behind in ribbons of green. And is such harmonious *vert* not the very principle of the rebirth? Of spring?

'My love,' he says, rising. 'My dearest heart.'

The kiss they exchange would not be out of place between brother and sister.

Eleanor sits, and settles herself. Bates flaps his hand to draw over a waiter, and sits down himself.

'How is Henry?' he asks.

'As ever,' says Eleanor languidly. 'An ideal husband. But how,' she smiles, 'how is the *hero* of the hour?'

'Alas,' says Bates, good-humouredly, 'I fear the hour is passing, and that this hero must bid it adieu. Do you read the newspapers?'

'Rarely.'

'The news from America's southern continent? From Peru?'

'I have heard something of it,' says Eleanor, with a delicious impersonation of languid uninterest.

'The new cometary arrival seems to have focused its attention upon Peru.'

'From the ocean?'

'The ocean,' says Bates, shaking his head. 'The ocean can never have been its destination. I wrote to the *Times* to express my view that ...' He stops himself. The smile that eases itself between his lips and widens across his face makes him look more handsome, and better humoured, than you have ever seen him. 'How clever you are,' he says, nodding at her, 'to tease me out of this humour of self-pride. Do not think I am unaware of the tricks you play. I owe you so much.'

'And I owe *you* something more material,' she replies. 'Or did you think I had forgotten?'

'My gift.' Saying the words gives him a deep sense of joyous well-being, in the deeps of his abdomen.

'Your gift.'

'Have you brought it?'

By way of reply she slips a small mahogany box from her handbag. It is the length of a man's hand, the width of a man's wrist, perhaps two inches deep; its cover is marked with the intricacy of Lilliputian work, in curlicues and lines, gorgeous little welts in the wood delineating blossom. Spring-blossom. Blossom.

'Thank you my darling,' he says, laying his hand on the box and drawing it across the table towards him. The waiter is here, so he must delay looking under the lid – although he wants nothing more, this moment, than to look under the lid – and instead he orders her a *verre* of hot chocolate. The fellow turns his back and slinks back inside the shop, to the chocolate mill and the steamer and the stove, the boxes and bottles of ingredients, to all the paraphernalia behind the bar, and Bates lifts the lid and holds the box before his face, angling the light right to be able to look inside. Inside is a perfectly tapered, delicate turd. He can smell its dizzying smell. He lowers the lid with that absolutely intoxicating sensation of foreknowledge that this small portion of his lover is now *his*, and his for ever.

'Thank you,' he says, simply, and slips the box into his pocket.

They sit in sunlit-caressed silence for some minutes.

'The riverside,' he says, pointing. 'Just there.'

'There?'

'It's where I first met your brother, your saviour.'

'I have two,' she said, dropping her face but looking up at him from under the brows.

'Two saviours,' agrees Bates, 'but not two brothers.'

She laughed. '*That*,' she agreed, 'might be an outrage too great. But, there, that was where my big brother and my true lover first encountered one another?'

'During the invasion. He carried me along the river's way to the Tower. And how is Sir Splancknunck?'

'Well.'

'The most liberating and extraordinary thing,' he says, after a moment, 'is the surrender of jealousy. I had not before realised, for instance, how intimately jealousy and hope are woven together in the human heart.' He takes another sip from his coffee. What is happening in his brain, now, where those tiny threads spurt electrical and al-chemical discharges from one to the other, of unimaginable density and complexity and intricacy, to form thoughts – what is happening is: he is considering how little he understood of love before. How scalar love is, *simultaneously*, small and large, the smallest and the very largest scales both at once. He loves Eleanor, of course. But, it occurs to him to admit to himself, he loves her husband too, he has won *that* battle over himself. He loves her big brother.

The sunlight goes, promiscuously, over roof and ground, over water and earth, each particle of light as large as the sun and as small as the smallest atom.

'How long do I have you?' he asks.

'Forty-five minutes,' she replies, easily.

'It is long enough. It is in the nature of love, you see, being infinite, that one minute of it is an eternity, and the whole eternity of it functions as a continuous present.'

'And to think,' she says, laughing, 'when I first knew you, that you were so tongue-tied!'

AFTERWORD

❀

It has often been my habit (and a bad habit too) to flick from my reading-place in the middle of a fat book to the end pages: teasing myself with the last paragraph perhaps, or reading whatever postscriptum or afterword the writer may have provided me. Often this deplorable practice results in me chancing upon spoilers that materially diminish my enjoyment of the remainder of my reading. If you are doing this same thing then don't. Go back. Read the rest of this novel and *then* read this afterword.

This story, beginning as it does from the point of view of Swift's Gulliver, always seemed to me to contain within it a version of the story of H. G. Wells's Martian invaders from the point of view of the true defenders of Earth: the microbes themselves. The novel you hold in your hands makes plain, I hope, how that perhaps counter-intuitive connection works. I brought in Voltaire's *Micromégas* not because I take any particular delight in the promiscuous recapitulation of the backlist of this glorious genre of ours, SF, but rather because it was necessary for the specific story I was telling. And besides, one thing that is defiantly true of Voltaire's splendid little fable is that it is already an extrapolation from Swift's original (giants twelve times human size? But *why stop there*! One-forty-four times, or greater still!), and any subsequent fictional experiment in the extrapolation of Swift's extraordinary vision ought, as a matter of mere courtesy, to acknowledge that. Other acknowledgements are also needful for this, the most long-drawn-out, carefully and indeed anxiously revised of all my novels. Having got into the habit of writing novels across a period of time to be measured in months it was challenging to write one whose gestation and parturition was measurable in years, but during that time I have received support from my wife Rachel and my daughter Lily; from my brilliant editor Simon Spanton; and from Steve Calcutt my agent. My knowledge of the nineteenth century, upon which of course this novel depends, derives in part from my other job as Professor of Nineteenth-century Culture at Royal Holloway, University of London, and I would like to thank that excellent institution in general and my eighteenth-century and Victorianist colleagues in particular. You can find them here: http://www.rhul.ac.uk/English/. They're good people.

An earlier draft of Part 1 appeared in *Infinity Plus*, edited by Nick Gevers and Keith Brooke (PS Publishing 2001), and also online at *SciFiction*, edited by the estimable Ellen Datlow. Particular thanks to them. Part 2 first appeared in the like-titled *Swiftly: Stories* (Nightshade Books 2002), which stands as a pendant to *Swiftly: a Novel*. At some point in the future I'll put together *Swiftly: Poems*, and that will then be enough *Swiftly* for the time being.

AR
London June 2007